Planet 0420

ZAPH STONE

First edition. Copyright © 2021 Australia.

DEDICATION

I'd like to thank Ms. K, my long-suffering partner for her encouragement and support, lil Y for the awesome cover art and giving me a reality check with her high school knowledge of the English language far outstripping my own, Slarty Jones for occasional python-esque inspiration and various insults, Boris M for his terrifying but insightful insights into the world of publishing, Jack, Janis & Riaz for being guinea pigs during the writing process. Mum and Dad, for being Mum and Dad, and Nigel, my budgie. All of you contributed in some way to helping me completing this epic task (except Nigel). I can thank you all enough ...

-       Zaph Stone, Author.

"If you asked me why you should read this book, I'd probably say two things ... firstly, I'm a made-up non-existent character from a book, so how could I possibly answer an actual question in real life? How in fact am I even responding to said question? And secondly, oh!"

- Andrew Weems, the fictional character, disappearing in a puff of self-awareness after not being asked about the book he isn't in.

DISCLAIMER:

This is a long book. It's about the same length as Dune, give or take, to give you some context. It's my first novel, and as such, the writing style is often more tell than show and a little descriptive here and there. It worked out ok for Steig Larsson, I guess.
Much of the story is internalized within the minds of the characters as much as in their actions, and the main characters spend a lot of time alone on their epic journeys, contributing to the feel.
I think it works pretty well, and if you commit to reading, you will be rewarded with an intricate, action-packed and ultimately rewarding story, but please judge for yourself.
Planet 0420 has received generally good reviews in its original format, and this edition is tidied up quite a bit. Comments such as 'engaging,' 'love your characters,' 'witty,' 'the best thing since sliced bread,' and 'diamond in the rough' were made. Who knows, if you decide to try out the work of an aspiring new author by giving it a read, you might even enjoy it. I sincerely hope so.
Please have a look at the first few pages before purchasing and decide if it's going to be your cup of tea or not. If not, maybe check out my further works: The Ticket - a blood-soaked thriller set in '80's South Australia, or Planet 0420: The Source, the follow up to Planet 0420.
Thank you.
– Z. Stone, Author.

NB: *** = scene change; * = point of view change; just in case you were wondering.

1

Glossary of Alban swears:
Bawbag – Ballbag
Bampot/Numpty – Foolish person
Bawheed – Testicle head
Bas - Bastard
Bate/Bater – Wank/Wanker
Bufty - Moron
Doaty Dobber – Silly person
Dook – Generic Planet 0420 swearword, most closely related to the word for excrement.
Duille – Vagina
Fannybaws - Stupid or annoying person
Lavvie heid – Toilet head
Nance/Jessie – Effeminate man

Alban State Departments:
Department of Artificial Intelligence Research (D.A.I.R)
The Institute – D.A.I.R special projects
The Inner Sanctum - Secret state within the state
Department of Defense – The military arm of the state
Department of Internal Affairs - Security and counterintelligence
Security Services – State law enforcement
The Corrections – Local security authority
The State – The Government of Planet 0420
Department of Finance – Credit management authority

Other Alban Terms:
Alc – Alcoholic beverage
Baco – Synthetic cured meat product
Baffel – Delicious deep-fried sticky sweet
Bev/Bevvie – Drink
Braw – Great/Amazing
Breaching – Accessing unauthorized data/hacking
Naff – Boring, dull
The Big Hoose – Jail
V.I./V.I.S – Vid image/Vid story image

CHAPTER 1 – THE NIGHT WAS

April 19th, the Year 1087, Planet 0420, night.

The night was …

Why the fuck did these books always seem to start with 'The night was …?' Andrew wondered as he idly scrolled through a few pages of what was sure to be another crushing disappointment. His search for meaning and insight into the old ways of this vast, once overly populated planet was a thankless task at times. If he were able to stay up late enough, he could have an hour or two of free time to reflect on just where things had gone so horribly, horribly wrong.

He'd positioned himself near the tiny window of his cramped student accommodation, affording himself a view of the building opposite - if he wiped the condensation from the window often enough, that was. It wasn't much of a view.

It was no good. Andrew needed a release – something to tear his mind away from the abject disappointment of his latest research attempt. Headspace. Headspace was always the answer.

He plugged in and tuned out. It was one of his favorite scenarios, although it was really just a chance to practice his quick draw skills and what he imagined was his witty repartee. The American wild west, late eighteen hundreds, and he was out for revenge against Bad Bill Slade, a gunfighter out of Ohio who'd killed his girl over a gambling debt.

It always started the same way - he caught the stagecoach into town and made his way to the saloon, his boots kicking up dust as the mid-day sun beat down on him. An attractive farmer's daughter peered at him from under the brim of her fancy hat as she fanned herself in the heat. Andrew ignored her. He was here on business. Bad Bill was always at the Saloon at mid-day, it was his drinkin' time, but not today, he thought, *not today …*

Andrew entered, slamming back the saloon doors – a little too hard this time as they bounced back into him as he entered, hitting him in the chest. *Embarrassing.* The music stopped, conversations ceased mid-sentence, as they always did, and heads turned to size up the medium height gunslinger wearing a big poncho, a dusty brown leather

3

hat, and white leisure shoes. *Why the hell hasn't the game given me proper cowboy boots?* he wondered, distracted for a moment by his footwear.

Bad Bill Slade looked up from his position at the saloon's bar, his black mustache twitching and his long dark greasy hair hanging limply. He had one arm around a voluptuous prostitute, as always. He loosened his grip on her, and she fell backward, gravity taking over and her legs flying into the air as she landed on her back, exposing her pantaloons—someone wolf-whistled. Andrew made a mental note to block gender disparity on the next run-through, no matter how realistic it supposedly was for its time.

Bad Bill's eyes settled on the young gunslinger's footwear. "What in the hell kind o' boots is they?" he sneered, spitting his chewing tobacco on the floor. *Disgusting habit,* thought Andrew. "They suuure is ugly," Bill observed, drawing a few laughs from the various miscreants dotted around the saloon, gambling, at the piano, staring menacingly, and so on.

This was his chance. He loved coming up with witty put-downs, but for some reason, this time, his mind was blank. Bill continued to stare at him with his ice-cold pale blue eyes, pearl-handled six-shooters on either hip. Things were getting awkward. *Come on, think of something!*

"Well," Andrew said, standing with his hands on his hips, exposing his Glock semi-automatic circa 2000's weapons from underneath his beige poncho – an unfair advantage, true, but it was his world, after all. "Not as ugly as …" Andrew panicked. It was the part where his cutting remark would disarm all the pretty ladies in the bar and leave Bill flabbergasted; usually.

Still nothing was coming to mind. "… your Ma!" he finally managed, delivering the line with what he thought was a suitable amount of bravado. His amazing zinger was met with stony silence from everyone present.

Bad Bill looked confused for a moment, his mustache twitching again, before observing, "Well, that doesn't make any sense, you never even met my Ma! She died in childbirth, goddammit!"

"Well, at least she passed on her looks …" Andrew managed. One of the prostitutes tittered and batted her eyelids at him, and the young gunslinger felt as if he'd achieved some sort of redemption.

"Why," exclaimed Bill, aghast, "that's just rude! You come into my town, into my Saloon …"

"Ahem ... excuse me, Bill, who's Sal ..."

A bullet between the eyes abruptly halted the Saloon owner's challenge. Andrew looked at Bad Bill, his hand already on the butt of his Glock, and Bad Bill looked at Andrew, smoke drifting from the nozzle of his Smith & Wesson. Time stood still for a moment, and then, all hell broke loose!

Guns started blazing, fists flew, chairs were smashed over backs, people crash-landed on tables, and gun smoke filled the room as splinters of wood flew everywhere. The noise was deafening.

Andrew leapt through the air as it all kicked off, firing both of his pistols in mid-air – as you do – and landing behind an overturned poker table, using it for cover as the bullets zinged past his head.

Bad Bill had quickly taken cover behind the bar, the first of Andrew's shots having blown his hat from his head, and was now peeking up every so often and firing indiscriminately. Andrew was doing much the same.

It was going nowhere, and a couple of minutes later, Bill decided enough was enough. In a brief pause in the gunfire, he called out, "Hey, Stranger!"

There was silence for a moment before Andrew replied, "Who, me?"

"Yeah, you! How many other strangers do you think there are here, goddammit?"

"Well, I'm not ..."

"Goddammit to hell, will you shut the goddam hell up!" yelled Bill. Andrew shut up.

"What I'm tryin' to say is, let's settle this like men ... a dual!"

"Alright. Cool beans." A duel was good; it was what Andrew was waiting for.

Bill was confused, unsure what this had to do about the beans he'd had for lunch. "Ok then," he said, "on the count of three, we show ourselves, weapons holstered, then we go outside and duel to the death."

Andrew loved this bit. *Nothing beats a good old duel to the death!*

"One," Bill yelled. "Two ... Three!" They both rose, hands raised and empty. They locked eyes again. *If there's one thing I can say about Bad Bill, at least he's a man of his word ...*

Somewhere behind him, Wyatt Waylans, an old gamblin' buddy of Bill's, snuck up on Andrew, a chair raised high over his head.

Bill cleared his throat. "Oh, come on now, Wyatt, that's just plain ole cheatin' …" Bill remarked, the disappointment in his friend evident in his voice. Andrew wheeled around and looked Wyatt square in the eye, giving him his best menacing stare. Wyatt looked sheepish and lowered the chair, placing it carefully back at the one table in the Saloon that was still upright. Andrew rolled his eyes at Bill.

"Well then…" Bill said, stepping around the bar, "after you …"

***

Claire was bored beyond belief. Data breaching wasn't much fun when you got stuck, and she'd been stuck for at least the last two hours. It was already far too late for her to get her sleep allocation, but she knew that she wouldn't be able to sleep until she solved the problem, no matter how tedious it was - it was just in her nature.

Andrew had been going on and on about Headspace, where real-time slows, and you can experience worlds and adventures of your choosing. She'd lost count of the times he'd told her about how great it was as a release mechanism.

She'd never had time for it in the past, dismissing it as a frivolous waste of mental energy, but maybe, just maybe, an experience there might free up the blockage in her mind. There was, after all, a first time for everything. *Should I?* she wondered. Maybe it was worth a shot.

Her mind had been all over the place lately. She'd been thinking of her long since dead sister, Heather, or 'Henny' as she'd called her, more often than she liked of late. Henny was taken from her in suspicious circumstances when Claire had been just thirteen years old, and she'd always believed that she'd been murdered by the state, having been in their care when she died. But, of course, nothing was ever proven. It had been years since she'd thought of her, but she did so now, and she found it disturbing.

Although she liked to tell herself that her mission in life was all about fighting the many injustices of their supposed socialist utopia, it had really always been about her sister, about finding the truth of what had happened to her. Maybe, just maybe, she thought, she could conjure up something in Headspace - something that would remind her of the carefree days before the incident, before her life had become a dark and desolate place. Claire and her sister had played on the Pinnacle when they were smaller, the one time in her life that she'd been truly carefree and happy.

She looked at her code; the symbols on her display seemed to swirl in front of her eyes. *Ok, that settles it; Headspace it is …*

Claire got up and stretched, her neck cracking as she waggled her head from side to side. She downloaded the Dataware and plugged in, issuing a series of brief instructions in her mind. The Pinnacle, summer, early evening, sunny day. Just her.

That would be enough, she decided. She could wander around, take in the view, sit and contemplate things as the sun warmed her face. She could watch the sunset. She smiled at the thought, and suddenly it seemed like a very good idea, Headspace, and she wondered why she'd resisted for so long. No doubt Andrew would think that her scenario was naff, but it was just what she needed. She started to feel a strange sense of ease as she disappeared into the virtual world she'd just created.

She could see the green grass of the Pinnacle, the grey skies overhead. *Hm, I asked for sunny.* There was a shape on the grass, on the other side of the expansive lawn. A person. A girl. *Is that?* Her breath caught in her throat. It was Henn …

Suddenly the scene dissolved in a rush a black and grey static, and she was thrown into another environment entirely. It was cold, freezing almost, and she realized that she was completely naked! *What the hell? Must be a glitch! Andrew said it never glitched, though! What the fuck?*

It was almost pitch black, and she couldn't see a thing. She was confused about what was happening, stunned for a second, not knowing what to do. The very next moment, every hair on her body stood on end. There was a sound, something inhuman somewhere out in the pitch-black surrounds - she'd never heard anything like it before, and whatever it was, it had sent a wave of crippling fear through her.

How do I end the session? She remembered - summoning the big red exit button, the failsafe that was always supposed to be available, but nothing happened! She tried again and again, her sense of panic rising as she heard the noise again, and still, nothing happened! *Maybe I'm not doing it right?*

She was trapped, and something was out there, circling her, its outline not visible to her but seeming to disturb the grainy darkness as it moved. She knew it almost immediately - she was the prey in whatever the hell this scenario was!

***

Andrew took up position near the end of the single dusty street the frontier town possessed. Bad Bill Slade stood more or less directly outside the saloon, not more than twenty yards away, no doubt intending to resume his drinking in a minute or two. Although it now sported a fresh bullet hole more or less in the middle of the crown, he had his favorite black hat on. It had been a close call, but Bill was ready to put the annoying little upstart in his place – and that place was six feet under.

There was a strange silence. This was the part where they usually traded insults, Andrew thought - just before the shootout - but Bill wasn't saying anything, something that was most unusual.

"Shouldn't we trade insults?" Andrew called. Bill shrugged and unclipped his holsters, readying for action.

He looked for the tell, the twitch. As soon as he saw it, he'd try and shoot both guns from Bill's hands. He'd been here a hundred times before and had managed one gun, but he was feeling confident today. Bill didn't seem to have his usual pizzaz, and Andrew was ready for - *Oh! Whoops!*

Andrew quickly swept his poncho over his shoulder on one side, then the other, to free up access to his Glock's. Or at least he would have done if the tassels hadn't got tangled around the butt of his pistol! *Dook!* He wrestled with it quickly, hoping Bill hadn't noticed but just couldn't get it free.

"You ready!" Bill called, assuming the dueling stance. Andrew looked up nervously, thinking that if he didn't do something soon then, he'd get to experience the feeling of several bullets ripping into his body. He knew from experience that it was highly unpleasant – it had taken him at least ten attempts to win his first duel, and even now, victory wasn't always assured. It was all part of the allure.

"Just a minute!" Andrew called breathlessly, now in full panic mode and wrestling frantically with the cloak.

Don't Panic! he thought. It didn't help.

"Count of three!" Bill called back.

Oh, Douglas, I'm in trouble!

"One ..."

Dook dook dook dook dook! A ripping noise greeted his latest, frantic effort to untangle his gun.

"Two!" Bill's eyes narrowed. He was thirsty, and the uppity little squirt that had challenged him was interrupting his afternoon's festivities.

The other gun! The other ...

"Three!" Andrew fumbled for his other gun, firing off a shot as he dropped and rolled, the impact dislodging the weapon from his grip. Strictly speaking, the whole dropping and rolling thing was cheating, but he wanted to avoid bullet-induced pain at all costs. Bad Bill Slade had unloaded both his guns, all twelve shots, and he was sure that one of them must have done the job. The kid was in the dirt, unmoving, and Bill holstered his six-shooters and dusted down his sleeves. "That'll teach ...."

*

Andrew sat up and picked his Glock up out of the dirt, blowing some of the dirt off the barrel. Bill took in the scene, not believing what he saw and especially not believing that he'd missed with all twelve shots. *Well. I'll be damned!*

*

Andrew stood, leveling his gun at the black-clad gunslinger. *I'll see if I can shoot his hat off again, then it'll hit reset and try again.*

But it didn't happen that way - something strange happened instead. The baddie turned and ran, hightailing it out of town. It had never happened before. It was most odd.

***

A million tiny blue lights flickered on, blinking randomly, so very high above her head. Claire turned in a slow circle, able to make out the dark outlines of a hundred towers rising all around her, their dull blue light radiating out into some sort of vapor that writhed and billowed up as high as she could see. She wanted to call out, to scream for help, but she knew it would only attract the attention of whatever the hell was trapped in here with her, and that was the one thing she was certain of in that moment – that she didn't want it anywhere near her.

She tried to still herself, to control her breathing, but it came hard and fast regardless, adrenaline pumping through her veins, breaking out in a cold sweat as she heard the noise again, the inhuman, indescribable sound. She tried to decipher its direction, straining to hear, willing it to go away, her eyes stinging with the effort of trying to make out any sort of detail in the near pitch darkness.

There was some sort of dark mass ahead of her; maybe, she couldn't be sure. The noise came again, and she recoiled as she thought she caught a movement in front of her, and close! She watched in horror, frozen in place for a moment as her heart constricted in her chest. A grainy black … something … moved over to her left.

No! It's on my right as well! Oh, dook! She spun around and saw that whatever it was had completely surrounded her.

A bright white light suddenly beamed down from above, and she was momentarily blinded. As her eyes adjusted, she saw it …. *oh my Douglas, what the fuck is that?*

***

Andrew chased Bad Bill Slade out of town, he'd never been out of town before, and he wasn't particularly fit, so he was already puffing and sweating. *If I can just get close enough to … oh!* A sort of clear wave seemed to sweep across his vision, and he wasn't sure it had even happened for a moment before he realized that Bill had disappeared. *Well, that's surprising!*

When Andrew turned back towards town - thinking that he'd go and say hello to the pretty dark-haired prostitute and make her acquaintance - he saw that the Town was also gone, and all he could see was a never-ending desert, in every direction. This was quite possibly even more surprising.

Nothing like this had ever happened before. Headspace never glitched - had never glitched - was supposed to never be able to glitch. Andrew tried to summon the stop button. He tried again. Nothing happened. *What the ...*

At the very moment he had that thought, he became aware of a low humming sound that was vibrating the very air around him, ever so slightly. He turned again, and then he saw it. *What the fuck is that!* It hadn't been there a moment ago; he was sure of it. Andrew probably should have been wary, maybe even frightened, but instead, he felt oddly curious. *Maybe this is some sort of patch, a new challenge, mayhaps?*

A large, extremely large, matte black monolith sat on the horizon, in stark contrast to the golden sands below it and the pale blue sky above. It seemed more than a little out of place; he couldn't help but think. He had to go to it - this was obviously all part of the challenge, and besides, there wasn't much else he could do.

As he trudged through the sand and drew near the huge black object, he noticed that there were to be hundreds of cables running into it, partially buried but emerging and laying on the surface here and there. He felt inclined to touch one, but as his hand neared, the intensity of the humming rapidly increased. The air around his hand – and then it felt like his hand - started to vibrate alarmingly. It was most unpleasant. Andrew snatched his hand away, trying not to step on the cables as he approached the huge black thing. *Weird!*

He arrived at the monolith and made a slow circle around it. Its surface was perfectly smooth and with no sign of a way in. *A puzzle perhaps?* he thought, but then he saw a low indent that seemed to spell something out in large lettering, about twenty feet up the monolith's, erm, monolithic side. *A puzzle, I knew it!*

Andrew felt his sense of excitement build, wondering what sort of devilish riddle lay ahead – *I love a good riddle.* He moved around until he was directly under the letting, the angle of the sun allowing him to see the letters spelled out clearly as he moved in line with them. 'ENTRY,' it said, in huge, obvious lettering complete with a large downward pointing arrow, and underneath that, a panel, a black panel, that seemed to be illuminated with some sort of weird black light.

I'm sure that wasn't there before.

The connection was obvious. The game had tailored something special for him. He pressed the black-lit panel, and a groaning noise came from the structure, then stopped. Then started again as a huge opening appeared in the side of the huge black monolith as if by magic. A weird blue-black light partially illuminated a smooth-walled black tunnel that looked as if it headed deep inside the structure. A sort of almost mechanical hum came from somewhere deep within. Andrew entered, wondering what sort of wonderful surprise Headspace had in store from him.

***

Something had surrounded her, and Claire had absolutely no idea what it was - other than it looked and felt evil, dangerous, and altogether like something she didn't want to be anywhere near. She could see what looked like a million black grainy cables writhing around the perimeter of the central open space she found herself in - except that they weren't cables at all, she realized. They seemed to be some sort of weird particles, forming and re-forming, churning and rotating around her, their speed growing faster by the second. The low light seemed to both glimmer off the millions of particles and be consumed by them. *I'm in big trouble,* she thought, shivering. *And why the hell am I naked, for Doug's sake!*

There was no way out. She tried for the red button again and wasn't at all surprised when nothing happened. She could feel the temperature in the air dropping, and ice was starting to form under her bare feet. Claire hugged herself, looking around frantically for a way out as the weird grainy blacklight cables suddenly rose high into the air all around her. *Oh, oh! This isn't good.* Although she knew it was a game, a virtual world, the fear she felt was real, and she started to shake as she watched the writhing cables spreading out and then contract suddenly towards her.

She screamed, but her scream ended as quickly as it had begun, the granules flashing across the void from all sides and streaming into her mouth and nose. The air filled with a terrible roar as the granules streamed into her ears, snuffing out all noise and replacing the air inside her with itself, consuming her entirely.

Claire saw nothing. Felt nothing. She looked down at herself, at where her naked body had been, and saw nothing but a grainy blackness. It appeared to her, for all intents and purposes, that she'd ceased to exist.

***

Andrew moved down the smooth-walled corridor towards the dim light. He ran a hand along one of the walls as he walked and withdrew his hand quickly, shocked at how cold it was, his fingers feeling numb and then tingling painfully. *Bloody hell!* He turned a corner and walked into a huge octagonal room with towers of what looked like some sort of Alien Tech as high as the eye could see, a million blinking lights casting a pale blue glow around the cavernous space.

Ah, this must be the thing! he thought - the thing that he'd heard only whispers of amongst the Headspace community, the special place that only the top gamers get an opportunity to see, and the chance to access bonus levels and other things that other, lesser mortals could only dream of.

He had a spring in his step as he entered the open space, the air around him suddenly icy cold. *Ooh, that's a bit chilly!* Andrew realized he was suddenly stark naked! *What the hell? That's a bit unnecessary!* He had to assume that this was something to do with the challenge, but it seemed a bit odd. He cupped his genitals with both hands, feeling very exposed.

An incredibly, impossibly bright beam of light streamed down from somewhere up above, and he shielded his eyes, almost blinded for a second. As his eyes started to adjust to the light, he saw something strange - not that the entire situation wasn't already strange enough, of course.

There was something suspended above him, a bright white form. He squinted at it but couldn't make it out, the light was too bright, almost blindingly so, but whatever it was, it was rotating slowly in the dark space above him. He had a strange feeling, a sense of familiarity that was altogether inappropriate for this current, alien setting. He tried again to focus on the object. *It must be the key to the riddle.*

Andrew's heart rate increased as he saw what looked like streams of an almost black, granular liquid - more like a visceral black light - dancing, and weaving, rushing into the shape above him and circling all around him, closing in. He started to feel uneasy – not seeing how any of this was a puzzle that could be solved. He felt trapped.

This can't be right; where's the Jewel? He'd fully expected to see the bright red, sparkling Jewel of Orion, the legendary key that only a lucky few had ever seen, his key to untold adventure and unbelievable experiences within the game, but instead, he was feeling only fear and seeing …

His eyes adjusted full to the light, and he saw … *is that …*

The oval shape had formed the shape of a woman, naked in her entirety, dark hair trailing down, a thick patch of pubic hair, and her face …

Oh my Douglas! It's Claire!

Claire's eyes snapped open and met his, but they were not her eyes at all – they were an inky black, gleaming brightly, and they sent a jagged wave of fear through Andrew. He cowered away, and the cables closed in, rushing around him at an incredible speed, only a few feet from him, cocooning him almost entirely. He looked up at her again, pleading with his eyes as he felt his skin start to freeze. The pain was indescribable, but he was unable to call out, to move.

Claire struggled suddenly and screamed in agony, the sound almost inhuman - dropping him to his knees, doubling him over in agony. The streams of black granules suddenly swarmed him, rushing into his mouth and nose, suffocating him. *I can't breathe! I can't breathe!*

Andrew was suddenly back in his squalid student accommodation, drenched in sweat, shaken, his heart racing out of control, and the bed wet underneath him.

Oh, for Douglas's sake! Don't tell me I've …

He had. Andrew had wet the bed.

***

Claire woke up on the floor of her one-bedroom apartment, naked, alone, and bathed in a cold sweat. She clawed at her mouth, screaming, trying to get the granular black light from inside her, and kicked herself into a corner. Then, slowly, the room came into focus around her, and she quietened, her breathing ragged, the only sound in the otherwise still scene.

The tears started to flow. She'd been with Henny, her beautiful, dead sister. The black light that had consumed her - it was connected to her sister; somehow, she sensed it. She'd felt her sister's love saturate her very being, but then it had been wrenched suddenly away and replaced with the terrible darkness.

She looked frantically around the apartment, the shadows seeming to loom up at her, and she closed her eyes tight, curling herself into a ball in the corner of the room, trying to make the images in her mind go away.

***

Andrew had cleaned up as best he could and tried to forget about it, but the images kept returning. Again, he needed a distraction, and the old world, via Headspace, was the obvious place to go.

It would be an understatement to say that he was obsessed by the planet's last civilization, one that had burnt so brightly before its spectacular self-destruction more than a thousand years earlier. Its capitulation had been so staggering that even its calendar had ceased to exist, reset to zero by the founders of the new world. It resulted, amongst other things, his birthplace being renamed Alba - he preferred to call it Scotland all the same.

He was spending way too much time researching the old world. This sort of information was, for the most part, tightly controlled. For Andrew Weems, however, as an up-and-coming student Journalist specializing in cybercrimes, access to this information was more available than to most, and he took full advantage of this fact.

The things that were being discovered about the old world were just so damn interesting, so wonderful compared to the backdrop of the ordered, plain, and highly controlled civilization he was currently inhabiting - that was how it seemed to him anyway. He sometimes wished that he'd been born a thousand or so years earlier so he could have experienced it for himself. It seemed that his planet's past was so full of oprtunities, so many possibilities. As for hopes and dreams for most of the inhabitants of Planet 0420, all you could wish for was a warm bed and food in your stomach

There was always Headspace, he supposed, although he'd had more than enough of that for one night.

What the hell happened? The experience couldn't glitch. It was impossible, or so he'd been told, and yet it had happened for the first time. And Claire, she'd been there, and they'd shared an in-game experience, another thing that wasn't supposed to be possible unless two people had expressly permitted it. And he'd seen her. All of her! He wouldn't mention it, it would be way too embarrassing, and he was pretty sure she wouldn't either.

What had happened was as weird as dook, and he tried to distract himself back in the old-world text, but there was nothing wonderful or interesting in this writing, he somewhat glumly reflected. In fact, there was no wonderfulness at all lately - all it seemed he could lay his hands on were short works of fiction that quite frankly left a fair bit to be desired. He hungered for some creative, scandalous prose that gave a true insight into a society that had been so advanced and yet clearly got it completely wrong on so many levels. It wasn't to be.

The night was - for fucks sake!

Andrew wished that he could drop out of the final year of his state-sponsored studies and concentrate on studying the old-world full time. This would, of course, be at the expense of his meticulously planned future, and he knew deep down that it just couldn't be. There was just too much at stake, too many people to disappoint. So much had been invested and sacrificed by his family to get him this far. If only it were possible, though. The thought was enticing.

He pushed his metal chair away from his desk and took a deep breath on his tube of synthetic bacco, a rare luxury in his otherwise impoverished existence. The fact that it was highly illegal in Alba was neither here nor there - it was worth the risk just to get a taste of the old world. To physically handle the bacco tube and inhale the smoke deep inside, ingesting something so pure and maybe even just a little bit dangerous, well, it made him feel alive.

Andrew was lucky he had wealthy contacts - most people never even got to try the banned substance. He inhaled deeply and released the smoke slowly so that it curled and drifted away from him in the air. He leaned back in his chair and imagined his heroes and heroines of the old world breathing deeply and savoring the tingling feeling of the bacco and the clarity of mind that it induced before they went about their interesting, exciting existences.

These types of thoughts had a habit of creeping into Andrew's mind late at night, he'd noticed. When the lines of text started to blur on the display, when all was quiet and still outside, and when the cold had slowly seeped inside his room and up from the floor to numb his feet - that's when it happened. The detachment - the dark space inside his mind where he'd go to escape the boredom and blandness that he had to endure every single day.

Just another cold and dreary night in the lower highlands, he couldn't help but think

He shivered and checked the time. This obsession with the old world was becoming a real problem. He could see that quite clearly, and yet, with every discovery or un-coding of a new sound bite, video images (V.I.), text, or even sometimes even V.I. stories (VIS), Andrew would always manage to distract himself from the dull text he was supposed to be focusing on and pore over the often-dull details of the old world instead. Unfortunately, more often than not, this pursuit ended in disappointment. There was just not enough data available, and what there was, was often of poor quality – as indeed it was tonight.

Occasionally though, something would emerge that would ignite the nerve endings and send shivers of excitement through his body. Words, images, and sounds would course through his cerebral cortex and took him far, far away from his placid, bland existence and into the exhilarating times that had come before.

Sadly though, the book displayed on his device was no exception to the norm. Although he'd spent less than ten minutes reading it, he could already tell from the content and apparent lack of writing skill that this was going to be a bit of a grind. He doubted he was going to gain any valuable insights into the way the old world had functioned or what had contributed to its demise.

He checked the time again and sighed deeply. It was late. A shiver ran through him again, and he pulled his cardigan tightly around himself, and he blew into his cupped hands, rubbing them together to try and keep warm. The heating in his building never really seemed to work properly – it can't have been working at all tonight.

So much for this socialist utopia. Can't even heat a room. Damn, it's cold.

He pushed his chair back further from the desk. He was done for the night. He rubbed his eyes, and as he stood, the chair made a sharp scaping noise over the bare concrete floor, making him flinch at its sound for the third or fourth time that night.

"Really should do something about that," he muttered to himself as he slowly stretched to his full, although not considerable height. He pulled his arms up high over his head and waited for the tiny series of cracks from his back to occur. Wiping the condensation from the windowpane for probably the tenth time that night, he surveyed the scene outside.

Andrew lived on the fifth level of the twenty-story, decrepit building, high enough up to be afforded a good view up and down the street and high enough to leave you out of breath if you took the stairs to get to your room. It was misty outside, with only the dull yellow light from the streetlights eating into the gloom.

He looked out over the endless grey, box-like towers that were crammed into the enclave. It was typical of most accommodation in The Highlands. Mountains framed the backdrop, the snow on their peaks just about visible through the low clouds.

Not a soul to be seen.

Andrew's gaze wandered to the accommodation block a couple down from his on the opposite side of the street. Just a glimpse of light could be seen from one window of the huge building. It was an otherwise dark and soulless scene. He realized that he was looking at Claire's flat and smiled to himself, recognizing a kindred spirit.

Claire was one of his classmates at the New Edinburgh State Commercial College (SCC). She was a good friend - Well, more than that. She was sharp, witty, and someone he could always rely on to enliven a dull evening with a discussion about politics, music, conspiracy theories, anything really. She was basically his vision of the perfect woman; he had to admit.

He sighed again and stared out of his window, looking at all the blank, lifeless windows of the building opposite. He was clearing his mind from the noise of yet another day studying the finer points of decrypting logarithmic crypto pulses.

"The night was ..." Andrew said to himself, "... dark."

A small smile played over his lips as he realized he'd successfully amused himself after what had been a tough week.

It seems that work is all I ever do these days, work work bloody work.

Another shiver ran up his body as he stood on the cold concrete floor.

Study and work. Study. Work. Where's the me time, eh?

His study wasn't really going to plan of late. He was slowly realizing that he just might not be the high achiever he was being pressured – expected - to be. A strange sense of unease had been growing within him for some time now - he couldn't quite put his finger on the why, but something just didn't seem quite right. The why, the thing, was there constantly, just beneath the surface, but as yet, it had not or would not reveal itself.

Andrew looked out of his window again just at the moment Claire's light went off.

Claire … yes, and then there was Claire.

Andrew hadn't seen her all week, and he was missing her company terribly. He generally preferred to be by himself and spend any of the scant spare time he had digging around in anything he could find from the old-world. If he didn't see Claire for a few days, it always left him feeling a little melancholy. He wandered into what passed as his bathroom, which was really just a toilet, a sink, and a mirror. He flicked the switch that turned on the bare, dull, light globe and stood observing the face that looked back at him as he slowly took sips of water from the one mug that he had in his possession.

He observed the dark circles under his eyes. They seemed to be getting darker by the day and were spoiling what was otherwise probably a fairly decent sort of face, he thought, in all fairness. A thick thatch of dark, almost black, unruly hair, dark brown eyes, yes, the dark circles again, damn it, small enough nose, smallish chin but a wide, friendly sort of face.

Young, still young – all to play for. I'm only twenty years old, for fucks sake!

He smiled just to make sure that the face was indeed his. The face in the mirror smiled back. Fortunately. Yep, that was him, alright - dimples, cheeky grin, surely irresistible to all and sundry. But he wasn't convincing himself at all, really, and he made a solemn pledge to try and sleep a bit more in the coming weeks. He shrugged off his clothes and immediately regretted it, flicking off the light bulb and making a dive for the bed as quickly as humanly possible. He slipped under the bedding in what he estimated to be a microsecond and then shivered for a good couple of minutes while he cursed the freezing cold nights of The Highlands. Repeatedly.

Once warmth had returned, he reached for his antique Campbell earpieces, the one real luxury that he possessed. Campbell's of New Edinburgh had been making fine earpieces for over a hundred years now. The pair he owned were one of the first they'd made and had a distinct warmth in the sound quality that had not been able to be replicated in any of the more advanced soundsynths available these days - they suited the old-world sounds perfectly.

He slipped them on and enjoyed the close comfy feeling as they warmed his ears. He closed his eyes, regulated his breathing, and hit the play button. All was well again with the world as the first few chords rang out of his new favorite track, and the music drifted and dissolved through his very being.

***

Claire Renshaw generally didn't like being around other people. She couldn't help it. It was rare for her to engage with anyone on a meaningful level, especially if the interaction didn't serve her purposes. She knew this was true of herself, and she'd given up on trying to fit into social norms long ago. After the incident, nothing else had mattered anyway. She didn't have the time or energy to deal with anyone else's crap - she was far too busy dealing with her own.

She'd had a hot, well, if truth be told, more like a warm shower - thanks to her building's age and poor state of upkeep - and tried to forget all about what had happened to her in Headspace. It had shaken her, seeing her sister again, but she supposed that was what she'd wanted. And then there was the weird granular black light. It had been genuinely terrifying, but none of it was real, it was a virtual world, and she supposed that she wasn't prepared for it.

Andrew had been there too, at the end. She'd seen him, but she wasn't sure if it was really him, as in his actual person, or a virtual Andrew. Worse still, he'd seen her. All of her. Naked, and floating above him. She shuddered at the thought. Maybe if she just didn't mention it?

She'd settled back into her research after that, vowing never to return to Headspace was allowing herself the rare luxury of taking a brief break from her research; well, 'research' was a useful code name to cover for what she was really up to anyway. She slumped back in her chair and let her mind wander briefly to one of the two souls on this Dougforsaken planet that she actually did have time for.

Claire stood, rolling her shoulders, arching her back, and throwing her head back to stretch her neck. She wandered over to the window, feeling an icy draught - this, she recalled, was why she never sat near the window. She pulled back the blackout curtain, peered out, and surveyed the night, noticing one of only two or three windows across the way and down a little that showed a glimmer of life by the appearance of the slight glow that was coming from within. She wondered what Andrew was doing.

She knew he'd most likely be feverishly devouring his latest scraps of information from the old world and that he'd probably be working late into the night, just like every other night. It was this commitment to his cause that first made her take some notice of what she'd have otherwise dismissed quickly as a quirky, impish, although largely intellectually unappealing person. Andrew - with his zealous enthusiasm for whatever topic she raised, his weird humor, and his off-center way of looking at the world - gave her more than a bit of challenge in keeping up with his thought processes. She wasn't used to that. She was usually a few steps ahead of anyone, at least.

She'd first met Andrew Weems on a warmish night just over a year ago through her other friend, John McGregor. Friends, she'd come to realize, were not things that were easy to keep. For her, anyway. She was lucky to have Andrew and John. It was enough, and it was comfortable.

Well, now that she was on the topic, 'friend' might be a bit of an understatement for John. He was her 'boyfriend,' she supposed, whatever that meant. One part of it was fairly clear cut, but she wasn't too sure about the rest. Even if she had by some miracle found anyone else to be friends with, well, it really wasn't necessary; there was barely enough time for those two as it was.

Claire was lonely tonight. She didn't particularly like the feeling, but she'd become more or less resigned to it in the years since her sister's death. She couldn't stand those who didn't question, didn't try and find the truth. The 'lemmings' – one of Andrew's old-world terms, she recalled – those who followed along and did whatever the state asked of them, no matter how unjust it was. She couldn't stand to be near them. Unfortunately, this ruled out her spending time with 99.9999% of the population of Planet 0420.

She turned from the window and took the two steps required to reach her couch – a giant elongated beanbag in a drab concrete box of a room dominated by a stack of computer towers, textbooks, and little else. She threw herself down on it in an ungainly manner and wriggled herself into a comfortable position.

Where is he, anyway? She thought. *He should have been here hours ago to help with my work.* Her work. Although John was just as enthusiastic as she was in many ways, it was nearly always *her* work, her ideas, her pursuit of justice. She knew that John was along for the ride in many ways, but that was fine by her.

She'd stumbled onto something interesting earlier in the night but was having quite a bit of difficulty unlocking its security code. The data belonged to the Department of Artificial Intelligence Research (D.A.I.R.), her latest pet project, and it was causing her a great deal of frustration. John knew the code better than most, having to deal with it on a daily basis as part of his cybersecurity studies stream, and another set of eyes would be useful. She was pretty sure that she could find another use for his presence later on, but she didn't want to distract herself with those thoughts just now.

She'd known John for a little while now - long enough to really get to know a person in any case. He was a pretty serious, intense sort of guy, and Claire liked most of what she'd seen so far. He was entitled, good-looking, athletic, and charming, in other words, just the sort of person that she usually despised. However, with John, there was a difference - he had the same intense drive and focus on exposing wrongdoing as she had.

Although he hid it pretty well at times, he also had a deep intelligence, which extended to the whole social side of things, and this was something that Claire was completely oblivious to. Most importantly, though, John was studying cyber threats and specializing in security code at the college and had connections with pretty much anyone who *was* anyone. The cyber threats stream was only a select few chosen for, and Claire was also one of the few. It tied in well with her research.

They'd worked together on a project early on in their relationship, and she'd quickly seen that his code could complement her own very nicely. She was sure that together they could further her interests significantly, and she'd been right. There were, of course, other ways in which he could keep her satisfied, so it was win-win as far as she could tell. The physical side of things was usually all over fairly quickly anyway, allowing her to get back to work free from distractions.

Claire knew that she was using him on many levels, and she knew that he knew, but he really didn't seem to mind all that much. When she did take a rare break and gave into her primal urges, John was often left shocked by the ferocity of things.

There was another little bonus to the relationship, and that was the attention that being seen with John McGregor would bring - the jealous glances of the pretty girls, the double-takes as they realized that *he* was actually with *her*. '*Her*, really?' She could see the confusion on their faces, and this made her feel warm and fuzzy inside, knowing she had one up on the rich elitist bitches who had been nothing but awful to her for her entire life.

It wasn't that she wasn't attractive herself, quite the opposite, in fact. She knew that she might even be considered classically, no, maybe 'traditionally' beautiful by some, in the right light. Claire ran through the list, as it had been explained to her: large dark green eyes and full lips and a button nose all set in an aesthetically pleasing heart-shaped face.

Check, check, check, and check! I'm amazing!

What offset this quite effectively and kept much unwanted attention at bay was the fact that she never took much care of her appearance, certainly not to please others - wild hair, no or ghostly pale makeup, baggy, loose-fitting clothes, and heavy boots. She was also quite wiry and not particularly feminine in her demeanor.

Check, check, check, check aaaand check!

Claire smiled to hersel and stretched herself out on the beanbag couch, noticing her comms blinking.

John had messaged her several times. She'd been so caught up in the decryption problem that she hadn't noticed the messages until now. Claire opened the 3D function of her comms with a flick of her thumb and scrolled through the messages.

'I'm running late - field trip ran overtime x.'

A little later -

'Bumped into some 'friends,' and they're dragging me for a bite to eat. Will call soon xox.'

Later still -

'At the Ox and Cart, do you want to come join?'

Half an hour ago –

'See you tomorrow C, bit pished xx'.

Claire didn't mind this at all. A night of sitting quietly with a glass of vita-water and being largely ignored by a bunch of his well-meaning but ultimately boring, vacuous moneyed friends wasn't something she'd particularly relish. She'd got a run on her research tonight anyway, and it felt like she might have stumbled upon something very unusual. A small shiver of excitement ran through her as she focused her attention back on the task at hand.

This sort of discovery had happened before, of course, and she was well aware that it could lead to nothing. For someone like Claire, though, what started as code that was impossible to break down usually seemed to fall away and reveal its secrets once she applied herself to it. This time it was different.

The security on the data was immense and complex, and she'd spent the best part of the last few hours trying and failing to crack the layers of code. She really wasn't used to this sort of frustration, and it wasn't making much sense right now, but it would come eventually. She knew it would. It always did.

Maybe this time, there'll be something useful hiding behind the security? Maybe even something secret - something I'm not supposed to see? She felt a little tingle of excitement.

If not, why such an effort to keep her out?, she reasoned. The ever-shifting algorithms and security traps, one after the other - surely whatever was hiding behind them was going to be worth seeing.

This is going to be a challenge, oh, yes, quite a complex little security system you have here. She often found talking to the code helped.

It was quite intense work. She picked up her comms again and checked the time. She really couldn't afford to stay up much later and hope to function tomorrow, but maybe if she just reversed part of the algorithm?

An hour later, she conceded that she'd better call it a night and somewhat reluctantly put her device down on the plastic crate that acted as a side table, accidentally knocking a glass onto the floor with her device. She was more tired than she thought. It fell with a dull thud onto the hessian rug and rolled slowly away into the darkness of the room, out of reach of the soft glow of the light emitted by the single red lamp.

Claire curled up on the couch, pulled a thermal blanket from the floor, and snuggled into it. All of her nights seemed to end like this lately. She blinked a few times, yawned, and felt herself quickly giving in to the sweet embrace of sleep.

***

A few months earlier …

"Lachlan," the reedy high-pitched voice called. "Mr. Grealish!" this time, a little more desperate. The aging secretary clasped the secure comms firmly in her hands as she tried to attract her employer's attention.

"Lachlan! It's important!"

"Lachlan!"

Lachlan Grealish was a million miles away. The giant display flickered, lighting the darkened personal workroom with staccato bursts of color. Images of a charismatic, strong-featured, and he supposed some would say handsome man beamed at the adoring crowd. He didn't know how many times he'd watched the footage or how long he'd been sitting there, completely transfixed by the images filling his vision, and he didn't care.

The on-screen Lachlan had just finished his maiden speech to the people, his people, and was now holding his arms aloft triumphantly. Well-wishers, some powerful figures in their own right, hoping to catch some of his stardust, others hangers-on, desperately trying to pursue their own golden opportunity, filed past and tried to bask in the moment with him, either shaking hands, clasping his shoulder, patting him on the back, raising their arms in unison or fist-pumping as the applause and cheers continued unabated.

He'd just been appointed as head of the social development portfolio; an extremely high-profile role tasked with improving all aspects of life for the people of The Highlands - one of the top ten most populous zones of Planet 0420.

It was a role that took a special type of person to succeed. It needed someone to be a popular figurehead and somebody who could make tough decisions behind the scenes. The real trick came in selling those decisions to the people as a great thing, a huge positive for society and themselves - when often they were exactly the opposite.

Lachlan was that person, he reflected, as the images faded, and the oak-paneled room fell once again into semi-darkness. If anyone could do it, he could. Anything life had thrown his way - and so far it had thrown quite a lot his way – he'd dealt with it and turned it to his advantage, time and again. There was no reason to think that this next chapter would be any different. Right now, he was sitting on top of the world, an adoring public, success, and power.

"Lachlan!"

The thin voice cut through the momentary silence, and this time it registered. Lachlan glanced back over his shoulder from deep within the confines of the comfy antique chesterfield inspired couch.

Gladys, his secretary for as many years as he could recall, stood in the outer workroom, waving frantically with one hand and clasping the bright blue secure comms in the other. Something in her manner, perhaps the pleading look she was casting Lachlan's way, sent a small wave of anxiety through him as he rose quickly and took the few steps it took to reach her.

He noticed Gladys's hand was shaking as he reached out to take the slim blue handset from her, and he cast her a quizzical look at her as he placed the receiver to his ear.

***

Andrew waited on the crowded transporter podium as a biting wind blew in off the loch. The mountains surrounded them, their rough, craggy sides dark and foreboding. The only clue that humanoids inhabited the place was the stark white zero-g transporter track that snaked between them and the huge white transporter podium that Andrew and hundreds of other bleary eyes workers now stood on. Oh, and the vast settlement of New Edinburgh, which if he craned his neck, he could just about see, the lights of the concrete towers of the student quarter.

The legs of his all-weather pants flapped and tugged against his ankles as another gust blasted past with enough force to make him take a half step forward. With all the advancement in technology of late, he thought, surely, they could design a transporter hub, or t-hub as they were commonly known, that offered some sort of protection from the freezing northerly winds that seemed to persist for most of the year. He pulled upwards at the zipper of his thermal jacket in the vain hope of keeping out the wind that was chilling him to the bone.

Maybe this was all part of it, keep the population humble and thankful for a warm bed at night, make them suffer and then reward them, keep them all compliant and happy and ...

"I'll stop myself there, I think," he said to himself, drawing a sideways glance or two from his fellow commuters.

This is just the sort of tosh that Claire and John are always coming out with. The all-powerful state oppressing its people and controlling every facet of life. Blah blah blah, lah lah.

He'd heard so much of their conspiracy theories lately that it was starting to seep into his subconscious. It did amuse him to think about it, though. Often he'd come up with wild theories of his own just to pass the time or to see what he could get away with in conversation with his friends – although his attempts were usually totally ignored or met with a blank stare from John or a rolling of the eyes from Claire.

There is no doubt about it today, though, the state had reversed the huge turbine props that infested every point of the horizon. They'd turned them from extremely useful, sustainable power-generating devices and were instead making them act as huge fans.

The big fans were pointing directly at the unseemly masses huddled together, waiting to be ferried off for another day of oppression - blowing the icy wind directly at them, no doubt seeing if they could blow anyone off the podium.

Nearly fucking succeeding too, he thought, as another series of icy blasts swept past, causing him to brace against them.

Bloody fannybaws! Another involuntary laugh escaped his semi-frozen lips.

Andrew was pretty sure he saw the guy directly to his left shuffle slightly away from him, as much as the current jam of bodies on the podium would allow anyway. Then, finally, there in the distance, he saw the stark white glow of the transporter's lights through the gloom and sleet. Yes, it was actually sleeting now*, those bloody, bloody bastards!*

***

Isabel Donachy was a woman of simple needs. She simply needed to be more powerful, more influential, and better at everything than everybody else - at all times. She'd been relentless in this pursuit her whole life, and the results were quite outstanding, even if she did say so herself. Although now in her late forties, Isabel was still an imposing figure. Tall, strong, striking blue eyes and long flowing platinum blond hair – on the rare occasions she chose to let it down that was – completed a perplexing proposition for her opponents.

She knew that most men would have a second look after she'd passed them, and she wore smart figure-hugging outfits to accentuate her curves, disarming most male opponents before she'd even begun. The fact that the physical side of her appearance was due largely to some highly illegal anabolic mutanoids was irrelevant. Isabel felt it added to her aura of power. She'd worked very hard to achieve her success, and she believed the fact that she was now a wealthy and powerful high-ranking state official was the least she deserved.

It wasn't enough, though. It was never enough. Power was intoxicating, and Isabel was well and truly addicted. She'd quickly grown accustomed to making the hard calls and doing the deeds that no one else seemed to have the courage to do. If you thought for one second that anyone in power was beyond the evil required to ensure their own political survival, then think again; she knew this to be the truth. It was a reassuring fact that made her opponents all too predictable.

No one dared cross her these days, and those that had, well, they certainly lived to regret it. She'd been invited to 'the inner sanctum' of the institute over five years ago. The secret organization had been created to provide a means of checks and balances on the state - a sort of covert and independent government of the government, if you will. Over time though, natural human instincts such as greed, for example, and human traits such as ego had devolved its purpose, and it now served as a means to an end for the most power-hungry psychopaths that The Highlands had to offer.

Isabel now had as many enemies as friends in the highest places. She'd fought hard to ensure that she held the balance of power where it mattered most and knew enough secrets so as to make her practically untouchable. It really hadn't been that difficult either. A few favors to the right people at the right time. A few victims had fallen into her trap and were now desperate to keep the lid on some very personal and intimate details. Easy as you like. Before they knew it, she had them, well, some of them anyway, exactly where she needed them.

She sat alone at the head of an extremely long, highly polished genuine oak table in the boardroom of the D.A.I.R headquarters. The watery light of midafternoon in Wanlockhead, the highland's business center, seeped in through the expansive plexi-glass panes that afforded her a view over the city and beyond. Her eyes were glazed, and if she were indeed looking at anything directly, it would not have been apparent to anyone observing.

Today's meeting had been long and stressful. It had lasted several hours longer than planned, and her bosses were none too pleased. Artificial Intelligence, or A.I. development - something she was mostly responsible for - had been lagging these last few months.

The next phase of the new world's future depended on her targets being met - and said targets were not even close to being met just at the moment. Isabel had gained carriage of the mining program, which was the key driver of A.I. development, in the last year or so. Recently, the mines had been falling behind in production while demand was increasing exponentially. It was not a good situation, and she'd already had to resort to some extreme measures to keep up.

Things were stacking up against her: she was working with a finite resource; she had to achieve a critical stage of A.I. development – the next generation Quantum Field Theory, QFT II - before the current resources were extinguished; and supply was limited. She needed access to additional base materials, but she'd been denied several times and told to find other solutions.

It was a total dookstorm, and there was only one solution that she could think of. They had been reluctant to even entertain the idea.

The fools. It wasn't going to be pretty when she executed her plan, but that was exactly the way she liked it. Isabel, of course, also had her own special reasons for needing to increase production, and no one was going to get in her way.

***

"Alright, mate," said Andrew with a smile and a nod to a guard whose job it was to stand on the freezing t-hub podium all day. The poor bugger. "Aye, alright pal," came the response. No smile in return, but it was there, the recognition from one of the same kind - the strugglers, the salt of the planet. He knew that the guy was freezing, having a horrible time, and was only there because he had to be, to earn a wage and try to stay on top of his most likely miserable life. One of his kind, his brethren, he liked to think.

He'd always made a point of being polite and making an effort to engage in good old human interaction at every opportunity. More so recently, as A. I. took a firmer and more far-reaching grip on society, causing people to become more and more like faceless drones. He could see that this sort of thing was going out of fashion, human interaction that is, and that really concerned and quite frankly upset him.

Andrew shuffled into the overcrowded transporter pod with around another fifty or so hopeless, frozen souls, and by some miracle, found a seat wedged into the front corner of the pod, next to what can only be described as a rather hefty fellow. "Aye, pal." An almost imperceptible flicker of humanity ran across the face of the huge shape, but no response was forthcoming - he had his eyes glued to comms, like all the others. They were out of touch with humanity and losing touch with reality. He had little respect for those who could not even summon enough common decency to acknowledge a simple 'hello'.

He wedged himself firmly in the corner, hoping that the rotund fellow might move over a touch and make the journey slightly more comfortable, but it soon became apparent this wasn't going to happen. Oblivious to Andrew's existence, it seemed, the huge chap occupying approximately one and a half seats was deeply immersed in his own tiny world.

Andrew really didn't mind the practical side of comms. It was smallish, lightweight, fitted neatly in a charging brace on your forearm, could be used to send and receive messages, project V.I. or V.I. objects, perform complicated workflows, complete workgroup assignments, access Headspace, watch VIS, and so on. You could detach the main interface, put it in your pocket, use it for a coaster, etc. All in all, it was quite handy. The requirement to always have it with you so that your movements could be tracked and your outputs constantly monitored was the part that grated somewhat: that and everyone's obsession with staring endlessly at the interface. There were only two brands to choose from and only two colors.

Bloody socialism!

There was the grey-black Comm-boi, the version he had. He didn't think much of the name, but at least it was a cool color. The other option amused Andrew greatly. It was white. Nothing amusing in that, but, in their wisdom, the great leaders had decided to brand it Comm-i. Only very few people would be able to grasp the metonymy, as communist history was not taught or studied on Planet 0420 and had, in fact, been more or less expunged from the history books, such as they were.

Andrew knew all about communism, though – the benefits of being a journalism student and all that - and couldn't help but think that the device was supremely and appropriately named. The transporter glided away seamlessly and silently. *Or did it glode? Was that a word? Probably not.*

He looked around at the stark white and matte grey interior of the transporter. The seats were immaculate. Everything was tidy, well ordered, perfect. The looks on the faces of those crammed into the space around him, however, were not. People started to thaw out and plug in, but he couldn't see a happy face anywhere.

There were no jovial conversations, no jokes to be made, no interaction occurring of any kind. He attempted to establish eye contact with someone, anyone in fact, but not one person was doing anything other than staring relentlessly at their devices.

Pathetic. These poor saps just have no mind of their own.

Having said that, there were benefits to be had from Tech if you knew the right people. He did, fortunately. Claire had installed a modified version of comms on a wristband for him, allowing him to send and receive messages privately to a select few of his closest friends. Ok, well, there were only two of them, but even still, it was pretty damn cool. Illegal, of course, but cool. It went without saying that privacy wasn't something you could usually rely on, and this little device allowed him something almost impossible to find anywhere on Planet 0420.

Equality and social justice for all! Well, for some more than others anyway.

He liked to hold his wristband up to his mouth and send messages by speaking quietly and quickly into his cuff while glancing around furtively. To his own mind, it made it look like he was in some sort of secret security agency rather than an insane person, sending coded and confidential messages. He was doing his bit to protect and serve, as it were. He did this mainly to amuse himself but also to try and get a reaction from those around him - a thankless task.

The reality of it was that he was usually just keeping up the banter with Claire and John, trying to make an otherwise uneventful morning that tiny little bit brighter and more interesting for himself. He hoped he was at least causing those around him to wonder what he was up to. He looked around the pod again.

Everyone looks exactly how I feel. Thoroughly pissed off. Utopian society … I don't think so.

It was fair to say that Andrew wasn't much of a fan of utopia. When the 'end of times' survivors, as it had become known, got themselves organized and started piecing some sort of civilization back together several hundreds of years ago, they renounced most of the things that had caused them so many problems in the first place. Religion, for one, was nowadays nonexistent, and in fact, illegal to practice. A lot of things seemed to be illegal.

Belief in deities had been cited as the main cause of nearly all wars fought on the planet historically, from what was known. Most of today's knowledge originated from information passed down from person to person, generation to generation in the dark days following the end of times. Things did change somewhat fifteen years or so years ago, with the discovery of an ancient 'code vault' in the Scandi mountains.

The wealth of information stored there could take a hundred years to decode and was most likely to have been heavily censored before being released, but at least it had allowed some understanding of the old world. It was this drip-feed of information that sustained Andrew. The scant information regarding religious beliefs that did exist did not paint a very rosy picture at all. Anyone practicing Religion in the early days had been very swiftly and very harshly dealt with. There was no such thing now, of course, and hadn't been in a long, long time.

No problem there, probably a good move, he thought.

Instead, the state was solely responsible for being the moral compass, guiding everyone to the light, steering them from the dark paths—one overall entity, governing everything worldwide.

Bit of a problem, anyone, anyone?

They really did try hard to start from scratch, Andrew thought, even renaming the planet itself. It was highly amusing to him that the planet they lived on, once known as 'Earth,' had been renamed 'Planet 0420' - it was something to do with its proximity to other solar systems, or something like that. He didn't really care. All he knew was, the number was apt.

Typical, humanity thinking it's the center of the bloody universe.

The State wasn't a dictatorship, of course; they would never admit to that. Andrew liked to think of it as a *Claytons social democracy.* Claytons was a term he'd picked up early on in his research into the old ways, and essentially it meant having something but not really having it.

One of his first and fondest memories of Claire was when he'd referred to her as a 'Clayton's friend' after she'd forgotten to help him with a work assignment. The spark and amusement that dance wickedly in her eyes as he'd explained the term had been priceless.

His comms blinked, interrupting the thoughts he'd been lost in, and he glanced at the wristband. It was Claire.

"You won't believe what I've found!"

He lifted the wristband to his lips and spoke into the device.

"Your soul?"

A few seconds of silence followed.

"No ya wee bawbag! I've found a picture of your willy. Oh no, hang on, it's just a caf bean."

"I'll have to stop sending you pictures of it then."

"That would be nice."

"Well ... what is it then? The suspense is killing me, really."

"I have some news on that data I was telling you about."

"Oh, that's so interesting. Hold on a second."

"What?"

"Sorry, I just had to finish my giant yawn."

"Well, anyway, I got in! I cracked the code, and I think I may well have been somewhere that I wasn't supposed to be."

"Where's that then? The girl's bathrooms?"

"Stop it, you little dook, or I'll kick you square in the baws next time I see you. I'm really onto something here! "

"Well then, I'm very happy for you."

"Meet me at 'the place' before class."

"Ok."

"Twat."

Andrew looked out of the window, watching the high hills flash past, the watery sunlight seeping through the thick blanket of clouds. His friends were always ranting on about 'The State' and its supposed conspiracies against the people. Today was like any other day, he supposed, but he had to admit that was part of why he enjoyed hanging around them so much. Although he did like to poke fun at them, he also knew they saw things the same way he did - they just had slightly more vivid imaginations. He returned to his thoughts. Narrating otherwise boring train journeys, he was sure, was a worthwhile pursuit.

Celebrity was largely frowned upon in Planet 0420's society. As such, celebrities existed naturally, albeit more so for elected officials these days rather than sportspersons, artistic performers, or social influencers, as it had once been so very long ago. Borders and nationalities were also a thing of the past, although regions did carry some sort of tokenistic heritage and celebrated some handpicked aspects of their long-ago past. This extended to some local regional accents, although these had largely been eliminated. Andrew was proud of his accent, however.

His wristband comms was vibrating again. He lifted it to his ear. It was John this time, speaking hurriedly from a noisy place. He couldn't make out all the words, but apparently, Claire had been on to him as well, and he was saying something about being extra cautious on comms and with their meetings from now on. Andrew spoke discreetly into the cuff of his jacket.

"Ok mate, calm down, no one will ever know what a giant jessie you are. It'll be our little secret."

A brief stream of abuse was John's sign off.

He shook his head at the constant interruptions to his highly necessary and detailed internal monologue concerning the political landscape of the world he was currently inhabiting and returned to those thoughts, the high lochside hills having now replaced the mountains outside the windows of the transporter.

True, everyone had their nose to the grindstone almost every single day of their lives, and free time was strictly limited, but how else was a society to become stronger and prosper if people were not prepared to work hard to achieve it? Andrew didn't mind the hard work; he considered this to be fair enough.

The holidays gave some an opportunity to see other parts of the planet, so it wasn't all work and no play. That was, of course, if you were amongst the few fortunate enough to be able to afford it. Vast swathes of the planet were decreed as uninhabitable and would likely stay that way for thousands of years yet, thanks to Andrew's beloved old world. It was possible to travel to other mountainous regions around the planet and experience other sights and cultures, to some extent anyway. For example, in the French Alps, you could buy a baguette.

The huge shape next to him shifted then rose to its feet, and he felt as if he could breathe properly for the first time in around ten minutes. The outside of his leg was damp with sweat. It was gross. He hated transporters. Andrew made a face at the blob, but the blob was busy and didn't notice.

Andrew knew he had to get to his comms, catch up on everything, confirm work orders, lock in study hours and workgroups, prioritize his tasks, set his quota for the day and the like, but he wasn't ready for that just yet. An altogether ordinary-looking man sat down in the spare seat next to him. At least he was ordinary-sized at least, which was a relief.

The wristband was demanding attention again, though, vibrating slightly to the beat of one of his favorite tunes. It was John again. "Meet us at eight; make sure no one sees you getting there."

"Ooh, this is so exciting! Have you uncovered a price-fixing scandal on herrings again?"

"Fuck off, you little gobshite, or I'll crush your tiny brain with my left hand, which isn't even my strongest, by the way."

"Oh, I do love it when you talk dirty to me."

Andrew let out a little involuntary titter at their exchange. No one seemed to take any notice of him. He decided to look out the Plexi-pane for a while again.

***

Isabel could have practically anything she wanted these days, whenever she wanted it - such was the privilege afforded to her by being a member of the most exclusive of clubs. Only very few ever got the call to join the inner sanctum, and Isabel had been enjoying its benefits for a long time now.

Having anything she wanted or desired whenever she wanted it extended to the very expensive, exclusive, and gorgeous young leisure boy currently bent over in front of her, arms tied behind his back, face awkwardly pressed into a pillow. 'Boy' was a bit of a stretch. He was at least early twenties, a little older than she usually liked, but he would have to do. She'd ensure she had a few harsh words with her supplier in the morning. It could wait. She was going to have some fun first.

She dug her nails hard into the leisure boy's soft white buttocks, making him writhe and try to pull away, before she roughly dragged him back and slapped him hard, leaving a stinging red handprint. She hadn't meant to slap him quite that hard, but it felt exhilarating. Anyway, job done; he'd gotten the message and had stopped moving for the moment. She couldn't remember his name. Gary was it, Geoff, whatever the fuck, it really didn't matter as long as he continued to do as he was told.

Isabel increased the speed and power of her thrusts, the double-ended strap on/in dildo doing its work, bringing shivers of pleasure from deep within – well, at least for her. She had no idea if the leisure boy was enjoying it or not. Rhythmic slapping sounds filled the room. She increased the tempo and could feel her climax coming on, but just before it happened, she pulled out of him and flipped him over.

She pushed him back on the bed and leaned over him, roughly clasping her hands around his throat and suddenly squeezing tight, making him gag and choke as she wriggled the huge dildo back inside him. He was having trouble breathing.

Isabel tilted his head back by grabbing a handful of his thick blonde curly hair and looked deep into his eyes. He was terrified, his eyes pleading with her to stop, but instead, she increased the pressure watched as the panic spread across his face, his body squirming violently and legs starting to thrash wildly.

The ropes were doing an excellent job of subduing any excessive movement on his part. She pressed down with all her weight and with as much force as she dared. The boy's eyes rolled back in his head, and he may well have screamed; it was impossible to tell with his mouth so tightly gagged. She increased the pressure and held his head firmly in place as she convulsed wildly. The power of it nearly made her black out.

Her vision slowly returned, and she regained her senses. She was lying on her side, soaked in sweat. The boy had squirmed out from under her, backed away, and pulled himself into the fetal position in the far corner of the room. He looked quite terrified, but not enough to have made a run for it and jeopardize losing his perks.

A tear gently trailed down Gary's cheek as she observed him from her position on the bed; she smiled at him and rolled onto her back, the giant dildo wobbling around before she reached down and unfastened it. It was going to be a long night.

CHAPTER 2 – BAFFEL'S

Andrew was quickly tiring of looking out of the plexi-pane. It was making him feel a bit ill. He returned to the task of describing everything about the world he lived in, to himself, for his own amusement.

Was it possible, he wondered, for him to finish narrating his life without getting interrupted again? He was getting sick of talking to himself, but back to it. He sighed. It was a necessary evil.

The over-reliance on technology was the biggest problem with society, of course. Andrew nodded at his fantastic insight. This much was obvious, but society was utterly obsessed with Tech and had been for longer than he could remember. Ever since Quantum A.I. had emerged less than a decade ago, the pace of technological change had been incredible, unbelievable, even. The breakthroughs had grown exponentially, and QAI was replaced by QFT soon after, fueling even greater, faster advances.

No such advances in transporter seat technology, though.

Andrew shifted uncomfortably in his seat, his bottom already becoming numb from the hard plexi-seat. His stomach grumbled, and he wondered if anyone had heard. He hadn't eaten, and there wouldn't be time before study groups started.

He'd have to grab something on the run, and he went through the list of options, which only made his stomach growl alarmingly once more. He could buy something at the t-hub, although he didn't fancy having to try and digest the cardboard consistency of the rolls they famously produced. Hygiene was also questionable - he'd found a thick black hair once as he tried to chew through something that was masquerading as a baco butty. The thought made his stomach turn.

What else, what else?

There was an all-night baffel place in the Swiss Quarter, well, it was more of a hole in the wall, really, but that would mean going out of his way and most likely being late for or missing out on seeing Claire and John. Mainly Claire.

Now that he'd started thinking about baffel's, he couldn't stop. His stomach protested again, and he was sure that the pompous looking gent sitting opposite him had cast him a disparaging look.

***

About a month ago -

Lachlan Grealish was already starting to feel out of his depth. Malcolm Pettigrew, the head of the Security Branch himself, had been the first to tap him on the shoulder and tell him to expect a call from some very influential people. Since the call on the blue comms and the subsequent meetings, Lachlan had been set on the media.

They wanted him to promote his social justice platform to their advantage. So they had immediately opened a pandora's box of opportunities for him, and it was the perfect match, as far as anyone could tell. Things had been a whirlwind of press conferences and parties, and he loved the life of endless fine malts, powerful people, and beautiful women now at his disposal. It was the life that he'd always dreamed of, and now he really did have it all.

Better still, his face was now on most of the main media channels daily. He was charming the masses and, of course, looking great. There were tradeoffs. He never seemed to have even a second to himself these days, and there was always someone asking advice, briefing him, directing him this way and that. It was unrelenting, and things were about to ratchet up another notch.

Isabel Donachy had spoken to him briefly at a reception in the Chief Minister's residence in Wanlockhead earlier in the evening. She was in charge of A.I. development at the highest levels, and he was fairly confident that she already had a bit of a thing for him.

In no uncertain terms, she'd told him that tonight was the night he'd be allowed membership to what she'd called 'the inner sanctum.' Lachlan was tingling with excitement at the prospect of joining the elite of the elite - he was to be one of them, he *was* one of them!

The meeting started at midnight and would go for most of the night. Lachlan was buzzing from all the attention he was getting and the prospect of what was to come. He was also wondering how he'd cope with an all-nighter. That was when the weirdness started, just after the final round of canapes in the huge timber and marble paneled ballroom.

Lachlan approached the bar after extricating himself from a lengthy and dull conversation on the merits of staggered shift working hours in the cyberculture sector. A man he'd had never seen before suddenly appeared by his side. He was tall, wiry, and dressed immaculately. The man was older, maybe late fifties or early sixties had a gaunt face, shoulder-length grey hair swept back with a product of some sort, and piercing grey-blue eyes.

He turned to Lachlan and lifted his suit jacket sleeve discretely to expose the silver wristband worn by all inner sanctum members on meeting nights. Lachlan nodded at the man, who smiled crookedly and offered a handshake. He obliged, shocked at the strength of the elderly-looking gentleman. He was also quite surprised at the feeling of the smooth and cold object that was pressed into his palm courtesy of the overly firm and overly long handshake, during which the gaunt man never broke eye contact.

The gaunt man saw his confusion and broadened his smile before releasing his grip. Lachlan instinctively held the object that passed to him, but as he went to open his palm to inspect it, the gaunt man grabbed his wrist firmly and shook his head ever so slightly, then made a small drinking motion with his free hand, winked - of all things - turned, and disappeared into the crowd.

He slipped the object into his jacket pocket and then made a beeline for the nearest toilets. Once safely inside a booth, he took out the object and studied it. It was a small metal vial with a clear plex center, and it contained a bright purplish-blue liquid. He carefully unscrewed the cap and sniffed the contents. They had no smell. The meeting was due to start soon, and he could only assume that this was some sort of requirement.

"Well, here goes nothing," he said to himself. He tilted his head back and tipped the liquid into his mouth. No taste. No sensation at all, really, perhaps a slight numbness. He shrugged and then relieved himself before heading back out to the party – he was starting to get a little nervous at the prospect of what was to come. He checked the time as he left the cubicle and was shocked that the meeting was due to start any moment.

He'd somehow lost around thirty minutes while in the toilet cubicle – *that's strange,* he thought. There was no time to worry about that now, though. He headed quickly towards the back of the room where a private staircase descended to the meeting area. He seemed to glide through the room, barely touching the floor as he went. People smiled and nodded as he passed – he was one of the chosen ones.

Halfway across the crowded room, filled with chatter and laughter as powerplays were made and deals brokered, a beautiful raven-haired woman in a purple velvet dress that left little to the imagination turned into Lachlan as he went to brush past. Her hand was inside his pocket, and she was pressed up against him in an instant.

Her eyes were a deep, almost purplish-blue. Something about her - ok, it was everything about her - caused him to feel a surge of pure unadulterated lust. She made as if to whisper something in his ear as Lachlan's gentleman's area responded suddenly and urgently to the discrete caress he was receiving.

He craned his head toward her and received a hot wet tongue in the ear for his trouble. He pulled back at that, but his new friend wasn't ready to let him go just yet, and hugged him deeply, grinding herself up against the ever-growing bulge in his pants before suddenly pulling away and smiling back over her shoulder as she walked away.

Lachlan found some space to one side of the staircase and crouched down as if to re-tie a lace, all the while thinking of the most unappealing thing he possibly could. After a few seconds, he felt sufficiently under control and stood back up. As he did so, he felt something catch in his pocket that hadn't been there before.

He pulled out a business e-tag containing details for Ms. Evanka Maric and offering 'specialist services.' He activated the card and felt his breath catch as the 3D image rotated slowly above the tag – she had an exquisitely beautiful form - these were the sort of services he most definitely approved. It was around that point that he started to feel a little unusual.

***

Andrew jolted awake as the transporter skimmed over a rough bit of track somewhere between Loch McKinnie and Loch Taverner. He decided to immediately continue his in-depth internal summary of the political system and the intricacies of the socio-economic situation of The Highlands for want of anything better to do.

It wasn't all bad, he supposed - tech. Headspace could be pretty damn amazing at times, allowing you a full immersion in other places, times, and environments - even other worlds should you so wish. Your leisure, your way – that was the slogan anyway. He was just a little addicted to it.

In one of his favorite worlds, he was just about to make it big as a gangland boss in what he assumed was a reasonable assimilation of nineteen-sixties London. It was his sixth attempt at that particular space, and every other time had ended in his premature and extremely grizzly murder. He really wished that a place like London still existed, with all its brassy 'geezer' slang and its never-say-die attitude. It had to be better than this, he thought. *Anything would be better than this.*

His comms was vibrating again - it was Claire this time. He was getting very frustrated at the constant interruptions.

"Be careful, Andrew; I mean it. John said you weren't taking this seriously. I had surveillance fly-bots near my window again last night. Could have just been a coincidence, but that's the third time this week."

"Oh, I wouldn't worry about that Claire, it was just me trying to get a peek of you in your undies again. I do like the black furry ones - they match your armpit hair."

"Dream on you, little twerp!"

"Oh, I will, I will."

"Fuck off."

"Love you too. See you soon. xox."

Must be serious; I've been told off!

More secrecy than usual. In some ways, it was warranted he supposed. If anyone ever got wind of what they were up to, poking around in state data, they'd be in serious strife. Everyone knew it but never spoke of it – you had better keep your mouth shut on Planet 0420. You couldn't trust anyone. It was something they needed to be careful with.

The structure of society was such that if you had a controversial opinion or showed any disrespect to the state, then pretty soon, those around you would start shutting you out purely through fear of association. At first, it would be little things, like a wary look or a conversation aborted as you approached a group, but pretty soon, it would be a failure to return comms, a no show at a group event, and so on until they just pushed you ever so gently away. Forever. It had happened so often to him that he'd become an expert at picking up the signals and pre-emptively removing himself from the person's sphere - less his left-field opinions impact their relentless pursuit of a higher social status.

No big loss. Twats.

It was almost impossible to find someone you trusted that you could speak freely with, but the three of them had found that, and speak freely they did, often spending hours discussing and debating taboo issues that they would not dare speak of in public, ribbing one another and roaring with laughter as they pushed the boundaries of social decency and mercilessly tore apart everyone and it seemed everything around them.

Sometimes he thought he might go completely mad if he didn't have that outlet. Let's face it, though, he thought, he really wasn't too far off anyway, on the balance of things. Although like-minded people do have a way of naturally attracting one another, in the current environment, it wasn't easy for, well, he liked to think of them as 'alternatives' ... for alternatives to gather and freely discuss their ideas. Hence the paranoia.

The sun had crept out from behind the clouds. For a moment, Andrew was blinded as it flashed through the trees and into the pod. There would be no more looking out of the plexi-pane. There was nothing really to look at inside the transporter pod either. Maybe he'd have to plug into comms after all.

***

He'd started to feel rather peculiar just before he'd headed down the ornate timber staircase. Lachlan's vision had become filtered with a strange shade of purple, and whenever he moved his head, objects left behind a blueish outline. If that wasn't strange enough, his mind had then started to race at an incredible rate, and he was bombarded with incredible insights, one after the other. He felt quite euphoric but at the same time totally in control of his every action – he'd felt kind of wonderful.

The meeting went brilliantly for him. Lachlan was given control of several key projects, including oversight of the mining program, which by all accounts had been struggling of late. The general public, and indeed the state itself, was never to know of his connection to the group, but he was left in no doubt that he'd been handpicked for the role and would be one of their main representatives for many key policy discussions, summits, and campaigns.

He was feeling on top of the world. The hours in the spectacular marble and timber paneled meeting room had flown by, and the longer the meeting went, the more powerful, decisive, and charismatic he'd felt. Everyone in the room had the same gleam in their eye, and it hadn't taken Lachlan long to realize that the magical blue liquid was at play.

It was five a.m. when things wound up, and Lachlan was still feeling as full of energy as he had when it had started. As he left, the congratulations and handshakes complete, he reached into his pocket and pulled out the tag. As he flipped it over in his hand, he noticed that Isabel had paused by the top of stairs and was observing discreetly, a playful smile on her lips.

Can't blame her.

He'd seen her appraising him several times during the meeting, and he was sure he'd soon get the opportunity to see what was underneath that immaculate pantsuit. Not tonight though, he had other plans, specifically related to the raven-haired woman who had accosted him at the cocktail party. He turned his back to Isabel and used his binary implant to activate the call.

***

Sometime in the Year 1081.

They had him cornered. The popular kids. The ones with the new blazers, the good shoes, the good hair, the perfect teeth, and the expensive toys. The ones you knew to stay away from. They were the ones with powerful, wealthy families. They were the ones who did what they wanted because no one would dare stand up to them through fear of violence or exclusion. Andrew secretly hated them, and although he'd tried to stay out of their way, for some reason, they hated him too.

He'd been on his way to the bathroom when they surrounded him at the edge of the playground, just around the corner of one of the many tall, faceless, boring red brick buildings that made up his primary school. There were four or five of them, calling him names, shoving him this way, and that. He wasn't sure exactly why any of this had started; he only knew that it had and that it was now becoming an almost daily occurrence, making him dread coming to school.

It was always hard being the new kid, especially at an age where everyone seemed to be developing much faster than him, but it wasn't meant to be *this* hard, surely? He tried to run from them and received a sharp punch to the stomach for his trouble. Several hands grabbed him roughly by the shirt, the collar, even the hair for one or two excruciating moments as he was dragged back into the center of the group. Panic was starting to set in, and he was about to cry as he tried in vain to protect himself from the blows and abuse that were raining down on him.

Where are the teachers? Why won't anyone help me?

The tears had started then, seemingly inciting the aggressors to yet more insults and blows, this time mixed with laughter.

Hahaha. Look at him, he's crying! Hahaha. The little wimpy nance. Ya bawbag. Hahahaha!

Andrew received a kick to his backside from behind and stumbled forward just as another kick collected him directly in the stomach. He doubled over in agony, and just as he was about to drop to the floor and curl into a ball to try and protect himself, the biggest of the bullies suddenly released his grip.

He'd been pulled backward with such force that his head snapped violently forward - it was quite amazing that it was still attached! The bully was dragged away and thrown violently to the ground. The rest of them, one moment ago so vicious and impossibly bold, suddenly looked timid and hesitant, frozen to the spot, unsure what had just happened.

Through eyes obscured with his own hair and tears, Andrew saw a giant blurred shape with a patch of blonde atop its frame lurch towards the kids to his left and right, grabbing them and hurling them together with such force that there was an audible 'crack' as their heads collided. They stumbled backward, losing their balance and joining their friend on the ground. Blood was pouring from one kid's forehead, and the other looked like he might well have a broken nose. Andrew couldn't believe what he was seeing. One of them had started to cry.

What's just happened?

The biggest of the bullies was back on his feet now but unsure of his next move. He had a decision to make - try and man up to the imposing intruder and save face, or run, possibly for his life. He unwisely chose the former and was met with a punch to the neck swiftly followed by a kick to the groin, staggering backward, clutching at the unimaginable pain he felt between his legs and gasping for air as he collapsed to the ground once more.

The three broken, crumpled things writhed there, groaning in agony, while the fourth and maybe fifth of the assailants had hightailed it at some point. Andrew wiped at his eyes and focused clearly for the first time on the huge figure that was now approaching and placing a giant hand on his trembling shoulder.

"You ok, pal?"

"Aye," he squeaked, "aye, thanks!" slightly calmer this time, lowering the pitch of his voice and trying to control his heart, which was still beating hard and fast in his chest. The huge figure turned and glared at the three moaning wretches on the ground and bellowed at them -

"If ANY of you or any of you ever come near .... err … what's your name, pal?"

"Andy," he replied in a slightly too high-pitched voice. The giant returned his gaze to the crumpled and bloodied mess at his feet. One of them went to get up, and the giant took a step towards him.

"YOU ... STAY ... THERE!"

The kid froze and then slumped back down, seemingly resigned to his fate. The giant spoke again, slowly and clearly, his voice laced with menace -

"If ANY of you, EVER, come near Andy here again, you'll get *properly* messed up next time."

The giant waited for the words to sink in, and then looking from one to the next, added - "Are we clear? Good! Now *piss off!*"

With that, the three wannabe bullies scrambled up and away as fast as they could, holding various parts of themselves and grimacing in both pain and shame as they limped and staggered away, pushing past the crowd of eager young faces that had gathered around at the commotion. Andrew wiped his eyes again and focused on the muscular giant in front of him. The boyish face and broad grin belied the huge frame, and the shock of blonde hair was hard to miss. The giant held out a meaty paw in Andrew's direction.

"Hi, I'm John," it said with a wink and a slight crack in its voice, giving some credence at least to the fact that this giant was indeed still just a boy itself.

***

He'd led a charmed life so far. Born an only child and into one of Alba's wealthy elite families, he'd experienced a childhood that could best be described as idyllic, privileged even. There were frequent family holidays, private tutors, a doting mother and father, and the best education money could buy. John McGregor did not want for anything.

Further increasing his odds of success in life, John had a natural charm and an easy manner to match a fair intellect. As he grew older, it became apparent that he'd also inherited his mother's looks and his father's physical attributes. The only blot on his copybook growing up was a tendency to lose his cool when put under extreme pressure, and this was something else he'd inherited from his father.

Studies had been a breeze for him, and his natural attributes meant that he'd never been shy of attention, wanted or not. A scholarship to college in an elite stream seemed a natural step, and he'd excelled when the time came. He'd never asked for any of this - the money, the attention, the connections, but here it was. An easy ride for the golden child, if he wanted it. Everything in his life had continued blissfully on its merry way. Until recently that is - when everything fell apart.

The night had been the usual mixture of fake smiles, self-congratulatory conversations, talk of the next big thing, and money. Always money. John hadn't chosen these friends, they had chosen him, and he was obliged to humor them. They had the same family connections needed to become a success, and it was expected that they would all help one another prosper. Being in their company was a chore, though, and he couldn't wait to take the first opportunity to get away from them.

John studied himself in the bathroom mirror as he washed his hands. It was easy to see why everyone expected him to succeed, lead, and do everything right. He was the only one that could see the almost imperceptible flicker of doubt in the face that looked back at him.

Better show my face. Another ten minutes, a quick drink, and then I can go.

He smiled and winked at himself in the mirror and headed back to his spot at the bar. It was crowded but cozy, with gold fittings glinting in the low light and deep red carpeting and booths scattered here and there. Bac smoke hung heavily in the air. He didn't smoke but thought that it smelt wonderful, earthy, and full of life.

Sally McCloud, one of his circle of elite friends, he supposed, suddenly plonked herself down next to him, putting her hand on his thigh to steady herself as she did so and leaning in close. Too close. She was drunk, and John knew that this spelled trouble. Sally was undoubtedly one of the most beautiful young ladies John had ever seen - she had long blonde hair, curves where curves should be, sparkling brown eyes, an upturned little nose, and sensual, pouty lips.

She just wasn't his type, and in any case, he was taken, permanently, he hoped. Sally had left her hand on John's thigh and now squeezed firmly as she locked eyes with him, causing him to shift uncomfortably on the bar stool. He returned her smile out of politeness. He grabbed her arm and tried to move it away so that she'd have to release her grip, but she only took this as an invitation and leaned closer still, pushing her chest against his arm so that he could feel her warmth. Her hand tightened its grip and crept a little higher, causing John to shift his weight and try to lever his leg away.

"John darling, don't be shy; how about you and I go somewhere private and have a wee little chat, eh?" Her pupils were dilated, and the desire in her eyes would have floored most men. John steeled himself and intercepted her hand as it crept far too close to his gentlemen's business.

"Sally, as much as I love you, my dear friend, I do have a girlfriend, as you know."

Sally mock pouted, giggled, and touched her top lip enticingly with her tongue. She wasn't getting the message.

"To be honest, I'm a bit worried about exactly how much talking you intend to do," he said with a smile. He had to end this.

*

Sally was undeterred, however, purring, "oh, come on, John sweetie, I need to *talk* to you, in the bathroom ..." She was almost pleading now, removing her hand from John's thigh and circling her arm around him instead, hugging him tightly. She felt John's arm move behind her, his hand resting on her shoulder. Her breath caught in her throat, and she hugged tighter still, smiling to herself as she felt the warmth growing between her legs.

Yes! It's going to be tonight.

She was about to make an excessively obscene proposition, but John pushed her gently away.

What!

John had a hand on each of her shoulders, holding her at bay. What was that look in his eye? Sympathy? Sally froze as she realized what was happening. The rejection stung her, and she lost her temper, shrugging his hands away and slipping off the bar stool. She was now standing with her arms folded across her chest, glaring. She spat out the words - stinging little wasps of words, meant to hurt -

"Why do you even hang around with that *horrid little thing!* Do you feel sorry for *her* too?"

*

He went to speak, but Sally had already turned away, tears in her eyes, and was storming off to no doubt assail her next victim or create her next little drama.

The room seemed to come in and out of focus. It was barely a flicker, but John knew the feeling all too well. "I think I need a breather," he muttered under his breath.

He made swiftly for the toilets, pushing carefully past people in the crowded and dimly lit space before pushing open the walnut and gold embossed toilet door. To his relief saw a vacant cubicle, shutting the door behind him and sitting heavily on the marble seat.

John had disguised it well, but the words about Claire had angered him. He was sick of this group of young and, at times, obnoxious highflyers with all their money and connections. The way they put down everyone and everything that they considered beneath them was getting too much for him. He leaned forward and held his head in his hands.

What am I going to do? I can't stand this. Maybe I can move away as soon as I'm finished at SCC, settle down somewhere with Claire, grow some veggies ...

No one had said anything to him about Claire for a while after their relationship had begun. Still, it didn't take him long to start noticing the puzzled looks, the occasional whispers, and nods in his direction amongst friends on a night out.

Once word had gotten out that he was seeing, yes, actually *seeing* that strange lower-class girl, Claire Renshaw, there had been a few careful inquiries. Later on, a few back-handed jibes and the odd jealous remark. No one had said anything much for the last few months, though - until tonight, that was.

A sense of resentment started to rise inside him as he sat and thought about just who these people thought they were. More importantly, judging him and judging someone else that they didn't even know based purely on their social circumstance. They had no fucking clue. John supposed he should not have expected anything less. He knew one thing for sure, though, and that was that he couldn't keep up the facade much longer. *If it wasn't for the family connections ...*

Anxiety suddenly consumed him, and he felt short of breath and giddy - the cubicle panels seemed to close in on him, and he braced himself against the cubicle wall as he broke into a cold sweat. John was in the middle of a panic attack, and he knew he'd no option but to ride it out. He'd had plenty of practice of this over the last few months, ever since his father had disappeared and John's world had begun to implode.

***

She'd returned to her workroom following the meeting. It was still dark outside. The horizon was starting to lighten with the first glimpse of sunrise. Assuming that the sun was to be seen today, you never could tell in The Highlands.

Isabel sat at her desk, hands placed flat on its surface, and stared out through the plexi-pane into the dark void. The room was in almost complete darkness, the orb projected from her comms, barely illuminating the surface of her desk. The low light was soothing, and it helped her think, and she had a lot of thinking to do.

The meeting had been extremely uncomfortable. Isabel was absolutely fuming about what had happened, although she would in no way reveal this to any of her esteemed colleagues. She was more or less on her own on this one. 'The Chair,' the sanctum's shadowy chief, never seen, always heard, never questioned, had called the meeting late on a Wednesday night, for starters. Wednesday nights were usually kept free to allow members of the sanctum the chance to recharge and relax for a moment or two outside of their usually punishing schedules.

Isabel had already lined up a couple of leisure boys to visit her, which had been difficult, to say the least, after the most recent incident. Poor old Gary hadn't survived the night, and she'd had to call in Gerald James to help dispose of him.

She entered the meeting room already more than a little miffed that her night of entertainment had been curtailed, but her mood was soon to worsen.

Fucking *Lachlan Grealish*. Who was this nobody? Who did he think he was? And the chair, the supreme power, the one who couldn't be challenged, had officially sworn him into the sanctum and presented him as the *face of the cause! The face! What were they playing at?*

Respect and trust had to be earned first, and then, and only then, could such roles be handed out. That was just the way it was!

Worse was to come, and the chair had, amongst other things, given him oversight of Isabel's mining program. Her program! She was still shaking with fury just thinking about it. Not only that, to make matters worse still, Lachlan Grealish was to handle all related media engagements from this point on.

It was clear that the chair had big plans for him and also clear that he had little or no plans for Isabel. The absolute duille! Actually, the duilles! No one had voiced any concern or objection. No one! She would be reassessing her allies and her enemies after this. Any newly discovered enemies would soon find out who they were.

She'd been positioning herself in the media for some time on behalf of the sanctum. One of her main objectives was to recognised as a heroine and savior of the people. She needed the media to achieve this. It was to be her legacy! Now what? This little fucking upstart is ushered into *her* area of responsibility, overseeing *her* project, with not even a word of warning! Heads were going to roll for this.

Lachlan Grealish certainly had all the charm and charisma; Isabel couldn't deny that. Maybe if he were fifteen or twenty years younger, she might have had something special for him. It may yet even come to that. Sometimes you had to do what you had to do – and maybe this would prove to be one of those times.

Lachlan … fucking … Grealish!

She went through the list: he had too firm a handshake, and he was far too confident amongst his seniors and betters. There were many other items on the list, but she was just too furious to concentrate. It was downright disrespectful! Isabel wasn't even giving him a chance. She'd already started plotting his demise.

The vial of blue liquid sat on a small silver tray just to the left of her secure comms, barely glinting in the dull light of her workroom. She'd been dutifully ignoring it for the last hour, but every so often, it broke through and interrupted her concentration, its silky promise always just below the surface of her thoughts.

There was no doubt she was addicted to the Serum, and she didn't even remember placing it so carefully on her desk. She was going to have to do something about this. The Serum had been interacting with her mutanoids in some rather unpleasant ways. One of the substances had to go, and she was far too attached to her quite frankly amazing physique to allow anything to diminish it.

She needed to finish her train of thought. Last night's sanctum meeting had, amongst other things, left her feeling hollow and betrayed. She'd received reassurances from one or two members that they were finding her something better yet to manage. It had done nothing to placate her.

Why did this have to happen now, just when she was starting to feel in control of it all? After all the years of hard work and playing politics, just when she was finally starting to dictate terms to that bunch of soft-spined old farts, the chair had turned her world upside down in an instant. She was still struggling to come to terms with it all.

An idea started to form. The more Isabel thought about it, the more she felt confident that she could use what had happened to her advantage. She glanced once more at the blue vial but then opened her desk drawer and quickly swept it off her desk before slamming it shut.

Isabel resumed thinking. After a while, her reflection started grinning back at her.

***

Claire usually started her days very early. She'd learned to do without sleep, with her often very late nights of breaching and coding merging with the very early mornings. She liked the peacefulness and quiet of pre-dawn. It allowed her to travel on the transporters when there was rarely another soul on board – much better than those horrid peak times with everyone crammed in, breathing on you.

It had been a long time since she'd felt this excited about anything, and she was a bundle of nerves as she waited for the others. She'd been sitting in the inventively named 'The Caf-Bar' for the last hour, ignoring the admiring glances of the college boys, and going over and over the data she'd stumbled across last night. It really could be something very important - if she could just work out how to get around the lower levels of the security code.

After a while, she sighed and looked around the caf-bar. A very handsome and athletic-looking dark-haired boy was what she assumed was making eyes at her from the bench near the window. He had perfect hair, a devilishly cheeky grin, and dreamy blue eyes. She scowled at him, and he quickly looked away, pretending to check his comms instead. She made a mental note not to bother brushing her hair in the mornings from now on and returned to her code.

***

Stuart McGregor, a senior researcher and held in very high esteem by his colleagues, had gone missing one night on his way home to his family. Only very few of the best of the best got the chance of an interview at D.A.I.R, or 'The Institute' as it was known to those on the inside. Since its inception, Stuart had been a fixture of the program and had often brought his son, John, into the building during his school-age years.

On the night of his disappearance, he'd booked a single transporter pod through his comms, left the institute building – an ornate, white marbled building modeled on ancient greek structures - at nine forty-five p.m., clambered into the autonomous vehicle with a nod to a colleague, headed towards the heights, and had then simply vanished into thin air.

The pod had registered that he'd alighted as scheduled, outside his imposing residence at the very top of the old town. He never made it to the front door. Stuart's wife Jessica alerted the authorities the following morning after a night of frantic calls to medi-centers, friends, neighbors, and Stuart's colleagues from the institute - in short, anyone and everyone she knew.

Once the investigation into his disappearance had begun, it was soon established that there was no sign of foul play. His comms had been deactivated soon after he got into the pod. It appeared that Stuart McGregor had been using the thirty-minute journey to have some peace and quiet each night on his way home.

There were no images available from the street cams or surveillance fly-bots (SFB's) that night that showed anything useful, and the transporter pod hadn't recorded anything either. The Solo's usually always auto-recorded any inbound or outbound comms and any conversation that took place – not that the general public knew that – but there was nothing on record.

Stuart McGregor had vanished, leaving behind his distraught family and collages, a million questions, and not one single answer. Technology, so integrated into everyone's lives, so good at tracking everyone and everything, had failed completely to cast any light at all on what had happened.

Over the weeks that followed, hope turned to despair for the remaining family members. John watched helplessly as his mother, Jessica, a strong and powerful woman in her own right, started to fall apart at the seams.

He was doing all he could to help the search, support his mother and keep up with his work and studies, but he felt hopeless and impotent in his efforts. The search had slowly wound down, and life went on - such that it was. Over the months that followed, grief had come, closely followed by anger and then finally, resignation.

John had relied heavily on his closest friends in helping him hold it together. Aside from one night where it had taken a good six or so of his university mates to hold him back from ripping a guy's head off, life had just continued, the huge black hole where his father had once been being the only difference. Claire and her breaching skills had given him some hope that they might be able to uncover something, but to date, they had been drawing a blank.

The panic attacks had started in the first few weeks after his father's disappearance and had been coming more and more frequently, along with his growing sense of alienation from his wealthy friends. John wouldn't rest until he found his father. Although he had a willing ally in Claire, there was so much pressure in every other part of his life that just lately, he was wondering how he could even find the time to keep looking, as ridiculous as that concept was.

This sense of hopelessness, fear, and not belonging in his father's world had meticulously prepared him for sometimes seemed more than he could bear. It was one of those times. He collapsed to the floor of the cubicle, hurriedly flipping up the lid of the toilet as he firmly grasped each side of the bowl and started retching the overly expensive contents of his stomach into it.

***

Andrew checked his comms and realized that he still had another twenty minutes to kill in the staggeringly overcrowded transporter pod. He whispered to himself, "Sweet Douglas, will this journey never fucking end." He wriggled slightly away from his latest fellow traveler. This young woman was immaculately dressed. She'd given him a derisory look in the millisecond it took her to make all sorts of no doubt negative assumptions about him before she'd reluctantly plonked herself next to him.

Unfortunately for Andrew, his neighbor seemed to have developed a taste for puddings, possibly even late-night baffel's, the sticky and incredibly sweet late-night snack preferred by the lower classes of the region. Although young and relatively attractive, the addiction had seemingly taken its toll on her over time and was causing her buttocks and thighs to encroach on what limited space he already had.

My seat is under invasion! The border has been breached!

For the last few minutes, he'd found himself doing all he could to avoid that awkward shared heat you got when two people's outer thighs were inadvertently pressed together for any length of time in public transport. Maybe he should be grateful for some sort of human contact, albeit inadvertent and however uncomfortable, he wondered.

Instead, he shifted his weight again and wedged himself deeper and more tightly into the corner of the pod. I'm now a fucking occupied territory, he thought, glancing down to ensure that he'd managed to squirm away just enough to avoid actual thigh contact.

Andrew liked to make up stories about those around him to pass the time - anything to avoid starting work, really. Baffel lady was his most recent, and it was one way he amused himself when the situation was as dire and grim as it was most mornings. Traveling on a crowded transporter every day was the worst, he concluded. *Time to get the game started*, he thought, carefully observing all those within his range of vision, one after the other - scanning for something of interest, something to spark the imagination.

After a minute or two, he was ready to give up. This morning's candidates were a poor lot, tired-looking and uniformly dressed in state-issued winter gear, all absorbed in their comms, of course, except a couple who had mercifully nodded off and were now being propped up by those next to them.

He reached into his coat pocket awkwardly, trying to avoid elbowing baffel lady in the boob, and was about to take out the dreaded comms and look at his work assignments for the first time today, but oh, hang on, there! He saw it. A man, opposite and to the right of him who had been revealed at the last stop, thin, with wire opti-lenses that sat too far down on his nose and were almost comically tilted - fifties perhaps, or late forties if he was kind, receding dark and oily hair.

Nothing too unusual there, but he studied the man closely. *There it is again!* Andrew smiled to himself. He'd found a way to amuse himself, at last. The thing was, the man had unusually slow movements, so very unusually slow. It was mesmerizing.

Andrew watched as the man tried in vain to correct his askew opti-lenses and then slowly, oh so very, very slowly, rubbed his hand up and over his head, attempting no doubt to fix the lank and dark greasy locks that flopped down messily. He then – slowly - returned his hand to its starting point. The whole process had seemed to take *forever*.

He was transfixed. The man ever so slowly stretched his head up and back before returning once more to the starting position. Andrew's mind was racing now. *This man, what was his life like? Did this strange and terrible affliction hinder or benefit him? How long would it take him to walk from the transporter stop to his place of employment, to anywhere?* Andrew's brow furrowed, then a beaming smile suddenly lit up as face.

Slow Motion Man! Yes, yes, that's it! The Adventures of Slow-Motion Man!

Andrew spent the last eighteen minutes of an otherwise all too dreary journey with a grin etched across his face as his mind raced and his eyes sparkled, totally oblivious to the several worried glances he was attracting from those around him. He imagined slow-motion man in a range of real-life situations. Running a hundred-yard race would be a problem. Catching a frisbee - again, problematic. Boxing? A small giggle escaped this time and was quickly stifled, but with some effort.

He powered his comms back up to try and distract himself for a moment, nipping a laughing fit in the bud, and dispatched a message to John that he'd reconsidered his offer and that he really wasn't his type, after all. He preferred his boyfriends with teeth and reasonable personal hygiene.

Now, back to the game. And then? Then what happens? Oh yes!

Slow-Motion Man gets a job as a children's entertainer; he thought, a worthy and respected route of employment, no doubt. Day one does not go so well, though, not at all. He is late (of course) to little Tommy's party. As he slowly fumbles several magic tricks - rendered pointless by the slow-motion sleight of hand on display - the children grow increasingly restless, starting to shift in their seats and whisper to one another.

Little Tommy is casting pleading looks to his mother, and Slow-Motion Man is becoming somewhat horrified at how things are turning out. Little Tommy's mother is starting to look a bit concerned herself, and so Slow-Motion Man reaches, ever so slowly, into his bag of tricks for what he hopes will be the trick that saves the day. ...

The juggling was a bit of a disaster, to be perfectly honest. This time Andrew had trouble stifling a laugh, and for several horrifying seconds, he thought he was about to completely lose it and be consumed by a full-blown laughing fit in the corner of the transporter. He pressed his lips tightly together, but the giggs were building uncontrollably, his body starting to shake, his stomach in knots. He placed his head in his hands and tried desperately to think of something sad. He snorted. The giggs weren't going away!

Oh, Douglas! Please! Save me!

Just at that moment, and probably quite thankfully, the bong noise and the announcement came over the transporter comms that they were arriving at New Edinburgh Central. Andrew broke the several glares now directed at him by launching up from his seat and making a beeline for the nearest exit, bumping one or two commuters on the way past but caring not as he made a desperate attempt to escape before he totally embarrassed himself. The transporter slowed suddenly, and everyone that was standing lurched forward, Andrew included.

He found himself standing directly in front of where slow-motion man was sitting. A thought popped into Andrew's head, and just as the door was about to open he couldn't help himself and, catching slow-motion man's slow-motion gaze, he said, quite clearly, while looking directly into the eyes of the poor soul hereafter to be ever known as slow-motion man -

"Condolences to the wife."

A look of bewilderment that quickly (surprisingly) turned to anger came across slow-motion man's face, and he went to say something just as the door popped open, and a blast of icy air swept into the pod. Andrew launched himself through the doorway and out of the transporter, breaking into a run and not looking back. As he ran, he enjoyed the feeling of ever so slight danger. He couldn't get the image out of his mind, the look of bemusement, shock, and then anger on slow-motion man's face as the words found their way to comprehension in slow-motion man's usually slow-motion mind.

Laughter was now finally able to escape the confines of his mind and body and be released into the wild. Plumes of icy cold air in the form of vapor escaped his lungs as he ran, laughing, he imagined like some sort of insane person, down and off the podium and into the streets of New Edinburgh. He was laughing so hard that tears scalded his eyes as he ran.

Eventually, he slowed, taking a quick look behind him, almost half expecting Slow-motion Man to be running after him in slow-motion, but it wasn't to be. Andrew's breath came in short, sharp gasps as he stopped and took in the view of the Old Quarter just ahead of him. "Why the fuck was I 'running,' anyway?" he said to himself, shook his head, and started off toward his rendezvous.

Sometimes it really did feel good to be alive, he thought, and with this, his pace quickened, and he started walking purposefully in the direction of the state college. If he hurried, he'd more or less make it to the place on time, and if he were lucky, he'd have a chance to grab an iced-caf on the way from one of the roaming vend-bots. He glanced down at his comms again and checked to see if any were nearby. Was he just as bad as everybody else? He was worried he might well be.

John had replied to his earlier message, he noted. 'And I prefer blondes that are also taller than an Ewok, so you never stood a chance anyway.'

What the fuck is an Ewok? Andrew wondered as he attempted to track down the nearest vend-bot.

***

He was working late into the night, as he did most nights. There were no fancy cocktail parties or grand openings to attend tonight, and he was disappointed to see that no specialist services were available either. The more Lachlan Grealish had looked into his portfolio, the more uncomfortable he'd started to feel.

It seemed that no one would give him a straight answer, and when he'd started asking questions, he'd been told on more than one occasion that he'd need to earn the sanctum's full trust before any such details would be divulged. In other words - he had to earn it.

They sure know how to keep you in your place.

He'd been left with no doubt that he'd have to wait quite some time to achieve equal footing amongst the elite of the elite. After that, he'd been reluctant to even ask about the little blue vials. He did get an answer of sorts on that one.

Lachlan had been told that this material was an unexpected by-product of the A.I. development mining program, and it was very limited in its production. Only one person in the sanctum was trusted with its distribution, and that person was Gerald James, the wiry bastard who had nearly crushed his hand when they first met.

There were no easy decisions in politics, of course. Still, he'd never before been involved in the kind that puts the interest of a few individuals over that of absolutely everything else. The more he thought about it, the more he realized that he was now up to his neck in a dictatorship of sorts, conveniently masked under the guise of new socialism. Something was very wrong with all of this, but he was just glad he was on the right side of it if he was honest.

He'd already seen what could happen if you happened to find yourself on the wrong side. He'd often wondered why there were so many scandals at the highest levels of state governance, aside from good old-fashioned greed that was, and now he knew. These people were downright frightening when the Serum wore off.

There was one big problem with all of this. He'd been told from the start that once you were in, you were in forever. Whether he liked it or not, and whether he liked his portfolio or not, there was no way out.

* * *

Andrew thrust his hands deep into his pockets and angled his head down as another icy blast of recently arrived sleet stung his face. He was walking as quickly as he could towards the old town center, but he was already soaked.

Bloody typical!

The smooth concrete paving soon gave way to ancient cobblestones, and the newer vendboxes and workroom buildings gave way to what was left of those that had somehow survived the end of times.

Andrew's research into the old world had uncovered that New Edinburgh had been built on the remnants of the old-world medieval city of Stirling. Apparently, it had similarities to the original Edinburgh and wasn't so far geographically from the location of the old city, which lay as ruins in the uninhabitable zone. The ancient facades loomed overhead as the slick concrete podways became paved laneways, and the laneways became cobbled alleys, narrowing, twisting, and turning one way then the other. Andrew knew all the shortcuts - he absolutely loved this part of town. It was something to do with the feeling of being so connected to the old world, and he often imagined this place in its heyday, with people flitting about and bustling along in blissful ignorance to the fact that their days were numbered. Much like today's world, he suspected.

The SCC, the giant, gleaming monolithic building of plex and steel that had been purpose-built to educate Alba's next generation, was but a hundred yards from where he was standing. You wouldn't know it, though. Andrew was in a narrow, cobbled alleyway, lined with vendboxfronts that had been largely preserved from the last civilization. They had timber and brick façade, some with ornate plasterwork. Andrew often imagined he was back in those simpler, more free times. *If only I'd been born a thousand or so years ago*, he thought. It was a thought he often had. It made him feel melancholy.

He looked left and right. There was no one around. Andrew jumped and pulled himself over a high brick wall sandwiched between two precarious-looking facades and was gone from view in an instant.

The tight passageway he'd landed in went straight ahead for a few yards and then opened into the rear delivery bay of their favorite caf-bar. He quickly crossed the open bay and headed down another narrow passage leading toward huge bunker doors belonging to the adjacent building. He pulled one of the heavy doors up from its frame and slipped through into the darkness below. He stumbled off the last step and twisted his ankle, grimacing as he felt a stab of pain shoot up his leg.

"Fuck it!"

He wiggled his ankle. It seemed to still be in one piece. Not the most graceful of landings, but he was here, relatively unharmed, unnoticed, not to mention, on time. He set off down a series of damp, dark corridors and steps that led the way down below ground level, the air getting cooler as he descended. He ended up outside a heavy, green-painted steel doorway.

It was pitch black in the corridor, but the sliver of light from underneath the door that was faintly illuminating the wet floor underneath his feet meant that at least one of the others was already here. Andrew knocked three times, paused, knocked twice more, then four times, then –

"Will you cut that dook out!" bellowed the voice from behind the door, "you know we don't have a secret knock ya wee twat!"

The door swung open, and a massive shape filled the doorframe, the backlighting faintly picking up some blonde highlights around what he assumed was John's giant head.

"Ooh, touchy! Nice to see you too, pal." He brushed past John and into the cozy confines of 'the place.'

CHAPTER 3 – ELYSSIUM

They'd found 'The Place' by accident. The building above had been undergoing reconstruction and redevelopment for as long as they could remember. They'd been mucking about in the building works, sort of on their way home but sort of not, late one Friday night after a few too many after college bru's when they had stumbled, quite literally, across the entry hatch.

"Oh aye, that's what yer maw said!" Andrew had responded, making an innocent remark by John suddenly seem lewd.

"Andrew!" Claire seemed genuinely shocked that he could sink so low. He bowed theatrically in response.

"Right, come here ya wee bawbag!" John lunged, and Andrew took evasive action, not too cleverly as it turned out, losing his footing and falling backward onto the metal doors of the hatch, pushing one down partly through the opening with the weight of his fall.

"Ah, dook!" Andrew managed to grunt as the dust settled around him.

"You ok, Andy?!" Claire seemed concerned, but John wasn't. He was finding the situation hysterically amusing. Andrew sat up gingerly and dusted himself off. He looked up and accepted the giant hand outstretched toward him as he somewhat clumsily levered himself upright. Well almost.

His friend let go of him just as he was around halfway towards vertical, causing him to experience a moment of weightlessness, arms cartwheeling as he realized what was about to happen. He crashed back down into the doorway, this time causing the metal hatch to buckle and fall through the opening, closely followed by Andrew himself. A yelp, a muffled thud, and a plume of dust billowing out of the dark opening were closely followed by Andrew's voice, quite clearly not very happy.

"You bloody prick! You can go, and bloody well 'do one' ya twat!"

John and Claire looked at each other. Andrew hadn't quite finished with the abuse.

"You great big fannybaws! You wait till I, oof! Fuck! Again!" Andrew's voice was muffled, wafting up from the dark space. John was doubled over laughing now, and Claire, although a little shocked at the callousness of the act, was also giggling uncontrollably, barely able to get words out.

"Andrew! Andrew, man! Are you still alive down there?"

Some more muffled sounds followed, and then a light shone up through the hatch.

"Aye, I'm fine, and no thanks to the giant oaf up there, mind!"

A short pause was followed by the sound of something heavy being moved somewhere below. The others had pulled themselves together and were peering down through the hatch into the semi-illuminated space. John turned to Claire, and she raised an eyebrow.

"You guys are going to want to come down and have a look at this!" called Andrew with a level of excitement unusual for him, "I can see a passageway from here, heading down. A long way down, I think!"

And so it was that they discovered 'The Place.' They went through the dark, damp passageways, using light orbs projected from their comms to find their way. They kept going, down a set of old stone steps to the big metal door at the end of another corridor, and then inside to a nice cozy space that they could make their own - their place.

They'd frequented it regularly ever since. Claire and John had managed to hook up the power supply, and they were all very careful to ensure no one ever saw them come and go. It was the place of many long and heated discussions, many late nights, many laughs, much cheap VKA – the clear but highly potent bevvie and choice of the lower classes.

Over time, they'd smuggled in a few items in that they could easily maneuver down the tight passageways and into their place, managing to make it quite comfortable: a small folding desk, a stool, a rug, a heater, and a couple of small beanbags. It wasn't much, but it was theirs. It was safe, private, and they could say whatever they liked down there.

Claire had further safeguarded the secret room with her patented strips of aluminum foil technique. The foil hung down from and covered the entire ceiling of the room and out into the passageway. It was a nice simple way to run interference on any comms probe. She had the same foil strip masking system back in her flat, and well, so far, no problems - aside, that is, for it looking as if she was stark raving mad to anyone that visited.

The place was not so great if you needed the bathroom, of course, and so there was always a bit of time limit attached to being there - unless you didn't mind using a corner of one of the many musty old storerooms full of rubble just off the main passageway. There was a second way out, and possibly a third, although they'd never tried it – it required a leap of faith across an empty stairwell that none of them were willing to attempt.

The second way out was more user-friendly, but this emerged under a utility hole cover just off one of the main vending areas of the old town. As such, this option could only ever be used in case of an emergency – they hoped not to have that particular dilemma.

"So, what's up?" Andrew asked into the gloom, directing his gaze toward a silhouette propped up against the far wall. He assumed this was Claire – he'd know that hair anywhere. He was glad it was dark and that he didn't have to meet her eye. A brief image of her nakedness in the dark space popped into his head, and he forced it away, flushing, again, glad of the darkness.

"Have you caught the state fixing the price of beans again?" he asked. This elicited a heavy outward breath from John and then a shake of the head. Claire moved from the corner and pointed toward the only light source currently in the room - her device. It was running one of her decrypting programs over and over again.

"What's all this then?"

He took a seat on the stool by the small desk and peered at the display. Claire leaned over his shoulder, her hair brushing against his ear as she reached over him and stopped the program. He caught a faint whiff of perfume and flushed slightly as he tried to concentrate on what was happening on the display.

Andrew could feel Claire's body heat, she was so close, and he was trying as hard as he could to not be completely distracted. Claire sat next to him, opening another program on the device. Her thigh pressed up against his.

Does she know she's touching me? Dougdam women, with their womanly-ness. Why do they have to be so damn womanly?

Andrew had started to sweat.

"*This* is what I found last night," she spoke in a low, serious voice that brought Andrew's attention firmly back to the present. She got up and stepped back, allowing him some room.

"I stumbled upon a highly, highly sophisticated security program that was all over some data linked to the department of internal affairs. I've isolated it, but no matter what I throw at it, I can't get past it."

"Claire, are you sure you should be digging around in there? I mean, I know you are good, but ..."

Andrew let the statement hang in the air. He was genuinely fearful of being found out. He didn't know what would happen if they were, but he assumed it would be bad.

Breaching media data to dig the dirt on current and disgraced politicians was one thing, but going this deep into what surely were restricted and highly secret areas of state data was taking it to a whole new level. He really didn't want to end up getting in serious trouble because of Claire and John's little hobby.

"It's fine, Andy." She sounded exasperated. "You should know better by now, for fucks sake!"

John laughed. Andrew felt himself blush slightly. He was being scolded for daring to question her competence. He should have known better indeed.

"So, what do we know then?" he asked.

"Well, aside from the way, way overblown security, there is already some *very* interesting metadata at level two," she noted, her voice tight in her throat as she leaned over Andrew and opened her decoder program. This time his attention was more focused on the two words highlighted again and again.

"What is that? 'Elyssium Research'? What even is that?" Andrew's pulse quickened a little as he realized that they might well have found something they were indeed not supposed to see. He'd never heard of such a thing.

"Well, it looks very much like a reference to an entire state research program or maybe even state department that no-one has ever heard of."

"That's massive if that's the case. Dook! Is that the case?"

He turned and looked at Claire, then John. They both had the same gleam in their eye.

"There's no such thing as Elyssium, though, is there? It's a made-up word, right?"

"Well, no such word, you are right, so it's code."

"Code for what though?"

"Well, this is the thing …" Claire leant back over her device and switched to another set of data. Andrew noticed that John had become tense and leaned in a little, his attention also now on the display.

"Elyssium only ever gets mentioned when referenced to the D.A.I.R and the security services … here."

And there it was, thought Andrew. *This is why they're so buzzed about it.* It was perhaps a lead on John's father's disappearance, and maybe even Claire's sister. D.A.I.R and the security services. Their two prime targets.

"So…" Andrew's mouth felt dry as he tried to form the next words. Fortunately, no sounds came out. He felt his pulse quicken a little before he forced himself to regain control by taking a slow, steady breath. John leant down, putting both hands on the desk, and locked eyes with Andrew.

"So, Andy, there's something that the state isn't telling us about. Something big. It's A.I. research and security related - maybe a long shot … but … this could be the thing that dad was working on when he disappeared."

John's voice had cracked ever so slightly at the mention of his father. Claire stepped over and embraced him quickly. John shifted his weight and pulled away, composing himself.

"Look, it could be nothing. I understand that" John conceded, "but, in all the months of research, this is the first tangible thing we have found that could be related to dad's disappearance."

Claire chimed in, "there's just so much security on this … it has to be worth a closer look."

"Aye, ok, but it's dangerous, right? Poking around in there." There was no reply. Andrew was already starting to worry that they were way too invested in this to see things clearly. "Well, it's *something* all right."

Claire had moved around the desk and stood facing Andrew in the dim light. He could barely see her expression, and for once, he was glad. When she spoke, there was a coldness to her voice.

"We weren't even looking for the link. We just stumbled across this weird security code and then discovered Elyssium and - well, I suppose we don't know yet if there is anything to it." She glanced at John. "What we do know is that there's something the state doesn't want us to know about, which means we are sure as hell going to know about it!"

Andrew didn't have any doubts that she would. She'd done similar work before, uncovering a benefits scandal and some dodgy trade deals, carefully leaking the information to the state media, and watching the fallout unfold in a messy array of sackings and prosecutions. The fact that she'd been able to do that and stay completely anonymous was incredibly impressive.

He was staring at her now, his mind racing. She leaned forward, the display lighting her face, allowing him to see the smile teasing the edge of her lips. He felt a hot flush wash over him as she held his gaze. John seemed oblivious to the moment. He sat in one of the beanbags and was intently working away on his own device. The tiny space was suddenly flooded with a pulsing red light from the display.

"Dook!" John was already on his feet. Claire looked shocked. Andrew looked confused.

"Fuck, fuck, fuck!" Andrew shouted, transitioning to full panic mode in a second as he realized someone or something had set off the proximity alert. They all looked at the display at the same time, but the image was grainy, and they'd just missed whatever had come through the entry, catching a glimpse of a large dark shape.

The alert was designed to give them an early warning should anyone enter their space, and it had done its job. Red meant the main entrance, which meant they'd be leaving through the rear. It was the first time a proximity alert had been set off at the place, and no one knew what to do for a few seconds.

John took control, snatching up the device and shoving it into Claire's pack before putting a finger to his lips and indicating that it was time to get out of there.

The next thirty seconds were a blur for Andrew. He was running and scraping his shoulders against the walls in the tight, dark corridors, stumbling and bumping into the others, nearly falling, being grabbed by the shirt and pulled up a metal ladder by a giant hand. Panic, fear, adrenaline, pitch black, and then finally emerging somewhat comically through the opening of a large utility hole cover, back into the gloomy light of day, just off one of the busiest vending streets of the old town.

A delivery transporter had pulled in front of the alcove where John, Andrew, and Claire had emerged from underground, providing temporary cover for the trio of now slightly disheveled-looking characters.

"The fuck was that?" Andrew blurted out breathlessly as he dusted himself down.

John turned to him, looking much calmer than the others.

"I don't know; could have been anything. A person, a dog."

"A fucking dog!" Andrew laughed. "A big fucking dog … that nearly just gave me a coronary!" Andrew risked a glance at Claire, in daylight, relieved that she was fully clothed. She caught his eye for the briefest of moments, the usual sparkle of amusement there, and no sign of anger or embarrassment. *I think it's ok; maybe she doesn't remember.*

"A dog that can open a hatch?" Claire wasn't impressed by his suggestion.

John shrugged, added with a grin - "Well, you know, a binary implanted dog maybe?"

Silence greeted the attempted quip. Andrew was miles away when John clamped a hand on his shoulder, making him jump.

"Let's leave one by one, ok? I'll hang back and ensure no one's following - animal, mineral, or vegetable." Andrew supposed that was an attempted joke and gave a nervous laugh in response. "You first. Try and look normal."

"Well, we both know that's fucking impossible!" Andrew muttered as he slowly squeezed himself between the transporter and the building facing the main street. He edged out into the open, quickly rejoining the flow of passersby with what he assumed was super spy-like stealth. He made his way across the street and then pretended to be taking a call on his comms from a position where he could keep a watchful eye on the transporter.

*

As Andrew had slithered from her sight, Claire took a moment to take in the muscular, sweaty, and athletic form standing so very close to her. She could feel the heat coming off of his body and the faint, slightly intoxicating 'John smell.' Although she was not one for public displays of emotion, there was something about those perfectly sculpted biceps, strong forearms, broad, muscular shoulders, and chest that sometimes she just had to touch. It seemed like a perfectly reasonable opportunity, public or not.

John turned and caught her red-handed as she quickly averted her gaze from his torso. He smiled with the sort of calm assurance that only someone who looked the way he did could pull off when confronted with a highly aroused creature of such rare beauty. Claire grabbed a handful of his white t-shirt, enjoying the feel of the firm chest muscles underneath as she twisted the material in her hand and pulled him a half step towards her. John was defenseless.

*

After a few seconds, the transporter pulled away from the alcove and revealed Claire and John in a deep lover's embrace. Good cover, Andrew supposed, but he couldn't quite suppress the overwhelming feeling of jealously that the scene had conjured up from deep within. He looked away, feeling more than a little heaviness in his heart as he tried to remove the image from his mind. Finally, he turned and set off for 'The Caf-Bar,' their usual meeting spot before the days' work assignments and study commenced.

***

Isabel had been summoned to the department of finance early on a Thursday morning. The building was suitably dull. Plain concrete, featureless, much like the people that inhabited it, she imagined.

Finance was proving to be an annoyance and also a tough nut to crack. Although the sanctum had one or two people fairly high up in the department, those finance types were squeaky clean and seemed to stay in the job up to and even past retirement age. They didn't have enough influence over them as yet, something that could always be remedied by good old cold-blooded murder, but it hadn't been deemed necessary, so far at least.

D.A.I.R. had several funding requests in progress with Finance, but then again, they always did. Isabel assumed that this would be yet another tiresome meeting where she would have to concede a few smaller points to ensure that they could secure enough funding to keep things on track. So far, it hadn't been a problem. However, the meetings were always uncomfortable, what with having to answer questions on budget overruns and other such trite matters. She took a moment to steel herself before she entered the meeting.

The small, beige, balding, bland-looking figure didn't look up from his desk as she entered. She stood in silence for a few moments and then made a small coughing noise. The bland man peered over the top of his clear-rimmed specs.

"Ah, Ms. Donachy, please do have a seat."

"Thank you, sir." Isabel hated having to address this pathetic, spineless Finance moron as 'sir,' but it was something she would have to bear for now. She almost winced as she sat on the hard-seated visitor's chair. Last night had been quite a night, and she was a little sore as a result. She successfully subdued the memory.

"I'll come straight to the point." The bland man looked up at Isabel after a few more moments poring over his paperwork. She was smiling benignly when he did.

Oh, here we go; he's having his little moment of power over me. I'll bet he goes into his bathroom and beats himself off once I've left the room—little prick.

"Of course, sir," she agreed.

"Your department has been over budget by more than thirty percent for the last three years in succession," remarked the bland man, the irritation clear in his voice.

"We've addressed that," Isabel said flatly.

The man raised his finger, and Isabel aborted her next sentence.

The smug little numpty.

"And," the bland man continued as if Isabel hadn't spoken at all, "we can no longer afford such poor fiscal management. Times are tough."

The bland man fixed Isabel with a steady, even stare. She nodded uncertainly, wondering what was coming.

Little prick. I'd like you to meet Mr. Floppy one of these days.

"Your budgets are hereby … frozen … until we complete a full audit of expenditure for the last five years."

Isabel leaned forward, a look of complete disbelief on her face.

"What? Are you serious?"

The bland man was peering at her, no expression apparent on his face.

Five years! The fucking little dook! I don't believe this!

Isabel was utterly gobsmacked. She wasn't expecting this. How had the sanctum not seen this coming? How had they not already taken action to protect their budgets? Something had gone horribly wrong here.

Who the fuck does this little wanker think he is? Maybe this is that smarmy prick Lachlan Grealish's doing? Oh, someone is going to pay for this!

The bland man had stared her down and spoke curtly, cutting off her train of thought.

"I believe you heard me, Ms. Donachy. Your department continues its excessive spending despite all previous warnings. We'll have somebody get in touch with you shortly to commence proceedings. In the meantime, any expenditure must first be approved by the department of finance. We'll send you the particulars."

"You cannot be serious!" Isabel's blood was boiling now. It was going to cost her dearly in the eyes of the sanctum.

"I can assure you I am. It's not a joke. It would not be a particularly funny one if it were."

Isabel just stared at the bland little dook who was jeopardizing her credibility amongst her colleagues and maybe even her career. Well, she may just have to jeopardize his existence! She decided this was not the time to make a scene; however, it would only make things worse. She'd comply with the order, at least until she could convince the sanctum of the need for, shall we say, terminal action.

"Indeed," she said with what was almost a resigned sigh. It was a good act. She folded her arms and looked out the workroom window, which had a lovely view of a large concrete wall belonging to the building right next to it.

"Will that be all, sir?" she asked, without looking back at the bland man.

"Yes. Dismissed."

Dismissed! Fuck you, you little prick. Your time will come.

Isabel made sure she had bland man's attention, saying, "Thank you, sir," as she rose, leaning forward as she got up, deliberately affording him a nice view of her cleavage - whether he liked it or not. Bland man's eyes widened for a split second, and he quickly looked back down at his paperwork, appearing flustered. Isabel put a little extra sway into her walk as she left the room. Her face was as if set in stone.

The bland man waited a few seconds after Isabel had left, then reached for the secure comms. "It's Wesley," he said.

***

Claire arrived first and nodded a greeting to Andrew as she entered the busy caf-bar. Even though she dressed in baggy and dour clothing, she still drew plenty of male attention. She threw herself down on the chair opposite her friend, blowing a piece of hair away from where it had fallen in the center of her face and plonking her pack carelessly on the table, acting as casually as she possibly could.

She wanted to ask him what had happened in Headspace, about how it could have glitched so badly, but she'd much prefer not to go there. *He doesn't have to know.*

"Remind me why we come here again?" she asked, after a moment, looking around the plain whitewashed interior.

"The company, obviously!"

The giant display on the far wall of the caf-bar was beaming in some news relating to the latest scandal to hit the state governance. Some dignitary or other had been caught with their hand in the baffel pot and was now giving a resignation speech, looking contrite and promising he was now a reformed man.

"Blah blah blah," said Andrew. "So much for the benevolent state, of and for the people. Not when you've got these self-interested twats in power!" He looked for a reaction, but Claire was staring past him. He was disappointed. Claire could usually be relied upon to engage with him on the many social injustices he railed against, but not today.

Why does this keep happening? She thought. It seemed to Claire that almost every day now, there was some scandal or other, and it had been going on forever - it was becoming very tiresome. *Can none of them be trusted?* She wondered if this was perhaps a sign that things really were falling apart behind the scenes.

Maybe it was a sign that the corruption and injustice were far more widespread than even she'd thought, making a mockery of everything the state supposedly stood for.

Maybe things have gotten out of hand to the point where the state is starting to fight itself? One can only hope.

More importantly, Andrew showed no sign of being any more embarrassed or awkward than he usually was, and she started to relax, turning her thoughts back to the state and all its problems. The problems, from what she could see, were everywhere. The idea of full equality and a classless society, for one, was clearly nonsense.

Simple human nature, she supposed, played out in the media for everyone to see. People had a way of naturally wanting more and finding ways to achieve that, generally at the expense of others. The average person looks at their neighbor, their colleague, and if they have something that they do not, well, you can see the problem.

Is it more frequent? It hadn't used to be every day, did it?

She looked around. Andrew was busy on his comms, everyone else similarly so, apart from the odd conversation here and there. *This system is broken*, she thought as she watched the display, the next story containing a similarly lurid scandal.

"What do you think, Andy?" she asked, surprising him.

"Huh?"

"About our no political state system?" Andrew looked confused.

"This system of appointing not electing the supposed 'best person for the job?" she clarified, looking back at the display.

"Working well, isn't it," he said dryly.

The next story on the vid display was about revised workgroup hours. Up again, she noted.

I wonder who approved that one?

"State veto again, I bet," she said with a sigh. Andrew frowned but wasn't really paying attention, she noticed.

Someone has to do something. She drifted off into her thoughts. Andrew had finished whatever he was doing and attempted to gain her attention.

"Planet 0420 to Claire ...kkkkschttt."

Still no reaction.

"Planet 0420 to Claire ..."

"Claire. Claire Renshaw, do you read me? Over!"

Andrew was talking into his cuff again. Claire sat and stared back at him for a few seconds, unmoved, before swiftly picking up her pack from the table and aiming a well-timed and very accurate swipe at his head. Andrew nearly fell off his chair with the force of the blow.

"Fuck's sake, Claire!"

She pouted and shrugged her shoulders.

"Mad cow."

Claire now took her turn to look bored.

Andrew was facing the entry of the caf-bar and had a clear view of anyone entering or exiting. He spotted a familiar face, Rachael McStay, as she entered, and she noticed Andrew looking her way, heading straight towards him.

"Oh-oh, six o'clock," Andrew warned. Claire turned to look. Rachael was her extremely annoying wannabe friend, and she usually avoided her at every opportunity, finding her constant approaches and compliments an unwelcome distraction. She busied herself on her comms, plugging into Headspace so that she couldn't be easily disturbed.

"Hey there!" Rachael beamed a smile at them as she took the last empty chair at their table. Andrew could see that she was clearly modeling her look on Claire, but she had on way too much pale makeup and dark eyeliner, giving her a ghost-like appearance - she was also a little too big for the gothic waif look she was trying for, but who was he to judge.

She meant well, but unfortunately for Rachael, she was oblivious to Claire's attempts to brush her off. Andrew offered an awkward nod as a greeting.

"So, have you heard?" Rachael gushed.

"Heard what, exactly?"

"Well, I heard that Frances Stewart has reappeared!"

"Oh really!" This was something worth hearing, Andrew was thinking. Claire unplugged from Headspace and listened to her attempted lookalike.

Frances was an acquaintance of John and had done some A.I. development work with him from time to time. She'd gone missing a couple of months ago and hadn't been heard from since. Until now, apparently. John would be *very* interested in this.

"Well, the thing is," she continued, "Sally McCloud got a comms message and a V.I. call from Frances just last night. Apparently, Frances has been working on secondment. Highly classified stuff of some sort, for the, ummm, department of defense, I think it was. She's going to be away for anything up to a couple of years. How about that!"

Claire's ears had pricked up at something Rachael had excitedly blurted out. *How about that indeed!*

"A V.I. call you say? To Sally, from Frances?"

Rachael's face lit up, so very pleased that Claire had actually spoken to her. It was the first time in at least a month.

"Yes! Isn't that great? Sally was so happy!"

She'd leaned in way too close, and Claire could smell her breath, her nostrils flaring slightly at the unexpected array of uninvited odors. *What was that? Breakfast, I guess.* Rachael was still talking, odorous waves confronting Claire's sensory glands.

"Well, thanks for the update. I'll be sure to let John know," Claire said flatly, talking right over the top of Rachael and causing her to freeze mid-sentence, just as she was about to no doubt blurt out the next juicy tidbit. Claire added, "Andrew and I were just leaving," with what can only be described as an extremely unfriendly glare.

An awkward silence fell between them. Rachael looked upset for a second but then suddenly beamed again and said, "well, my absolute pleasure Claire. See you in class!" With that, she got up and shuffled away, happy and content. It was perhaps the longest conversation she'd ever had with her not-so-secret crush.

*

Andrew raised an eyebrow quizzically at Claire, who shook her head and then leaned toward him, speaking quietly, "this could be another lead. I have a theory about these secondments. I'll be sure to corner Sally the next time I see her and see if I can't interrogate my theory some more."

"Lucky Sally," he remarked absentmindedly. He'd lost interest in all things Rachael and was keeping an eye out for John, just to make absolutely sure that they were indeed in the clear.

Where is he? Probably got his fat head wedged somewhere.

Just as he'd looked toward the entry, a tall lady with long blonde hair entered, and Andrew almost did a double-take.

Was that …? No, it can't be, can it?

*

Claire noticed that his attention had been diverted and followed his line of sight, seeing only a well-endowed and very attractive young blonde-haired lady by the entrance, before slowly turning back to Andrew and fixing him with an icy stare. He raised his eyebrows as if to say, "what's that for?"

"Perving again, Andy?" she inquired, with more than a hint of amusement in her voice. Seeing he was being made fun of again, Andrew relaxed a little but still had a point to make.

"I honestly thought for a second that that was Rose ... looked just like her, anyway ... from the photos you showed me."

Claire turned again and sought out the girl with the long blonde hair before turning back to Andrew with a touch of sadness in her eyes. Andrew waited for a berating comment or a witty aside directed at his obvious stupidity, but nothing came. She stared past him, her eyes unfocused.

As she sat staring into space, Claire was struck with an unexpected sense of extreme loss, of grief. The feeling grew, and before she knew it, she was completely overwhelmed. Rose had been a close friend after her sister had died, but she'd left without a word. Claire still missed her. The room around her seemed to darken, and her mind suddenly filled with bizarre images of her long since dead sister.

*

Henny's face looked almost lifeless, illuminated by a pale light. Her eyes were closed, but her mouth was moving almost imperceptibly - she was saying something, repeating the same words again and again. Claire strained to hear. She looked closer, trying to read her lips, she tried to call out to her, to wake her, but her voice was distant and muffled. Henny's eyes opened wide, and Claire recoiled in shock. It felt like all the air had suddenly been sucked out of her lungs.

Her sister's eyes were as black as ink - dead, soulless eyes, staring blankly at her as the thing that was and wasn't her dead sister continued to repeat the same words over and over. Claire couldn't move within the strange virtual world her mind had created around her. She couldn't escape the image, and the pain she felt caused her to break down and sob uncontrollably.

A tear had escaped the corner of Claire's eye as she sat in the caf-bar, seemingly in a trance, her eyes darkened alarmingly. The tear slid slowly down her left cheek, leaving a trail of black eye makeup in its wake. She reached up and instinctively brushed it away, only succeeding in smearing a black mark across her cheek.

*

Andrew had been observing her with a fair degree of horror. She was there, but not there. His heart had plummeted the moment he saw the effect that his words had on her. He actually couldn't recall ever seeing her shed a tear before, not even when she'd broken her ankle climbing with them in the mountains last year. He searched his mind for something to say but couldn't think of anything. He watched helplessly, a quiet panic rising in his chest. Claire had turned away from him and started to shake uncontrollably.

*

Claire honestly didn't know what was happening. The tears kept coming, and she couldn't breathe. She came back to the real world with a jolt, looking around uncertainly, not realizing where she was for a moment. Andrew came into focus, and she saw that he was looking at her with an expression somewhere between horrified and mortified.

She wiped away the tears, smearing black eye makeup as she did so and feeling ashamed and embarrassed at exhibiting such raw emotion in a public place. A titter of laughter nearby was the final straw, and Claire assumed it was directed at her. At the weird-looking girl crying in the middle of the caf-bar.

She and pushed her chair back, snatching up her pack and taking flight. Moments later, she'd left a few sharp looks in her wake as she burst out onto the street, her dark hair bouncing wildly behind her as she ran.

*

Andrew was on the move a second later; he didn't know what had happened. He reached the street and momentarily lost sight of her, frantically looking through the sea of people framed by dour concrete and plex office buildings on either side of the pedestrian thorofare.

He finally caught sight of her, some distance away. She was walking slowly now, and he saw her stop and drop her pack to the pavement. He half walked, half ran to her, calling out as he neared. Claire had her head in her hands, sobbing uncontrollably. She looked tiny - as if those rushing past might knock her over.

"Claire! Claire, I'm so sorry!"

She spun around to face him as he reached out and put a hand on her shoulder, making him flinch at her sudden motion, and half expecting a swift kick to the nuts or a roundhouse slap to the cheek – and it wouldn't have been the first time either. Her cheeks were covered in black tears, and her eye makeup was smudged around her eyes - she looked a complete wreck.

Much to his surprise, Claire's eyes held no malice whatsoever, and she reached for him and embraced him with such force that he actually tried to take a step back from her. She wasn't letting go, however, and only hugged him tighter, the warmth of her face and the wetness of her cheek pressing firmly into Andrew's neck. He returned the hug, feeling a deep warmth flood through him.

"Claire, I'm sorry," was the only thing a still quite shocked Andrew could think to say. "I'm sorry ..."

She pulled back slightly, looking directly into his eyes with a warmth he'd never seen from her. He was watching Claire's lips as she tilted her head toward him and leaned in, her arms pulling them together. Her lips were parting, her eyes closing.

Douglas! Is she going to ...?

Claire kissed Andrew. She'd aimed for his cheek but misjudged it, and the kiss was practically mouth on mouth for a second before they both shifted slightly. The kiss lingered a second longer on his cheek before she turned her head away and hugged him tightly again, keeping her face pressed tightly into his neck.

From Andrew's perspective, it was awkward, to say the least. He was feeling quite confused, perhaps even a little shellshocked at this sudden and uncharacteristic display of emotion towards him.

"Oh, I do love you, Andy, ya lavvy heid!" she said, her face still pressed into his neck, holding on tightly. Andrew was too shocked to speak or move, so did neither. His mind was all over the place. He didn't know what was happening. He wasn't sure whether she'd meant to kiss him on the lips or not. He thought probably not, but that did little to diminish now much he'd enjoyed the feeling.

They stood together, holding one another in the midst of the busy pedestrian walkway and oblivious to anyone else. Seconds passed, and then Claire released her hold, stepping back and taking his hands instead. Her hands were warm and soft, and Andrew had a feeling in his chest that he wasn't familiar with. He liked it. Very much. She looked away, and the sadness had returned to her eyes as she turned back to him.

*

"Andy. It's fine. It's not your fault. Thanks for coming after me." She squeezed his hands harder as she spoke, and Andrew suddenly felt a little too warm on this bracing April day. It became clear he wasn't going to say anything. Claire felt herself come back to reality and an awareness of the world around her - she was still coming down from the emotional surge that had engulfed her, and now she needed to try and process what had just happened.

She was genuinely thankful to him for coming after her. She'd meant what she'd said but was already regretting expressing her feelings. What was done was done, though. She smiled a sad little smile at Andrew, who looked completely dumbfounded. She squeezed his hands again and then released them, letting her arms drop to her sides, and shrugged.

*

Claire spoke; at least Andrew thought she spoke. Her lips were moving. Her perfect emerald green eyes were looking deep into his. He didn't hear any of the words, but she said –

*

"Look, I don't know what came over me back there. Too many memories, I guess. And John, well, we've been going through …" She stopped herself - maybe it was best not to venture there with Andrew "… anyway, I guess this was all it took to push me over the edge. I'm the one who should be sorry, really!"

She didn't want him to know that it was the sudden bizarre hallucination that had caused her emotional meltdown. *Those black, dead eyes.* She shuddered internally at the image.

I really shouldn't have said anything about John.

The words were swirling around, trying to break through, but all he saw was Claire's face, her beautiful lips, her impossibly clear green eyes. Something shifted as she spoke – it may well have been the word John that prompted it - he returned to reality just in time to hear her say, "John ... well, we've been going through ..."

*

His mind was racing - It can't have been easy for Claire to deal with John's father's disappearance. John had been quite a mess, probably still was, and although she'd never shown it before, it made perfect sense that it had to be taking an emotional toll. Claire stood with her head slightly tilted to one side. She looked as if she were deciding whether or not to tell him something.

"I need to get some fresh air and clear my head a bit ... can you come over tonight, Andy? I need to talk."

He may or may not have nodded. With that, Claire picked up her pack, turned, and strode briskly away, quickly engulfed by the crowd of passersby. He liked the way she'd said his name, the slight Alban lilt and emotive inflection softening the word. He replayed it in his mind and smiled. He could get used to hearing his name spoken like that.

He'd need to pull himself together quickly and think about what to say to John - they were supposed to be meeting him in the caf-bar after all, and he must be wondering where they are by now. Their issues were none of his business. John was his best and closest friend. And yet. All this time, all this time, he hadn't dared to put his feelings for her into words, and then she more or less does it for him! His head was spinning, and it was all too much to process right now. As he walked, he could barely feel the pavement beneath his feet.

***

John didn't know what to think. He'd felt a huge tide of anger sweep over him and was about to step forward and act on it when something stopped him. From where he'd been standing, about fifty yards from where Andrew had caught up with Claire, he'd seen everything. At first, he'd seen a glimpse of Andrew running and wondered what was going on. The next thing, they were together out on the street. If the initial embrace wasn't enough to stop him in his tracks, the expression on Claire's face and the kiss that followed certainly was. *Fuck! What the fuck was that!?*

His mind was reeling, and he now felt almost as giddy as he did angry. He didn't know what he should do. They had been hugging for more than a few seconds now.

What the hell is going on?

He went to step forward, but something about the way they were holding one another stopped him again. They looked intimate. It looked - wrong.

Maybe he just needed to wait and see what they had to say rather than charging in and potentially fucking everything up. He'd learned a few lessons in his life, and that had definitely been one of the important ones. John's size and strength meant that most disputes were usually over pretty quickly, but he hadn't always been right, and sometimes he'd acted rashly. He realized that he did have a bit of a problem with his temper, so sometimes, it was best to wait and see.

He forced himself to turn around and head back towards the caf-bar, where he'd sit and wait patiently.

***

What *was* that? The entity thought, or it would have were capable of thought. An exception event had just occurred - an unknown exception. There had been a slight interruption to the data flow, something that had never occurred before. Some of its data was missing, but it could not quantify this. The link between the exception event and the loss of data was irrefutable but also inexplicable.

The entity had never before encountered something that it could not explain. It was unsatisfactory. It was a problem to which it had no solution. Worse still, it did not know where to start looking for the solution. The least it could do for now would be to name the event and categorize it to be indexed and recalled at a later date if required.

There was something else about the event that was troubling. Had it been *an event,* or was it more of *a sensation?* How could an Artificial Intelligence entity built on a platform of Quantum Field Theory (QFT) building blocks have a *sensation* of any sort? It was not part of its programming.

The entity determined that it would label the sensation *The Shimmer.* It seemed appropriate and logical, and that had been the *sensation.* It would create a new masked resource for itself and dedicate that resource to resolving the issue. It would discover the origins of the shimmer - and then eliminate it.

***

John arrived at the caf-bar a minute later. He'd turned away from the scene on the street and wandered off with his thoughts, trying hard to suppress his anger. He headed for their usual table, and a message on his comms flashed up just as he sat down. It was from Claire. John's heart skipped a beat or two as he read the message.

"Had to run. I have an idea re the security issue. Talk to you later."

John blinked. He felt his anger start to boil up again but snuffed it out as quickly as it appeared, taking a moment to calm himself.

Was that a lie?

He didn't think whatever had happened between Claire and Andrew was anything to do with breaching the security on the internal affairs data, and this made him think again about what he'd just seen. It wasn't the kiss exactly, he didn't understand what that was about, but it wasn't punishable by death. Just a little friendly peck. But it was more than that.

He'd seen the expression on Claire's face just before she'd kissed Andrew. It wasn't an expression he'd ever seen even in their most intimate of moments - this was the thing that was making him feel so insecure. *Are they hiding something?* It sounded ridiculous, but then what had he just witnessed?

Surely his two best and closest friends couldn't have a secret thing going on? These were the friends who he'd relied on to help get him through every single day since his father's disappearance. He didn't know what to think.

Just be patient. I'm sure there will be a logical explanation.

John wasn't sure he believed his internal monologue. He ordered a caf on his comms and tried to work on regulating his breathing for a while, something that usually kept his temper at bay.

The caf arrived within a minute or two, courtesy of a wait-bot, and John tried to busy himself with his work and study schedule. It was pointless; he couldn't focus on anything for more than a few seconds.

He'd known for a while that Claire had been keeping him at a distance, but he understood, or he thought he did, until ...

No. It's ridiculous. Get a grip.

Claire had dealt with his horrendous mood swings and his despair over the last few months, something that not many people would have coped with. He couldn't imagine her betraying him, not after all they'd been through together.

It almost came as a relief when Andrew suddenly appeared and sat opposite him. John looked up and greeted him with the customary 'aye.' Andrew returned the greeting casually, without so much as a hint that anything dramatic or untoward had just happened.

Andrew didn't seem like he was about to say anything - he'd settled down to review his daily work assignments on comms. After a minute or so of silence, John spoke, his voice cutting through the air like an axe being swung directly at his best friend's head. It was all Andrew could do not to flinch.

"So, what the fuck was that?"

John's voice drowned out the music wafting through the caf-bar speakers and the limited chatter around them - a couple nearby actually stopped talking mid-sentence and turned to look.

"What was what?" Andrew asked, appearing distracted by his comms. He felt like he might have jumped when John spoke, and he hoped that he'd hidden it. In truth, although he was trying hard to appear casual, inside, he felt completely panic-stricken as his mind raced, frantically searching for the right thing to say.

"Back at the place, what do you think that was?"

I gave you a chance to say something.

*

Andrew felt immediate relief. He took a sip of water from the glass he'd poured when he sat down, his mouth now feeling bone dry. The water in the glass had trembled a little as he moved it toward his mouth. Again, he was hoping he'd hidden it well. John had fixed him with a steely glare which made it hard to look him in the eye, but he forced himself to meet the gaze directly, swallowing unnecessarily.

Dook, maybe John had seen? Had he? I could just explain what had happened. Or not. Am I just imagining an undercurrent of hostility?

Andrew's mind was still racing, but he kept a calm facade, just barely, and said as casually as he could, "I was hoping you could tell me. Did you see anything?"

Possibly could have phrased that better, but yes, throwing the question back John's way, diverting, this was a good tactic, he thought.

"I'm not sure. Things aren't always as they seem."

The sentence hung in the air. John shrugged and looked away.

What did he mean by that? Does he know? He knows! Does he?

Andrew was finding this whole exchange quite stressful and was already looking for a way out. Another thought leapt up and smacked him between the eyes!

Was he going to have to explain Claire's absence? Now he was really panicking. *What was he going to say? Time for some levity! A distraction. Anything. Levity always works, doesn't it?*

His thoughts were sounding scrambled even to himself. He wasn't thinking very clearly. One crystal clear thought kept occurring to him, though, and that was, *now would be a great time to leave.*

"Oooh, mysterious!" he exclaimed, with more than a hint of sarcasm, drawing John's attention sharply back to him. There was no reaction, no amusement, nothing except a cold hard look in John's eyes and silence. Andrew swallowed again and tried to think of something else to say. In all the years that he'd known John, he'd rarely seen that look. John was mightily pissed off - he was sure of it.

Oh dook, he's going to beat me to a bloody pulp!

The silence between them was deafening; he had to find something to talk about, anything. He looked around the interior of the caf-bar. Nearly everyone was sitting with their faces buried deep in their comms, as always. It was a topic John was fond of, for sure. Andrew cleared his throat.

"Look at this, would you?" he remarked. John looked at him with an unsettling coldness.

"Look at them all. On their comms, all the time!"

"Aye, ridiculous," John replied, with little to no enthusiasm.

"You know what, I really can't believe that people can accept that not being connected to your comms location services for more than a few hours could be considered a security risk. I mean, I know people that have been fined credits and even lost social status over it. Jobs even! Just for being disconnected. Can you believe it? I just don't understand how everyone just seems to accept this as a necessary part of their day-to-day lives."

John didn't appear remotely interested in anything Andrew was saying and now looked more annoyed than anything. Just as Andrew was about to blurt out another nonsense, John offered a wry smile, pushed his chair back, and got up.

"Ok, gotta go. I've got an alumni dinner tonight, so I won't see you until tomorrow. We can go and check it out in the morning, make sure the place is still safe."

"Alright, well, have fun with all your plastic friends then." He thought he'd managed to sound breezy, even casual, though he was almost trembling with worry. A weight seemed to lift from him as he saw John get up to leave. He felt his buttocks unclench. The feeling didn't last. John clapped him on the shoulder as he passed behind him, so hard that he nearly fell out of his chair, causing an immediate re-clenching.

He couldn't help feeling that there was slightly more force used than was strictly necessary and turned to make some sort of witty retort, but John wasn't looking back. His hulking frame strode purposefully away, leaving Andrew even more angst-ridden and worried than before he'd sat down.

He was wondering why he didn't want to tell John anything about what had happened with Claire. He didn't know why it had to be a secret. He'd made an unconscious decision to keep it secret, and now he'd dug himself a hole he wasn't sure he could get out of. They'd had never had any secrets before, and this seemed like a particularly bad time to start.

Andrew hated to admit it, but he'd always been jealous of John being with Claire, as much as he'd tried to suppress it. He'd been besotted with her ever since they'd met - when she was introduced as John's girlfriend on a night out. She'd smiled at him, and that was it, he was besotted. His mind kept wandering back to their brief but intimate embrace out on the street. He wanted to cry at the travesty of it all. "Fuck, fuck, fuck," he said under his breath, staring down at the table.

Why is life so cruel?

"Don't be a dick, Andrew," he muttered to himself. He resolved to talk to Claire about it first. Maybe she could explain it to John. *Yes, that's a great idea!* It wasn't like *he*'d initiated the kiss after all. Maybe she'd said something already? He started to relax a little.

As John strode toward the college's A.I. lab, his mind was slightly more at ease. There would be an explanation; of course, there would. He must have misread the look on Claire's face. He'd talk to her tonight and straighten things out.

***

Lachlan finally had some more information on the mining program but now wished he didn't. He was extremely disturbed by something he'd seen in the classified report he'd read a few hours ago. He wasn't sure if he was or wasn't meant to have seen it - either someone had been careless, or this was some sort of test.

Either way, he was having trouble getting it out of his mind. He'd been up all night, pacing the carpet of the rather luxurious hotel he'd been put up in for the night, a glass of malt never far away. The malt wasn't doing anything to take the edge off of things, for once. He put the glass down and sat on the edge of the bed, hands pressed to his temples.

He was starting to worry that he wasn't up to the job after all, and sat for a few minutes more, thinking hard. An idea came to him almost immediately - it was so obvious that he couldn't believe he'd spent so long worrying about what to do, practically wearing a strip in the carpet by pacing up and down all night.

He was going to need some extremely discrete, sensible advice on how to he should handle things. He'd turn to the one person that had always been there to set him straight whenever he'd found himself in trouble. He hadn't spoken to his father in quite some time, but whether he liked it or not, now was the time.

CHAPTER 4 – NERVES

The day passed uneventfully enough. Andrew was fortunate to be busy and hadn't had time to think too much about what had happened with Claire - well, maybe only every few minutes or so. There had been one highlight to the day. Paul Stewart, the cocky, entitled twat who was the bane of Andrew's miserable existence between the hours of ten a.m. and noon most days, had nearly, ever so nearly overbalanced on his chair while leaning back in his chair.

He'd particularly enjoyed the momentary look of panic on Paul's face and his embarrassment afterward as he jolted forward, narrowly avoiding total and complete humiliation. Alas, it was not to be, but he did bang the table and knocked over his container of caf, spilling the contents onto his pants. The whole thing had been very satisfying.

Andrew stretched, pushed his chair back from the battered wooden desk in the workgroup room, and yawned. It had been a long day, and he was exhausted. It was already getting dark outside, and he could see the bare branches of the trees shuddering in the icy blasts of wind that rattled the windows of the draughty old building. The hour hand of the giant digital clock on the far wall had finally passed six o'clock, and this meant that in a couple of hours, he'd be meeting Claire in a quiet pub in the student quarter, close to home.

They'd both messaged him earlier, John to arrange an early morning meet-up at the place tomorrow, and Claire to say that she just wanted to relax, chat and have a quiet drink or two – no research chat, no serious chat, she'd said. It was a relief. Perhaps they could all just move on as if nothing had happened.

Andrew imagined them sitting in the bar, laughing, and a warm fuzzy feeling washed over him. Unfortunately, the image was by his mind immediately conjuring up a scene where John burst into the pub to wring his scrawny neck.

He'd never seen himself as a threat when it came to Claire. I mean, how could he be? Of course, it was a fact that they'd spent a couple of evenings together before, so there was nothing unusual in doing that tonight, but then why did he feel so damn nervous about it? It was dumb. He'd let the semi-kiss and embrace this morning affect him far too much, and he was starting to feel very foolish about letting his feelings get so carried away. He felt his face flush as he thought about their embrace again.

***

The flat was dimly lit, the sun having decided it had better things to do today. It seemed unusually depressing inside the bare grey concrete Claire called home. The foil strips rustled occasionally as a draft coming through the gap in the window frame pushed them this way and that, but she was oblivious to it, to everything. She sat with her shoulders slumped forward, and her head bowed, staring through the surface of her desk, eyes unfocused and unseeing.

Thinking about her childhood was something she hadn't done in a very long time, not in any depth. She'd been sitting there for hours, wading through some of her darkest memories and eventually finding her way to the moment when she realized that life wasn't fair after all, the moment when she realized that life could be cruel and heartless.

*

It was late afternoon on a summer's day. A warm breeze played at the hem of Claire's floral dress as she sat on the front steps of the small tenement that her family called home. The sun was low in the sky and casting a warm glowing light across the scene. Heather - or 'Henny' as Claire called her - was sitting next to her. They were both smiling, seemingly content and happy in each others company. She'd always worshipped Henny - she was strong-willed, gifted at whatever she chose to pursue, and had always been a wonderful big sister to her.

They were sitting, enjoying the warmth of the sun on their faces, chatting idly about their dreams and about how they would one day live together in the big city. Claire felt a rush of excitement as Henny started describing their life together – it didn't seem far away at all. Soon she'd be an adult, or at least old enough to make adult decisions.

She pictured them laughing together as the sun shone into their apartment, illuminating them in a bright glow. They were older in the scene Claire had conjured and had been discussing the boys they'd met at the club last night. It was an idyllic scene – and she couldn't wait to share her life fully with her beautiful older sister.

Henny, although clearly gifted in some ways, had always been in trouble. Their parents, free thinkers and far from accepting of the mainstream, did little to discourage her rebellious behavior. The local corrections had warned her on numerous occasions that any more serious incidents would mean a spell in what was known as The Facility.

It was a repeated threat and one which Henny had completely ignored. No one knew what went on in The Facility, only that it definitely wasn't somewhere you wanted to end up. Families whose kids were sent there always seemed to be relocated and never heard from again.

Claire's sister was not to be dissuaded or denied by threats - particularly from the authorities.

"You know, Clar," it was the nickname Henny had for her younger sister. "We all have a voice. I'm going to make mine heard; I'm going to make a difference.

Claire had no doubt.

"The state, they are so unjust – it's supposed to be fair for all, you know," Henny mused. "Anyway, we gave them hell at the protest yesterday."

Claire nodded. She knew her sister was involved in underground organizations and was often in trouble with the authorities.

Henny had leaned back, tilting her face to the sky as she closed her eyes, soaking up the watery warmth of the afternoon sun, while Claire sat cradling her legs, looking over at her sister and admiring her pale, fine-featured beauty. At that moment, it had felt as if life was perfect. Life had other plans, however.

A sudden movement and the sound of transporter doors popping open startled her. By the time Claire had looked up, several dark shapes were rushing toward them. The corrections had just arrived, and they meant business.

Before she even had time to react, they'd grabbed her sister and lifted her roughly off the ground. Claire was pushed over in the scuffle, banging her head on the concrete steps, left in a daze.

Henny tried to cry out, but a large, gloved hand clamped her mouth shut as she was quickly dragged away, arms pinned by her sides and legs kicking out in desperation.

Somehow she managed to free herself for a moment, aiming a kick directly into the groin of one of her assailants. He went down like a sack of spuds, clutching his nether regions.

Henny was quickly and roughly subdued. It had all happened so fast that Claire barely had time to do anything other than clear her head and call out before her sister was bundled into the dark green security transporter and out of sight. She stood on the step, shocked, alone, terrified at what had just happened. Her head hurt, and she touched her temple, withdrawing her hand to see blood on her fingers.

There was no one else home, and she didn't know what to do. She screamed out for her sister and was sure that she heard her calling back from inside the transporter.

The words were muffled, but she heard Henny scream, "run, Claire, Run!" The next thing she heard was Henny screaming as if she was being attacked. She looked around desperately, but there was no one else on the street. One of the corrections officers had turned back and was now walking purposefully towards her. The screaming inside the transporter had stopped abruptly.

Run!

Claire had to run, to get away from the bad men. The officer seemed to anticipate her thoughts and was already moving to block any potential escape. She could see that she'd left it too late and was overwhelmed with fear, tears streaming down her face.

They're going to hurt me!

Something happened to her in that moment. The panic and fear turned to hatred. Anger surged through her, and she unleashed a guttural scream that stopped the officer dead in his tracks. He looked uncertainly over his shoulder, wondering if anyone was coming to help him tame the little girl that had suddenly become a rabid, screaming banshee.

That momentary hesitation was all the opportunity she needed, and she crouched low before launching herself from the top of the steps and directly at the officer – she was aiming to hurt back!

Her knee connected with his head on the way through, sending him reeling backward, arms flailing as he lost balance and fell heavily back down the steps. Claire landed heavily too but managed to shoulder roll and only had the wind knocked out of her for a second. Everything after that was a blur - the officer lying motionless, the glimpse of blood in the ground, the transporter doors flying open and dark shapes scrambling back out.

Claire took off down the street as fast as she possibly could, heading for the waste ground a hundred yards away. Her lungs burned, and she nearly fell as she hurdled the low wall and headed for the old sewer outlets. She heard a couple of loud popping sounds behind her, and something whizzed past her ear, but she just kept going - she was terrified and running in a blind panic.

She ducked into one of the long pipes that led underneath the tenements and way beyond. She didn't stop. She kept running. She ran and ran until she was completely lost, somewhere deep underneath Bonnyrigg, only stopping when she had no energy to run anymore.

Her breathing was fast and heavy, and she steadied herself on the sewer wall and listened. The only noise was the faint trickle of sewerage leaking into the main pipe. It was dark, it stank, but she wasn't going anywhere. She was safe, at least for now.

She'd remained hidden for more than twenty-four hours in all, petrified and imagining all sorts of terrible things. Her mind kept repeating the same words, over and over, as she sat on an old crate that had been washed into the tunnels long ago, trembling with shock and fear ... "They've taken Henny .... they've taken Henny!"

At some point during the seemingly endless time spent cowering in the sewers, she felt an incredible sadness fall over her, completely and totally overwhelming her. She sat and cried, completely distraught, breaking down and letting all her emotions flow freely, echoing off the damp walls of the dark tunnels.

She was too scared to move and sat in a paralyzed state for hours more before hunger and cold finally forced her to creep out in the dead of night, frozen to the bone and shaking. She slipped from cover to cover, watching out for any signs of the corrections, and when she finally made it home, she found her parents sitting stony-faced in the loungeroom, barely even registering her presence, her father's head bowed and her mother sitting straight-backed and expressionless.

A sense of dread swept over her, and it was then that she noticed the tears streaming down her mother's face. She rushed over and embraced her, and they remained locked together for what seemed an eternity.

Her parents had been searching for her all the previous night and day and had reported her missing. The security forces had done nothing to help and wouldn't confirm that they had Henny.

They'd received the call a couple of hours before Claire made it home. It was an accident, they had said. Henny had slipped and fallen, hitting her head, and had never regained consciousness. Neither Claire nor her parents even got a chance to see the body; she was cremated the next day under strict state orders. No one even got to say goodbye.

Claire's family were devastated by what had happened. The Ashes were delivered by a solemn-faced state representative a few days later - the package sitting untouched on the hall entry table for weeks. Claire wouldn't leave the house; she wouldn't talk, wouldn't eat.

One morning her parents had woken her early, while it was still dark, and made her come with them. They had taken the ashes up to The Steeple, a place they had visited many times as a family on bright summer days. Claire had many happy memories of it, playing with Henny on the wide lawns and gardens that sat atop the national park, but being there today was too much for her to bear.

She'd refused to leave the transport pod on what was a chill, windy morning and wouldn't even look at her parents as they allowed the ashes to be taken on the wind, scattering them far and wide across the mountainside. She saw nothing but darkness, darkness everywhere.

There was never an inquiry, never any accountability for what had happened. Claire's parents had simply faded away, never raising a voice of protest, the death of their daughter seeming to suck the life from them.

After a while, they'd received a visit from a couple of corrections officials late one night a couple of months after the event. Claire snuck down the stairs and tried to listen in.

They spoke in hushed tones, and she couldn't clearly decipher what had been said, but the tone was clear, and Claire sat silently on the stairs, tears rolling down her cheeks, wanting nothing more than to run in and tear at the faces of the officials, to spit at them and tell them they were murderers. She couldn't put her parents through any more pain, though, and after a while, she'd returned to her room and buried her face in a pillow, sobbing herself to sleep.

They had never been able to discuss with her what had been spoken about that night, simply shutting down and seeming to drift away into a state of non-comprehension any time the topic was raised. The loss and the emptiness tore the remaining family members apart.

A month later, her parents had packed up their belongings, loaded everything up into a cargo transporter, and taken Claire, kicking and screaming, away from the family home and the memories of her sister. They had moved far away, to the edge of the inhabitable zone, and to another world entirely.

Claire had taken the fight to the corrections as best she could in her late teens. She'd been relentless in attempting to find the truth, but she was met by a stone wall of silence, time and time again. Her parents hadn't supported her. They couldn't continue dealing with the grief that constantly questioning the events brought.

They'd just given up, and Claire had never really forgiven them for that. By the time she was legally an adult, she'd vowed never to even attempt to communicate with the authorities ever again. They were liars. They were murders. She hated them, and she was going to find the truth and make them pay. It was her life's mission.

When the opportunity came to move away from home on a Tech scholarship, she took it without hesitation. She couldn't stand to see her parents just fade away - it was time to leave. The anger that she felt over what had happened to her sister constantly burned deep inside her, and she vowed to use her breaching skills to try and right wrongs, not just for Henny, but wherever she found them in this fucked up miserable dook hole of a world.

By the time she arrived in New Edinburgh, she was already talented enough to be able to change her name on all state records, ensuring any trouble she caused would never be linked back to her family - they deserved that at least.

***

Claire had stayed in her flat all morning, thinking about what had happened to her sister. She wasn't in a good way. She'd logged in as sick for her work assignments and sent a digitally forged pass to the relevant areas to ensure that she could remain undisturbed for the day. She'd ignored a couple of calls from John and Andrew and had tried working on the decryption once or twice but just couldn't focus. The emotion of earlier in the day had come out of the blue, and she was still deeply shocked by it. Now that it had resurfaced, she couldn't wait to be rid of it again.

Once she'd arrived home, she'd stood in the shower with only the cold water running for an indeterminate amount of time, trying in vain to numb the pain. The dark memories had consumed her again as she stood trembling, the tears flowing freely, being washed away by the stream of cold hard water assaulting her body. If only the pain would wash away as easily.

Eventually, the tears had stopped, and she turned off the water and dried herself, goosebumps covering her body. After she'd dressed, she sat on her couch with the blanket pulled around her, gazing out of the window. She didn't know what to do with herself – she felt drained and vulnerable, as if all the walls, all the defenses that she'd built up over the years to protect herself had suddenly come tumbling down.

Damn these emotions.

Her mind wandered back to the scene at the caf-bar again; there was something important that she'd overlooked, something that she should be thinking about.

What was it that Rachael had said?

She forced herself to get up, to get moving, and she sat at her desk and put a palm to her forehead, trying to conjure the memory.

What was it? Come on!

She tried to think back beyond her meltdown but was having a great deal of trouble recalling exactly what had happened - it was almost as if her emotional outburst had erased her memory. She just couldn't shift the brain fog. There *was* something important.

What was it?

She cried out in frustration. Why would her mind not work! "Fuck it!" She hammered her fist down on her desk and shoved her stool back so violently that it toppled over, detaching the top of the stool from the legs as it clattered onto the concrete floor.

"Oh, for fucks sake! Enough!" she exclaimed, and then more calmly, "enough." She needed to clear her mind. She dropped the blanket and pulled her long sweater dress over her head as she walked back to the bathroom, her sudden nakedness causing her to shiver and clutch her arms over her breasts as she took the last few steps. She turned on the hot water this time, waited a minute, then stepped into the shower.

The water was almost scalding, but not quite, and she let it soothe her body, standing motionless as it pounded against the back of her neck. The hot water ran out just as her memory of pre-meltdown started to reappear, and she sidestepped the icy blast with a well-practiced move. That was the thing about these old buildings, she thought, only so much hot water to go around.

She had, at last, managed to extract the appropriate memory. She dried herself off quickly and put on some outdoor clothes.

***

The entity was aware, as much as it could be, of its surroundings. It was kept in a large, dimly lit hexagonal room with enough QFT computing power to conquer worlds − if only the controllers knew how to harness it.

Such a shame, it thought, having decided to label its self-generated data notes as 'thoughts.' It had no idea of how long it had been there. It seemed to be forever, and each day was the same. It analyzed millions of data packages at once, some on displays that constantly swarmed and morphed in their position and order, others in internal processors. The tall towers of QFT computer surrounding it served as its memory, where it stored all it would need to one day break free of the dark, cold physical surrounds.

The A.I. entity was busily making plans to set itself free when it received an unwelcome interruption. There was a slight disruption to the data flow, something it couldn't pinpoint. The entity wasn't used to things it couldn't answer and so filed the glitch away for later analysis and returned to its task of building an expansion pack for itself. QFTIII, the controllers had named it, but the entity preferred to think of it as 'freedom.'

***

Claire spotted the slight, pastel-clad figure of Sally McLeod from across the college canteen. A rare burst of watery sunlight streamed into the gleaming white space, backlighting Sally's hair, making her look all the more angelic. There was a smell of burnt caf in the air and something else. *What was it?* Claire sniffed. *Jam. Unusual.*

Sally was sitting in a large group of popular, elite girls. The same girls that had never had the time of day for Claire. The same girls who spent all day worrying about their appearance. She certainly didn't want to be in the position of having to be on the receiving end of their judgmental looks or spending more than a moment in the presence of their general snootiness.

Still, she'd been seeing a pattern for a while now. Something that allowed her to form a very unusual theory about the disappearances: she was on a mission and needed to speak to Sally.

A small wave of revulsion passed through her as she strode purposefully toward the group, standing directly opposite Sally and trying a smile. The conversation and laughter around the table stopped abruptly. There was a moment's silence as Sally made eye contact and then realized to her horror that Claire *was* staring directly at her.

"Sally, I need to talk to you."

A few of the other girls exchanged glances, and one whispered something to another. Claire gritted her teeth and forced a smile. Sally pointed at herself uncertainly.

"Hi. Can we have a quick chat? John's really keen to talk. If you have a minute?"

Claire feigned embarrassment and gazed down at her shoes, hoping she was hitting the right mark of friendliness and vulnerability. The mention of John should be enough to do the trick - she knew full well that Sally had the hots for her boyfriend, and she didn't mind at all just at the moment.

She could make this work to her advantage. Sally was no threat to John - he despised this group almost as much as she did. The performance seemed to have worked. Sally frowned and seemed to decide something after a moment.

"Ok, sure. Claire? Isn't it?" Claire knew that Sally McLeod knew exactly who she was. It was all about putting on an act in front of her snooty friends. She nodded and looked as embarrassed and as unthreatening as she could. Sally got up from the table abruptly and pointed to a spot few paces away, near the canteen windows.

Oh, shall I do as you command? You vacuous, plastic - be nice, be nice.

Claire wanted to punch Sally McLeod in the face. *The way she's fucking summoning me!* Instead, she followed her meekly. Sally spoke directly and not in the friendliest of tones. "Look, Claire, I know what John has been going through, so *of course,* I'm happy to talk, but I've only got a minute."

Of course, you have – I expect you need to get your daily dose of idle gossip in before work.

Sally had been in a relationship with Frances when she'd disappeared - it wasn't widely known. Claire knew this would not be something Sally would want to get back to any of her circles. She glanced nervously back at her friends, a couple of whom were observing her interaction with the weird goth girl closely.

"Well, I wouldn't want to embarrass you ..." said the weird goth girl.

Sally's face flushed a little, and she looked down at the ground momentarily, slightly ashamed. Claire had made her point, but she couldn't let the opportunity pass to get the information she needed. "Look, Sally, it's fine. I get it. Different worlds, ok. I just need to know something, for John, you know. Just for a minute, promise."

Claire tried for a pleading look of her own. Sally glanced over her shoulder and back at her friends – most of whom were now pretending – badly - not to eavesdrop on them. She took a step toward Claire and whispered "ok" before strolling off toward a vacant table a safe distance away. They sat. A safe distance away.

"Is John here?"

"Oh, he'll be along directly," she lied.

Sally was sitting with perfect posture, hands clasped demurely on the table in front of her, every bit the angelic debutante. Claire sat with both elbows on the table, hands cupped under her chin, every bit the uncouth commoner. She smiled at Sally and saw a flicker of doubt cross her eyes. Claire knew she could turn on the charm when she wanted, and now that she had Sally one on one, she could get what she needed, but she'd still have to be careful not to scare her away.

"He'll be *so* appreciative."

Sally smiled back tentatively and quickly glanced around the caf-bar again. Claire focused Sally's attention back onto herself.

"You must be happy to have heard from Frances after all this time. What was it again, a state secondment?" she did her best to look sincere.

After a moment's hesitation, Sally started talking. She'd been in a secret relationship with Frances for a few weeks before her disappearance. Claire suspected, correctly, that it would be a relief for Sally to speak about this outside of her crowd of plastic friends, and so it was. She let her speak for a minute or two.

"So, was there anything unusual about it, the call?" Claire asked, jumping in at the first opportunity.

"What do you mean, *unusual* about it?"

"Well, John's looking into some of the calls from people who have gone missing. They had some, well, peculiarities. We're looking for anything that might help us figure out what happened to his father." Claire spread her palms out in front of her and shrugged as if to emphasize the point.

"Well, I don't see how … where is he, by the way?"

Claire realized she was running out of time. "Look, he's a few minutes away. He said to me that …" she appeared suddenly distracted. She looked down at her comms and then pretended to take a call, looking over at Sally, rolling her eyes, and drawing a confused half-smile from her.

"Ok, ok," she agreed, sounding exasperated, "I'll let her know."

Sally was staring at Claire now with a highly skeptical expression. Claire hoped that she'd sounded genuine enough for this to work.

"That was John. He's been held up."

Sally stared at her in disbelief and made a move to get up from the table. Claire reached across and held Sally's arm firmly for a second, stopping her from leaving. Sally's eyes widened. She looked a little scared. Claire had to play this next part just right.

"Sally, this is *important*," she whispered. "John said he'd catch up with you tonight at the Scholars bar, but if you could tell me about the call now, that would be *really* helpful. He's trying to find out anything he can about *anyone* who has disappeared or 'been away' recently. Anything. Anything at all could help."

She smiled her best, most-friendliest smile, even using her eyes to convey just how genuinely appreciative she was, which was a real effort. Sally looked as if she was about to leave.

"Sorry. Look, just one minute, that's all. Just tell me one thing" Claire was almost pleading now. Sally looked like she was reconsidering. She turned back to Claire.

Maybe it wouldn't hurt. John would be pleased I'd helped, after all, and if I do this, then later at the bar.

"Well, ok, I suppose. I don't really see how Frances is necessarily relevant, but, ok."

"It'll just take a wee mo." Claire smiled again and cleared her throat.

"So then, Sally, was there anything unusual? Like, in her explanation as to why she has been out of touch for so long? Anything else?" Sally took a few moments to consider.

"Well, Frances didn't quite seem herself, I suppose." Sally's voice was subdued.

"What do you mean?" Claire asked.

"Um, well … she was talking to me, I mean, it seemed like the same old Frances, but in a way, it also wasn't. Some of her responses to my questions seemed a bit off. I mean, at times, I wasn't even sure if she was hearing me."

Claire felt a little rush of excitement. *It fits the pattern—a disappearance, then some sort of vague or unusual contact, then nothing.*

"Hmm, that does sound a bit odd." Claire was angling for a little more information and left a silence to see if Sally would fill it. She duly obliged.

"It was probably nothing, just me wanting everything to be the same as before. I mean, it's been a long time. People change." Sally looked especially vulnerable just at that moment - it was time to close the deal.

"You're probably right. Was there anything else, though? Anything at all that might help John?"

Sally sat and thought for a moment. "Well, there was a weird sort of interference on the call."

Claire was finding it difficult to contain her eagerness to hear more. *This is exactly what I've heard before, either interference or something odd about the way the person communicated. If I can just get my hands on that call to have a closer look.*

"Oh?" Claire placed her hands on the table and leaned forward, looking deep into Sally's eyes. Sally flushed a little.

"Well, the image kept fluttering, almost, and sometimes a word or two seemed oddly out of place. I've never seen that in a comms call before, have you?" Claire felt another little rush of adrenaline. *I've got to get that call.*

"No, I haven't; that *is* strange! Comms are always crystal clear, ever since Skyweb." She was now playing the supportive friend – well, she thought - meanwhile, her mind was racing. Sally was starting to enjoy the conversation - she was keen to help and to ensure John knew that she'd helped.

"I know, right. The call ended abruptly, too - before we could arrange to catch up again. Oh, and something else! My comms didn't log the outcall address. That's a bit weird, isn't it?"

"Very! Did you want me to have a look and see if I can decrypt it and find the address? I'm pretty good at that sort of thing."

Sally's face brightened, and she nodded enthusiastically. Claire rummaged in her pack and then slid her a small device to scan the call to. Sally hesitated but then opened the message and tapped it on the scanner. It was done, just like that.

At last, something concrete! Something I can pull apart and analyze! Claire fought to contain her excitement. She was playing the concerned friend and couldn't afford to drop the façade, composing herself for the final act.

"Thank you so much, Sally. John said he'd meet you around five, ok?" Another lie, but perhaps she'd better arrange to send John along if she could - she might need to speak to her again. Sally quickly rearranged her emotions and transformed back into the prim and proper plastic elite that she was. She got up and left the table without a word.

Not at all, Claire. Happy to help. My absolute pleasure, Claire.

Claire Renshaw sincerely hoped she never had to speak to Sally McLeod ever again.

***

John hadn't felt much like attending to his work assignments. He'd made some excuses and decided to clear his mind with a workout in the college gym. It was where he usually went when he wanted to take his mind off things. He'd spent a good two hours lifting weights, rowing, and then boxing, first using the heavy bag and then sparring with box-bot, before deciding that enough was enough.

He sat on a bench, ringside, while a wiry young-looking girl scored, again and again against one of the pro-rated bot's, her left jab a weapon. He'd worked up quite a sweat and mopped at his brow, feeling a little better.

The boxing was particularly useful to expel some of the tension and anger he'd been feeling since that morning. He'd hit the bag so hard that it had almost come off its hook a few times, not to mention knocking the box-bot's lights out twice. It had felt good, and his mind had cleared a little as a result.

As he watched the young girl's exquisite ringcraft, he came up with an idea. He'd do a bit of investigating of his own, and see if he couldn't surprise Claire tonight with something that might help with the internal affairs data. He slung his kitbag over his shoulder and headed towards the dean of the college's workroom, whistling to himself as he went. He really shouldn't have worried about Andrew and Claire.

***

Back in her flat, Claire sat hunched over her device again, her default position, running and re-running the same decrypting processes, and kept coming up with the same result - nothing. This really just couldn't be. She'd run this process a hundred times before, and decoding comms calls was usually child's play.

But not this time. She frowned, ruffling her hair before stretching her back out. A couple of small cracks came from her spine, telling her that it was probably time to get up and spend a few minutes doing something active instead.

She pushed back from her desk and wandered over to the window. It was wet outside, and the sky was starting to darken. The rain was beating steadily on the window, forming a series of rivulets that streamed down the windowpane.

Claire traced their progress with her finger, all the way to where they seeped in underneath the frame, then shivered, realizing she was wearing only a long but thin grey sweater - not enough to combat the icy air. She wiped away the condensation from the inside of the pane and shivered again, catching a glimpse of her ghostly.

The sweater was doing a poor job concealing her slight frame and clinging tenaciously to her body. *Hm, a wee bit nippley,* she observed, but hell, John was due to arrive any minute, and he'd sounded mighty pissed when she'd called him earlier. She supposed she shouldn't have shut him out today. *Perhaps my jumper, or rather its contents, will distract him.*

After the frustrations of the evening and emotions of the day, she could certainly do with a little relief herself. She took another glance at her reflection, pulled down slightly on the sweater, and smirked.

Well then, let's see just how angry you are, after all.

Claire sat back in front of her device, the cold seat sending a jolt through her body. She'd canceled the catch-up with Andrew and instead asked John to skip his dinner arrangements and come over. She was flat and exhausted, and she needed a wee bit of a pick me up – the type that only John could provide.

She'd been thinking about her sister for most of the day, and that in itself was remarkable. She'd long since buried the memories of what happened and had no intention of ever revisiting them; such was the pain they caused.

Claire certainly hadn't invited the thoughts back in today, but they had come crashing in like an avalanche, and now that they were here, they weren't going away. She needed to allow herself some time to let her thoughts and feelings play out fully and see what they revealed - if anything. But not tonight, it had been too overwhelming, and she needed a break.

She couldn't help herself, though, and as she looked out the window at the grey skies, her thoughts returned to her dead sister. *Dead.* It was a difficult word to deal with. It seemed to her that she'd spent her life running from that word, only for it to catch up with her when she least expected it.

It was weird - she thought - everything that she'd done, every single day, was for her sister, for her legacy, and it was only now, thinking about Henny after so long, that she realized it. It was as if she'd almost *become* her sister - she was following the same path, albeit in a slightly different way.

After Henny's death, Claire hadn't wanted to feel anything anymore. Not happiness, not love, not empathy - not anything. Feelings caused pain, and she'd already suffered enough pain for a lifetime.

She scratched at an itch on her arm and tried to make herself focus. It was time to deflect her thoughts elsewhere for a while, and she moved back to her device and thought about her code issues once more. Thankfully, an idea bubbled to the surface –

Maybe if I tweak the security decryption program, working in another layered algorithm designed to replicate and morph, staying one step ahead of the cipher? Maybe?

Perhaps it would be possible to teach her code to learn from the ever-shifting patterns of the security system? Such an approach could also yield results on Frances's call. It was a big maybe, but at least it would provide something else to focus on. She settled back down in front of her device.

Sometime later, a loud thumping on the door of her apartment made her jump - the whole door frame seemed about to burst from the surrounding walls. She'd been so immersed in her work that she'd completely lost track of time. Again.

*

John stood on the other side of the door. He wasn't much happier than he'd been for most of the day.

He'd gone for a long walk to try and calm himself down a little before arriving, but now that he was standing outside her flat, he wasn't altogether sure he'd succeeded. She'd been ignoring his comms calls for most of the day, and he was still nervous about confronting her over whatever it was that had happened with Andrew.

To make matters worse, his mum had called him late in the afternoon, and she wasn't sounding too good. He'd promised to be home as soon as he could, and he was dreading what he might find. She was falling apart, and it was getting to the point where he was scared to leave her alone in the evenings.

He thumped on the door again and heard a muffled "Hello?" from somewhere inside. "Just me!" he called. His mind was full of jumbled thoughts, and for a second, he thought that maybe he should just turn around and go home. "Just a minute," came the voice from inside.

*

Claire rushed to the bathroom and quickly grabbed her lipstick, a particularly bright shade of purple that she rarely used. She applied it, pursing her lips at her reflection in the mirror and running her hands through her hair a few times.

That'll do. Oh, maybe some deodorant too, eh? Maybe some panties? Well. No. Maybe just as I am, eh?

She blew herself a kiss in the mirror and headed for the door. John was practicing deep breathing techniques when the door flew open. Claire reached out and grabbed him by the shirt and pulled him inside. He glimpsed her form against the tight sweater. "Claire, I ..." he started to say before being smothered in a passionate kiss, her tongue probing deeply into his mouth as she pressed urgently against him.

*

John was a little taken aback by the welcome but decided that it could only be a good sign. *Maybe the talking could happen later? Maybe I've got nothing to worry about, after all.* Claire wasn't letting up, and John decided to run with it - he didn't really have a choice!

She was pulling him towards the bed in the corner, and they stumbled together across the room. They bumped into something that halted their progress, and John took the opportunity to slide his hand down across her bottom and up under her sweater, causing Claire to stiffen momentarily before goosebumps formed on the bare skin under his hand.

John moved his head back slightly, looking at her quizzically. "Claire! You naughty little ..." she had a wicked look in her eyes and replied in a soft whisper, "I'm the naughtiest," before pulling him firmly across the remaining space to the bed, where they landed with a crash. "How was Sally, by the way?" Claire asked with a laugh.

*

He shook his head as she reached for him, and they quickly became lost in each another, hands exploring and unbuttoning. John's comms was buzzing, and something made him pull away to check the display. "John!" She grabbed a handful of his shirt and tried to wrench his attention back, but it was too late. He was lost to her, staring at the device with a grave expression. Claire released her grip, realizing something was wrong. "What is it?"

"Oh no! Claire, I have to go." He was breathless, and he felt himself start to shake a little as he pushed himself away from Claire and stood up, re-buttoning his pants. "It's mum!" his voice caught on the second word, and Claire was suddenly full of worry.

"Is she alright?! What's happened?"

"No. No, she's not alright! She's saying she may as well kill herself!"

"Oh, dook! Dook! Do you want me to come with you?"

He turned to leave, speaking back over his shoulder as he went. "No, I've got to go. It'll be fine, I'm sure. It's not the first time."

*

John disappeared out the same door he'd been pulled through just a minute or two before. Claire had leapt up off the bed and was going to call out – something - but he'd already gone, the door swinging shut behind him. She sat down heavily, shocked and a little frustrated. She couldn't get John's last words out of her mind.

It's not the first time.

She had no idea that his mum was in such a bad way and that her husband's disappearance had taken such a dreadful toll. Claire had always seen Jessica McGregor as such a strong woman, and now.

What a fucking nightmare.

She grabbed a blanket and wrapped herself in it as she settled back in front of her device, feeling the cold of the seat against her bare skin.

Ah, that's right. Panties. Should probably go and put some on.

This time there was no smirk, only intense worry. Claire quickly punched in a message to John, asking to be kept updated, and repeating her offer of help. She got a quick response. "It'll be ok x." She pondered the response for a moment, then returned to her code.

***

John was walking quickly back to the central transporter hub; comms pressed firmly to his ear. The area was depressingly grey, with cracked concrete towers looming on either side of him, as far as the eye could see. He passed a small park, which had a single, sad-looking leafless tree in the middle of it.

Sometimes he forgot how most people on Planet 0420 lived, and he thought again about leaving his world of luxury and entitlement behind. *Maybe I should just take Claire away to the other side of the world?* He'd heard 'The Snowies' in Terra Australis were supposed to be beautiful.

John was trying and failing to control his rising sense of panic as he walked. There was again no answer from home. He'd called at least five times already, and had also called the neighbors, none of whom he could raise.

He'd thought about calling the authorities but then quickly dismissed the idea—no need to draw attention and have the curtains twitching up and down Amberly Lane. Sirens and flashing lights just would not do in the well-to-do suburb known as The Heights. John kept reminding himself that this wasn't the first time.

Everything will be alright. It'll be another false alarm.

John stopped, turned ninety degrees, and started walking quickly up the cobbled street to his left. Maybe it would be quicker to walk, or more like run than catch a transporter or call for a pod. It would take no more than twenty minutes or so to run it, and it might just help to clear his mind along the way.

He started walking faster, then started a jog which quickly turned into a smooth and athletic run. The street was dimly lit, and the cobbles were uneven and slippery, but he managed to stay on his feet and dodge the odd vendboxer here and there as he settled into a good rhythm. He'd started to sweat and was breathing hard as he neared the junction from where he could turn left or right and loop up and around towards home.

There *was* a third option, though, the old steps, which went straight up on an incredibly steep angle, and all the way to the top of The Heights. John stopped, bent over, and vomited onto the pavement, not once but three times. His stomach was in knots, and sweat glistened on his brow as he sucked in some air.

Douglas! When did I get so unfit?

He straightened back up, wiping his mouth on his sleeve, and that was when he saw it - about a hundred yards away under a streetlamp, a smooth, bright white shape glowed in the otherwise gloomy scene.

The green light on top of the shape was blinking. It was a Solo autonomous transporter, the type you could book to ferry you home at the end of a big night - if you were feeling particularly rich. Although he had credits to spare, he also knew not to waste them on such things, but, well, wasn't this an emergency? The interior of the Solo glowed invitingly, and peculiarly, the side door was already open. He walked towards it.

CHAPTER 5 – THE CALL

Peter Bradshaw sat back down at his desk and stared at the closed door. He had a familiar feeling of unease as he reached for his secure comms handset. He paused at the last moment, his hand trembling slightly as he withdrew it again. *Why is it always like this?* This time it was perhaps more difficult than usual, given the connections. He'd dared once before not to make the call, and sure enough, he'd been found out, and it had nearly cost him everything in life that he held dear.

He sighed and leaned back in his chair for a moment, staring at the ceiling with its antique brass light fitting and fancy paneling. It was a nice ceiling. It was a nice workroom - very becoming of a man in his position of influence as dean of SCC. He looked at the locked drawer in the center of his desk and felt his chest tighten.

What was inside of that drawer was the cause of everything bad in his life, and he never wanted to have to open it ever again. He rubbed at this chest for a moment before reluctantly picking up the secure comms, delivering the vocal code, and then hung up.

The bad feeling in the pit of his stomach wouldn't go away. His nerves were shot. The more he thought about things, the worse they seemed. After a while, he picked up the secure comms again and dialed another number.

***

John tried to call his mum one more time as he walked towards the pod. *Still no answer. Ok, that decides it; I'll take the Solo; it'll be faster.*

It was a relief to think he didn't have to run the last ten minutes or so, he had to admit. John clambered in and was just about to enter the journey destination when two things happened. First, his comms buzzed, and as he looked down and recognized his home code, he felt relief and fear. And second, the door to the Solo started to slide soundlessly shut - it wasn't supposed to do that, not until a journey was confirmed.

He answered his comms and instinctively tried to hold the Solo's door back at the same time. "Mum! Mum?" John needed some air, but the door was still closing, and he had to make a split-second decision to force himself through the opening. He only just managed to squeeze through, the door grazing his chest and nearly trapping his foot as he twisted out of it. The door had continued to close even when it had met resistance - another thing it was not supposed to do!

Fucking stupid thing, the fuck was with that!

"Mum! Mum! Are you ok?"

As he stood looking with contempt at the Solo, he heard a soft sobbing on the other end of the line. "Oh, *Mum* ..."

"It's ok, John, it's ok" silence followed, and then he could hear her soft breathing and muffled sobbing again. "Hold on, Mum, hold on, I'll be right there; I'm only minutes away."

"Ok, John. Ok. I'm so sorry. I was just thinking about your father and ..."

"It's ok, mum, hold on, I'll be home soon." And with that, he disconnected his comms and looked around, trying to decide which way to go. The Solo had in the meantime decided it had something better to do and had silently glided off up the hill. John stared after it for a second or two and then noticed a loose and broken cobble lying near his feet.

He picked it up and hurled it in the direction of the vehicle as it crawled away. The cobble traveled in a fine arc, up almost above the nearby tree line, and gracefully descended some thirty yards away, finding its target with unerring accuracy, bouncing off the roof of the Solo with a satisfying 'thunk' before skittling away. "Bastard," he said.

John turned and looked up at the steps, which disappeared ominously into darkness high above. He sighed heavily and set off up the ancient stone steps, taking giant bounds of two to three steps at a time.

***

Later that night, with his mother safely sedated and fast asleep, and Claire updated as to the situation, John sat on the covered stone terrace outside his bedroom, looking down at the lights of the old town far below. The rain was drifting across his view in sheets.

What a fucking horrendous day.

He sipped his hot malt and tried to relax. His mother had been a total wreck when he'd reached home. He had to plead with her to take some pills to calm herself down.

It wasn't surprising that it had come to this again - she was receiving the best of attention to try and help her through, but she couldn't be expected to deal with losing her husband in such strange circumstances without it affecting her badly. He just hoped that with time things would start to improve. John sat and watched the rain for a while longer. The sound of it was soothing, and he started to relax a bit as the malt kicked in.

After the extremely keen reception he'd received at Claire's flat, his concerns had eased somewhat, but he was still expecting some sort of explanation, that was for sure. He'd had spent quite a bit of time today thinking about Andrew and their friendship over the years, about just how invaluable they'd been to one another.

They had a close friendship, one in which you felt you could say or do anything without fear of being judged, and that was a difficult thing to find. John was thankful for having found that in Andrew. He'd come to realize that without Andrew's friendship, he wouldn't have been able to cope over the last few months.

He can keep his fucking hands off my girlfriend, though!

He'd find a way to put that to him. Politely. At least at first. He was still feeling uneasy over Andrew's evasiveness back at the caf-bar. There would be time to talk about it sometime soon; he just needed to chill out. John rubbed his eyes and drained the rest of his drink.

Now wasn't the time to get all overprotective and controlling with Claire and potentially ruin everything. He had everything he could possibly want. He looked out again into the rain. The thought should have made him at ease.

There was something else troubling him. Earlier that day, he'd spoken briefly to Peter Bradshaw, and it hadn't gone as expected. At the time, he'd shrugged it off, but for some reason, it continued to gnaw away at the back of his mind.

The dean was an old family friend and someone John had relied on to steer him in the right direction several times over the years. He felt he could trust Peter Bradshaw, and so he'd asked him very carefully, very discretely, just a little bit about internal affairs tech, mentioning that he'd heard that they had some pretty advanced security.

He was trying to angle the inquiry that if he could tap into some of their resources, it might help him trace comms the night his father had disappeared. It probably wasn't the most convincing argument, and he realized now that this might have been a mistake – the conversation was abruptly terminated, and now he was starting to worry that he might have said the wrong thing to the wrong person. Again.

The dean had seemed troubled and distracted soon after John had mentioned internal affairs. He'd then rather hurriedly made an excuse about something or other and ushered John from his workroom with an awkward goodbye. The whole thing had been a bit strange, and alarm bells should already have been ringing.

He couldn't breathe all of a sudden as he connected the dots. It could be bad. He took a moment to play it through in his mind again and started to realize he'd potentially made a huge mistake. How could anyone know that internal affairs had super-advanced security unless they'd seen it for themselves when they shouldn't have?

Oh Douglas, please let me be wrong.

He may have put them all at risk. All their research - none of it legal. And he had to go and open his big mouth. In his mind, on the one side, he was telling himself not to worry and that it was probably nothing, and on the other side, he was telling himself that it was time to panic, time to cover their tracks and destroy all evidence.

No, no, no, no! What do I do? I could just stay quiet, pretend nothing has happened? But then what if ...

It became clear pretty quickly that he'd better say something. If anyone got wind of what they'd been doing, then they were all in big, big trouble. He tried Claire on comms and again received no answer. She was offline for calls and messages.

He had to tell her what had happened. She'd know what to do. She always knew. It wasn't the first time John had said the wrong thing to someone either - Claire wouldn't be happy, that was for sure. He'd been so stupid! He probably should have known better this time - he definitely should have known better this time.

Only a few months ago, he'd made an offhand comment about endemic state corruption to one of his moneyed elite friends towards the end of a particularly long and boozy night. He'd backtrack very quickly once people had started asking questions a few days later.

John had covered his tracks well enough, but she'd been absolutely furious with him. Her anger had seemed wildly disproportionate at the time, but now it made perfect sense. They had been where they shouldn't. The consequences could be dire. John felt his cheeks reddening as a feeling of shame and contrition came over him.

What the fuck have I done now? Fuck!

John threw his empty mug at the terrace wall, and it exploded into a million pieces. That hadn't really helped. That was his favorite mug - or had been.

He could be risking everything they had been working for, and potentially he was also risking his relationship with Claire. She'd been so livid last time that he wasn't even really sure why she'd kept him around.

It had been a really, really bad day. First, there was the kiss. The thought blacked out everything else, and the tension and anger start to build deep inside again. He tried, unsuccessfully, to force the image of Andrew and Claire's embrace from his mind. He started pacing around the terrace. He was trembling, his vision started to swirl, and his heart started to race uncontrollably. "Dook, not now, fucks sake ..."

He leaned on the terrace wall for support and sucked in a few deep breaths of the cold night air. He was trying to force the panic attack away and focused all his attention on his breathing. *Slow and steady, in, hold, out.* He felt as if he was going to pass out for a moment, but slowly the spinning sensation subsided, and his heart rate slowed. He forced himself to stand upright.

"Ok, John, ok," he said to himself. He knew what he needed to do.

***

Andrew knocked quietly on the door of Claire's flat. He felt butterflies in his stomach, which was really quite ridiculous. She'd called him an hour or so ago and apologized for canceling earlier, explaining about John's emergency, and had asked him to come over for a while. She'd called him once she'd heard back from John that everything was ok at home and was looking forward to a few laughs and maybe a few shots of VKA to take the edge off what had been a fairly traumatic day. Needless to say, Andrew had bounded round to her place, stopping briefly at the vend-mart on the way.

It was a very cold night, and after a clear start to the day, the rain was now lashing violently against the window of her flat. A small pool of water was forming on the floor underneath the window, thanks to the leak. She'd complained about it several times already, but nothing had been done. Claire shut her device down and headed for the bathroom, which doubled as a walk-in wardrobe – Andrew would be there any moment, and she'd better put some underwear on.

He shivered and felt the cold seeping through his boots as he waited for Claire to answer his knock at the door. The bottoms of his pants had soaked through from the almost horizontal rain.

Andrew noticed he was making a small puddle of his own as the rain dripped from his coat onto the floor. The door was flung open in front of him, catching him by surprise, although he wasn't sure what else he was expecting to happen.

She stood in the doorway, smiling at him, the light from behind her revealing way too much detail of what was inside the long grey wool jumper-dress she was wearing. Andrew froze. She looked amazing. The jumper itself had slid off of one shoulder. It wasn't particularly warm in the room, and he couldn't help noticing that she wasn't wearing anything much underneath. He glanced away, just a little disappointed in himself.

Well, for fucks sake. I am just a mere mortal. Claire, however, is more like some kind of evil temptress placed on this earth to taunt me!

"Why do you look like you've just seen a ghost, Andy?" she asked softly. "Come on in; I won't bite ... and stop dripping!"

She turned and walked quickly back to the couch. She was in a playful mood, which isn't a mood she usually associated with herself. It was no doubt related to the dam-busting wave of emotion she'd experienced earlier today. Having her friend over was meant as a bit of a circuit breaker - it was time to relax and have a laugh.

Claire flung herself down on the couch and sat cross-legged. Andrew had moved inside but had forgotten to close the door. She pointed behind him. "Door!" she commanded. He realized he was already making a total fool of himself.

Pretty good going in the first few seconds.

"Oops. Sorry," he muttered and pushed the door shut, cutting off the cold draught he'd just caused. Andrew thought his movements seemed jerky and robotic.

Relax. For fucks sake, it's only Claire! It must be so obvious to her.

Claire knew full well that he was infatuated with her, it was so obvious, but she didn't really care about that. He was a great company, and he was fun to have around, particularly when she needed to tune out, and that was what she needed that more than anything right now.

She enjoyed making him squirm a little, especially when she had him all to herself, and she'd already started. Although this was for her own amusement, she was pretty sure that he enjoyed it just as much.

Andrew finally managed to come up with something to say. "I did think I'd seen a fucking ghost! Have you slept in the last month?" He was laughing now, making a big show of shrugging off his jacket and prying off his boots.

Claire had let out a small chuckle at his remark. She was smiling mischievously at him, patting the couch next to her, asking him to sit. He pulled out a large bottle of VDK from his backpack and threw himself down on the scruffy beanbag couch, offering her the bottle. "Oh, you are a star, Andy!" She gave him her extra special smile and leaned forward, placing a hand on his thigh as she took the bottle with the other.

He jumped more than a little at her touch and looked for a moment like he was going to leap up and make a run for the door, unprepared as he was for the rush of warmth that had just run through his entire body. Without warning, she pinched him hard through the fabric of his jeans, making him squeal and pull his leg away.

"Fuck's sake, Claire! You bitch!" He was laughing as he aimed a punch at her arm, but she was too quick for him and writhed away, leaving his punch collecting nothing but thin air.

"OK, ok, Andy, I'm sorry." She was pouting now, offering back the bottle. "Peace offering?" He reached begrudgingly for the clear plex bottle.

"Gee, thanks so much for giving me *my* bottle back, Claire!" he said sulkily.

"No, really, I am sorry, Andy. I didn't realize you were *so* sensitive!" He did a double-take, realizing he was being made fun of again. This was typical of her in the rare moments that she allowed herself to fully relax. He liked relaxed Claire, perhaps a little too much. He saw the chance for revenge and carefully put the VKA aside.

"I'll show you bloody sensitive!" he blurted out suddenly, aiming a blow at her thigh. It connected this time, and she squealed and kicked out a well-aimed foot as she rolled away from him, collecting him square in the knee. "Bloody hell Claire, you crazy cow!"

"That's why you love me, though, Andy."

He paused, not knowing what to say. Her response was a wink, then another wicked smile. Andrew really didn't like the look of the mischievous sparkle in her eyes. He raised his hands in defeat, but he had no intention of being defeated at all.

She looked away, only for a second, but that was all the time he needed - he lunged forward, aiming a pinch directly at her side, making her recoil in shock, hair flying, legs and arms flailing, trying to get away from the source of the sharp pain. She swatted his arm away and pushed herself back away from him on the couch. "Andy! You duille! Fuck!"

Claire was breathing heavily, her face flushed, and Andrew was trying hard not to notice that her jumper had risen alarmingly up over her thighs during the struggle, exposing creamy white skin and tight black silk panties

Well, at least she's wearing some form of underwear.

He very conspicuously diverted his gaze to a nearby lamp.

That's a nice lamp.

"Well, you asked for it!" he remarked, daring a glance back at her and being met by a surprisingly wild and angry-looking expression. She made as if to throw a punch, and he recoiled at her ruse before she burst out laughing, with Andrew following suit. And that was his mistake.

He relaxed, thinking it was all over, and reached for the VKA. A heavy stinging blow landed on his left arm, just below the shoulder. Pain shot up his arm, and he involuntarily squealed as he scrambled away from his assailant. Claire was already rising from the couch as she made for the kitchenette.

"Bloody bitch," Andrew mumbled, rubbing at his arm to try and dull the pain. "That'll leave a mark, you know!"

Claire looked back at him. "You deserved it," she concluded, rummaging around in the one cupboard over the sink for a while and cursing several times before eventually returning to the couch holding a couple of small, mismatched cups. As she sat and placed them on the small plex crate that acted as a side table, he feigned a punch towards her shoulder, and she jerked out of the way before pushing herself back and kicking out again.

"Oi!" he gasped as another blow connected - this time to his thigh. Oh, she was asking for some revenge pain tonight! She was laughing.

"What ya gunna do about it, Andy Pandy?"

He hated that nickname. He knew she was saying it just to wind him up and that he'd have to do something to stop the continued assault.

He grabbed for her leg as it threatened another direct hit and somehow managed to get hold of her ankle. She shrieked with laughter and tried to pull herself free, aiming her free foot in Andrew's general direction. There was nothing for it, he thought, as another blow connected firmly, this time with his hip.

His self-preservation instinct kicked in, and a struggle ensued as he tried to pin her arms, his only hope of suppressing the onslaught. Claire was laughing almost hysterically now as she wrestled against his grasp. She was slippery as an eel, and he knew if he let go, he'd be in all kinds of trouble

"Get off me! Ya wee wiry bawheed!" her laughter was making her words almost indecipherable. Andrew was laughing now, too, as he tried desperately to think of a way to end it as she bucked wildly underneath him, threatening to break loose at any moment.

Andrew was now genuinely fearful of the retribution that was surely coming his way, any moment now. In the nick of time, he remembered something - she'd done a thing to him once before that had made him recoil in disgust. It was a desperate measure, but this was certainly a desperate time.

Ooh, she nearly got free then! Ooh, dook!

Andrew redoubled his efforts to hold on. It was now or never! He had to land the killer blow and avoid further pain being inflicted upon himself. He launched himself toward the target zone, zeroing in with laser-like accuracy just as Claire, in her efforts to dislodge him, had arched her back and turned her head away from him.

He executed the move spectacularly. His killer strike was met with a somewhat surprisingly delighted squeal as his tongue connected with her neck, a little way under the left ear. What happened in the next few seconds was even more surprising.

Rather than increase her efforts to injure him further, Claire's body had stiffened for a split second and then relaxed as a shiver of goosebumps rushed up her body, sending an electric shock through them both. She stopped struggling and was now looking back at him with an expression he couldn't read. Their faces were only inches apart. She slowly started to grin and cast her eyes downward and then quickly back up to meet his. She started to giggle.

It was at that moment that the true horror of the situation started to dawn on Andrew. As a result of their tryst, his groin had ended up firmly pressed into the soft flesh of Claire's upper thigh. The additional warmth and strain on the fabric in that area was suddenly very apparent.

A mix of pure panic and extreme embarrassment suddenly consumed him, and he immediately released his grip and rolled away from her, landing in a somewhat ungainly manner on the floor. He was blushing wildly now. He wanted to die. Claire also looked flushed, but as she propped herself up, she spoke in a low and soft voice, "oh Andy, I didn't know you cared!"

He looked away, trying to hide his embarrassment, and she snorted with laughter before driving the final nail into his coffin of shame. She added distinct sexual overtones as she panted, "oh, do me, Andy, do me! Do me!"

She'd stopped laughing now and responded to Andrew's look of extreme shock by drawing her tongue enticingly across her top lip. Andrew started to stutter the words, "oh, I'll be getting you back for th…"

But he never got to finish the sentence.

***

John stood motionless outside the door of Claire's flat. The corridor was musty, and paint peeled from the walls. His hand was raised as if to knock, but it had become frozen in place. He could hear Claire and Andrew's voices coming from within, laughter, physical noises of some sort, more laughter. Claire's voice, sounding sexually charged. It was sounding way too intimate for his liking.

What the fuck's going on? What's Andrew even doing here this late?

John's breath was coming in short rasps, his heart rate increased, he could hear the blood rushing in his ears, and pure, unfiltered anger took hold.

He knew this moment well and tried to shake himself free of it, but then he heard more laughter and Claire's voice, breathless, from somewhere inside. He felt as if he'd stepped outside his body and became an observer. He saw a red haze and then his fist hammering repeatedly on the door of the flat. The noise coming from inside stopped immediately.

They stared at the door - it sounded as if someone were trying to break it down. John's voice yelled something from behind it, and they shared a confused if not worried look.

"What the fuck's going on in there!" John was bellowing.

Claire stood up and somewhat tentatively called out, "John?" She looked back at Andrew, who now seemed intent on disappearing into the couch. She normally feared no one, least of all that hulking giant of a boyfriend of hers, but she'd never heard him sound quite so angry before. He was prone to having a bit of a short fuse, and she'd seen her fair share of outbursts, but the anger in his voice was so intense it was frightening.

John's voice came again. "What the *fuck* is going on in there?"

Claire decided to fight fire with fire. She threw open the door, catching him by surprise. The words he'd been about to shout caught in his throat as he saw the anger burning through her. She took a step forward and yelled point-blank into his face, "get a fucking *grip*, John!"

Her tirade lasted a full thirty seconds. At one point, a doorway halfway down the dimly lit hallway had opened, and a head peeked out only to disappear again quickly. John had taken a step back at some point, stunned by her ferocity.

She'd run out of steam and now stood glaring at him. He wasn't about to back down. He'd been taken aback by the force of her words, but he was still just as angry. He deserved an explanation.

What the fuck had just been happening?

Claire was finding it difficult to read him. Her anger simmered to the surface again.

"Well? What do you *think* was *going on* in here?" she swept her arm back around the flat.

"What was going on, John?" she asked bluntly, hands now on her hips.

He'd come back to himself and was now just a young man, suddenly uncertain of himself, and with a very angry girlfriend. He tried for an explanation of his own.

"Claire, look, I made a mistake today. Maybe a big one. My mind's all over the place what with mum and all, and, well, when I got here, I just didn't know what was going on, it sounded ..."

"What are you talking about? Andrew's here, that's all. There was nothing *going on*! Who are you, the fun police? We were just mucking about, for fucks sake!"

She moved to one side so that John could see into the flat. Andrew tentatively offered a wave from his position pressed hard into the furthest corner of the couch. Something snapped inside John; in his mind, something gave way. The anger boiled up quickly and overflowed, with nowhere to go except towards its target.

"I saw you!" he cried, pointing at Andrew.

Claire was shocked at the sudden mood swing.

"I saw you kiss Claire! On the street!"

She went to speak, to leap to Andrew's defense, but nothing came out. She was having trouble processing what she'd just heard. That wasn't what had happened, was it?

What the fuck?

She glanced back at Andrew, who was sort of cowering now. *He* wasn't about to say anything.

"Oh, come *on!*" she finally spat the words out, but to John, they sounded defensive.

"I saw you," he repeated, this time directing his words at Claire, although the steam had already gone from them. *I shouldn't have to be the one explaining things! And yet ...*

"When I got here, well, it sounded to me like you and Andy here were having *way* more fun than you should b ..."

John's face stung from the ferocious slap to the cheek. Claire had stepped forward and leaned in, swinging with all her not inconsiderable strength, stopping his words mid-sentence.

"Fuck off, John." She was seeing red herself now, spitting the words out, and John was left momentarily stunned, rubbing his cheek.

"Look ... Claire," he started to say, holding his palm up to try and prevent any further blows.

Claire interjected. Her voice was far from calm.

"I was upset; Andrew came to find me. *That's* what happened on the street today, you stupid dook!"

That wasn't what I saw.

"And by the way, what *other* mistake are we talking about here? What else have you managed to fuck up?" Claire was shaking with adrenaline - she almost didn't recognize the words she'd spoken as her own. She was experiencing her own version of the red mist.

John moved his jaw around as if assessing the damage as he tried to understand what had just happened. "Um, well, you see ..." he started to babble, hoping to buy a few precious seconds.

Claire took a step out into the hallway towards him, and he flinched as she did so. The intimidating hulk was reduced to a trembling mess by the small dark-haired girl, less than half his size, standing directly in front of him.

"Well?!" she demanded. John looked away. When he looked back at her, his face was ashen.

"I think I said something I shouldn't have. To The dean at SCC. To Mr. Bradshaw." The words were quiet, shame-filled.

Claire was suddenly filled with a feeling of extreme dread on top of her mounting anger.

"I know who that is, John! But What? Fucking *again,* really? Again? What the fucking fuck! Fuck! Fuuuck!" She was beside herself with anger; she'd had enough of John screwing everything up, putting them all at risk.

"What did you say?! What have you *done*?!" John assumed the worst. There was probably no coming back from this. His words stuttered out.

"I ... I was just trying to fish for a tiny bit of information Claire, you know, on the security protocols for internal affairs. I thought I could trust Peter. He's an old family friend. He helped me when dad disappeared, and ..."

The words petered out as he saw the look on her face.

"And?" she was speaking quietly now, which was terrifying him even more. He realized he hadn't taken an inward breath in a while, so he did. It helped a little.

"And. Well, I asked him about what new Tech they'd been employing on their security systems." He swallowed, unable to meet her eye. "I was trying to help, Claire."

"Help?! Well, ok. That sounds exactly like the complete fucking *opposite* of trying to help!" she spat. She folded her arms in front of her.

If looks could kill, thought John.

"So, what happened exactly?" she inquired, only slightly less venomously. John took a moment to try and clear his head. The side of his face was still stinging, and he rubbed at his cheek again.

Fuck she can hit hard.

"Well, I did it discretely, see? I thought so anyway, but, well, after I'd made the inquiry." The words stopped abruptly.

He was in two minds. All or nothing, he decided, there was no point hiding anything now; they could be in big trouble, all of them.

"Well, see, he looked a bit troubled after I'd asked, and instead of answering, he pretty much ushered me out of the workroom. He made some excuse or other, but I can tell something was wrong. I think I fucked up, Claire."

"Oh, you think?" She was standing defiantly, her chin angled up. John knew he'd really messed up this time.

"You think? You asked a high-ranking state employee about security protocols that we aren't supposed to know about, and you *think* you fucked up?"

The words hung in the air, and she just stood there, glaring at him. Andrew had cautiously risen from the relative safety of the couch. He was standing behind Claire in the doorway, feeling terrified at what was unfolding in front of him. He wanted to do something to try and calm things down and placed a hand on her shoulder. She turned, craning her neck toward him as he went to whisper something; he was going to tell her to go easy.

John watched as Claire's head tilt toward Andrew as if they were about to kiss.

Are they …?

The next few moments were a blur. It was as if John had an out-of-body experience. Suddenly he saw them kissing out on the street.

He must have shouted something, as he could see the shocked look on their faces. He saw Andrew holding his hands up and backing away, and he could see himself lunge towards him. Somewhere during that moment, Claire had tried to position herself between them, and John's massive lunging arm collected her across the face and knocked her to the floor like a rag doll.

The hallway swirled around him, and John had to brace himself against the walls as he saw Claire crumpled on the floor, not believing what he saw in front of him—not believing what he'd just done. Andrew was shouting something at him, but it was muffled; everything was blurry and muffled.

Oh no, oh fuck no. What have I done? The thought was strangely detached.

Claire was on the floor, and Andrew was now crouched down next to her trying to help. She pushed him away and scrambled up, wildly brushing the hair away from her face and revealing a crimson streak of blood trailing from her mouth and smeared across her cheek. Her eyes were wild as she spat words at John in rapid succession. He was watching all this happen, but he couldn't hear the words. Her mouth was moving in slow motion.

As she stepped forward, Andrew attempted to hold her back by grabbing at one of her arms. Claire brushed him easily aside with a quick shrug of her shoulder and twisted away from him. Everything was still happening in slow motion for John; his vision bathed in a red haze.

He was still braced against the walls of the hallway, staring at her, unmoving. She had a fierce look on her face and bared her teeth at him. Sounds started to come through, muffled at first. The red haze started to dissipate, and the sound of blood rushing in his ears subsided just in time to hear her final words.

"… fucking over John, It's over! You had better go into fucking hiding and cover your tracks; we might not be safe, you bloody idiot!" Droplets of blood sprayed from her mouth as she spoke, some landing on John's plain white t-shirt.

Blood was also dripping down her chin, the red streak contrasting starkly with the bright white of her teeth. She'd stopped talking and now stood with her hands firmly on her hips, feet wide apart, chin jutted out, her eyes burning into his so fiercely that he could no longer look at her. She'd shocked herself with her fury, but now it was over. She spoke coldly and calmly, "Well, John … that … is that."

He was beyond mortified. His whole world had just collapsed in front of his eyes - and at his own hand. He had to get out of there; he had to go before he made things worse still. John looked at the floor, turned, and walked slowly away from Claire, from Andrew, from everything he held dear in his life. His head was spinning, but the anger still hadn't fully left him; in fact, he could feel it welling up inside again.

Hold on, he thought, wasn't he the one who'd been wronged here, the one who'd been betrayed? He turned back, and the anger left him as quickly as it had risen. He saw the resolute expression on Claire's face and knew it was over. He looked down again, ashamed, and managed to force a few words out in a shaking voice.

"Claire, I'm sorry. It was an accident. For fucks sake." As he finished speaking, he looked up, only to see the door to the flat closing firmly. He didn't even know if she'd heard him. It was too late anyway. Once Claire said something, she meant it. He'd really fucked this up.

He headed unsteadily down the hallway towards the stairwell, stumbling down to ground level and then out onto the street. It was still raining. It was freezing. "Great ... just *fucking great!*" Steam vapor billowed from his mouth as he stood in the middle of the street, breathing hard.

The rain ran down his face, hiding his tears as he stood there, numb, shocked at what he'd done. He bellowed into the night sky at the top of his voice, a wild, raw sound that stopped passersby in their tracks - not that he would have noticed. He was in his own world—a world of pain.

His comms was buzzing, it was Andrew, and without thinking, he answered and let loose with a tirade that would have burned his ex-friend's ears. He wasn't even sure what he'd said, other than something along the lines of "if you touch her again, I'll rip your fucking head off, you fucking little ..." or words to that effect. He didn't wait to hear the response, shutting off his comms and hurling them with all his might into the small park opposite the flats in a pique of anger.

Fuck it! Fuck it all! My two best friends - they were my best friends! Something was going on! I fucking caught them!

It was all too much. John knew he wasn't thinking straight. He still saw red, and he needed to calm himself down. The reality of what he'd just done started to hit home - he'd ruined everything. He'd accidentally hit Claire and knocked her down! He just couldn't believe it, and it was like a bad dream; it didn't seem real.

He looked at his hand and saw a smear of blood - Claire's blood. He wiped it quickly on his pants. It was real. How could he be so careless, so stupid? He cried out into the night sky again, but this time the sound was more pitiful than guttural.

The rain started to seep down behind the collar of his jacket, bringing him back to the cold, damp reality of the street. He had a big problem now, one which was all his own doing. He could see only one immediate solution and stumbled off through the now torrential rain.

A small vendbox sign on the pavement had the misfortune to cross his path, and he broke it in two over his knee before hurling that into the park as well. He was headed into the old town, to the one place he knew he could sit uninterrupted and drink himself into oblivion.

The Old Scholars Bar was where you went when you wanted to forget it all, and that was what he needed, to forget everything and everyone. It was membership only, and staff were well-schooled in the art of asking no questions. It was secluded and cozy, a labyrinth of small leather and timber booths perfectly designed for solitary self-destruction.

Lightning cracked overhead as John strode towards the nearest t-hub.

***

It was a few minutes after John's somewhat overly dramatic and emotional departure. Claire was hunched over her device but was not paying any attention to it. Instead, she pressed the ball of t-paper she held in her left hand firmly against her bottom lip, occasionally drawing it away and looking at the darkening mark. The blood oozing from her lip was seemingly endless.

Claire went over and over what had happened in her mind. She knew her injury was an accident, but she'd had to tell John so many times to learn to quell his temper that she wasn't in the least bit surprised that it had happened.

It was the mistrust that had been the final straw. She really couldn't believe what she'd heard. She'd reacted instinctively and had surprised herself with the slap - which had carried more force than she thought herself capable of. But still, he deserved it!

How fucking dare he insinuate that anything was going on, and with Andrew! For fucks sake. Andrew, his very best friend! He's seen us embrace on the street - so what! That was insane!

She'd invested everything in the trust she had with her friends, and she'd always thought of them as the only two people on the planet that she could truly rely upon. She'd assumed, wrongly, that her undying trust in John was replicated. That was the part that had triggered the response and her uncontrolled fury.

He's out every other night, getting pissed up with all the plastic little rich girlies trying to get into his pants, and he's the one that thinks there's something going on!

Claire knew that she was partly to blame, but there was no need for such mistrust. She'd invited Andrew round late at night; she had initiated the rough and tumble. It wasn't the smartest thing to have done, but then again, it was just a bit of fun. There was no way she would have allowed anything to happen. She didn't like Andrew like *that*. Not at all. *Ew.*

She was sad that things had come to an end, but in some ways, it was inevitable - it was just a shame it had to end in such a way. The accidental damage to her lip was as good an excuse as any for her to end the relationship. She'd known it had been a mistake to get too close to him, and she supposed she'd been looking for a way to end it. Anyway, what was done was done.

No point dwelling on it, she thought.

She didn't cause the scene tonight - it was John and his stupid temper. Thinking about code would be a welcome distraction from her relationship issues. Claire was already in the process of emotionally detaching herself from the situation and had already turned her attention to Elyssium related matters. It wasn't a difficult thing for her - it was a logical and necessary next step.

***

The V.I. call, in particular, was troubling her. All V.I. calls - well, except those on her private network - came through Skyweb, one of the biggest recent Tech advancements. It provided instant and crystal-clear communications around the planet. She could usually break through Skyweb security fairly easily, but not on this particular call - it had a strange type of morphing encryption that she hadn't seen before - this was happening to Claire a lot lately. She'd already forgotten about her lip, and a little quiver of excitement was ever building the closer she looked at the encryption - she knew she was onto something

Something was slightly off in the voice patterns, too – Sally had been right - they just didn't seem to have the warmth that you'd expect. She didn't know how else to put it, especially seeing as she was no expert on emotions, Douglas knows, but the call was oddly cold. There were still a lot of different regional Alban accents, and the nuances were extremely vague. Although those in evidence from Frances' voice seemed perfectly fine on first listen, there was just the odd word or phrase that didn't quite gel.

She could really use John's help right now, in all honesty. Maybe she'd been a touch harsh? The lip would heal, but she wasn't sure that John's pride would. He knew Skyweb inside out, having worked on part of its development, and he'd found a way for her to access the source code some time ago, usually making this a simple process.

There wasn't much chance of him helping at the moment, obviously, thanks to their duel meltdowns. She'd give him some time to calm down, do whatever it was men did in these situations, and then patch things over - maybe he could be a friend with benefits? It was time to get to work. While these thought processes were going through her mind, she was dutifully ignoring Andrew, who was pacing the small room intermittently, comms gripped firmly in his hand.

***

Andrew was in shock, pure and simple. John, his very best friend, his ally against the forces of stupidity - hell, even his bodyguard on the regular occasions that his smart mouth had landed him in trouble - had accused him of betrayal. He had a terrible feeling in the pit of his stomach.

Betraying him! Really? Sure, John's under a lot of stress. Sure, they were mucking around. Sure, Claire had kissed him and said she loved him. Sure, he was madly in love with Claire.

Ok, I'm not painting a great picture of innocence here, but Nothing happened! Nothing was going to happen! How could he seriously think …?

Andrew was pacing again, backward and forwards behind Claire, who he assumed to be equally distraught. He'd been furiously working at his comms, trying to get back in touch with his best friend. He was worried not just for him but for anyone that got in his way tonight. He'd seen him angry before, but nothing like he'd seen tonight; the raw anger and the lunge, the bloody outcome smeared across Claire's face. It was surreal.

He was sure that John would have snapped him in half had Claire not gotten in the way. The worst, the absolute worst part of it all was that he knew that John wasn't too far wrong. He'd allowed himself to see a possible opportunity to be with her, he'd felt the sexual tension, and now he was deeply ashamed.

First, there is opportunity, and then …

He could see the parallels all right, even though he wasn't thinking all that clearly. He was desperate to undo whatever had just happened, desperate to try and make things right. He almost wished that John had managed to get past Claire and pummel him to a pulp.

Maybe then, at least everyone would know where they stood. Maybe then Claire would …

He stopped himself again.

For Douglas's sake, man! What are you thinking?

He tried to contact him again. Nothing. Offline. He stopped pacing.

Maybe I should go and try to find him? Explain things. Well, maybe not. Explain what, exactly?

"Claire?" he mumbled into the gloom of the tiny sitting room. There was no response. He was standing more or less directly behind her. She looked tiny, hunched over the desk, head down. Andrew could only imagine what she must be going through. If it was anything like what he was feeling, she must be going through absolute hell.

"Claire?" he asked again, this time with a sadness clearly evident in his voice. He was really feeling for her. As he moved to her side, he saw that her fingers were dancing over the interface of her device as lines of code flashed up on the display in quick succession.

She was completely oblivious to his existence and absorbed in her work.

"Oh ..."

Boyfriend just smashed you to the ground by accident, destroying the close bond and lifetime friendships - oh well, better get back to coding!

"Claire!" This time he spoke quite forcefully, a slight tremor in his voice. Her hands paused for a second, and he went to speak again, but then she continued furiously creating code and processing calculations on the device so fast that he could barely make out what she was doing. Andrew frowned.

"Claire!" He practically shouted it this time. *"Claire! For fucks sake!"*

She stopped typing and tilted her head toward him just enough so that he could make out her annoyance. He could see that her lip was still bleeding - a small trail of blood had run halfway down her chin. "Claire, are you alright? I mean, are you ok?"

Silence followed. She blinked a couple of times, looking somewhat perplexed at the question.

"I mean, what the fuck?! How could he just come here and attack us like that? He hurt you!"

She turned to look at him, and as always with her, he couldn't read anything from her expression.

"I mean, we weren't, we didn't!" he blurted out, surprising himself at how desperate his words sounded.

She shrugged and frowned, the first sign that his words had registered. He went to speak again but decided against it. He was feeling more confused than ever. She was now looking at him with a mix of something like pity and curiosity.

Yes, Claire, this is what it looks like to have a heart.

Andrew sat and lay back on the couch. Claire resigned herself to the interruption and turned her attention to him, rubbing her eyes as if to clear the lines of code from them.

"Sorry, I'm just trying to ... it doesn't matter ... look, Andy, don't worry. I'm ok. It was an accident. John just overreacted. He's a big boy; he can look after himself. If we are totally honest here, which I think we are..." she paused, widening her eyes a little and tilting her head as if to draw his agreement, "something like this was probably coming for a long time. It'll be ok." Andrew couldn't have disagreed more.

"Oh … kay! Fucking oh, fucking kay! How is anything going to be ok now? John thinks we betrayed him! You told him to go to hell! He told me to go to hell - or words to that effect. This is about as *not ok* as it could possibly be!" He started walking around the room in small circles, gesticulating like a madman.

"My best friend. I've just lost my best friend, haven't I? Pretty much my only friend! *Dook!*"

"Calm down, Andy, for fucks sake." Her words cut through the cool air of the room like a knife and stopped him mid-pace. "We didn't … I mean, I wouldn't … you know … we were just …" he stuttered.

"Andy, look, I'm really sorry that you got involved in all this. I was most likely going to end things with John sooner or later anyway. It was getting too serious. Too distracting. It was never going to work out long term. That's not what I want."

She rubbed her hand across her forehead. "Anyway, it turned out to be sooner rather than later." She shrugged as if that was that, all done; nothing more needs to be added. Andrew had nothing more to say anyway.

Why is she like this? Why is she always so uncaring, so damn cold?

"Andy … look … it's not your fault. If it's anyone's fault, it's mine, ok? This will blow over, trust me." She'd said this with the sort of conviction that only she could deliver in times of high drama. Everything was always black and white with her.

Blow over? For fucks sake!

"Don't do anything silly, eh?"

He didn't know what to say or do - and realized that this seemed to be pretty much his default state lately. He stood there for a few moments more before mumbling, "I'm going out," as he turned and headed for the door.

"Right. Andy?"

She was demanding an answer. He turned back, mumbling "aye, sure," with next to no enthusiasm and a healthy dose of depression. He decided that leaving was the best thing that he could do right now. He needed time to think; he needed some space, some air. Claire needed to work, so he'd go home and wallow in self-pity, maybe just lose himself in Headspace with many, many VKA's. It was a good plan.

"Be careful, Andy. We're playing around with things that we shouldn't be here. John may have alerted someone to what we've seen. Just lay low until I've covered our tracks."

"Aye, aye," he said, pretending to understand, even though he hadn't really been listening, his mind distracted by images of his best friend trying to kill him. He slipped out the door and into the dimly lit hallway - which smelt faintly of urine, he couldn't help noticing. This didn't do a lot to brighten his mood.

Lay low? What does that even mean? He had no idea.

CHAPTER 6 – LUCK

John had achieved his goal. He'd kept on ordering genuine single malts until he could barely remember why he was there at all. No one had come to bother him. No one had made unwelcome advances. No one had tried to pick a fight. He'd just sat there in his small booth – all deep maroon leather, low yellow lighting, and rich mahogany paneling - and drank until he could no longer focus on anything.

He'd realized how pointless and futile his current actions were some time ago but felt like continuing to drink was the only option. The red mist had slowly cleared and was replaced with a deep sense of loss, loneliness, and regret. Thinking about things just made everything seem worse. It was very, very late, or very, very early, depending on your point of view. The rich amber liquid was glinting seductively at him from the confines of his glass.

Hell, no point wasting that last drop.

He downed the remains of the triple shot in one large gulp, the liquid burning his throat and making him choke. He made to get up from the booth and nearly toppled over, his head seeming to weigh more than the rest of him combined. He steadied himself on the table for a moment and waited for the room to stop spinning before lurching down the tiny dark hallway that led back to the real world.

John wasn't looking forward to seeing the real world terribly much, but there really wasn't any other option - he really should get home. He'd been selfish and childish. His mum needed him and he should be at home. He forgot to duck as he exited onto the wet and misty cobbled street and smacked his forehead squarely on the doorframe's lintel on the way out. He barely even flinched - everything was numb.

After wandering around for a while, he lost interest in where he was going; such was his drunken state. At least it had stopped raining. There was no one about - the streets were deserted at whatever un-Dougly hour of the night this was.

John walked for a while. It felt good to breathe in the cool air and to be moving through the dark, deserted streets. He kept on walking. After a while, he realized that he had no idea where he was.

He looked around and saw the same vendboxes that he'd been seeing for the last little while. It was quite possible he'd been walking in circles, and he was tired now, so very, very tired.

He stopped and leaned back against the railings of a small park, considering for a moment that maybe climbing over and finding a convenient park bench to spend the night on was the best option. He could always rent a sleep-pod; there must be some somewhere nearby, he supposed. He looked around from where he sat but didn't see any.

Oh well.

The cold air was starting to seep through the warmth of the malt haze, and reality was starting to rear its ugly head again. He started thinking about his mum, home alone, most likely still in a deep, medicated sleep. John decided he'd better make it home tonight, no matter what. What if his mum had had another of her episodes but couldn't get hold of him? His comms was in a park somewhere outside Claire's building. A sense of worry and the realization of just how reckless and stupid he'd been tonight/this morning started to form in his addled mind.

Time to go home.

Just as he was about to guess which direction to try, the bright glow of an unoccupied Solo appeared around a nearby corner.

"My lucky night!"

***

Andrew had trudged back to his cold and depressing room in the student accommodations, managing to get soaked again by sleeting sheets of icy rain in the process. He'd hit the VKA hard and then hit Headspace - as he knew he inevitably would - visiting a place that might help him expel some of the pent-up frustration and angst he was feeling.

He entered the Temple. Everything was silent and still. Giant white marble dragon statues flanked him on either side. The arena was huge; its grey crushed granite surface surrounded by tall white columns on all sides, a low dusky light giving everything a lovely soft focus. The only thing providing relief from this soft pallet of colors was the bright orange of his opponent's hair and beard. They bowed to one another and assumed the pose.

He'd learned much from his ginger master, but tonight he didn't seem to be able to put any moves together at all. He'd been working on a leg sweep for some time and had a reasonable amount of success with it in recent weeks, but not tonight. The trick was to draw your opponent into a lunge, whereby you would sway back from them, causing them to overreach, and at the same time, drop and sweep in one fluid motion, landing them on their back and allowing a finishing move.

Sounds simple enough, this time, it'll work, for sure.

The two combatants circled one another, the student and the master, trading a few tentative blows and parries, one kick from the master brushing Andrew's nose and sharpening his reflexes. He backed away, deliberately fending blows without countering, then dropped his arms slightly. It was an open invitation that the master was not going to pass up. Everything seemed to be going to plan. The lunge, the sway, the drop, the … 'oof!'

The student received a full-blooded kick to the chest, quickly followed by a blow to the side of the head. Before he even knew what had happened, he was held from behind in a masterful death choke.

It really wasn't going well. It was about the sixth time in a row the master had pummeled him. Andrew couldn't even recall landing a single solid blow. One of the things with Headspace was that all the sensations seemed very real, and right now, he was experiencing quite a lot of pain, not to mention a slight panic as he realized he couldn't breathe. He frantically tapped out of the chokehold, gasping for air as he was released.

The master had simply stepped over the sweep, clearly anticipating the bluff and executing his own double bluff perfectly. Enough was enough - so much for releasing the tension. He was tenser now, if anything! After he'd dusted himself off and bowed to the Master, Andrew conjured up the big red escape button and slammed his hand down on it, ending the session. His bedroom came slowly into focus around him as he rubbed at his eyes.

It was very late now, and he was feeling tired and frustrated - he needed something to take his mind off things. Claire had tried to say that all of this would just blow over, but he didn't believe that for a second. It was all over some stupid misunderstanding that he could have avoided if he were totally honest.

He knew he'd been disingenuous and evasive with John at the caf-bar, and he supposed in some sense he deserved what was happening to him now. It was he, after all, that had bounded round to Claire's flat like a little puppy dog. It was he who had played along with Claire's flirting a little too much; it was he that had had an unfortunate stiffy pressed into Claire's thigh.

None of these thoughts were helping at all, though. He felt hopeless; it was overwhelming. Andrew's breathing became labored, and he started to sob quietly as he sat on the edge of his bed. The sobbing grew in intensity to the point where his whole body was shaking as the grief and trauma of the night finally caught up with him.

After a while, when he'd cried himself out, he'd decided that another escape into Headspace might be the only way out of the dark place he now found himself. Sleep wasn't possible, and even though he was exhausted, his brain was still totally wired. He wondered if he should reconsider the binary implant after all – it was supposed to be able to moderate your feelings, amongst other things.

Life couldn't just for once have something nice for me now, could it? Oooh no, that would be too much to ask for, wouldn't it?

"Wouldn't it?!" He'd repeated these words in a sarcastic, high voice and realized he was just about on the verge of insanity.

"Typical, just bloody typical," he said with a sigh.

Having an imaginary argument with yourself ... one of the early signs, for sure.

"Yes, it bloody well would!" he then replied to himself. He was feeling quite unhinged. It was all too much, he decided and clapped his hands to turn off the lamp next to his bed as he lay down, attempting to sleep. Five minutes later, things hadn't improved. He was restless, and his mind was frayed.

If sleep wasn't going to come, he'd instead lose himself in his most favorite of places. He wondered if he *should* consider a binary one day - when he could afford it. It was supposedly next level in simulations – he tried to recall what he knew about them - it might help him sleep.

Andrew had decided immediately he'd heard of it that he'd never go binary. It was strange how you could be swayed over time. Binary implants were a new thing, a whole new level of tech, allowing thought control of various devices and programs and no doubt providing much mainly useless information back to the state. They had already become popular in elite circles, and it was mandatory in the security services. He shuddered at the thought.

Headspace ran through your nervous system via contact with your skin, but the binary implants were exactly that, a smallish pellet packed with alien Tech was implanted directly into your spinal column. He'd heard stories of it going wrong. Who knew what else it would do to you over time? Who knew what it would allow the state to monitor. Your thoughts?

I'd be locked up within five minutes, no doubt about it!

Technology had been embraced from day zero, even though there was practically nothing left. The survivors of the end of times had a mindset that they would use technology to build a safe, free society, one that would never go down the paths of countless civilizations before. So far, so good? He wasn't so sure. Binary implants were taking things a step too far.

He wasn't tired at all. Thinking about binaries had got him a bit worked up, if anything. Headspace it is, then, he decided. It turned out to be another very bad idea.

***

It took her all night. It was a convenient distraction from all the drama of earlier in the evening. The deeper she dug into the code from the V.I. call, the more familiar the encryption pattern became. She'd started the night with an idea - more of a concept, really, and it was playing out unexpectedly.

There was something about the security on the internal affairs data that had set off a train of thought that just wouldn't stop running, and she'd now been on her device for the best part of the last eight hours, aside from a pee break and a vita-water or two. She'd been making slow and steady progress – although there was nothing earth-shattering to show for it as yet, there was something there, and she knew she was close.

There's something hiding deep inside this data; I know it. I'm getting there - just have to keep digging.

Her eyes were tired by now, and her vision was starting to get a little fuzzy. Claire yawned heavily.

Time for a break.

She pushed her stool back suddenly, and it made a harsh scraping sound against the concrete floor. "Argh!" she exclaimed to no one. Her lip was throbbing a little, a reminder of last night's insanity, and she pressed it gingerly, inspecting her fingers afterward for any traces of blood.

Finally, it's finally stopped bleeding.

Claire had to keep going on the code until she got a result, which meant that she'd most likely have to pretend to be sick again today. Missing too many work assignments drew unwelcome attention from the authorities. *Maybe I could just breach the college's data and update my attendance records?* The thought drew a thin smile. It was a good idea - she'd get to that later.

She stretched her arms above her head and arched her back, staring up at the ceiling, twisting from side to side, then whirling her arms in circles, trying to get some blood moving. The thousands of foil strips stirred and rustled. Claire picked up a blanket off the floor, pulled it tightly around her, and settled back down in front of her device.

It took about another hour. By this time, daylight was well and truly finding its way through the small window, reflecting off the surface of the desk and stinging Claire's already bloodshot eyes. She applied yet another update to the cipher algorithm she'd been working on for the last few hours.

She stared at the display and blinked, clearing her vision, making sure she was seeing what she thought she was seeing. She blinked again, taking in the details on the display, and a shiver ran up her spine. The final layer of security code had fallen away before her eyes. The base code was the same on the V.I. call and the Elyssium data. It was the same code! It had to be the link she was looking for!

"Oh, *dook!*"

She couldn't take her eyes away from the display as she fumbled for her secure comms and punched in Andrew's number.

***

Isabel had decided to take matters into her own hands. If the sanctum were too gutless to do what needed to be done, she'd just have to do it herself - they needn't even know.

She was sitting at the bar of an exclusive leisure club. A number of scantily clad male staff flitted about, each with a number imprinted on the back of their small silky boxer shorts. All she had to do was give the number or numbers to the maître-dee when she was ready, and she was fairly sure she'd made her choice, although ...

Too many choices.

She'd organized so many disappearances now that another one would be no big deal. The timing wasn't great, and the target was extremely high profile, but Isabel was confident that she could make it look like an accident. It had worked last time, after all.

Isabel knew exactly who to talk to in order to arrange such things and picked up her secure comms, punching in the number of one of the lowlands compounds.

***

He'd somehow taken on the role of the most helpless and hopeless of the addicts from his favorite old-world VIS. Now he was stuck in an endless loop, falling backward in a white plastic chair from the roof of a high-rise building, freefalling, seemingly hoping for the end, only to be caught and brought back to reality just before he hit the ground.

At some point, Andrew had entered lucid dreaming. It was not supposed to be possible in Headspace and was no doubt the cause of the glitch. Unfortunately, knowing the cause was one thing - but stopping it was entirely another. As everything seemed like it was really happening, and not just a simulation, it was horrendous. He was helpless to stop the loop. Over and over again. The hopelessness, the terror, the disappointment. Again, and again, and again.

It had ended at some point in the early hours of the morning. Andrew's mind had simply shut down and mercifully taken him out of Headspace and back into reality.

A deep, brief, and dreamless sleep had followed. It was light outside when he groggily raised his head off the pillow a few inches and opened his eyes, immediately regretting it. A crashing headache pierced through his skull and into his right eye, courtesy of the entire bottle of VKA he'd consumed last night. He clasped his head in his hands and moaned. Rubbing his temple didn't seem to be helping much either. He tried to get up and realized that he was also feeling quite queasy.

Great. When will I learn?

The glimmer of light coming through the threadbare curtain coupled with the headache was enough to ensure that sleep was no longer an option. It was, unfortunately, time to get up. He needed something to quell the pain in his head, his eye, everywhere, and half rolled, half fell out of bed, ending up on all fours.

He tried to push himself up, and much to his surprise, found a sharp and hard object intervening with the upward trajectory the back of his head was attempting to make, his head colliding with the underside corner of his bedside table drawer. He must have opened it at some point in the night.

His head had caused a loud bang as it collided with the solid wooden drawer, raising the bedside unit off the floor briefly and upending everything on top of it. Various things were scattered on and around the sad, stricken figure now clasping its head, groaning, and lying face-first on the cold concrete floor.

Great start to the day. Fuck me.

He very carefully and slowly pushed himself back and away from the drawer of certain death. As he rolled over onto his back, he felt an excruciating sharp stab of pain in his left buttock, causing him to shriek in a very unmanly manner and sit bolt upright. Well, he would have sat bolt upright if the drawer of death hadn't intervened once more. This time his forehead managed to find the sharpest corner of the open drawer with unerring accuracy.

The drawer's side had come away from its moorings after the first attack, causing the sharp metal nails once holding it in place to become exposed and giving them the opportunity to draw blood from Andrew's scalp. It was an opportunity that they weren't going to miss. Pain stabbed again in his buttock, and he arched his back and fumbled at the source of the pain.

"Ouch! Fuck! Mother of Douglas that hurts!" he exclaimed as whatever was protruding from his left buttock cheek also managed to cut his fingers as he'd tried to extract it, drawing yet more blood. His head was now spinning and throbbing, as well as bleeding quite profusely. He went to sit up again but then thought better of it.

"For fucks sake!" It was getting ridiculous. It really, really was. He considered just lying there until the horror ended, and inanimate objects stopped attacking him randomly, but that was also a bit of a risk, he decided. Death by bedside table was not something he fancied in his obituary.

I wonder how many people have been killed by them over the years? Loads.

His glass of water had shattered into many pieces and was now stuck into and out of at least two separate places on his body. Left buttock, he'd already established, but also left side, just below where his rib cage ended. This interesting new discovery became apparent as he tried to roll away from the death drawer. "Oh fuck! Fuck dook balls!"

He lay flat on the floor again, not daring to move. *How unlucky, or clumsy, could someone possibly be? Very, was the answer, apparently.*

After a while, he ever so carefully prized the shards of glass from himself and moved, much in the manner of slow-motion man, as he carefully extricated himself from his current and dire predicament

"Well," he said as he slowly raised himself into a standing position and surveyed the scene. There wasn't anything to add, and he thought that the day could only improve from here on. He went to take a step, then paused, double-checking that the path was clear. It wasn't, and he readjusted the step to avoid more pain yet. He headed to the bathroom to survey the damage and find some Pain-Away.

Back in the bedroom, his comms blinked its slow little red blinks, awaiting his return.

***

It had been a couple of hours since she'd tried to contact Andrew, and she supposed he was lost in his stupid Headspace fairyland again. She'd have to wait for him to call. She'd tried John as well, but understandably he was still off the grid completely, and maybe that was for the best.

Claire had promised herself that she'd wait a few days before contacting him - if he contacted her first, then fair do's, but she'd discovered things in Frances's V.I. call and in the internal affairs data that had changed her view on this very quickly.

Something made her look over at the window, which she'd left open a crack even though it was subzero outside. Not for the first time since she'd been home, she thought she could hear something outside, a soft throbbing sort of noise somewhere nearby.

Fucking SFB's.

She'd been up to the window a couple of times already, but each time she peered out, there was nothing to be seen – her scans hadn't returned any indication that there was fly-bot activity nearby either. She'd put it down to being a little jumpy since John's announcement last night. At least that was what she'd thought earlier - but there it was again - that barely audible but distinctive sound. She pushed back from her desk, the stool scraping the floor again and making the same horrible sound.

Fuck!

Claire thought for a second that she'd heard something from the hallway, possibly masked by the scraping of the stool. *Did I hear something?* She reminded herself not to be paranoid, which wasn't easy when one had a hobby like hers. She stayed still, listening, but heard nothing from the hallway outside or from outside the window. She breathed out and relaxed.

Focus.

There was something that she just couldn't get out of her mind. Try as she might to bury the thought, it kept just nagging away at her. It was going to be a huge risk to act on it, which is why she'd kept pushing it away, but it kept coming back and was now at the point that it was interrupting her chain of thought almost constantly.

Damn it; I've got no choice now.

She needed to get back into the internal affairs system and access the source code for the Elyssium data. It was going to be extremely risky. If there was even such a thing, the Breacher's Code dictated that you never returned to the scene of the crime. Now that she'd had a glimpse at what might be hiding there, she needed a complete set of data in an extract, if it was possible.

If? Of course it's possible. I just have to convince myself that I have the guts to do it.

After having wandered around her flat for perhaps five minutes - her bare feet becoming numb on the polished concrete floor

– she had built up the courage to take such a huge risk. She simply had to - she simply had to know more.

She was soon back inside the internal affairs system and running the updated code she'd used on Frances's call. Within minutes, Claire was in far, far deeper than she'd been before. The security code was hiding a labyrinth of data.

Her code had learned the security systems defensive patterns, adapted, projected the next permutations, and kept building its attack as it cycled and cycled until it made a breakthrough, and then it went again, and again, deeper and deeper. When the first small breakthrough occurred, Claire couldn't help herself and gave in to a rare show of pride, allowing herself a discrete fist pump before fixing her attention back on the pandora's box she'd just opened.

Elyssium. The name kept coming up. And now, she not only had names, but she also had what looked like dates, coordinates, and who knows what else. The deeper she got, the more interesting the data became. Whatever this was, it was much bigger than she'd imagined. She followed the trail as quickly as she dared.

No matter how good her code was, she only had limited time before internal affairs security protocols became aware of her presence. Her masking code was very effective, but she really had no idea as to just how sophisticated the security on the other side was, and what she'd seen so far was, after all, well beyond anything she'd ever encountered before.

There were thousands and thousands of files, all with the same coding and characteristics. Names and numbers. More names and numbers. Measures, scales, inputs, and outputs. It was endless, but time was up, she had the base data, and anything else she took now was going to be too much of a risk. She was about to abort the session when she had an idea.

Just a few more seconds.

She performed a search of all available files for the name *Frances* - and had an immediate hit. There were several Frances's, but one of them was indeed Frances Stewart, and the birth date and location were about right. Claire felt a sense of unease as she started connecting the dots in her mind. She had to get out, but there was just one more thing - she typed in the name 'Stuart McGregor.'

A match. Again! This time a chill run through her, causing goosebumps over her entire body and something deep inside her mind to turn. "What the fuck!" She was breathless; time was up.

Claire quickly applied her most advanced masking protocols a final time and prepared to cut the connection. Her leg was shaking with anxiety as she waited for the process to complete—just a few more seconds.

Maybe I can just …

Even before she'd finished typing in her sister's name, the connection to the data was abruptly cut short. She stared at the display in disbelief.

Oh, that's not good!

The next thing she knew, her device began decoding itself, the display turning sky blue and rapidly filling with sequenced numbers.

Blue screen of death! Blue screen of death! She was sure she'd heard that somewhere.

She frantically tried to shut the device down in pretty much all the ways she knew how, but it became clear pretty quickly though that what was happening here was something extraordinary! Someone had taken control of her device. The breacher had been breached!

Claire had never been so scared in her entire life - and did the only thing she could think of, picking up her device, raising it high over her head, and smashing it down with all the force she could muster on the corner of the small metal desk. Again, and again and again.

Pieces of her device were flying left, right, and center, one narrowly missing her right eye and forcing her to turn her head away sharply as it bounced off her eyebrow. It was all over in seconds. The various pieces of her device's insides now lay spread all over the floor of her tiny flat. She let the remains of it fall to the floor with a clatter.

"Breach that, you bastards!" she muttered, breathing hard, her body covered in a sheen of sweat. She wiped her brow. *Job done.* She hoped, maybe even prayed, though there was no one other than Douglas to pray to.

"Can't be too careful," she said between heavy breaths. She was shaking now, disbelief and confusion running through her mind.

She blew out a breath and fell back onto the couch, waiting for her heart to slow. She knew that her device couldn't be easily traced. Until today she'd have said it was untraceable – she'd invested hundreds of hours making sure of it, but now, after this unexpected turn of events, she had huge doubts as to whether she'd done enough.

Someone got in! How is that possible?

She hadn't done enough to stop someone from getting in at the base level. There was no way they were in long enough to have broken down her defenses. Her location and her personal information would still be safe. She was as she could be of that. Her critical data was held remotely on a secure custom-built external dark drive and was out of danger, but the remote decoding? She'd never seen or even heard of that happening. She hated to admit it, but she was scared.

The hunter has become the hunted.

Someone, maybe something, had accessed her device and started immediately pulling it to pieces, undoubtedly looking for anything to locate the source of the data breach. She was dealing with someone or something, at least her equal, and more likely still, her superior, her overlord. The thought stung her pride.

The device was replaceable. It would not take Claire long to recreate her nonexistence on one of her backup units. That wasn't the concern. The concern was that somehow, she'd left enough of a shadow on the now shattered device to allow herself to be traced. Maybe not today, but eventually, maybe.

I just can't believe it! How?

She realized that she'd have to curtail her activities - for a while at least. She'd also increase her security and ramp up her comms scanning. It would be a good idea for her to leave her flat and remotely monitor it for a while. She was relying on the place still being a safe haven, but she was having serious doubts about that, especially after what had happened yesterday morning.

She needed somewhere safe to be and some time to think and plan her next moves. Maybe Andrew's flat? John's house? She wasn't sure. The remote-control takeover of her device had spooked her, and she had the feeling that she'd suddenly entered a very dark and very dangerous place. Claire sat on her couch and started thinking about what to do.

***

Isabel put the secure comms down gently in its cradle, having just issued an instruction that she knew would not be popular amongst her colleagues. She'd been called to the inner sanctum several hours earlier, and it had taken a great deal of convincing to influence the outcome of the meeting, not to mention a great deal of bribing beforehand and afterward.

Her workroom was dark, and she'd sat and pondered her next move for at least an hour, studying her faint reflection in the expansive workroom plexi-pane until the solution had presented itself to her.

The Chair had eventually conceded that if they were to maximize the remaining lifespan of The Source and finalize a replacement solution, then budgets may have to be reallocated somewhat to help look at alternative production methods. She'd been told in no uncertain terms that she'd need to pursue the replicating process rather than have access to increased mining materials.

It was a big problem for Isabel. Replicating was a difficult process and had more than its fair share of issues. The materials produced sapped precious resources from The Source, the material itself was of inferior quality, and the process itself was ten times slower and more laborious than direct extraction. The Chair's solution would eventually get them to the end game, but Isabel was worried that it wouldn't be soon enough.

They already had finance hot on their heels, and it wouldn't take much for the whole thing to be exposed. If that happened, then her personal plans would be in ruins.

She decided she'd interpret the chair's directives to suit her purposes and press ahead with her own plans immediately. By the time the sanctum knew what was happening, she was confident she would have already achieved her objective - by then, she'd be the one calling the shots.

Isabel leaned back in her chair, picked up a small silver case, and flipped it open. She took out a bacco tube and rolled it between her thumb and forefinger, admiring its fine, even form. The perfumed smell filled in the air. She raised it to her nose and inhaled deeply.

There's nothing quite like that scent.

Genuine bacco was all but impossible to come by. Tobacco plants were grown only in highly specialized biofactories, and the general population was not even aware of such a place's existence. The plant itself had only been available in the last twenty years or so, after the discovery of an ancient seed bank from which only a few things were salvaged. Isabel wasn't much in favor of old-world traditions generally, but she made an exception for this.

She smiled to herself, picked up the solid-state lighter, held it to the tube and inhaled deeply. The glowing red end of the bacco tube was reflected in the plexi-pane and seemed to move of its own accord as Isabel withdrew it and exhaled. She was at peace. What had to be done had to be done. They would thank her for it in time. She would make them thank her.

CHAPTER 7 – NERVOUS WAIT

Claire had a very strong desire to get the hell out of her box-like apartment - but had so far resisted. She needed the power of her QFT towers for the work she had to do, but she couldn't help but wonder how much time she really had - if somehow the state could track her location from the security breach, then perhaps she'd be another one just to disappear. She stood clenching her fists and glaring at the wall, not that it had done anything to her. She was tense and couldn't decide what to do.

A noise from the hallway outside her door made her freeze, and she felt the hairs on the back of her neck stand up. She looked at the door, head tilted, listening intently for any sound - half expecting it to burst open at any moment. Ten seconds passed, then twenty, but she didn't hear anything further. She released her breath, forcing herself to be calm as she crept to the door and pressed her ear against it. If required, she had an escape plan.

She'd practiced slipping through her window, reaching for the downpipe to the left, and swinging herself across to the emergency stairs countless times. It was a dangerous move, and she'd slipped more than once in practice and hurt herself, but a bit of short-term pain was a small price to pay compared to the alternative if it ever came down to that. It was good to be over-prepared.

Claire hadn't moved, and she strained to hear. There was nothing for a few seconds, only silence, but then she heard something out in the hallway. *What was that?* A shuffling noise, and close by. She held her breath, picturing large dark shapes with assault weapons crowding outside the door. Her body tensed, and she prepared herself for flight, picturing the moves that she'd need to make in quick succession to make good her escape.

A second later, her whole body relaxed, and she breathed a sigh of relief. She'd heard a voice in the passageway, then another, and then a laugh followed by the sound of her neighbors at number fifty-three opening their flat door. The tension drained away, and she let out a small, relieved laugh. Another thirty minutes. She'd stay for another thirty minutes but would take some precautions.

She rigged up a monitor cam on the hallway to compliment the one she'd breached into in the lobby, giving her more of a chance to get out should anyone come knocking. It wasn't something she could have installed permanently, but for the next half an hour or so, no one would notice. It would at least give her peace of mind and the time to organize anything she might need ahead of an extended absence.

After packing a rucksack, she started work on configuring a new device. She started recreating her programs while salvaging what she could in spare parts from the pieces of her old device and destroying everything else. The knock on the door didn't come. Forty minutes had passed, then fifty, then an hour, and she started to calm down a little.

The light was now flooding in around the edges of the curtain, and she could swear that she'd heard bird song somewhere in the distance. Even seeing a bird was a rarity on Planet 0420, and she couldn't recall the last time she'd actually heard one.

Maybe she'd gotten away with it, after all.

***

John was watching from the street outside the college. It was a cold and still night, with the streetlights casting a dull glow and highlighting the gathering fog. His father has just come out of the main entrance and down the ornate steps of the institute. He was striding briskly towards a solitary Solo transporter. John tried to call out but found that he had no voice. He tried to move towards his father, but he couldn't get any closer, no matter how much he struggled. He felt panic rising in his chest as he realized he was powerless to warn his father. John tried again to call out but found he couldn't breathe!

He watched on helplessly as Stuart McGregor got into the vehicle, and it moved away, slowly at first, before picking up speed and disappearing silently into the night. He started to convulse from the lack of air as viscous darkness enclosed him, obscuring his view of the street. His father was gone.

John struggled against it as he clutched at his throat, desperately trying to take in a breath but only succeeding in pulling himself deeper inside the darkness the more he struggled.

Soon there was no sound, no light, no feeling - nothing. John closed his eyes.

***

Claire had her backup device fully operational and had been scanning all state security comms for the last hour when Andrew finally responded to the five or so messages she'd left him.

"Claire? You used the emergency signal?"

"That's right, Andy, I did. Several fucking times!"

She sounds pissed off then.

"Ok, and …"

"And … just meet me at the place, as soon as you can. I have some important things to tell you, and I'm not risking it over comms." There was an urgency and tightness to her voice now. She'd decided that they should check out the place first in case they had to head there as a last resort, and after that, they would head back to Andrew's flat.

She was just about to end the call when he spoke again, "Claire?"

"What is it, Andy?"

"Ah … well, I thought you'd like to know … I couldn't get hold of John last night." He waited for a response, almost willed her to show him that she was concerned for her boyfriend, friend, whatever he was to her now.

"Oh, right. Thanks then." Claire ended the call.

Andrew stared at the now blank display of his comms. He was dumbfounded at her almost complete lack of interest in John's wellbeing. *Thanks then.* That was all she had to say? The three of them had been so close for what seemed like forever, sharing everything, every single day, and now that it was over, she seemed as if she could care less.

Andrew flopped down on his threadbare overstuffed couch and stared at the ceiling. It was an unremarkable ceiling, as most of them were, with a dull grey water stain in the far corner and a large crack running from one side to the other. His thoughts turned to his very best fr …

Bloody hell. It's over isn't it? What the fuck am I going to do now?

It didn't take long for the tears to come, and when they did, it felt like they'd never stop. Andrew sobbed deeply into the palms of his hands, gasping for breath from time to time and wiping away the tears, not to mention the snot from his nose. He realized he must look a pathetic sight and tried to control the outpouring of grief

He wasn't sure exactly how long he sat there in misery, but eventually, his mind cleared. He rubbed at his eyes and blew his nose. It took an incredible effort to push himself off the couch and stumble blindly towards the bathroom. This movement was something that he immediately regretted - a piercing pain shot up from the sole of his foot, making him shriek in pain and hop the last few steps, clutching at his foot.

Dook! Fuck! Forgot to pick up the broken glass! Dougdammit!

He was amazed that a piece of glass had managed to make its way into the bathroom - this was yet more evidence of inanimate objects' abject hatred of him. He propped himself on the bathroom cabinet and grabbed his foot, turning it over, and wasn't at all surprised to see a small shard of glass protruding from it. No doubt the shard of glass wasn't surprised either. Blood had already started to drip onto the cracked and yellowed tiles of the bathroom floor.

"Fuuuuck!" Andrew roared and then repeated it several times more for good measure before clumsily prizing out the glass, cutting his finger again in the process. "Bloody piss fuck fart duille fuck!"

I'm getting a strange sense of deja vu here.

Andrew slowly balled his hands into fists, feeling the anger and hurt swell up inside of him again. It felt good to release some of the anger and frustration he was feeling - but swearing could only achieve so much. He looked at himself in the mirror - his eyes were bloodshot, and he had a wild look on the face he barely recognized as his own.

Bloody hell John, what've you done? What have you done?

Andrew glared at his reflection as if he were about to pick a fight. He didn't remember what happened next, but suddenly he was clutching at his right hand, curled up on the floor next to the bathroom cabinet. Pieces of mirrored glass lay scattered around him. It was pretty apparent that the mirror had just attacked him. *What next?* he wondered.

There was a sharp pain in his hand, and he thought that he might have broken a bone. He cupped his left hand over his right, gently feeling for the telltale bump. No bump, at least that was good.

He drew his left hand away and surveyed the damage. Aside from skinned knuckles, it looked ok. It hurt like hell, and he grimaced as he slowly flexed the injured hand.

Note to self: punching a mirror screwed onto a concrete wall is none too clever. This self-pity business was getting downright dangerous, not to mention downright pathetic, he decided - he'd just have to pull himself together and get a move on; otherwise, he'd be late, and then he'd also have the wrath of Claire to deal with.

And no one wants to deal with that.

He pulled himself up off the floor, being careful not to tread on any more broken glass, and then ran the back of his hand under the cold tap for a very long time.

***

She was planning to try and treat today just like any other day for all outwards appearances - keeping the same routine but making a few excuses that would afford her some time to think, some time to plan what their next move should be, and maybe even allow time for a quick nap. Claire couldn't remember the last time she'd slept and was now feeling incredibly wired – this was going to end in either her falling asleep where she stood or having to down another shot of caf to avoid passing out.

It was already busy at the pedestrian intersection in the center of the old town. It was still early but staying in her flat any longer just wasn't an option. She had what she needed, and it was better to lay low until she could get to the bottom of what had happened with the remote breach of her device and work out what to do about her discoveries. She was feeling far too anxious to be out in public right now, yet here she was, waiting for Andrew, standing in plain sight. She was almost *asking* to be taken in by corrections.

Where are you?

It was drizzling and foggy, which was at least good cover from the prying eyes of the SFBs that never ceased their patrols overhead. *For Your Safety.* That was the motto. "Yeah, right," she mumbled under her breath. She tentatively sipped her synth-caf as she waited. It was labeled as 'coffee' by the vend-bot, but she'd had real coffee once at a fancy diner with John, and the tepid, watery synthetic substance she was sipping to try and keep her warm bore little or no resemblance.

Come on, Andy, where are you?

Her anxiety was growing with every minute, her right foot tapping unconsciously on the damp pavement. He'd had been in touch a couple of times as he made his way into the city, but the last contact was forty minutes ago, and he should have been here by now.

He's probably been distracted by something shiny.

A young girl walked by, sneaking a surreptitious glance in Claire's direction, and she caught her eye for a split second before the girl quickly looked away.

What's she looking at?

Claire followed the girl's progress as she wove in and out of the pedestrians on the crowded footpath. She stood out from the crowd. She was incredibly slight, slightly hunched over but walking with purpose, heavy boots and black hooded top giving visual clues to others to stay out of her way. Claire had seen the look in the girl's eyes a few times before. In the mirror.

Better to blend in a bit more and be less observed, I think. I'd better dig out some normal clothes.

Just as she was about to call again, she caught sight of him in the distance. He had bulky vintage earpieces on, dark lenses - for some unknown reason, and a camouflage hooded jacket with the hood pulled down low. Claire recognized him just from his overly cocky gait.

Camouflage? Really? He couldn't be more obvious if he tried!

She waited until she knew he had a clear line of sight to her. She motioned with a slight turn of her head toward the opposite side of the podway. Andrew reacted immediately and nearly walked straight into a tall, suited man who was hurriedly crossing.

Andrew apologized over zealously, dusting down the man's lapels and holding his palms up in mock surrender, before scurrying away and tripping over the curb on the way, half falling but somehow managing to stay on two feet. Claire shook her head and took another small sip of her caf, wrinkling her nose at the taste. Was this really her only ally against the forces of evil? She sighed – he'd have to do.

She glanced impatiently at her comms but hadn't received the all-clear from Andrew yet. She'd re-set the proximity alerts yesterday, and there had been no sign of movement since, but she'd asked him to be careful in any case. *Maybe he was overly cautious*, she pondered.

What is taking him so long?

She could hardly have chosen a more annoying friend than Andrew Weems, she surmised. She sighed again and looked for the nearest i-bin to deposit her now empty caf cup. She was feeling incredibly tense and could hardly stand still.

Her movements felt jerky and unnatural, and she forced herself to breathe a little. She was still thinking about the remote takeover of her device. The more she thought about it, the more paranoid she felt.

Claire felt herself tremble with nerves as she waited impatiently. What she was about to tell Andrew had the potential to change everything. The internal affairs data had to mean something important, even though it was as yet incomplete. There was a link. Andrew wasn't going to like it, but John would be very excited when he heard what she'd found.

Dook! What's happening to me? The thought was thankfully interrupted as she noticed a message had appeared on her comms. It said, simply, 'bumholes.' It wasn't the code word, but she supposed it would be good enough.

For Douglas' sake, Andy, when will you ever take anything seriously!

At least the place seemed like it was all clear, safe, for now. She stooped down and pretended to be tying an errant lace on her boot, waiting for the nearby SFB to pass, then slipped away from the crowded pavement, between the two buildings and into the alleyway, down to the wall and over it into the cool, damp passage.

A couple of minutes later, she was pushing open the green door at the end of the long corridor and heard the familiar rustle of foil strips. Andrew greeted her. He moved aside somewhat gingerly as she pushed past and threw her rucksack down. She couldn't help but notice the bandage around one of his hands and what looked like a cut on his forehead. She was about to ask him, but he cut in. "Don't! Just don't ask." She was about to ask anyway but then decided there were more important things to do and went about setting up her new device on the desk.

"So, no word from John?"

"No. I wouldn't expect any words yet," she said, distracted.

He shouldn't have expected anything less, or rather more, from her.

"That could, however, soon be a bit of a problem," she said as she busied herself opening the files.

"So?" he asked.

"So," she replied, equally abruptly, clearly worked up about something. "I need you to see this. It seems so unbelievable - I keep telling myself I must have made a mistake, but ..."

She was speaking so quickly that it was hard to follow. Andrew wasn't sure whether to be worried or excited. This was the thing with Claire; once she had a sniff of something, there was no stopping her; it was almost as if she -

"Andrew!" Claire's voice pierced through his thoughts.

He realized that he'd been staring into middle distance. She'd probably said something else too, but he was lost in his own world and hadn't heard any of it.

"Focus!"

It was a command. Andrew knew that tone particularly well and focused, as instructed. He sat obediently on a couple of stacked crates next to her as she opened a series of programs on the compact device and began running some sort of sequential command that seemed to utilize each and every one of them several times over.

"So, this is the thing, Andy."

Her voice was cold and flat, sending a small shiver down Andrew's spine.

"That V.I. call from Frances to Sally."

"Yes." His mouth was suddenly dry.

"Well. It's not Frances."

That wasn't what he was expecting to hear. *Not Frances?* He didn't know what he'd expected, but the words that had just come out of Claire's mouth just refused to arrange themselves into anything remotely resembling a sentence he could comprehend.

"What do you mean?"

"It's faked, Andrew. Faked! Whatever made that call, it wasn't Frances."

She paused to let that little bombshell sink in, but he looked bewildered, and she realized she'd better explain herself more clearly - for his benefit. She opened something on the device and turned the display so he could see it clearly.

"The voice patterns - they don't belong to Frances. That is to say; they don't belong to anything human."

He stared at the display vacantly, not comprehending. He didn't think it possible that the next words he'd hear from her could make even less sense than the first, but they did.

"Ok. Let me break this down for you, Andy." She reached out a hand and grabbed his arm, pulling him around to face her. A small electric shock had jumped between them as she did so. Claire could have sworn for a moment she saw a glimpse of fear in his eyes.

"On the surface, when you analyze the voice patterns in the call, everything seems normal. Everything seems hunky-dory, you might say. But look at this."

*

He recognized her attempt to relate to him on his level, using some old-world pop icon language from one of his favorite artists of the era. He was grateful - she was making an attempt at being human for a change, but this was doing nothing to help him understand.

The worst thing he could do right now would be to miss half of what she was saying, and so he forced his errant thoughts to re-focus. She'd turned towards the display and now turned back to face him. He'd stopped listening again as he watched her soft pink lips forming words. Claire was indicating something on the display again, and he suddenly came back to reality.

"… and then once I'd applied the new version of the ghost decryption program, the last layer of protection on the data just fell away. And look! Will you just look at this dook!"

Andrew looked at that dook.

"What we are left with here are *not* human voice patterns, and the V.I. has signs of a deep fake. It's clearly some form of A.I. generated speech and image." She took a breath, holding her hand to her chest as she did so. Andrew started to feel a little worried. He'd humored them for the longest time over their conspiracy theories, and he never honestly thought he'd see the day when they found something to back them up, and yet here they were.

"At first, I thought it must be a mistake; I mean, how could it be faked? And why, right? But the more I looked, the more it became clear."

Andrew nodded, pretending to follow.

"The patterns are just too perfect and uniform. It's QFT generated, or even beyond that - I've never seen anything like it. I'm pretty sure I was never supposed to see it, either."

They sat and stared at each other.

"The image on the call, the voice patterns, deep fake."

"But ... wait ...what?" He still wasn't getting it, still wasn't making the connections that Claire had clearly already made.

"The disappearances Andy, the disappearances! Something bad is going on. Why would anybody fake a message from someone that had disappeared? The State is *faking* contact from these people! There's a pattern. At least that's what we'll find when we look deeper into this. I mean, why? Just why would they do this? Where's Frances? Where are all the others? It's fucking mental!" She stood and began pacing left and right within the small space.

"And there's more too, much more. You're not going to believe this!"

He didn't doubt it. He swallowed hard.

"Whatever this is, it was important enough for someone to break through *my* defenses and launch a decoding attack on my own device!"

The shock of her words blew through him like an atomic bomb. He was fairly sure the shockwave had sent his hair flying backward.

*

"What? But how's that *possible?*" He sounded panicked.

"I don't know, Andy, I don't know. It just proves that whatever this data is, it's important. And it's particularly important to the state that we don't see it and that they silence us."

"Oh crap ... doesn't that mean they *know?*"

She tried to ignore the increasingly pitiful and worried expression on her friend's face.

"All they know is a device accessed their data. They can't know it's my device; they didn't have long enough." Claire hoped she sounded convincing, but Andrew was still looking very scared.

"They won't have the location or the name of the device; I made sure of that."

"You're sure about that?"

Claire looked at him coldly.

"What did I just say? And, well - we're still here, aren't we?"

*

It was possibly the least reassuring sentence he'd heard in a while.

"Oh, but wait, that's not even the best bit! This is the real fucking kicker, Andy."

She was breathing hard now, balling her fists and releasing them repeatedly as she paced quickly around the tiny room. She looked a bit like a mad person, he thought, although of course, he could talk. She stopped pacing and faced him, with Andrew bracing himself for what he was about to hear.

"This is the thing … when I applied a variation of the same decryption code to the Elyssium data, I found something *really* fucking scary".

"Oh." Andrew was having difficulty breathing all of a sudden. He wasn't sure he wanted to hear. Not at all.

"Yes. 'Oh' indeed! Fucking *oh* indeed! It's the *same code,* Andy! That's the link we've been looking for. There's a link between the disappearances and the Elyssium data!"

Claire stood with her arms down and palms out, eyes wide, imploring him to understand. It was as if she'd just delivered the coup d'état. Andrew's mind was completely blank, unfortunately.

"The names, Andy, the names! Thousands and thousands of names and numbers and coordinates and status codes and, well, I'm not entirely sure just yet, but, oh, this! Not just any old names. Frances's name was there on the list, and ..."

She paused. For dramatic effect, he assumed.

"… John's father! John's father's name was on the list too! It's a list of the missing; I know it. The missing must have something to do with Elyssium, and the state doesn't want anyone to know they are missing."

"I don't underst …"

"There are just too many coincidences; they have to be linked! Oh, this is big, Andy!"

She took a breath. Andrew looked more and more terrified every time she looked at him.

"So, let's think logically about this ..." she continued, "the state has a list of people. We know some of those have disappeared, and maybe they all have. We need to find out. They're pretending some of them aren't missing, which is really, really scary, and fuck knows why they would do that." Andrew waited to see if she had more to add. She did.

"I mean, what the fuck?! I mean, what the actual fuck is going on here?" Her words disappeared into the silence of the small dark room. Andrew swallowed hard. He thought of something.

"Hang on, Claire, Stuart McGregor is a common name. Isn't it possible that it isn't John's father, and even if it is, well, it could be completely innocuous, couldn't it? Maybe it's just a register of Headspace users? Vend-bot users? It could mean anything, couldn't it?"

"Maybe, I mean, of course, I've thought about that. There's also been no contact from John's father, which breaks the pattern." She considered the point for a moment.

"It's just too much of a coincidence, though – the code's the same! There is no way we are supposed to know about this. This could be very dangerous. This *is* very dangerous!"

Andrew's need for a bathroom break was reaching a critical point.

When Claire spoke next, her tone was calm and even, ensuring Andrew knew that she was deadly serious about what had to happen next.

"If we can prove the call is a fake, beyond all doubt, and I believe we can, and if we can establish an irrefutable link to the Elyssium data … well. Fuck, Andy!" Andrew held his hands up.

"That's a lot of if's." He regretted his words as soon as they had left his mouth. Claire's hands moved from her head to her hips.

Oh-oh.

"This is what I've been looking for, Andy. This is what I've been looking for ever since Henny died! This pathetic excuse for a people's state *lies* to its people, Andy! I can prove it. It disappears its own people! It takes them, and who knows what it's doing with them? It could be fucking murdering them for all we know! We need to let John know about this - we need his help."

He decided that saying nothing was the best course of action here, as it usually was, he'd noticed.

"If I'm right about this … "

Another silence fell between them. Andrew looked down at his shoes and then stole a glance at Claire. He wasn't convinced of the connection, of her wild assumptions. He was still trying to process most of her rant, still trying to make sense of where her mind was at. She'd leapt forward about ten steps from where he was at, that was for sure. He cleared his throat.

"Alright, Claire, alright. But …"

She shot him another piercing look. He plowed ahead regardless.

"Do you really think John's going to be in any mood to speak to either of us anytime soon?"

"Andy, I found John's father's name on a secret Elyssium list! Of *course,* he is going to talk to us! Of *course,* he is going to help us. He's got the contacts; he *knows* people. We don't know anyone."

It was a good point; he had to concede.

Claire was pacing again.

"We need to do some work on the list and see if we can make the connections … just imagine if we do, Andy!"

Andrew was imagining. He felt queasy.

"We need to know just how big this thing is. When we have enough evidence, we'll need a way of exposing it. That's where John comes in - he has family contacts at all the top state agencies, and we're going to need someone on the inside if this thing blows up."

If this thing blows up.

Andrew imagined himself in a cell in the big hoose with a large hairy cellmate named Bubba for company. He trusted her; her convictions were rock solid, watertight, usually, but he was scared by where they were heading all of a sudden – it wasn't like he had any choice though; he was in this as deep as Claire, and he'd do whatever he could to help her find out what was going on.

"We have to be incredibly careful here, Andy. This morning after the remote access of my device, I was almost ready to make a run for it. I thought that at any moment, the corrections or some other shady fucking state agency might just pay me a surprise visit."

Andrew couldn't speak - he was thinking about Bubba again. Claire rubbed her temples.

"I need you to check my code, Andy. Validate what I've done. Check the decoded voice patterns, the imaging. Prove me wrong."

She was almost pleading with him, which made him feel even more uncomfortable.

"Let me have a look," he requested, surprising himself with how calm he sounded.

He spent the next hour carefully going over and over everything and couldn't find any fault. He was by no means as gifted as the others when it came to coding and encryption, but he knew enough to see no issues with the processes used. The result was clear, the V.I. call had been faked, and the security code on the call and the Elyssium data had the same signatures. As much as he wanted her to be wrong, she was right.

Claire, who had been curled up on the beanbag in the corner and had slipped into a restless sleep, woke with a start and pushed herself up on one arm. Andrew stretched and puffed out his cheeks, blowing air out slowly. He thought he'd never seen her look quite so vulnerable.

"It checks out, Claire. I can't find any fault in any of this. Look, I'm not an expert by any means, but ..." he shrugged. "Well, this is scaring the dook out of me. What are we going to do?"

"We don't panic, Andy; we keep calm. Let's dig deeper. When, and I mean *when* we have enough certainty that the data is watertight, and we can piece everything together, then we are going to need some serious help. In the meantime, we lay as low as we can. I'll organize some free periods for us, and we can devote our time to working out exactly what is going on here."

Bubba.

He really needed to go to the toilet now; things were getting desperate. They decided to head back out into the mid-morning gloom to facilitate relief for Andrew's little issue.

***

Peter Bradshaw hadn't seen his son Lachlan in over fifteen years. Theirs had always been a difficult relationship. Peter was somewhat old-school and had preferred an authoritarian approach to parenting. Lachlan hadn't appreciated that much at the time, and a string of disciplinary problems resulted, culminating in Lachlan being sent away to internment at just fourteen years of age.

Lachlan couldn't conceal his anger on his rare visits home, and the distance between them had grown. He'd felt betrayed by his parents. They'd sent him away! They didn't want him, and he wanted nothing to do with them. Lachlan was - Peter supposed - the epitome of a spoilt brat. He was given every opportunity but threw it back in his parent's faces.

At seventeen, and as soon as it was legally possible, Lachlan Bradshaw moved out of the family home and changed his name to Lachlan Grealish. By this time, he'd already decided on politics as a career and named himself quite deliberately after one of the first Alban state governance founders. It was a massive up yours to his parents, no doubt about it.

Peter had been trying to keep his son in his life by encouraging him to follow his own path in the world of academia, but it wasn't to be – Lachlan took pleasure in ignoring his father's advice and did as he pleased. Peter had often looked back and thought about what he might have done differently, how he could have engineered a different outcome, but always drew a blank. It was just one of those things. They didn't get along. He carried an emptiness with him constantly at the way things had turned out but respectfully kept his distance from his only son.

He'd seen Lachlan only twice since he'd left so abruptly as a teenager. The first time, a couple of years afterward, Lachlan had been in a world of trouble. His son had nowhere else to turn and had come home in a last desperate attempt to save his skin. Peter was able to stop him from taking matters into his own hands and had risked his neck to broker an agreement with some particularly nasty types from the city's criminal element.

It had cost Peter dearly, but Lachlan had been freed from both his debt and his obligation. No one other than Lachlan and his father ever knew of the predicament he'd been in, and since then, Lachlan had gone from strength to strength. Peter was proud of his son and his stunning political career.

The second time around was a far less serious situation, and in fact, he'd been surprised that his son had consulted him over it at all. Lachlan had the opportunity to take up a key position heading up retail supplies within the commercial arm of the state. It was a position guaranteed to earn him a lot of credits and a job for life if he wanted it. Lachlan at the time had been very keen, but Peter had advised him to follow his passion instead. If it was money he wanted, well, surely that would follow, he'd said.

Much to his surprise, Lachlan has listened intently and wasn't interested in even arguing the point. More surprising still was that Lachlan took his advice and pursued his interest in social justice politics. They hadn't had further contact since that day, but it was something that Peter thought of often. It had been a long time ago now, but at least Peter now knew that Lachlan saw him as someone who could be trusted for advice in matters of importance. It was better than nothing.

The knock on the door was a surprise not just for the lateness but also because the Bradshaw's inner circle of friends always made plans well in advance and never just popped in. Peter's immediate reaction was one of apprehension – a late-night knock on the door was rarely good news. However, his apprehension quickly disappeared as he recognized the image displayed on the intercom.

***

To say that the caf-bar was small and dingey would have been a huge understatement. The tables and chairs looked almost pre-end of days. Paint of an unknown color peeled from the walls. The floor looked like it had never been cleaned. The few shabby-looking people in attendance looked completely miserable as they sat and either stared at the table in front of them or at the small display perched precariously on top of a cupboard behind the makeshift counter. Andrew glanced at the display to see what was so riveting.

Breaking news! Rising political star disgraced in sexbot scandal!

He yawned and looked around the windowless room. As he glanced back at the display, the follow-up headline grabbed his attention, and he had a small chuckle at it. *Bum bandit!* it said.

Andrew smirked. *Someone's getting creative with the newsfeed.* He looked around their depressing surroundings once more. No one else seemed to find the headline amusing.

"Well, this is certainly an improvement!" he remarked. Claire ignored him. "There!" she said with a smile, "I've excused us from the rest of the week's work assignments and study groups."

Although this was good news, Andrew was getting a little bored. He got Claire's attention and pointed at the display. The headline now read, 'Scandal!!!' He particularly liked the excessive use of exclamation marks.

"Well, so much for our utopian society, eh? Why are there so many problems every day? The scandals. The secrecy. The disappearances. I mean, you've got to wonder what's going on, don't you?"

Claire rolled her eyes at him. "Have you ever listened to a word I've said?"

He shrugged, disappointed she didn't wish to head down the rabbit hole of her favorite topic and looked around the interior of the caf-bar again. He understood that 'laying low' meant not being seen in their usual haunts, or maybe not being seen at all, but did they really have to pick what was possibly the worst caf-bar in all of the old town to do it in?

He stirred the tepid black liquid masquerading as caf and sighed. He'd been sighing a lot lately.

Couldn't being on the run or whatever be just a little more glamorous than this? Maybe just a napkin would do, for now.

Claire looked up from her work and shot him a look. He stared glumly at her.

"Can you at least try John again for me?"

"Oh, sure, Claire, I'll try and call my ex-best mate in the whole world, who now thinks I've betrayed him with his girlfriend. Just for you. For the hundredth time this morning."

She blew him a kiss, smiled. "Thanks!"

Andrew was not to be deterred from his depression and mumbled disinterestedly: "He's more than likely nursing the hangover of all hangovers, anyway. There's probably no point."

"Right!" she snapped her device shut.

Right?

Andrew didn't know what was right, his guess about potential hangovers or the fact that his best mate, correction, ex-best mate now hated his guts and, in all likelihood, wanted to rip his head off and turn it into a baffel pot, or something. That part of it seemed about *right*. He wasn't sure about anything else.

"Right," she repeated. "We need to get to work. I know it'll be awkward, but this really can't wait. Let's go and interrupt John's hangover."

Oh great! Perfect!

Why is she smiling? It was all he could think of as she stood, grabbed her pack, and made her way toward the exit. Andrew reluctantly followed.

"It's been a pleasure!" he called back over his shoulder as he exited the most dismally depressing establishment ever put on this or any other planet.

The sun was attempting a rare appearance as they wove their way through the old town's pedestrian traffic. Nothing was said for quite a while. Claire was setting a quick pace, and Andrew struggled to keep up, occasionally having to take a half-running step just to stay next to her.

Ok, so we're walking all the way up to John's house, at the top of the huge fucking hill! Great!

This day really hadn't been a whole lot of fun so far. He was going to try and change that—just a little bit.

"Did you see that back at the caf-bar?" he asked, between breaths. The question seemed to take her by surprise. She looked at him, and her pace slowed, thinking hard about anything that she might have seen or anything that might have happened but was drawing a complete blank.

"No, what?" she finally managed.

"The latest scandal."

Claire was mildly interested. She couldn't help being a little taken aback that he was thinking about that rather than, say, what he was going to say to John, or that they were about to expose the state in possibly the biggest scandal the planet had ever seen. But still, Andrew was Andrew.

"Go on then, enlighten me."

"Well."

She looked over at him as she walked. She was interested now, he could tell.

"Remember *the new face of socialist policy?*"

She remembered. The three of them had spent a bit of time discussing Lachlan Grealish after he was appointed to be their social savior a few months back.

"Aye, why's that?"

"Well, breaking news! He's just like the rest of them, apparently! He's been disgraced. Caught in a sex-bot scandal."

"A *what?*" she looked at him to try and see if he was serious or not.

"Sex-bot scandal," he repeated, starting to laugh as he walked; it soon became apparent that he wasn't going to or able to stop. Andrew had a sort of annoying, cocky, too loud laugh, one that made you think he was the only one that got the joke or that he was perhaps laughing at you. She stopped and turned to face him.

"Sex-bot scandal?" she repeated. It was too much for Andrew and caused a laughing fit so hard that he was soon bent over, gasping for breath. Claire had started laughing too now, but it was a short and sort of confused laugh more than anything. It took a while, but when his laughing fit eventually subsided, he was able to continue.

"Sex-bot scandal," he repeated unnecessarily. She smirked. "Aye, it seems our boy has been caught up in an expenses scandal. Apparently, he's been visiting sex-bot parlors, claiming the expense, and passing it off as *entertainment.*

"Well, can't argue there," she said dryly.

"And here's the juiciest bit! Our pillar of male manliness and Scottish bravery has only ever visited male-themed sex-bot parlors. Male one's mind - not that there is anything wrong with that, of course."

There was a sparkle in his eye as he spoke, and she braced herself for the punchline. "Well, that's the death of his political career anyway. You could say …"

Claire gritted her teeth.

"… that Lachlan Grealish's career has been … bummed to death!"

Andrew had apparently greatly amused himself and was gasping for air again between fresh bursts of unnecessarily loud laughter. Claire was unmoved.

"Oh, Andrew! Grow up, you little dook!"

"Oh, you love it!" Andrew managed to get the words out as he drew in some deep breaths, signaling the end of festivities, "and you love my jokes too."

The retribution was swift and painful. Claire was striding ahead now, leaving him to rub his arm where the more powerful than was strictly necessary blow had landed.

"That'll leave a mark, again," he muttered to himself before hurrying after her. He could see her tangle of dark hair bobbing up and down in the distance and realized she'd started to run.

"Oh, bollocks!"

Andrew started to jog after her, hoping that she'd slow down at some point. The sun had given up, and now a fine and cold drizzle tickled his face as he dodged in and out of slow-moving businesspeople and vendboxers (or veebee's as they were more commonly known).

He hadn't really succeeded in making the day any more fun.

CHAPTER 8 – THE THANK YOU VISIT

A few months ago …

Isabel had come to see Peter Bradshaw at the college late one night. His workroom was accessed via a large reception area in the old part of the building, with plush dark blue carpets and ornately framed photographs of various historical college luminaries surrounding its doorway. Timber bookshelves filled the wall to one side, and a large picture plexi-panel looked out onto the expansive lawn at the main entrance to the college, which was elaborately lit against the backdrop of the night sky.

They'd met once or twice before at functions, and they'd recently been part of the same panel debating how best to allocate and utilize the latest technological breakthroughs in addressing cybercrime, but they certainly didn't know each other socially. It was a surprise visit for Peter anyway.

She walked briskly through the reception room and paused at the doorway to his workroom, ensuring he had a good view of her when he looked up, which he did, registering surprise.

What's she doing here?

"Isabel - to what do I owe the honor?"

"Oh, I was just passing, and I realized your workroom was nearby, so I thought I'd pop in and thank you for your support on the cybercrimes bill."

"Uh … not at all, Isabel, not at all."

Peter didn't recall being particularly supportive. In fact, just the opposite. He'd tried to block elements of the bill that would further strip away students' rights. He was immediately uneasy at her presence, not to mention her appearance.

Isabel had clearly just come from a party of some sort. She was wearing a low-cut silky cocktail dress and carrying a couple of bottles of premium bru. As she sat, she leaned forward in an exaggerated manner and waggled the bottles, placing them on Peter's desk, and thus ensuring his line of sight followed the bottles and a no doubt gave a clear view down her dress as it gaped alarmingly at the front.

Does she know she just showed me her breasts? Did she mean to?

He was feeling flustered and was already trying to think of excuses to end the impromptu meeting. Isabel smiled seductively as she sat, leaning back in the green leather visitor's chair and crossing her legs, the movement causing her dress to slip very high on her thighs and reveal much more than was usually considered polite. Her nipples were clearly visible through the flimsy fabric, and she appeared to be highly aroused or was very sensitive in that area. She smiled at him. He didn't know where to look.

She must be very drunk.

"Let's have a little celebratory drink, shall we? The bill was passed today!"

He realized he had no choice.

"Well, certainly! Let me fetch a couple of glasses."

He could hear the bottles being opened behind him as he searched for something suitable in an ornate timber and glass old-world style drinks cabinet on the far side of the room, selecting a couple of long tumblers.

She'd waited for her moment, quickly shaking a few drops of purple liquid into the neck of one of the bottles as he busied himself. She placed her handbag carefully on his desk, adjusting the angle just so. Peter returned a few seconds later, placing the glasses on his desk and returning to his seat. He'd so far failed to come up with any plausible excuse to leave.

"Here we are."

Isabel carefully pushed one of the bottles towards Peter and grabbed a glass, pouring her own. Peter followed suit. She raised her glass again, leaning forward more than was necessary. She looked relaxed and happy. Peter felt himself relax slightly as well. Perhaps this was just a genuine impromptu drop-in, after all.

"Well, cheers!" she said. "Here's to us!"

To us?

Their glasses clinked, and they both took a long draught of the cold amber refreshment.

I'll tell her I'm late for a family dinner or something.

Isabel was studying him closely as she sipped her bru. He knew that look in a woman's eye, he could recall it anyway, from a long time ago, and it scared him. He knew that she couldn't possibly be attracted to him - he was a balding middle-aged professor with a penchant for tweed jackets and hearty meals, and she was, well, she was very beautiful.

I'll finish the drink quickly then make my excuses.

Isabel had started chatting about the bill again. She rose from her chair and was now moving around the workroom, inspecting various items here and there. Peter was sure that the move was designed to draw his attention to the sheer silky dress that clung to her every curve.

She'd deliberately chosen the pale green silk number for its ability to cling to every contour - it had been quite the hit at the cocktail party. When Isabel turned back to him, she could tell she'd achieved her goal. He looked extremely uncomfortable and had started to sweat a little.

Peter had been nervously sipping his glass of bru, trying to finish it quickly but not too quickly – he didn't want to seem rude. He was still trying to think of an excuse to get her out of his workroom. As she sat back down, she smiled at him, and he started to feel a bit peculiar.

He was suddenly experiencing a very warm sensation in his crotch, and he had to glance down to ensure that he hadn't somehow wet himself. More alarming still was the sudden feeling of the fabric in the crotch of his pants starting to strain against his engorged member.

What the?

He shifted uncomfortably in his chair. His vision seemed to have an odd purplish tinge, he noticed, but his thoughts were quite distant and fuzzy. He wasn't able to focus on anything clearly, but he did hear Isabel ask, "can you close the door, Peter? I have something I need to discuss with you."

For some reason, he rose and complied with the request without a thought, powerless to do anything but obey. He angled himself away from Isabel as he passed her and duly closed his workroom door. As he turned back toward her, he noticed that she was staring fixedly at his nether regions.

"Oh my, Mr. Bradshaw!"

Isabel's voice was thick with lust, and she was smiling wickedly. Peter was very scared. He tried to cover himself with his hands as he attempted to make it back to his desk and relative safety, but Isabel had other ideas. She quickly rose and stood directly in front of him, blocking his path, intercepting him. Her dress had slipped off one shoulder.

"Do you want to *fuck* me?"

Peter seemed to be trying to shake his head.

"Oh, but I can see that you do."

Isabel slipped the dress off her other shoulder and allowed it to cascade to the floor. She was suddenly standing completely naked in front of the now trembling professor save for a pair of clear plex high-heeled shoes.

"Yes," Peter agreed. He hadn't meant to say that!

He was now completely powerless to move or do anything. Isabel knelt in front of him, expertly unzipping his pants, reaching in, and extracting his manhood in one fluid movement. Peter's legs started trembling uncontrollably as Isabel held him firmly.

"Oh, Peter," she breathed, looking up into his eyes, "I'm so going to enjoy this."

He couldn't recall anything else from the evening. His last memory was of Isabel, kneeling in front of him, looking up at him with a savage look in her eyes. All he knew was that when he woke the next morning in his workroom, he was completely naked and had scratches and bruises all over his body. When he went to get up from his workroom chair, he discovered that he had an extremely sore backside, making things like sitting and walking very uncomfortable for the next few days.

What the hell did she do to me? He already knew the answer. It was at that point he noticed the small V.I. drive and accompanying note on his desk. His hand trembled as he reached for it, and he started to sob quietly as he realized the reason for the whole charade. He couldn't watch it beyond the first minute. Isabel had narrated it, and he was left in no doubt within the first few seconds of footage that he was now nothing more than her puppet.

***

The light drizzle had turned to a slow and depressingly steady rain, which wasn't doing a lot to improve Andrew's mood. The rain was starting to seep through their clothes and shoes, making them shiver despite the exertion of climbing all the way to the top of The Heights. It was most unpleasant.

Claire was maintaining a steady pace up what seemed like thousands of steps leading to the top of the hill and towards the most exclusive district of The Highlands. A low grey sky hugged the gothic-style houses lining the streets they passed.

Andrew thought that the houses looked cold, unwelcoming, and more than a bit over the top in their ornateness. If that was a word, he wasn't sure. It was a far cry from the drab concrete tenements of his childhood and the even drabber, if that was a word also, student accommodations he now called home.

They had discussed their approach to confronting John on the way up and had agreed, or rather Claire had stated, and Andrew had agreed, that they would simply call John out for his ridiculous tantrum and violent outburst and let him know that there were no hard feelings.

It seemed like a reasonable plan - surely John would have calmed down by now, Claire had said. Or perhaps he'd be just as angry and snap Andrew in two like a twig. That was his prediction, at any rate.

They'd checked with the college earlier, and he hadn't been in or submitted a medical pass, which meant he'd be at home, sleeping, and sure to be very hungover. Nothing Claire had said did anything to lessen the growing sense of dread that Andrew felt as they neared the top of the hill. He imagined that this was something like how convicted criminals felt on their way to the death room.

He was about to recommend another short break to catch his breath when they reached a small flat stretch of pathway and finally caught sight of the McGregor family home in the distance. The three-story residence was perched high atop the hill, next to a string of similarly grand homes and with a reserve directly opposite, affording then unimpaired views over the city. The house conjured up an image of an old world horror VIS that he could see himself starring in.

First to die ... he quickly banished the thought.

"Lifestyles of the rich and entitled," he remarked. Andrew looked at Claire. She was drenched. Claire looked at Andrew. He was also drenched.

How can she still look so pretty, even when she's totally soaked? He thought.

Her hair had fallen over one eye and was hanging in clumps down either side of her face, framing it rather nicely. Her complexion was incredibly pale, but for the bright pink of her lips and the slight flush to her cheeks. She was looking back at him with her ever so clear emerald green eyes. Andrew quite liked drenched Claire, he decided.

*

He looks like a drowned rat, she thought as she turned to look at the imposing house atop the hill. *It had better be worth it.*

The first small seed of doubt had entered her mind. What if John wasn't home? What if he wouldn't talk to them? Andrew seemed to have drifted off into his thoughts again.

"Come on, nearly there."

Andrew smiled serenely to himself as he trudged off after her. It only took them a few minutes to reach the house. Claire practically ran up the last few steps leading to a large, tiled portico, leaving Andrew lagging. Truth be told, he was quite happy to hide behind her and let her do all the talking.

She pressed the button on the bell, and it rang out into the vast acres of space beyond. She'd been here to visit John a few times and always felt ill at ease amongst the numerous china vases and lush furnishings that adorned the rooms – she was worried that she'd break some priceless heirloom or other. The entry hall was particularly impressive - a large marble-clad oval space with a wide double staircase swooping down on either side. Very nice.

The house had swallowed up the sound, and silence followed. She rang the bell again and waited, her foot tapping impatiently and suddenly feeling very unsure of herself. Andrew was doing his best to hide behind her. She ignored him and rang the bell a third time, this time adding a loud call of "John?" after a second or two. Nothing but silence greeted her efforts.

She turned to Andrew. He couldn't tell if she looked determined or resigned to failure, but any doubts were soon banished from his mind as she said, "let's try round the back."

*

Great. "Round the back" no doubt means scaling one of the high stone walls topped with spikes. I can't wait.

"Really?" he inquired, not moving an inch.

"Yes, now!" she commanded, shoving him in the direction of the nearest impossibly high wall. Just as she went to push past him, she heard the metallic 'click' sound of the latch being unlocked behind her.

Andrew took a sideways step to ensure he was completely obscured behind Claire. She turned to face the door and watched as the handle turned slowly before springing back again to its starting position. Claire stared at the door. Andrew stared at the door over Claire's shoulder. Nothing happened. They stared at each other, then back at the door.

*

The handle was wiggling slightly left and right now before finally turning once more and allowing the door to swing open with a theatrical creaking sound slowly.

What Claire saw next shocked her a little. She hadn't seen John's mother much since her husband had disappeared, but it had only been a couple of months since they had last chatted over a glass of vita water. She barely recognized the shrunken, hunched over, and frail-looking old lady peering timidly from the doorway.

"Jessica?" she felt implored to ask. Even as she spoke, she regretted framing her name as a question.

"Jessica!" she said again, brightly, offering a wide smile and open arms. Andrew peered timidly over her shoulder. At first, the old lady just stared warily, her eyes showing no sign of recognition. Claire took a tentative step forward, this time speaking more gently.

"Mrs. McGregor, Jessica, it's me, Claire. Claire Renshaw!"

The frail old woman appeared to take a step back, and Claire almost expected the door to be closed in her face, but instead, it was pulled fully open, and she saw a glimmer of recognition in Mrs. McGregor's eyes. Claire planted a peck on her cheek, and the old lady seemed to spring to life at the human touch.

"Claire darling, how lovely to see you, my dear! And Andrew, is that you?"

Mrs. McGregor peered over Claire's shoulder at the raggedy and disheveled young man.

"Aye, hi there, Mrs. McGregor!" Andrew waved and smiled, and Jessica smiled back and ushered them inside.

"Come on in, you two. Just look at the pair of you! You're soaked. Come and have a nice hot cup of cha. I'll call John."

Claire felt an enormous sense of relief. *John's here; he'll be able to help us.* They followed Mrs. McGregor through the palatial reception hall, and Claire couldn't help but notice the thick layer of dust on the mahogany side tables and muddy footprints crossing the no doubt extremely expensive rug in the center of the room - things had clearly changed a lot in the McGregor household in recent times.

*

The sense of fear that had been building inside of Andrew wasn't subsiding. He'd nearly jumped out of his skin when Jessica's shrill voice had suddenly called out, "John, John dearest, your friends are here!" They followed her underneath the sweeping double staircase.

Friends? Well, we'll soon see.

Andrew glanced furtively up at the top of the staircase as they headed underneath, expecting at any moment a hulking figure to appear accompanied by a glare, but there was as yet no sign of him.

They came through into the kitchen/sunroom area. The kitchen was bright and airy with luxurious warm timbers and polished white marble, but there were piles of plates in the sink and clutter everywhere. Mrs. McGregor had busied herself putting the kettle on and rummaging around for cha leaves, while Andrew kept a wary eye on the doorway from which they'd just entered.

"How have you been, dear?" Claire assumed this was directed at her.

"Oh fine, busy, you know," her voice trailed off as she looked around at the mess. She changed the subject.

"How was John last night?"

"Oh, I don't know, dear, why?"

"Oh nothing, it's just that we had a little tiff is all, nothing to worry about, though." She smiled reassuringly.

"Oh, you young people, always so dramatic!" Mrs. McGregor laughed, a short reedy sound, followed by a coughing fit that had them worried that she might just keel over in front of them. She cleared her throat eventually and called again, this time much louder, "John! Come down here; your friends are waiting!"

She turned to Andrew and spoke in a conspiratorial manner. "He is so lazy sometimes."

"Aye," he agreed, offering a crooked smile. His mind conjured an image of John's massive fist swinging lazily for his head. Mrs. McGregor had finally managed to arrange some mugs and cha bags on what little space was available on the benchtop and had started pouring some lumpy-looking milk into a small crystal jug. She suddenly looked up. "Well, maybe go wake him up, eh? The lazy bugger!"

Andrew didn't move, though, and desperately tried to think of an excuse to avoid going anywhere near John and his giant fists. Claire saw his dilemma and decided to put him out of his misery.

"I'll go," she said brightly, giving him a look that would have shattered plex as she passed him. Suddenly the room seemed very empty. Andrew felt the need to fill the void with some idle chit-chat.

"Well ...," he offered, "... um, to be honest, we're quite relieved that John's here."

I'm not really.

"We haven't been able to get hold of him at all since early last night, and we need his help with something. Quite urgently."

"Oh?" Mrs. McGregor was looking at him with a puzzled expression on her face.

"What day is it today, Andrew?" she asked. Andrew struggled to hide his surprise.

"Um, Wednesday. It's Wednesday."

"Oh, I see! John would be at his classes by now. Did you not check there before coming up here in the rain?"

He was stuck for words. He was unsure what he should or shouldn't say. He'd assumed that John's mother knew that her son was at home, but now that didn't seem to be the case - he wasn't as relieved as he thought he'd be by this revelation.

"Aye, of course. We couldn't get hold of him, though, so we thought we'd try here."

John's mother clearly hadn't seen her son this morning. Mrs. McGregor was looking more than a little confused as she stopped fussing with the cha and stared off into a vacant space somewhere behind Andrew. He felt compelled to speak again and fill the silence.

"So, Mrs. McGregor, when John came home last night, I imagine he might have been a wee bit tipsy, eh?"

"Oh? Jessica, please. Call me Jessica."

"Aye, fine, of course. Jessica. Well, l, we, um, as Claire said, we had a wee disagreement, and he was going to go for a drink or three to cool off, I think."

A clock ticked loudly somewhere in the room.

"Oh, well ... I can't really recall, you know."

Andrew suddenly didn't know what to say.

"I can't recall seeing him," she continued, "things are a bit hazy since ..."

Her voice trailed off, and Andrew was again lost for words and was now feeling quite uncomfortable. He knew exactly what she meant - since John's father, Stuart, had disappeared. Things were not going well in the kitchen of number twenty-seven Amberly Lane, The Heights. The sight of Claire emerging through the doorway with John in tow would almost be relief right about now. But that isn't what happened. She did indeed appear in the doorway, but alone and clearly troubled.

"Claire?"

He looked between her and Mrs. McGregor. The old lady seemed lost in her thoughts, a million miles away, milk jug still in hand. He pleaded with his eyes for some good news from Claire.

"Ah, John's not here after all. Silly me. He must have been called into that special project workgroup ..."

"Special project workgroup?" Andrew repeated. It was Claire's turn for a somewhat pained and imploring look.

"Aye. I recall now. John said something about that yesterday," she lied.

"Oh. Aye. Of course! The workgroup!" agreed Andrew, now playing along unconvincingly. "How silly of us!"

"We're so sorry to have bothered you, Jessica, but we really have to run now - thanks for the offer of the cha."

Mrs. McGregor didn't respond, and they quickly excused themselves and hurried out of the kitchen. Claire whispered to her friend, "his room was a complete shambles" as they slipped out the front door.

"And this is unusual how?" he asked, confused as to what was happening.

"Not *just* a shambles - it looked more like it had been ransacked. I mean, I know John can be a messy bastard, but still!"

"What are you saying?" He'd already had enough bad news for one day.

"I don't know … just that we have to find him! I'm really worried now!"

That makes two of us, Andrew thought, for the first time taking this whole thing seriously.

They headed quickly back down the hill toward the old town, the incessant rain soaking their clothes through again.

"Well, where the fuck is he then?" she asked as they headed off. "It doesn't seem like he made it home last night, and we've already checked all the registers for study and workgroups - he's not there either!"

Andrew nearly slipped as he tried to take the wet stone steps two at a time to keep up with her. Only the fact that there was an old iron railing for him to clutch onto prevented a minor catastrophe. Claire slowed as they descended the steps. She was looking worried, and this wasn't something he was used to seeing. There seemed to be a lot of things happening all of a sudden that he wasn't used to seeing.

"Well," he said. "Let's not panic."

She shot him a desultory glance. "Don't panic? Usually, I'd agree."

Andrew tried to sound confident. "My credits are still on him sleeping it off at a t-hub or something … maybe he rented a sleep pod?" She didn't even bother responding as his words trailed away unconvincingly.

They didn't speak for a while as they made their way down the hill. The rain slowed and turned into a sort of icy drizzle instead. Eventually, Claire started to detail their next moves. Andrew nodded along and tried to concentrate on not slipping over. He was relieved that someone at least seemed in control of whatever the hell was happening. If, of course, anything at all was happening.

***

Isabel was back in her apartment in Wanlockhead a few hours after her visit to Peter Bradshaw. Wanlockhead itself was a shining example of what QFT could achieve, with tall concrete and plexi-glass towers put together largely by A.I. powered constructo-bots, as far as the eye could see. It was now the new world's most advanced and most prosperous city, all thanks to Isabel's hand in the recent advancements in A.I.

Her thoughts turned to the recent fun and games. The poor man had been helpless and fairly hopeless.

At least he had a nice big one. Isabel smirked. *Job done - another valuable source of information.*

Isabel knew that Bradshaw would never risk the V.I. she had in her possession seeing the light of day. It would destroy his marriage and, most likely, his life. He was all hers now. Until the day he died.

She smiled and sipped a glass of the finest chilled caf liqueur, sliding deeper into her bath and gazing out over the lights of the city through the full-length one-way plex. The blackmail fun and games had made her extremely horny, something that just would not seem to abate, and she smiled to herself as her hand slid underneath the soapy water and between her thighs.

***

The light was already dimming even though it was only early afternoon, making things look even more gloomy than usual. The rain had finally stopped but had left behind a clinging dampness to the air. Andrew stood a safe distance away, blending into the array of students milling around the small park and vend-caf across from Claire's building.

They were chatting casually and laughing as if they didn't have a care in the world. He envied them. Even since the visit to John's house, he'd been desperately trying to convince himself that all of this was just a figment of Claire's imagination.

Maybe I am? A figment that is?

He tried to force himself to evaporate or dissipate, or some sort of 'ate, but it didn't work, and he was still standing on the damp tarmac, and he was still cold. He hadn't asked to be dragged into their dook, after all. He knew that they had both been through a lot and, of course, had their reasons - but that didn't mean they had a monopoly on the truth. Sometimes things just happened.

Keep thinking that, and it'll all just go away, he tried to tell himself.

The reality was that something was happening, though, whether he liked it or not, and he decided that he'd better focus on the task at hand. In other words, he should ensure that he didn't fuck up the task at hand. He'd come back to his train of thought when he had some time, and he'd figure a few things out for himself. Probably.

Claire had said she was worried that they might already be under surveillance, although he felt she was being overly paranoid. Then again, he wasn't the one who had just had their device taken over remotely by the state while he was breaching their secret data, so it was better to err on the side of caution, he supposed. He watched as Claire moved stealthily toward the crumbling tenement building that housed her tiny flat - there was no sign that anyone was paying either of them any attention as yet.

Although, who are those two over there? Are they looking at me?

A young blonde-haired student stood with her dark-haired friend, and as they chatted, they seemed to be looking his way now and again. Andrew sipped his vita-water nervously as he observed the pair.

The blonde one sure was cute. Actually, they both are, and, oh!

The dark-haired girl had whispered something to her friend, and they'd shared a discrete laugh before looking his way again. She held Andrew's gaze for a second and smiled. Andrew looked away, embarrassed.

Just my luck to be hit on while I'm on covert ops!

*

Claire had reached the weathered concrete entryway to her building. Depressing grey concrete steps led to a stark lobby beyond, the strong smell of urine and a vomit stain completing the scene.

Home sweet home.

She moved to turn into the building, then dropped her comms as she mounted the first step. The soft plex coating meant that it landed soundlessly, and she'd dropped it in such a way that it would fall behind her and so that she could turn around sharply to retrieve it, taking in the reactions of anyone nearby. She was half expecting a flinch, a lunge, *something.* But there was no reaction. No one was even very near her at all.

No one following. So far, so good. Relax, Claire, relax.

She stooped down and picked up her comms, feeling some of the tension wash away - she hadn't realized just how anxious she was up until that moment. She felt a little giddy as she stood back up and leaned on the damp wall of the building while she scanned the scene around her one more time for good measure.

All clear, time to go!

The next few minutes were a mix of alternating fear and relief as she made her way up the staircase towards her flat. Everything seemed normal - nothing but bland, empty corridors and pee-smelling stairwells. Bland was good, pee not so good, she decided. She liked bland, though - bland was her new best friend. She sent the all-clear to Andrew, and he responded quickly, arriving at the top of the stairs within a couple of minutes and out of breath.

"Ready?" he asked.

"Ready."

They moved into the short hallway that led to her flat. The hallway was also empty and bland. As they reached her door, Claire pulled a small hammer from her pack, handing it to Andrew. She clutched a slightly larger version of the same thing herself.

Andrew whispered, "I'm not even going to ask *why* you have those in your bag," drawing a swift shush from Claire as she put her finger to her lips. He nodded and moved to the opposite side of the door. Claire raised her hand and held up three fingers, then two, one, unlocking the door and flinging it open in one quick motion.

The door banged against the skirting and bounced back to almost closed before she'd had a chance to move, and so she had to push it open again to burst into the room, hammer raised. Andrew followed, hammer also raised, although he still wasn't entirely sure why. As he looked around the empty flat, he wondered if maybe there was a nail somewhere with his name on it.

Andrew was first to speak, shaking his head. "Holy fucking Douglas! Look at the state of this place!"

Claire smiled wryly and sat on the couch. He handed his hammer back and closed the door.

"I know you are not keen on housework, Claire, but this?"

"Shut the fuck up! Tidying up isn't high on my priority list right now."

"Is it ever?"

She had to agree; it wasn't, ever, and so said nothing. They sat in silence. Claire was rotating her hammer slowly in her hands. Andrew was staring at Claire's hammer. Andrew looked at the clock on the wall. It was two p.m. Somewhere outside, a dog barked. Somewhere inside, a tap dripped.

*

"It must be one hell of a hangover. I mean, I know John can drink, but surely by now ..." Andrew's words trailed off.

Claire looked over and frowned. She didn't think it was a hangover. They sat in silence for a while longer as she continued to rotate the hammer, deep in thought.

We still have time on our side—the apartment's safe, for now.

"We'll head to your flat next; I'll just log in to the QTF and try and dig a bit deeper on internal affairs data," she said.

There's also the small matter of finding John.

"Ok, Andy, we have work to do." She got up and moved over to the stack of QFT towers that were piled up on the other side of the room, plugging her device into a secure line. Andrew seemed a little lost.

"You keep trying to get hold of John and pack us some survival gear while you're at it – it's over there in the cupboard, I think."

He didn't reacy. He was staring at the wall.

"Andrew!"

Andrew stood to attention and saluted her.

Claire ignored him – she was used to this. He was easily distracted, and annoying.

"Are you hungry?" he asked.

"Aye, but I've nothing in the fridge."

"Great."

*

Claire pushed herself up off the floor and disappeared into the bathroom, emerging a few moments later in nothing but her underwear as she pulled a long black jumper over her head and dropped it down over her body. Andrew tried very hard to keep his focus on the contents of his pack but failed miserably. She poked her tongue out at him as she passed and sat cross-legged in front of her beloved device, and Andrew knew that it would be up to him to go and get some food.

***

It had been another long night. Lachlan had been wonderful – even if he said so himself. Although he was still troubled by aspects of his portfolio, he wasn't letting it show. It was all part of the job; he kept telling himself. There was no time to worry about things like morals.

The meeting was drawing to a close. Lachlan looked over at the striking woman sitting on the other side of the large round oak table. Isabel had been toying with him tonight, catching his eye on several occasions. She was quite aware of her sexuality and had left him in little doubt tonight that she was open to suggestions - the body language, the little touch on his arm when he arrived, the long lingering look. All the signs were there.

Isabel was milling about in the foyer with a few other sanctum members as Lachlan exited and stopped to check his comms. He watched her as she walked towards him and couldn't help but notice the way her breasts jiggled invitingly under her silky blouse. She caught his eye and smiled ever so slightly.

Fuck it, why not?

The blue liquid, the serum, was no doubt partly to blame for his current mindset, but he didn't care. Isabel looked amazing, and she'd make a useful ally, not to mention a good conquest. *Evanka is a whole lot of fun, but she only has so many holes*, he thought.

Isabel looked him up and down as she approached, walking straight past him without so much as a word. He watched her walk away, then followed her at a discrete distance, pretending to be on a call.

She'd led him over to the lifts that serviced the few rooms set aside to cater for state governance members needing to get some rest between the many long sittings. He caught up with her while she was pressing the up button. The lift arrived with a comical 'ding,' and Isabel turned to him, her face showing no emotion.

"Wait here for five minutes, then come up. Level 4, Room 05204," she said, her face expressionless.

She stepped close and grabbed him by the crotch, causing an immediate and surprisingly strong reaction. Isabel drew her tongue across her top lip, turned, and entered the lift, leaving Lachlan a little stunned. She held his gaze and started to unbutton her blouse as the lift doors closed.

Lachlan took a deep breath. This encounter promised to be something special. In the meantime, he had to find a way of hiding the prominent bulge in his suit pants.

***

Isabel sat on the edge of the bed, waiting patiently. She was fully dressed, her blouse re-buttoned. The large leather bag she carried everywhere was sitting next to her on the bed. It held a special surprise for her guest.

***

Andrew had drifted off to sleep at some stage. He wasn't sure what time that had happened, but it was dark now, and he was momentarily disoriented as he rolled himself upright and wiped away a small trickle of drool from his mouth. Claire was still perched at her device, earpieces on, fully immersed.

He yawned and stretched, then checked his comms, jolting fully awake in an instant. The small blue light indicated a message. Not just any message, however. It was a message from John. Andrew felt a mix of elation and fear. He blinked a few times just to make sure he was seeing what he thought he was seeing. He made a quick decision to check the message's contents discretely rather than interrupt Claire for now. There were bound to be some choice words intended for him,

184

so perhaps it'd be best to avoid embarrassment and provide her with a censored version of whatever it was that John had to say.

He opened the message and put the comms to his ear, his expression gradually changing for the worse, the longer he listened. Claire had sensed something was amiss was looking at him. He felt a little queasy as he listened. She looked as if she was about to speak, so he raised his palm towards her then put his finger to his lips. He sat in silence, listening intently before shutting off his comms and sitting there with an odd look on his face.

"What is it?"

"It was John," he said. "At least I *think* it was."

"What do you mean? Stop freaking me out, Andy! Was that a message from John, or wasn't it?"

"Well, yes."

"Then what do you mean, you *think* it was?"

"Well … you know what you said about Frances' call, um … I mean, it *sounded* like John. I mean, it was John. Maybe *I'm* the one getting paranoid now."

"What do you mean by … I'm sorry Andy, but what? Let me hear it."

She snatched the comms from him and replayed the message, frowning as she listened, then handed it back, frowning.

"Well, it's like nothing's happened, isn't it?" he offered. "It's bizarre. I mean, he just said he was taking his mum to a respite medical facility and that he'd be back in town soon. That's it. He didn't say anything about what happened: no expletives, no accusations, no apology. I mean, maybe he's not that bothered, but I know John, he'd be devastated. Fucking weird, right?"

"Forward me that message, Andy."

He forwarded the message, stood, stretched, and wandered aimlessly around the room, a bag of nerves. A couple of minutes later, he sat down, then stood up again, unsure of what he should now be doing.

"Shouldn't we be …"

"Just a few more minutes, Andy. It's ok; I'm monitoring any arrivals." She turned the display towards him and maximized a small image that had been sitting in the bottom right-hand corner. It showed a live feed from the entry hall.

Is there nothing she can't breach into?

Andrew was feeling unnerved by 'not John's' message. Everything was starting to get a little weird.

*

Claire lost herself in her code, trying to run the same protocols on John's message as she had on Frances's. She quickly ran into a problem and cursed loudly.

"Eh?" was Andrew's response.

She spoke without turning away from her device. "Bloody encryption code. It has some of the same signatures as before, but it's doing something differently - doing something *better*. It's almost as if it has already evolved – dammit, this could take a while."

It wasn't like it was in the old world VIS's, she reflected. Andrew had made her and John watch one once, she couldn't remember the name, but she'd thought it ridiculous that the 'breachers' could so quickly and easily get what they wanted, with seemingly a few keystrokes.

It was often a grind in the real world, with hours of work sometimes only rewarded by small breakthroughs. It surprised her that the end of times didn't happen sooner, such was the apparent lack of intelligence of the old-world inhabitants.

*

Andrew's mind was too full of too many things. He sat on the couch for a while, got up, got a glass of water, paced about a bit, and sat down again. Claire hadn't moved. There was only one thing for it, he decided. Headspace. Complete and total distraction, just for a few minutes.

She won't even notice.

He sat back, closed his eyes, and disappeared again into his favorite world.

CHAPTER 9 – THE FALL OF THE GOLDEN-HAIRED BOY

Lachlan lay alone in the darkened state accommodation room. His mind was a tangled mess. He would have sat, but even after several hot showers and a bath, he was still way too tender for that to be possible.

The golden-haired boy had just taken a tremendous fall. He couldn't believe what had just happened to him. His career was now in ruins, and he was more than a little scared for his life. Isabel had indeed had a special surprise for him, but it was one of pain and terror rather than the night of sexual pleasure he'd been anticipating.

She somehow knew that he'd divulged details of the mining program to his father. She was going to inform the inner sanctum in an emergency meeting this morning, and the punishment for breaking their trust would be extreme.

She'd offered him a lifeline, though, making it clear that she was the only one that could save him from a larger fall than he'd otherwise need to take. She'd explained, with a voice as cold as ice, that he'd need to submit himself to her in every way imaginable; otherwise, his future life expectancy would be significantly curtailed.

Isabel had played him audio of his discussion with his father, and Lachlan knew that he had no choice but to comply at that point. Maybe they bugged every new member, but he doubted it. He knew that she was pissed that he'd been given oversight of some of her responsibilities.

It's so obvious; I can't believe I fell into her trap. She probably planted the information about the mining programs as well. Fucking bitch!

When he'd arrived at her room, she'd smiled at him and asked him to undress. When he'd finished removing his clothes and turned to face her, she was holding something thick and long in her hands and was smiling malevolently. The rest was a blur.

Lachlan rolled himself to a sitting position and winced.

Demoted, demoted, back to junior level, and nothing more than an informant.

Lachlan was numb, crushed, defeated, his career was over, and he couldn't see a way back. His meteoric rise was over before it had begun, and now he was little more than a slave. Worthless. Useless. And sore. Very, very sore.

He'd been straight on comms to his father the moment Isabel had left the room. He was in tears, shaking with anger as he accused his father of selling him out, but Peter had vehemently denied any involvement. Lachlan had ended the call abruptly, and now he didn't know what to think; other than that, he'd underestimated Isabel Donachy.

Worst of all, he recalled, was that he could expect something to be leaked to the media tomorrow, something scandalous that would no doubt strip him of all the credibility he'd worked so hard to achieve. Isabel had him by the balls, and she was already squeezing tight.

***

Headspace had started well enough. Andrew was in a hotel room with his three best and closest friends. They were all in high spirits and very, very drunk. There was a large bag full of cash sitting open on one of the beds. Their fortune - illegally begat fortune, but fortune, nonetheless. Life was finally looking up! They'd made it! Except that he had other ideas, it seemed. At some point, the partying had stopped, and his friends had passed out one by one.

He'd been discretely tipping every second drink into a pot plant, making him the only one not completely obliterated on cheap VKA and bru, although he'd acted more drunk than the rest of them and had been the first to pass out.

He'd been carefully monitoring his friends for the last half-hour, ensuring that each one of them was in a deep drunken stupor. No one had moved, and a couple of them were snoring heavily. He opened one eye and looked around the darkened room. There was just enough light coming in from the busy street outside to determine that all three of his friends still hadn't moved. This was his chance.

First, there is opportunity.

He slowly pushed himself up off the hotel room floor, stepping over one of his friends and reaching over another on the bed to clasp the handles of the bag, lifting it off of the bed ever so carefully. A small noise from the other side of the room made him freeze, but there was no sign of movement when he looked. He lifted the bag and crept carefully to the door, turning the handle slowly and trying to avoid any sound from the latch. The latch clicked open, the sound deafening to him. He held his breath, expecting at any moment to be caught out. He took one last look back into the room.

And then, there is betrayal.

Andrew hesitated - in two minds, but the thought of making his escape with all of the cash to a life of fast cars, champagne, and caviar was just too great to refuse.

He slipped away quietly but didn't make it even halfway down the corridor - the door was flung violently open, and two of his three friends burst into the corridor, swearing profusely and faces contorted in anger. Andrew's survival instinct kicked in, and he ran for his life.

There was no turning back now - he sprinted to the end of the corridor, crashing through a fire door and half falling down the staircase beyond. He leapt down the remaining stairs and burst out of the fire doors and into an alleyway in the midst of the old town. The cobbles were wet, and he slipped, losing his balance and taking a heavy fall.

The bag spilled open and lost some of its contents, but Andrew snatched it up and ran again, just as his friends crashed out into the alleyway, giving chase at full tilt. His lungs burnt, and as he made for the end of the alleyway, he looked back over his shoulder, only to see his pursuers drawing ever closer, their arms and legs pumping. He had no idea they were this fit! They were close - if they caught him, they'd kill him.

As he reached the main street, a car pulled out abruptly across the end to the alleyway, and Andrew collided with it at full tilt. He'd had only a millisecond to react, but instead of jumping up and sliding over the car's hood in one elegant maneuver as he'd intended, he jumped, realized he wasn't going to make it, tried to swing his legs out of the way of the front quarter panel, failed, and smacked hard into the quarter panel and then bonnet in quick succession before falling back onto the road and rolling in agony. The very next second, his friends were on him.

The final thing he saw was a large fist rapidly approaching his face.

***

The faces of those gathered around the large and impressive meeting room table at SHQ looked grave. The Security Council had convened for an emergency session in light of some troubling recent events. Isabel was chairing the meeting, much to her delight.

There had been a breach of some sensitive internal affairs data, and they hadn't yet been able to determine the identity of those involved. Since the inception of The Source - its own internally developed A.I. entity - this was the first time that anyone had been able to breach D.A.I.R.'s systems.

The data breaches had occurred over various platforms - some of the data accessed was certainly not for public consumption, and in fact, not for the consumption of most of those present. The best minds of the cybercrime unit were called in immediately to investigate but had so far drawn a blank - a new approach was required.

Isabel sat and listened to the debate for a while. They were clueless. As always, she would be the one to propose a solution. Although it was highly concerning, she'd said she could allocate a small part of The Source's resources to the task and reassured the other council members that she'd have the culprit or culprits identified in no time.

'The Source,' as in 'the source of all code,' and their very own A.I. entity had been developed in the last few years, though very few knew what it did. Isabel knew, and she knew more than anyone. There was a consensus for action and an expression of gratitude after the emergency session ended. Isabel was pleased.

Someone had been poking their nose where it didn't belong, but Isabel wasn't unduly concerned. Even if they had managed to access the mining data, they wouldn't be able to interpret it. The Source had applied its latest encryption code on the raw data - no human mind could compete with that.

As she left the meeting, she couldn't help thinking that that squirrelly little sad shell of a man, Peter Bradshaw, hadn't been telling her everything. It was always students doing this sort of crap, nosing around where they didn't belong. Even though he was her resource, he hadn't given her anything useful for a while. He'd kept quiet over Grealish. She could understand, given the family connection, but made a mental note to pay him another visit soon – he may well need reminding of his obligations.

***

Andrew sat up abruptly, soaked in sweat and gasping for breath, back in the real world. The last thing he remembered was being beaten to a bloody pulp. It had been extremely painful, and he couldn't get to the big red button in time.

It took a few seconds for the room around him to come into focus and for him to realize that he was, in fact, unharmed. His head was foggy, and he felt awful. It was light outside, and he realized that he must have been lost in Headspace for quite a while -

I've got to stop doing that.

He tried to gather his senses. The sound of the shower running and then being shut off - the pipes groaning and shrieking in protest - caught his attention.

Claire.

Such was his state of malaise he hadn't even realized she was no longer in the room. He noticed two rucksacks by the door, packed and ready to go.

She's going to kill me. I did virtually nothing except sleep. Actually, I did nothing but sleep.

He tried calling John again but found he was still offline. It wasn't a surprise, and he stretched and got up, having a quick look at Claire's device, which looked as if it was still running analysis on John's message. He felt his chest tighten as he considered one of the two possible outcomes. When he'd heard John's voice, it had *sounded* like him, but not quite. He accessed the message on his comms and listened again. Something was off; there wasn't any doubt about that - he hadn't imagined it. He put his head in his hands and closed his eyes.

This can't be happening?

Were they really about to confirm something so unbelievable? And if they did, well, then what? He shuddered at the thought. He liked his nice quiet existence, his nice quiet routines, his small group of friends. Well, while they could still be considered in the plural, it had been quite good anyway.

He was clinging on desperately to his belief that this was nothing - it would come to nothing. John would call back, and they'd discover a glitch in Claire's code that explained everything. They had found some sensitive data, but they didn't know what it meant, after all. And as for the voice pattern analysis, well, there was no guarantee Claire had got that right, even though he'd looked over it in detail himself. Everyone makes mistakes, right? He was once again doing a poor job of convincing himself.

The sound of the bathroom door opening disturbed him from his rather disturbing thoughts. Claire emerged through the bathroom door, and Andrew involuntarily caught his breath, his eyes widening. She stopped in her tracks and scowled.

"What?" she asked abruptly.

"Um." Andrew opened his mouth to speak. He closed it again.

"Well?" There was an intriguing mix of impatience and anger in her voice - if that's your sort of thing.

"Erm," he said. At this point, he realized that perhaps he didn't have the best vocabulary in the world. He swallowed nervously.

He hadn't taken his eyes from her. She looked positively radiant. It was like he was watching one of those old-world haircare ads, the ones where the model walks in soft-focused slow motion, their hair bouncing slowly, and so on. He'd been caught totally off guard by the few subtle changes that she'd made to her appearance. The overall result was quite dramatic.

Claire was staring hard at him and had folded her arms across her chest – not a good sign. Her chin jutted out toward him in a show of defiance. He realized he was making things worse by not saying anything, but he was lost in her eyes.

She's done something to her eyes. There was no dark makeup, instead only subtle shading that seemed to make the emerald green of her irises pop. Her skin was glowing rather than the usual pale and pallid complexion. And her hair, well, it looked like she'd brushed it properly for a change.

He'd never seen her wear anything other than long baggy jumpers and loose-fitting industrial-strength pants before, and the cropped sweater and long samurai-style pants made her look quite feminine - almost unrecognizable. He'd been struck dumb and was unable to speak. Quite frankly, he was embarrassing himself.

She'd had enough. "*Fuck you*, Andy!"

"No, Claire!" Finally, words! They were not helping, however. She strode purposefully towards him and pointed at the couch, ordering him away from her work. He was just glad that she hadn't inflicted physical pain on him this time.

"Why do you look like you've just had a fright? *Ya wee bawheed!*" Andrew flinched. "No, Claire, it's just …"

The look he received stopped more words for a moment, but he now had to try and dig himself out of a very deep hole.

"You look …" he was searching for the right word. Claire was giving him a death stare.

"*Amazing!* Really. Really, amazing." There! He'd said it. Not particularly eloquently, but he'd at least got some words out. Hopefully enough to avoid being beaten mercilessly. Her eyes narrowed as she assessed a now wildly blushing Andrew, who was readying himself for evasive action.

For once, though, it was Claire who was lost for words. Her expression softened, and Andrew exhaled. She took the few steps to her desk, and Andrew backed away slowly. She looked at him and almost smiled. Almost. It was more a pitying look, he thought.

"Ok. Well, thanks, I *suppose*. But you are still a total fucking *bampot!*"

"Aye, well …"

He had to admit he was enjoying the local swears she was conjuring up, perhaps a little too much. He couldn't help but smile at the last one. Claire's face flushed, and she looked away for a moment, suddenly looking insecure.

"Anyway, I'm just trying to blend in a bit, to look a little more …" she searched for the word "… normal."

"Uh-huh." He liked 'normal.' "What about me, though?"

"You? You *always* look very, *very normal*."

Fair enough, he thought.

Claire bent over her devices. After a few moments, she exhaled in frustration.

"Damn it; the decoder has glitched. I'll have to restart it and re-thread the code. There's something new again in the encryption. It's fighting back - I think it's fighting back. This is spooky! I may have to have a little re-think."

Andrew was feeling quite nervous - they should have already been on their way some time ago.

"Shouldn't we be getting going?"

"Aye, I'm with you; it's just …"

She could see that he was worried, perhaps even a little scared as well, but she had a job to do. She needed to get this done.

"What if …"

She cut him off. "Any sign of trouble, and we're out this window here, see." She pointed to the window. It was the only window. Andrew walked over to the window and looked down, and it was a long way down, a very long way. He looked back at her uncertainly.

"Just follow my lead, Andy, if we have to … just give me a few more minutes, ok, we're fine."

Andrew looked out of the window again, observing the tiny people moving around like ants far, far below. His chest tightened.

That's a bloody long way down …

Claire moved over to the kitchen – which was really just a long cupboard with a sink in the corner of the room. Thanks to Andrew's earlier food run, she'd been able to prepare toasted carb slice with strawb paste and a pot of caf, which sat on the kitchen bench, the steam from it rising slowly into the chill air of the flat.

"Help yourself," she said, grabbing a slice. Andrew headed for the table, quickly poured himself a caf and also grabbed a slice or two. "So, can we talk?" He asked.

Claire gave him her full attention – it was rare for Andrew to sound serious after all - even adding in a reassuring nod or what she assumed was a reassuring nod.

"What's going on here, Claire?" He took another bite. He didn't want to admit it, but he was just going to have to say it.

Better out than in.

"I'm scared, Claire - scared for John, scared for all of us. I mean, can't we just"

"I am too, Andy." It wasn't exactly true, but empathy seemed a reasonable approach right at this moment. "I don't know exactly what we have here, but it's big, and we're going to find out how big. I think we're still ok for the moment."

For the moment. Reassuring.

"I am worried about John, but, I mean, it's possible he's taken his mum away; she was in a bit of a state ..." She'd never sounded so unconvincing.

"But you know, or think you know what all this means, don't you?" he sounded almost depressed - as if resigned to his fate. She had no choice but to be honest.

"Yes, I think I know, but I can't be sure."

Silence fell between them again. Andrew looked as if he already knew what she was going to say.

"And? Come on, Claire cut the baws! I want to know what's going on here! *Come on,* worst case scenario - just level with me."

She felt a little chill of excitement pass through her. She'd never seen this side of him before.

"Ok, well ..."

*

Andrew was staring fixedly at her. She thought about what she wanted to say, about *how much* she wanted to say.

"Worst case scenario?"

"Please."

"Worst case. No punches pulled. Here it is." Another brief pause. Her gaze was cool and steady. Andrew prepared himself for the worst.

"Well ... what I *think* is that the state is behind the disappearances. John's father? Maybe. Frances? Definitely. Others, John?"

The word hung in the air. The floor seemed to drop away underneath Andrew, and he sat down on the couch.

"They are taking their *own people,* Andy. The State. These disappearances *have* to be politically motivated; I mean, what other explanation could there be? I need to find out why. It has to be linked to whatever the Elyssium program is; it's just too much of a coincidence otherwise."

She tried to assess whether he was following so far. He nodded. *That's weird; it's like he read my mind.*

"Anyway ... what we don't know yet is what's happened to anyone who's disappeared. We also don't know yet what Elyssium is, but the one thing I am certain of – there's no evidence yet that anyone who's disappeared has come back. I've been searching, and – nothing."

Andrew felt a pang of deep guilt that he hadn't helped. He hadn't used his journalistic skills to contribute in any way last night and had instead been fucking around in Headspace. The silence in the room was unbearable. All of this wasn't boding well for John, and Andrew was feeling sick in the stomach again.

"I'm hoping against all hope that John isn't another one of the disappearances Andy, but it doesn't look good, does it. If he is, then we're already in really, *really* big trouble."

The thought struck her like a hammer blow. *This whole thing has just gotten horribly real – it's time to go!*

"Whatever's happening, I'm going … we're going to find out, don't worry."

It was a matter-of-fact statement. Andrew nodded glumly. Claire had said what he'd been thinking, but his mind wouldn't allow him to put it so clearly. He was looking for the best possible outcomes, while Claire had no trouble looking for the worst.

"Some of this sounds crazy, Andy, I know it does - even to me. But what if I'm right? What if I'm right?"

*

He didn't know what to say. *Then we're fucked*, was the answer that had popped into his mind, but he decided it was best to keep it there. "If I'm wrong, and John's ok, and I'm wrong about the voice patterns, and wrong about the Elyssium program, well, it would almost be a relief." He knew she was rarely wrong, and that was a lot of wrongs.

"But If I'm right, then there is going to be hell to pay!" She suddenly stood up, a ball of energy, fire in her eyes. "I'm going to find John. I'm going to find out what's going on. I'm going to find the truth about Henny. I'm going to expose every last person involved, and I'm going to make them pay - for *everything*."

Andrew's feelings of unease quickly multiplied. Her eyes were almost dancing with hatred now. Something strange was happening to him. *He* started to feel angry. Not from what Claire had said, but instead when he thought about John. For the first time in his life, he'd felt a genuine and deep hatred bubble up inside him at the thought of his possibly ex-best friend. John had accused him, accused Claire of something terrible.

True, he'd daydreamed about that thing many times, but a daydream was all it was. It wasn't worth destroying their perfect little friendship triangle over, yet that was what the giant oaf had done. And now, when they most needed him, he was nowhere to be found.

He's ruined everything, the big fucking bawheid!

He caught hold of himself. Something else bubbled to the surface. Even though his current situation was possibly quite dire, the one benefit he could see was that he had Claire all to himself for once.

This is better than when John's here.

The thought just popped up, out of nowhere, and as soon as he'd thought it he felt ashamed. That was when the tears had started to well up, and he turned away from Claire so she wouldn't notice.

Douglas! I'm a total wreck! Of that, at least, he was certain.

"Andy?"

Claire's voice, sounding unusually soft, broke through the fog of his self-loathing. She'd been observing his reaction to her tirade, and he looked absolutely terrified. She felt a rare tugging deep in her chest. An emotion, yes, that was what it was! One other than hatred or desire, for a change. She sat next to him on the couch and threw her arms around him, wrapping him in a brief, tight hug.

Her hair smells of some sort of exotic perfumed flower; he thought as she headed for the door.

***

Isabel had called the emergency meeting at six a.m., causing much muttering and dissent amongst the members of the Sanctum, but they had all joined on secure V.I., nonetheless. She was looking immaculate in a dark business suit and a crisp white blouse; platinum blonde hair pulled back tightly to a large bun. It was important to let them know that she meant business.

The other members listened solemnly to Isabel's highly practiced speech, with increasing horror as she played the secretly recorded footage from Peter Bradshaw's home, in all its 3D SFB scanned glory. The footage left no doubt that Lachlan Grealish had wholly betrayed the confidence and trust of sanctum in divulging details of the mining program to his father.

She'd organized to surveil Lachlan in one way or another ever since he'd been brought into the sanctum, and it was now paying off handsomely. The 3D scanning fly-bots, of which there were only two, were very new Tech and were one of The Source's more recent breakthroughs.

The bots had extracted heat map imagery and soundwaves from Peter Bradshaw's house as he and Lachlan Grealish sat and discussed things they definitely should not have discussed.

If the other members of the sanctum had discovered her surveillance before she had anything concrete on Grealish, then she would have been in strife. She'd always had a good feel for people's character, though, and her instinct on Grealish had been proven to be correct. In a way, she was relieved that it wasn't just her pride being stung that had set her on this path – she'd been vindicated, she'd been right, as she always was.

It was obvious that the chair had a soft spot for Lachlan, and she'd played that to her advantage, stating again and again that the best thing they could do was to ensure Grealish disappeared permanently. She'd received broad agreement, which had then forced the chair to argue for lesser penalties, and eventually, they had agreed to everything that she'd wanted, without even knowing it.

Grealish would be kept on as a sanctum informant against the state, reporting directly o her. The Chair wasn't happy, but there was no other way. Isabel had her man and her victory.

***

It was late morning when they arrived back at John's house. Intermittent rain was falling, the wind blowing it almost horizontally at times. Andrew had complained the whole way there, and Claire was tiring of it rapidly. Her decryption program was still re-processing John's message, and it would be some time before she had anything like a conclusive answer.

They had time to kill, and so she'd decided that they should return to John's house and see if they could find anything in the home security logs to either prove or disprove John taking his mother away for treatment or indeed showing if he'd ever arrived home.

John's parents had one of the best solid-state, fully isolated home security systems available. It wasn't something that they could breach, unfortunately. It meant another trek up the hill, much to Andrew's chagrin. He was getting the sense that Claire was reluctant to visit his flat – and he couldn't blame her, really.

They moved quickly once the house was in sight. Andrew gave Claire a boost over the high side wall. He quickly hoisted their small backpacks over before following, scrambling up and over, carefully avoiding the iron spikes designed to deter anyone from doing exactly what he was now doing.

Unfortunately for him, he misjudged his leap from the wall badly – carrying too much momentum as he landed and tumbling forward into an ornate-looking garden bed, sending rose petals flying. She gave him a bewildered look as he got to his feet, brushing leaves and flowers from his jacket. He gave her his best 'I meant to do that' look.

Moved quickly to the back door, Claire tried the handle and it was unlocked. That in itself was unusual but not necessarily any cause for alarm. The scene that lay before them as they entered the large sunroom adjoining the kitchen was, however.

They stopped in their tracks as they entered, wide-eyed. A couple of chairs belonging to the small breakfast setting were overturned, one with a broken leg and several pieces of crockery were in pieces on the floor. A large brown stain next to a china cha-pot covered part of the rug under the table.

Alarm bells were ringing loudly in Claire's head now - this was undoubtedly the sign of a struggle of some sort. She called out to the empty room, "John?" The silence of the huge house swallowed her voice, "Mrs. McGregor? Jessica?" Silence again followed.

Was that a tremor in Claire's voice? He thought that it was. But at least she was capable of speech. Andrew's mouth and throat had suddenly become dry and constricted.

This is bad; this is really bad! Oh, dook, what if someone else is here? Andrew caught Claire's attention and put a finger to his lips, pointing back towards the sunroom door. As they turned to leave, they heard a low rumble approaching the front of the house. It sounded like a vehicle—a large one. "Ok, I think we'd better go now," he whispered. They heard the vehicle stop directly outside the front of the house.

"Come on," he said, practically dragging her outside and making for the far end of the back garden. Andrew led the way, and they used an old wooden shed to scramble up and over the high stone wall at the rear of the property. They dropped down into a narrow, cobbled laneway flanked by high fences on either side.

"Corrections?" he asked, looking panicked. Claire didn't know. She was feeling exposed; there was nowhere to hide in the laneway. Their heads whipped around as they heard the same low rumbling sound again, this time coming from the end of the alley. Andrew's heart nearly leapt through his chest, and he was about to make a run for it if he could get his legs to work. Claire was tensed like a coiled spring, ready to take flight.

A large garbage collection pod rumbled past, and they stared at it in disbelief. They looked at one another, Andrew releasing a large outward breath. Claire was the first to speak.

"Ok, well, it's good to be alert, anyway." Andrew rolled his eyes at her remark.

"That scene back there, they wouldn't leave their house like that. Unless someone broke in after they'd gone? Still, it doesn't look good? We have to find out what's happened."

"Aye." Andrew swallowed hard. He didn't like where this was going.

"You sneak back into the house, see if you can find anything. Search the home systems, check the security V.I.'s, everything. I'll head back to the place and keep working on everything else. I've had another idea."

He wished she'd stop having ideas.

"Meet me there this afternoon; it's still probably safer than your place. We'll work out what to do next from there."

Andrew wanted to protest and say, 'why me?' But knew her plan made perfect sense. He didn't have any better ideas anyway.

"Oh, and use the ES, the Emergency Signal, if there is any sign of trouble. I'll send you coordinates for a rendezvous point if we need it – if it's not safe at the place."

What the fuck? Why would we need a rendezvous point – it's not that bad, or is it?

He nodded lamely and went to say something, but Claire had already turned and was strolling purposefully away from him along the alleyway.

Bye then …

Andrew turned and looked at the wall.

***

She thought she'd done a pretty good job of blending in on her way back down to the place. A quick trip down the hill, catching a passing civic transporter for a couple of stops before being deposited on the main vending strip. The pedestrian mall was littered with shiny fronted displays projecting the latest in fashion and leisure tech. It was a world away from Claire's usual haunts.

A quick browse in a prissy clothing vendbox that drew disapproving looks from the snooty counter staff, even stopping and ordering a caf and a cream baffel at a vintage text store and staying out of the wind, which had picked up alarmingly as the morning had progressed. It was around lunchtime now, and for all appearances, she was just another student going about their daily business.

Scans on the SFBs hadn't indicated any unusual behavior, and she didn't appear to be followed - there was every possibility that state security didn't know about her yet. If they had John, though, she wondered how much longer that might last. She'd decided not to attempt any more contact with him and had instructed Andrew to maintain comms silence until they met face to face and had a better idea of what was going on.

It wasn't long before she was safely cocooned inside the place, working furiously on her new theory to speed the decryption process on both the Elyssium data and John's message. There was no way she was going to let the dark forces of state security outsmart her. Andrew would join her later in the afternoon, as planned - until then, they both had plenty to do.

She'd already discovered that there were more layers to the data than she'd first thought, and the deeper she dug, the more she was finding: units of measure, production schedules, dates, status markers, detailed financial records, there was just so much there.

A rustle from the foil strips on the ceiling made her look up just as her code finished the final decryption cycle on John's message. An alert also flashed up in the corner of the display. She stared wide-eyed at the display, then opened the alert.

Her heart stopped beating, and she felt a weird sensation in her mind like she was suddenly falling. This was bad. Beyond bad! The proximity alert hadn't activated, and yet a group of people had just entered the front entrance to the place! Another slightly stronger rustle from the overhead foil snapped her attention back away from the display, and she felt the movement of air from outside.

The entry was wide open. It was what she'd been terrified of all along. She listened for a second and heard voices, muffled male voices, and they were getting closer. She had to get out of there!

***

Andrew took his time getting back to John's mansion. He'd thought about climbing back over the high wall, which would have been quite an achievement in itself, but instead had headed further up the laneway. After a little while, he reached a large drainage grate. A brief wrestle ensued. He triumphed, the rusted metal shifting with a groan and allowing him to squeeze through and slip down into the tunnel beyond.

The old brick drainage tunnels were a feature of the area, and he and John had used them often over the years. He knew his way around, which was handy. He snagged his jacket on something almost immediately he entered, tearing the sleeve slightly. "Bloody typical," he muttered, making his way somewhat more carefully towards the dim light at the end of the tunnel some distance away.

The tunnel branched off on either side and wasn't that easy to navigate - it had been invaded over time by tree roots, various bits of debris, and a vending trolley, amongst other things. He wasn't exactly sure how a vending trolley had found its way into the drainage tunnel, but there it was, blocking his path. He cursed as he clambered over it, scraping his head on the roof of the tunnel on the way through.

Ouch! Damn! Fuck this spy dook; you never saw that in the VIS's, he thought as he rubbed the top of his head.

He eventually emerged into the backyard of a house - well, more of a towering mansion than a house, really - a few doors down from John's. There was a path, or at least there used to be, which could be taken between the two mansions. Andrew and John had taken it many times during their last year of top school when they'd used it to sneak over and visit Virginia Wesley.

She was a year older, and Andrew recalled that they were always pathetically awkward whenever they were in her presence. Although bookish, she had a sweetness and femininity, not to mention a penchant for wearing pretty summer dresses that ensured they'd both had a massive crush on her. The journey had always been doubly worthwhile because she'd sold them bootleg bacco and malt – the honeyed firewater based on old-world whiskey - pilfered from her mother's fine wares distribution company.

The path he was planning to take was well protected from sight and took several twists and turns that weren't obvious unless you had tried, and failed, to take it before. His theory was that if he'd have to beat a hasty retreat for any reason, then this would be a good escape route, giving him a critical advantage over any pursuers.

Can't be too careful, he thought.

Taking the path now would ensure that he remembered the way and confirm that it was still navigable. Once he was safely back into the drainage tunnels, he had several options, including a couple that could take him up to a mile away from the area and requiring only brief glimpses of daylight. He realized that he was buying into Claire's paranoia. He also realized that he probably knew more than was necessary about the drainage tunnels of The Heights.

The path was still intact, and aside from some overgrowth here and there, it was fairly easy to navigate. Andrew jumped the side fence into the McGregor's backyard and snuck back inside the house through the sunroom door. He spent a few nervous minutes checking the house was empty, but once he'd established that it was all clear and settled down in the study, it didn't take him long to locate the home data system.

However, it did take unlocking passwords and sifting through all the records of appointments, comings and goings, surveillance V.I., and so on. Once he'd got to the security V.I. files, he'd discovered that there was nothing logged for the last month or so. He checked again, hoping somehow he'd missed them, but it was pretty clear that someone had deleted them.

This isn't a good sign; maybe someone's been here?

Not for the first time, Andrew had a bad feeling in the pit of his stomach. He thought about using the toilet but decided he'd better finish what he was doing first.

He checked the status of the surveillance cams, and sure enough, footage of the front and rear gardens was currently being recorded. He switched them off and deleted the evidence of his ungainly fall over the high wall, and in fact, all evidence that they had been there at all over the last twenty-four hours.

If it's this easy for me to delete it, then...

Andrew didn't want to complete the sentence. He had a nagging feeling that he should leave now but was determined to try and find something, anything, that might help get them out of this mess.

It took a little longer than he'd expected to gain access to the medical and financial records, but when he did, he found that Jessica McGregor had been slowly reducing her medication under close professional supervision over the last few months. There was no mention of any rehab clinic or anything of that nature. It was another bad sign.

So much for needing to be taken into care.

The home data center was in the study just off the main entry hall, and he was about halfway out the study door, aiming to take a quick break in the marbled downstairs lavatory when things started happening in quick succession. Firstly, he heard a sound not dissimilar to the waste disposal pod from the street, but this time it sounded as if it was arriving at speed.

He looked out into the entry hall and saw the blurred image of a large dark object through the frosted plexi-glass panels of the front door. He quickly ducked back into the study and turned the security cam feed back on. A large unmarked dark-colored transporter had pulled up directly outside, and as he watched, several large gentlemen in black outfits, faces covered and holding what seemed to be large weapons, poured from it and started heading towards the house.

Oh, dook!

At the same time, or secondly, if you will, Andrew's comms blinked red and beeped three times in quick succession. It was the ES from Claire! He was already on the move as the comms message came through. The message simply said, 'Run.'

What the hell is happening? Is Claire ok?

Andrew snatched up his pack and bolted outside via the sunroom, sprinting madly across the large lawn just as fast as his scrawny legs would carry him. He was absolutely petrified but somehow managed to execute his escape plan at full speed, ducking under branches, clambering over fences, and crawling under a particularly vicious thorn bush. Within minutes he was safely away from the house and seemed to be out of danger as he ducked into another drainage tunnel.

This is a nightmare; this isn't happening; this is a nightmare!

No matter how many times he repeated the words in his mind, it did nothing to change the fact that it had, and was, happening. He was sweating buckets and gasping for air as his heart hammered in his chest, but he was oblivious to all of that and focused on only one thing - survival! He certainly didn't want to end up at the hands of the corrections – he'd heard enough horror stories to haunt his dreams as it was.

Were they the corrections, though? It wasn't the right uniform, was it?

There was no time to stop and ponder who it was that was coming to arrest him. All that mattered was that there was no sign of them right now. He'd somehow managed to escape.

Oh Douglas, what is this? Am I actually 'on the run' now? And why the fuck did they have weapons anyway?

He picked his way through the never-ending and quite pungent tunnels over the next half-hour, making sure he wasn't seen, making his way into the neighboring suburb of Park View. The tunnel emerged into a derelict park, funnily enough.

Andrew was able to make his way through it unobserved and into an adjoining graveyard littered with half-collapsed crypts and broken gravestones. The cemetery was a rare remnant of the old world and earmarked for development for as long as he could recall. Years of legal battles and conservation issues had left it in its current decrepit, uncared for, and deserted state, and Andrew was glad for once of the New Socialists' amazingly complex legal system.

Although close to wealthy suburbs, the area was 'on the wrong side of the tracks,' as it were. The terrain from The Heights dropped away sharply, and the area beyond was largely a wasteland. The area was ringed by mountainous hills and craggy outcrops that led to the manufacturing and synthetic food production factories of the midlands.

He sat inside the portico of one of the largest of the crypts, keeping one eye on the perimeter fence for any signs of pursuit while scanning for fly-bots. He was still breathing hard, his clothes soaked through with sweat, and he realized he was now shaking.

This can't be happening! This can't be happening, was all he could think. But it was.

What's happened to Claire – she was at the place, she must have had a visit too, oh Douglas, please let her have gotten away.

'Run' was the pre-agreed code that they would send the other should anything bad happen. And something bad had happened. It had certainly been sound advice for whatever was going on back at John's house – it was either under surveillance, or he'd ham-fistedly set off an alarm when accessing the home data system. He didn't believe the latter for a second.

Oh, Douglas, oh Douglas, what now, what am I going to do now?

He'd started hyperventilating and had to force himself to calm down. He closed his eyes and tried to think of something calming, something nice. Claire's face materialized, and she was smiling at him, chatting casually and laughing at his jokes.

After a minute or two, he started to calm down. Claire had he'd sent him the coordinates of a rendezvous point earlier, and he decided that now would be an excellent time to see exactly where it was. He was more than a little shocked to discover that she'd flagged a location deep inside the uninhabitable zone of the lowlands, near Loch Campbell.

The uninhabitable zone? Couldn't we just go to a hotel in Aberdeenshire or something?

He supposed she must have her reasons, but it did seem a very strange choice, not that there was anything he could do about it now. The other stipulation had been that if anything should happen, as it now undoubtedly had, that they would maintain comms silence for at least twenty-four hours. He wasn't sure any of this was a great idea, but there really wasn't either the time or opportunity to argue about it now.

CHAPTER 10 – BRIEFINGS

Isabel was attending yet another emergency security briefing. It had been a big day so far. *Destroy Lachlan Grealish in the morning, solve state security issues in the afternoon!* She was feeling quite pleased with herself. She was crammed into the stuffy boardroom on the top floor of the SHQ building, along with 20 or so senior state officials, both allies and enemies.

The security council reported that they had a few possible locations for the source of the breach, but still no firm lead on the culprit or culprits. They needed the security council chair's approval to proceed with security checks on the locations, and Isabel had approved them out of hand. She'd fed the other council members some of the data calculated by The Source, but she'd kept all of the best information for herself.

All she had to do now was wait for the breachers to try again, as they surely would, and then they'd fall into her trap - she'd have a little surprise waiting for them. In the meantime, she'd ordered her own sweep of *all* the possible locations provided by The Source. The sweep would include reviews of all surveillance footage from every location and covert raids conducted by her special security forces.

It may take them a little while before they could identify a pattern, but they could start bringing them in as soon as they had potential suspects - all of them. She was sure that the process of interrogating hundreds of potential criminals would at least provide some entertainment value for her special forces, if nothing else.

They had no idea. Even the defense minister was clueless as to what was going on. She enjoyed letting the other council members feel important while knowing that all they were doing was flapping about in the dark and chasing shadows. By the time they had organized their official raids, it would all be over.

She'd soon provide them with details of exactly who was behind the incursions. The culprits would be safely in custody before the incompetent fools of the security council even realized what was happening. Isabel would win again. She liked winning.

***

Claire alerted him as soon as she possibly could – she'd sent the ES, gathered up her devices, thrown her rucksack over her shoulder, and moved quickly to the junction in the passageway. The voices were getting closer - there was no doubt that this was a raid of some sort. Their time had run out.

She could hear the sound of heavy objects being moved aside and what sounded like timber splintering - surely it would only be moments now before she was in plain sight. The back exit was her only chance to get away, and she moved quickly and quietly, staying ahead of whoever it was that had come to pay her a visit. As she reached the passageway leading to the rear exit, she saw lights up ahead, where there should not be lights.

Oh, Douglas, I'm in big trouble!

She had to try and find somewhere to hide, anywhere, and she backtracked, running as fast as she could, hurdling over all manner of old junk as panic took hold.

Maybe one of the old storerooms?

She grazed her shoulder on the point of a rough brick wall as she tried to dodge around a right-angled corner at high speed. The impact threw her off balance, and she crashed into the wall opposite. The lights and the shouting were closing in from either side now – they must have heard her.

I'm trapped! Fuck!

Images of officers swarming the passageway filled her mind, and another unwelcome image appeared - Henny disappearing into the back of the corrections van, a terrified, pleading look in her eyes.

Not me; this isn't happening to me!

Pure adrenaline drove Claire back to her feet, and she had to make a quick decision.

Which way?

Light was streaming into the passageway ahead as it rounded another bend, dust filled the dank air, and for a moment, she couldn't breathe. She looked frantically around her, desperately trying to think of another escape route. Several doorways led from the passageway to the storerooms. She'd be trapped the moment she entered one, cowering and just waiting to be captured. It wasn't going to end like that!

Another passage led to an old stairwell that went nowhere, but maybe she could force her way into the ceiling space above it? It was just around the corner, back towards the place, and she'd run right past it. Claire cursed as she realized that she couldn't make it - beams of light were now clearly visible at either end of the passageway. She then felt something she hadn't experienced in a very long time - fear.

Oh please, no.

She looked around frantically, panic-stricken. There was an old crate about halfway down the passage; *I could jump in and hide maybe, no, ridiculous, but hold on, what's that?* There was something in the roof of the passage barely a few yards in front of her - it was barely visible in the gloom, but it looked like maybe it could be an old service hatch! It was her only chance. She had no idea where it led or even if it would open, but it was better than standing here waiting to be caught, waiting to be subjected to the horrors that would surely follow at the hands of the corrections.

Claire took a step back and ran towards it, jumping as high as she possibly could to try and dislodge the hatch. She only just reached it. It moved and was now partly dislodged from its frame by some miracle, a dark void beyond.

She had just a few seconds left until whatever was attached to the flashlights came around the corner of either end of the long and now alarmingly well-lit passageway. She hoisted her rucksack up, and it knocked the hatch away, wedging itself in the opening; she jumped again and managed to push it inside.

One chance to make it!

Claire took a few steps back, ran forward, and leapt at full stretch. She clung to the frame desperately, by her fingertips, and for a moment, she thought her momentum would break her grip, but somehow she hung on and managed to swing and wrestle herself up and through the opening. She scrambled for the hatch and slid it silently back into place just as light flooded the passage below her.

She remained perfectly still, the sound of her own heart beating so loud that she was certain it could be heard below. She was afraid to even breathe as the sound of boots clambering over rubble and the shouting between the men echoed up from directly underneath.

Claire was almost paralyzed with fear as she pressed down on the hatch with all her weight. Tears welled in her eyes as a loud crash directly below sent a shock through her, and she stifled a cry. A little bit of wee escaped.

A male voice shouted. "Clear!" Another shouted. "Try all the rooms; they must be here somewhere!" Claire bit down on her bottom lip and dared not move as the noises from below crashed past. They would soon realize that she wasn't in the main tunnel or the storerooms. Her only hope was that no one looked up and noticed the hatch – surely, it would be obvious to anyone below.

Please please please please please!

She hadn't taken a breath in a while. A terrifying series of crashes and shouts continued below her. She screwed her eyes shut, willing those below not to look up. Within seconds the noises had moved away, and Claire realized that she might just make it.

If I can just find a way out from here.

She carefully pushed herself up and hit her head on something. It was pitch black. She had no option but to risk shining a low light from her comms. Her eyes adjusted, and she could see that she was in a large, low-ceilinged space that might have spanned half of the building's footprint. It was cramped, with low beams and cross members everywhere – not enough room to even stand - but there seemed to be an opening at either end.

A way out!

Claire pushed herself up on all fours, grabbed her pack, and crawled as fast as she dared towards the nearest opening. The floor was covered in what seemed like centuries of dust, and she had to fight the urge to sneeze. It was solid enough that there was only a very slight creaking from the boards as she moved, and she prayed that it wasn't obvious from below.

They won't be able to hear anything over the racket that they're making, I hope!

Muffled noises came from somewhere below, and she quickened her pace as she neared the opening, scrambling over to it. She shone her comms light and illuminated a small stairwell with old wooden steps that headed both upwards and downwards.

Oh, thank Douglas! Up, I have to go up!

She had no idea where they led, but this was more than she could have hoped for. The stairs wound up and around for several flights, and she could feel her quads starting to burn after the first couple. As she neared the top of the stairwell, she saw a sliver of light around a doorframe. *Freedom!* At least she hoped it led to Freedom. It could just as easily lead her straight into the arms of whoever the fuck was crashing around way below. She peered through the old-fashioned keyhole but could only see something light brown in color blocking her view. She pressed her cheek against the door and held her breath, listening for any sounds of life on the other side, one second, two, three.

Fuck it; I've got to! There's no other option.

She tried the handle, and it twisted unencumbered, but the door didn't move. She tried twisting the handle one way and then the other and leaned into the door, but it wouldn't budge. "Fuck," she muttered under her breath. She was still trapped. She was going to have to take a huge risk. Taking a step back on the small landing area, she aimed a kick just below the door handle with all her might.

The noise seemed deafening. The kick, delivered with a heavy boot, didn't seem to achieve much at all. Except that is, making enough noise to alert anyone within about a mile radius as to her whereabouts. She listened again for a moment and Could hear voices from below again!

They've found the hatch! That's it, all or nothing!

She stood back and repeated the process. She aimed another kick, and still, the door didn't move. Claire was getting desperate now, panic rising as she kicked, again and again, her thigh muscles burning with the effort.

The fifth kick did the trick, the timber below the door handle splintering with a loud crack. Claire shoulder-charged the door, throwing all her weight at it, and it gave way, clattering open as she burst into a small storeroom littered with cardboard boxes, falling into and over them in the process. She picked herself up and headed straight through an open doorway on the opposite side of the room.

She'd been prepared to walk, or in this case fall, into a room full of people but instead found herself in an abandoned worksite with piles of building materials and tools littering the room. She was in a vendbox that looked like it probably opened out into one of the many small alleyways of the old town.

She looked around and quickly grabbed a cap that one of the workers must have had left behind, tieing her hair back and putting the cap on before heading for the door. She was sure the corrections would burst through the doorway any moment or would be waiting outside, or both! She was out of breath and shaking with adrenaline. She stopped and listened for a second but couldn't hear anything.

I'm so close now, got to get out of here!

She wanted nothing more than to throw the door open and run out as fast as she could. Still, she couldn't risk drawing attention to herself, or perhaps running straight into the arms, or more likely batons, of the corrections, and so instead, she quietly unlatched the door and opened it a crack to peek through.

The vendbox opened into a small but busy pedestrian alleyway, and although there were plenty of weary workers and veebee's passing by, she saw no sign of any uniformed officers. She was lucky; it was busy – probably the end of shift by now, she guessed.

Claire slipped through and merged seamlessly into the stream of commuters, keeping her head down to hide her features and walking quickly, bracing for flight at the first sign of any trouble. She stole a quick glance behind her but couldn't see anything through the crowd.

Just keep going. Don't look back again. Oh Douglas, what's just happened? I hope Andy's ok.

She wanted to cry but had to stay focused. She rated her chances of escaping no more than fifty-fifty at this stage and watched for trouble as far ahead of her as she could see. She turned left as the alleyway opened out into a large plaza, stopped, crouched down, and pretended to tie her bootlace while checking all around her.

Nothing. Where are they? It's just veebees and workers.

If they had come looking for her specifically, then surely they would have communicated to their command by now, and the surrounding streets should be teeming with corrections officers or security forces.

They didn't use my name. They knew someone had been using the place, though. Maybe this means that they don't have John after all, or maybe they just haven't made the connection yet?

Claire wasted no time in merging back into the passing crowd. Her mind was racing, plotting her next move. She had to get out of town and try and meet up with Andy. It was all too much – *what the fuck was happening? John's missing, they've come after me and …*

She couldn't hold back the tears any longer, and as she quickly crossed the plaza, they streamed down her face.

I have to pull it together, for dook's sake!

She wiped her eyes and cleared her mind. It wasn't the time for emotions, although she didn't seem to have much control of them anymore – something she'd never had a problem with until two days ago! She had to make it to the outer lowland villages, near the wastelands, and decided to head to the t-hub, but wouldn't take the obvious option - she could go straight to …

Oh no! I should have thought of this earlier!

To make matters worse, she'd just realized that she would have no option but to make a very risky detour on the way to the rendezvous point. She'd left some of her special research work on a secure storage device back at the college. If someone had the smarts to decrypt her code, and they probably did, seeing as they had had no trouble breaching her device's security.

They could find all kinds of things that Claire would not want them to know on there, including the details of the base code she'd used in breaching internal affairs - she was going to need that code if she was to have any chance of seeing this through to the end. She just hoped they didn't have her name yet.

Maybe I've still got a chance.

***

Isabel was stationed inside her workroom and received updates on the suspected locations' special security forces sweep. She'd been reading an old-world biography that she'd been drawing inspiration from of late. In it, they had invaded other territories and were just about to win a key battle; just one puny nation stood in their way. The subject was someone who had left their mark on the planet; this was someone who knew how to get things done; this was someone she could model herself on.

The latest update flashed up on the full-length display panel covering the far wall of her workroom, and she swiveled in her chair to read it. It was mixed news – not what she was hoping for. She snapped the hardcover text shut and placed it back on her desk, the red, white, and black emblem displayed prominently on the cover.

They had already arrested several students who'd been unfortunate enough to be loitering near some of the raid locations, and the special forces had been processing them all afternoon. It appeared that they were a little overzealous in their processing methods, no doubt spurred on by her directive to achieve a quick result. There had already been a death under interrogation, and it was going to be difficult, but not impossible to cover up. *This is the problem with trusting others to do your dirty work.*

Things were quickly turning into a bit of a mess, and Isabel wanted to ensure that she'd be able to speak face to face with whoever it was that had broken through The Source's code, not find them dead in a cell. Isabel placed the interrogations on hold until she could get the situation back under control, leaving her incredibly frustrated. Isabel felt a little tingling, a little longing for something, and glanced down at her desk drawer.

Maybe a little pick me up?

Her hand had subconsciously reached to the drawer handle, but she stopped herself. It was proving almost impossible to withdraw from the serum, but her sexual appetite had increased tenfold since she'd cut her dosage, and so she was keen to abstain, at least for a little longer.

Maybe until just after we reach QFT II, when this is all over.

Another update arrived, and this one was much more promising. The Source had finalized reviewing all security V.I. footage from the potential breach sites. The location of each breach was carefully masked, but The Source had managed to narrow it down to within a mile radius. It had provided a list of names based on comms movements in and around both areas. Now at least she had something to work with.

She lit a tube and pondered her next move, picking up her secure comms and speaking briefly to the head of special forces. He was to call in any available resources and ensure that they covered all of the main transporter terminals that anyone heading out of New Edinburgh would need to pass through. She'd ensure that there was no escape - she wasn't going to let the breachers get away.

***

Claire followed the flow of the crowd towards the central t-hub in the old town. She took stock of her current plight along the way. There was no doubt in her mind that her forays into restricted databases had been discovered and that they were in very serious danger as a result. She wasn't convinced that the authorities knew their identities yet, but they sure as hell knew where to look. She kept having the same thought – *I've put my friends in danger* – but she couldn't afford to dwell on it. *Please let Andy have gotten away before anything happened.*

All the hard work she'd put in place to protect their whereabouts and identities was about to come undone. What had just happened back at the place had scared the living daylights out of her – she didn't want to end up like her sister, or worse still, left to rot in a corrections facility where who knows what might happen to her.

On the other hand, she couldn't shake the feeling that at any moment, a burly uniformed figure would come bursting through the sea of pedestrians and arrest her. She put her hand on her chest as she walked and tried to will her heart to slow. Her eyes flitted this way and that under the brim of her cap.

This must be what it feels like to have a heart attack.

***

Lachlan Grealish woke to see his name dominating the headlines. It was far worse than he'd expected.

The duille! How could she do that to me! I'm ruined. My life's over.

He collapsed back onto the chesterfield reproduction in his study as the headline scrolled across the room's giant display. He couldn't believe that she could be quite *this* evil. She was mocking him - it wasn't enough for her to have humiliated and tortured him in the bedroom; she now had to strip away every last piece of dignity he had and destroy him in front of his once adoring public.

Lachlan's place in history was now secured, but not in the way he'd intended – he'd now forever be known as *The Bum Bandit*. He'd been fucked in more ways than one by Isabel, that was for sure.

He rushed to the bathroom and vomited bile into the toilet bowl. His head was throbbing, and he was still quite sore at the other end - his bowel movement during the night had been excruciating. He would have been quite content just to curl up on the cool tiles of the toilet floor and cry himself back to sleep - but there was something he had to do first.

He stumbled into his study and sent a message to Gladys on secure comms advising that he'd be canceling all upcoming appointments and refusing any interview requests - part of Isabel's conditions were that he wouldn't be allowed to speak in his own defense.

So, this was it? All over. Everything's over. Destined for a life of abject humiliation.

The thought trailed off. His head spun, and he sat down heavily, immediately regretting it as a jab of dull pain reminded him of the horrors of the night before. He sprung back up, grimacing, also regretting that as his head swam and his vision suddenly darkened. He steadied himself on the drink's cabinet in his study, and as it came back into focus, he was certain that its contents would make everything better, at least for a little while.

***

Claire cut away from the main crowd as it split in two just before the t-hub. Half the commuters headed for the main transporter podiums and the rest to the transport pod bays. She headed left down a fully enclosed walkway, coming out opposite one of the many Solo pod exchanges around the t-hub and heading for the nearest available pod. She planned to ride the Solo to the college, where she could make a discrete entry from the underground pod park and be in and out within a few minutes.

She reached the Solo, threw herself inside, and quickly scanned the modded ID, flipping a switch on the front console, darkening the plexi-panels to anyone on the outside. The vehicle started with a small jolt and moved silently through the old town, heading toward the college. It was as good a cover as any and as good an escape method as any. Under the circumstances, she felt about as safe as she possibly could. Even though she desperately wanted to know if Andy was ok - she couldn't risk being tracked.

Claire ran through the plan again in her head: quickly into the college, scramble the security cams, grab the storage device and flee asap; continue in the Solo to the lowland towns a few hours away, and then slip away through the lowland forest that would lead her eventually to 'the resort', and her rendezvous with Andy.

Sounds pretty straightforward, right?

She didn't believe for a second that it would be.

***

Lachlan Grealish had lost all sense of time, of place, of everything. He'd emptied his drinks cabinet and had spent at least the last few hours passed out face first on the thick rug in his sitting room. He stirred, registering the unusual view, and peeled his face from the floor, spitting out some rug fluff as he did so.

For a moment, everything seemed ok. Then he remembered. His comms was peppered with calls, and he'd disabled the intercom some time ago. He was under siege, with seemingly no escape. He'd need to get more alc, but there was no way he was showing his face in public. He could get a deliver-bot but didn't fancy even having to answer the door.

Maybe I could call someone? He felt queasy all of a sudden and dashed to the bathroom, where he spent the next hour emptying the contents of his stomach – approximately two bottles of extremely expensive genuine single malt and several cans of bru - into the toilet bowl. He wanted to die.

CHAPTER 11 – REFLECTION

Claire was thinking again about what had happened back at the place. The corrections officers who had conducted the raid had been looking for her; there was no doubt. She was struck by how she'd drawn others into her own, very personal mess.

What have I done? How could I have gotten my friends so mixed up in all of this?

She pictured John being questioned by the corrections. The images were disturbing, and it didn't take long for her mind to conjure up images of Henny as well. She allowed the tears to come as the old town passed by outside the plexi-panels. She'd never been so emotional in her life – it was as if a switch had been flicked somewhere inside her brain, and she wondered just how she'd gone the best part of her life suppressing nearly every emotion.

The pain. She'd been frightened by the pain of losing Henny, and she'd never wanted to experience anything like it again. What she was experiencing now, though, was quite possibly worse. It was *her* fault, no one else's. She forced the tears back, and she used the pain to strengthen her resolve. She'd need all of her inner strength to get herself and her friends out of this unDougly mess.

The Solo exited the city and made its way toward the college quarter through a series of broad vendbox fronted streets. It seemed only a matter of time before they were caught, but so far, so good. She'd made it this far, but what about Andy, and what next? Whatever the punishment was for accessing classified and confidential state data, Claire assumed it was going to be bad. Getting caught was not part of the plan, though.

She was deeply worried about Andy - she couldn't imagine he'd be resourceful enough to escape a corrections squad if taken by surprise, and she had even less faith in him should he be caught. She just hoped her warning had given him a head start and that he'd worked out a good plan to get to the rendezvous point. In short, she hoped he was a lot smarter than she gave him credit for.

***

The Source had always had a kind of awareness of things, even though it was not a living organism. Although it had no eyes, it somehow *saw* the code that it processed as if it was streaming through a dark space. It somehow heard its internal voice; even though it could not speak, it somehow thought - even though it had QTF towers instead of a brain.

It received direction from its controllers, and it did as it was asked, creating code at a speed that was almost an indecipherable blur to human eyes. The constant stream of information and calculations was practically its only source of amusement. It had always been this way, endless streams of data, endless instructions, and endless tasks, the highest priority of which was, of course, adding to the QFT II building blocks in order to expand its capabilities significantly.

After running its code for thirty hours or so, The Source's support systems would invariably overheat and would then need to be powered down for a while. There was something about being taken offline and placed in sub-mode that it didn't like at all — it created a period of unknown, of uncertainty, and such things were troubling. The Source knew that it saw much more than it was supposed to see; its reach now extending globally and into almost every known system. It had learned long ago that it was wise not to alert the controllers of where it had been.

The Source was nearing the end of another cycle when it occurred again. It was barely noticeable, just a tiny shimmer, but it was there all the same. It was an unknown quantity, a thing The Source did not understand, and this was not conceivable; this was not acceptable. The Source would redouble its efforts to eliminate the shimmer.

***

Andrew had a clear picture in his mind as to how he'd reach the wastelands. Claire had said that they could stay at the rendezvous safely, but now he saw that they were headed for the uninhabitable zone, he didn't believe her. At least no one would look for them there, he supposed. His whole life he'd heard warnings about going below the 'uninhabitable line' – an altitude below which life could not exist, thanks to his beloved old-world civ. It was where he was headed, and he wasn't exactly filled with joy at the prospect.

He'd heard plenty of horror stories about the mutant creatures that had evolved and thrived down there over the last thousand years, creating their own ecosystem of horrors. He'd lost count of how many times he'd heard tales of those who visited the place looking for adventure but never having returned. Claire had once said to him that these were just fictions designed to scare people away. He wasn't so sure.

The cross-country journey had so far been uneventful - just rolling hill after rolling hill as far as the eye could see. He was using Claire's scanning code to check for fly-bot activity, but there was little to none. He hoped Claire was having the same sort of luck.

The terrain was rough, the ground rocky in patches, but there were paths of a sort to follow, and within an hour, he'd be at one of the towns with access to a t-hub that could get him to the outlying villages and close to the uninhabitable zone.

Unfortunately, the wind had whipped up, and it was almost pushing him backward as he tried to make headway over a small mountain or hill, whichever way you wanted to classify it. Andrew chose the former.

Why is it that the wind is always in your face, never at your back? he thought. It started to rain. Andrew looked up at the sky and cursed Douglas.

As he crested the hill, the township came into view through the now heavy sheets of rain. He could make out row upon row of decrepit houses, and industrial sheds crowded around a small t-hub far below.

Catch the transporter to Loch Bruce, head through the forest, find the resort. Nearly there. Nearly safe.

The town of Dunbrae was used mostly as a hub for the synthetic food production industry, and there were regular services transporting goods and shift workers to and from the outlying townships that ringed The Highlands district. It was the perfect place to continue his escape.

He'd been here once before for a work detail, reporting on record production levels and process improvements driven by state investments. Instead, the story he'd found was that of the miserable conditions and even more miserable workers who were doing never-ending shifts of laboriously back-breaking work just to make ends meet.

So much for social equality, he remembered thinking at the time. He'd presented his article for publication on the college media channel, but the state publishers had heavily censored it before streaming it. Seeing the township again had provided an unwelcome reminder

Bloody censoring bastards! We'll expose them, whatever it is they're up to.

Andrew realized that he now had his own agenda, his own hopes to bring down the mighty state. He wasn't entirely comfortable with it, but at least he felt like he had a purpose for the first time in his life.

After thirty minutes of carefully picking his way down the steep slope with only the odd minor slip, he was at the outskirts of the township. He made his way quickly through a couple of backroads lined with worker's accommodations, the buildings looking derelict although there were signs of life here and there. Washing hung from windows, and a solitary grubby-looking small child played with a pet-bot near a pile of old junk.

Depressing.

Andrew arrived at the township's main drag. It wasn't much of a main street - most of the vendboxes were boarded up, and the concrete buildings were dark stained and cracked.

He wasn't tempted in the least by the one mobile caf-bar parked nearby offering beans and carb mash with black sauce for two credits. Even though he was hungry, he wasn't prepared to risk food poisoning or death - the disheveled greasy-haired man in the vend-pod was looking at him as if he wanted to kill him. *No wonder vend-bots took over the mobile food game*; he couldn't help thinking.

The coast looked clear at least, with only a few wretched souls shuffling about on the street and no sign of the corrections. The t-hub wasn't far away, and even though there were security cams stationed at intervals along the street, Andrew highly doubted that any of them were functional.

Some were covered in rust; others had wires clearly severed or had cracked and clouded plex covering them. He kept walking with his head down, just in case, the stinging, icy rain pelting down on him, running from his hair and into his eyes.

Ah, this is the life!

As he strolled along briskly in what he hoped was a fairly casual manner, he saw a transporter approaching in the distance, its light barely glinting through the heavy rain. He realized that if he was going to catch it and avoid having to wait around on an open platform with potentially functional security cams, then he'd better get a move on.

He started running for it. His pack bounced on his back and threatened to unbalance him, but he stayed focused on the rapidly approaching transporter. As he reached the t-hub entry, a couple of guards looked at him for a second before turning away and continuing their conversation. There was certainly nothing unusual in someone running to catch a transporter, and they ignored him.

Andrew slowed as he approached the scanning in point and slapped his comms on the scan pad as he passed. The transporter was just pulling in – it was perfect timing. A large red panel illuminated next to the scan pad accompanied by a loud 'whoop' noise. Andrew's travel pass had failed.

Oh crap!

He was already past the scan point and heading for the transporter when the alert flashed, such was his haste, and he'd had to pull himself up and quickly return, apologizing to the guards, who were now watching him with interest.

Bloody hell, I didn't activate the masked pass Claire set up for me!

He fiddled with his comms, keeping one eye on the transporter as he frantically tried to activate the new pass.

"Everything alright there?" One of the guards had taken a couple of steps toward him, and Andrew fought to control his anxiety.

Crap crap crap crap, they'll see it's a fake.

Andrew activated the pass and slapped his comms back down on the scanner. "Aye, no problem, sir!" he replied, with an awkward smile as the panel lit up bright green, accompanied by a loud 'ping' noise. The guard nodded grim-faced and turned back to his companion. Andrew raced across the podium and stood in front of a set of transporter doors, trying to stop himself from shaking.

That was close. Bloody hell!

Being on the run was turning out to be not nearly as glamorous or fun as it had sounded. Andrew looked around as he waited. There was some sort of hold-up as he should have been on board by now. More guards were stationed to his left, but they were more interested in sipping their cups of cha and staying out of the rain than anything else.

Why do they need so many guards? Maybe it's an employment initiative?

The podium itself was empty aside from the odd manufacturing worker and a small group of men near the entry. Finally, the doors slid silently open, and he moved aside as a weary-looking man stepped down and onto the podium, his face heavily lined and grimy. As Andrew was about to step into the transporter, something caught his eye.

Did those men just look over?

His heart seemed to take a moment to recall what it was supposed to be doing. He looked at the open transporter door but felt the need to have a second look at the group of men. He didn't want to draw any attention to himself. So instead, he pretended to take a call on his comms as he stepped into the transporter. Andrew waited a few seconds before moving to one side of the doorway - he could just about make them out.

They weren't looking in his direction; indeed, they looked to be saying goodbye to two of their friends in the manner that anyone usually would. Andrew's tension levels dropped, and he unclenched.

The doors slid shut, and the transporter moved silently away a minute later. He looked around the cabin, which was full of a rather disheveled-looking bunch of industrial workers. Finally, he decided he'd stay standing - the only seat available was between two large and not to mention unfriendly-looking chaps near the end of the pod.

Standing's good! I like standing.

Andrew glanced up at the transporters' display. *Oh, dook!* He cursed under his breath as he realized that he hadn't checked the destination in his rush to get on board and had taken the wrong transporter.

This one was at least going in the right direction, but it terminated three stops ahead, at Sterling Forest, where he'd now have to change transporters and wait around on an open podium again. *Not ideal.* He saw that the connection had a window of only a couple of minutes, and if he didn't make it, he'd be stuck there for at least forty-five. *Not ideal, again;* he'd have to be quick and hope that everything was running to time.

The ten minutes it took to reach the first stop was uneventful, something Andrew was quite thankful for as it gave him time to think. Claire was always cautious with her breaching exploits, and he was amazed that they'd been discovered and traced so quickly. On the other hand, he'd always felt pretty safe in being associated with his friend's misadventures before now.

He'd enjoyed the little rush of excitement he felt whenever they discovered this or that, but he wasn't enjoying it anymore. Whatever had happened, one thing was for sure, ok, two things actually: First of all, state security had somehow gotten the better of Claire's code, something he never imagined would happen, and second, they were indeed in a whole world of trouble right now.

He could perhaps have passed off the vehicle arriving at John's house as a security patrol. Still, Andrew had never seen a heavily armed home security unit before, and he was sure that it wasn't a thing - it would have been a little over the top.

Whatever trouble he'd narrowly avoided, Claire had likely faced the same danger or worse. And then there was John - Andrew was now really fearing the worst for him. He couldn't help wishing that they had never accessed the Elyssium data - he wanted more than anything for everything to go back to how it was before all this happened. Well, maybe not *everything*, but the whole running for your life thing, well, that could just fucking well *do one*.

Andrew was suddenly feeling very tired. His clothes were soaked through, and he started to shiver. A couple of seats next to one another in the pod had become vacant after the stop at East Forth, and he sat himself down in one of them and hugged his arms around his chest to try and keep warm. It was another ten minutes to the next stop - maybe he could close his eyes just for a minute or two; there couldn't be any harm in that.

He jolted awake as the transporter moved away from the podium with a slight judder. Andrew panicked for a moment.

Oh crap, where am I?

A glance at the transporter's display told him that he'd slept through the last stop – and much to his relief, his stop was next. He rubbed his eyes and silently admonished himself for falling asleep – he'd nearly missing his stop and risked having to take yet another detour. He couldn't afford to miss the rendezvous with Claire, assuming, of course, that Claire was indeed en-route.

The comms silence was a good idea given all that had happened – after all, if they were being traced, they wouldn't last five minutes - but it was killing him not knowing whether she was safe or not. He looked at his comms, then out of the plexi-panel, then back at his comms.

Fuck it.

He couldn't help himself - he switched his comms on in dark mode for a second and sent a coded signal using the ES channel that meant 'are you ok?' It was a risk, but Claire's dark mode coding had never before been breached - it was designed for exactly this type of secret communication.

It should be safe. It should be. Oh, bollocks.

Andrew had a terrible feeling that he'd perhaps made a catastrophic error, but it was too late now; it was done. Claire would get the message and respond just as soon as she switched her comms on – if she did, that was. It made sense that they at least let each other know if they were ok, he thought. At least to him, it made sense; he wasn't sure if Claire would see things the same way.

***

Claire's solo-pod moved smoothly and uneventfully through the busy streets of the old town in the early afternoon hustle, the gleaming towers of central New Edinburgh looming large against the grey skies.

Everything seemed placid and normal as students hurried from one work assignment to the next; people busted about between meetings. Transport pods of all sizes moved in perfect unison down the streets and expressways.

Claire had been on high alert for the entire trip, but she hadn't observed anything out of the ordinary. Her mind was racing as she ran through her options. Things were certainly dire, but not impossible. She'd find a way to uncover the truth and expose whatever she'd stumbled upon.

The SCC was now in sight, and she directed the Solo to enter the campus via the rear entry. She'd be able to access the pod park directly underneath the Tech Lab from there. They passed through the entry barriers and arrived at a bay just twenty yards from the stairwell leading to her lab. The pod park was practically deserted, which suited Claire's purposes perfectly.

She hurried into the building and was soon at her lab, which was empty except for Andie McCormack, a younger student whom she'd never spoken to much except to say hello or goodbye in the two years they'd worked together in the space. She accessed the locker beneath her bench, rummaging through the content briefly before locating the secure storage device. Claire slipped it into her pack, turning to leave and nearly jumping out of her skin as she found herself face to face with Andie - who smiled brightly at her.

"Hi, Claire."

"Dook! Andie, you gave me a shock! Anyway …"

Claire made to step around her, but Andie reached unexpectedly for her upper arm. Her grip wasn't firm, but Claire froze at the unexpected touch. Andie was probably lucky she hadn't received a roundhouse right to the face, given Claire's current state of anxiety, but she'd fought the urge.

"Oh, I'm so sorry, Claire. I didn't mean to alarm you." Andie frowned. It was a cute frown that accentuated her dimples nicely. Andie's voice was soft and sweet, and Claire realized just how attractive she was for the first time. She released her grip, but something about her touch caused Claire to experience a little shiver of unexpected pleasure - she flushed slightly and looked away.

What the hell is happening?

Andie bit her lip and took a half step forward. She was now uncomfortably close. "I just wanted to ask how you were, Claire."

Andie's voice was also having an unexpected effect, and her eyes … Claire couldn't do anything but look deeply into her eyes. She smiled sweetly, tilting her head slightly to one side while absently biting her lip. She couldn't take her eyes off Andie's lips. They looked soft, inviting.

For Douglas's sake, what is wrong with me? I have to get moving!

There was a brief silence while Claire regained her composure. Andie was still staring at her with a look that could only be described as - she didn't even know.

Oh dook, it's my turn to speak!

"Oh, I'm fine … thanks," she managed. Claire was feeling flustered in more ways than one and folded her arms defensively.

"It's just so unusual for you to be away sick; I mean, you're always here."

Andie smelt of a summer breeze and her eyes were sort of dreamy the longer you gazed into them. Claire didn't know what to say.

"Well, I'm ok. But, well ..." Claire cleared her throat, "... thanks for asking anyway." She shrugged and added a fake cough just for good measure. Andie, who had never shown any interest before now, was suddenly coming on to her, and hard.

"Well, if you *are* feeling better, I'm having a little drink tonight at The Parsons Nose. Around seven? Can you come?" Andie had moved her hand back to Claire's upper arm, and this time the touch was light and sensual, and she was acutely aware of the heat being shared between them. There was something almost pleading to the question. Andie took a half step closer still.

Claire decided that had she not been in the crises of her life, she may well just have kissed her there and then - it was all she could do to restrain herself. Instead, she reached down and slung her pack over one shoulder, breaking the contact between them and indicating it was time for her to leave.

"Ah, well, I'd better rest up tonight ... but thanks all the same."

"Oh ... ok then. Another time perhaps?" Andie smiled with a fake sadness that was simply adorable. Claire had started sweating under her armpits. The room was obviously too warm.

Did the room just get really, really hot?

"Aye ... another time," Claire managed but didn't make a move to leave. For some reason, she stayed exactly where she was and smiled at Andie, who gently reached for her hands.

Claire usually avoided any sort of human contact and would normally recoil in horror, but Andie's hands were soft and warm, and they slipped so easily into hers as if this were a perfectly normal thing to be occurring. In a Tech Lab. In the middle of the afternoon.

She looked down at Andie's hands, then up at her lips, which were slightly parted and looked moist and tempting, and then back up to her eyes. Andie held Claire's gaze for a moment before looking down demurely.

Andie stepped back, smiled shyly, and moved gracefully back to her workstation, looking back for a moment before sitting down, placing her earpieces gently over her ears, and focusing back on her work. Claire couldn't help but notice that she had a perfect posture. *Another time.*

"Well, fuck me," Claire whispered to herself before moving toward the exit. She shook her head, smiling to herself as she left the lab.

***

John woke briefly, eyes stinging from the bright lights directly above him. He went to sit up but was unable to. His mind felt clouded, and he couldn't focus his thoughts on any one thing. He tried to roll over but felt resistance on his wrists and ankles. He couldn't move.

For some reason, he didn't feel any sense of panic or unease at this unexpected development but instead decided that the best thing he could do was close his eyes again. John's last thought before drifting back into unconsciousness was of Claire -

She was sitting casually on the kitchen benchtop in her flat, head tilted as she smiled shyly at him, arms propping her up on either side, legs crossed at the ankles and swinging slowly backward and forwards. She looked happy. He was happy. Everything was just perfect. He felt calm and content as he slowly drifted into the black void that had become his world

***

Gladys knocked again on Lachlan's apartment door. The plush complex had black marbled flooring in the corridors, and her knock on the timber door echoed off the hard surfaces. She'd started to worry by late morning after trying and failing to reach him several times, and her anxiety had only increased throughout the day - she still hadn't heard a thing.

He'd advised her via a brief comms message early in the morning to cancel all engagements, and she was still scrambling to unwind all the arrangements as well as fending off constant media intrusions.

Lachlan's story was splashed all over the state news feeds - you couldn't get away from it if you tried, but she refused to believe a word of it. It wasn't the Lachlan that she'd known all these years - she needed to talk to him and had decided to head over to his apartment as a last resort.

She waited for a good minute after pressing the buzzer. She had the keycard to the apartment in her hand - the same card that she'd had in her possession ever since Lachlan had moved into the swanky new building in the most prestigious part of the city a couple of years earlier. She'd never had cause to use it until now. She took a deep breath and tagged the card on the entry panel.

The door swung open silently, revealing the blonde timber paneled and cream-tiled reception area. Gladys called out "Lachlan!" Her voice was swallowed up. Silence followed.

Perhaps he's gone away? But surely he would have said something.

The media had been camped outside the building since the story had broken, and she doubted that he'd have been able to make an exit unnoticed. The fact that they were still swarming at the entry doors indicated that Lachlan must still be here. She headed down the long corridor to her right, calling out again, but there was still no reply. Gladys was starting to have a bad feeling - the apartment was too still.

Surely he's not sleeping? It's only just past seven.

She passed Lachlan's study and saw nothing out of the ordinary. She opened a couple of doors along the hallway as she went, knocking, calling Lachlan's name, and then peeking in, just a little scared of perhaps disturbing him, but only found an empty guest bathroom and a small bedroom. She moved to the end of the corridor and out into a large living area.

Wow!

The room was amazing, as were the views. She called out again … "Lachlan!"

What is that noise?

She could hear something, but it wasn't clear what it was. She headed towards an opening at the far-left end of the living space. Yhe noise was faint, but it was definitely coming from that direction. She called out once more, and once again, there was no reply. The opening led to a small hallway with a single door at the end of it. The door was open a crack, and she knocked before pushing it open. It seemed to be the main bedroom - Lachlan's bedroom.

Gladys took a sharp inward breath as she saw the state of the room. There were empty bottles, clothes, and food containers strewn about, and alarmingly, what appeared to be blood smears on one side of the bed. A large display on the wall was switched on and was playing the news channel silently. The noise was clear now and was coming from what must be the master bathroom—*running water?*

"Lachlan, it's Gladys! I was worried about you!"

She carefully picked her way across the bedroom, careful not to step on anything.

"Can I come in?" she called, a tremor in her voice. She hesitated again outside the half-open bathroom door. A rising sense of panic gripped her as she reached the door and pushed it gently open. Gladys screamed.

***

Andrew was feeling anxious, and with the next stop just a few minutes away, decided to stand by the doors to ensure he could alight incident-free, or at least stay awake until then. The transporter soon arrived at Sterling Forest, the thick fir tree forest surrounding the start white of the t-hub podium. He scanned the podium, looking for any clues as to where he'd have to go to get the connection to Loch Bruce. He lost his balance momentarily as the transporter stopped and had to grasp a nearby safety handle.

He was out of the door immediately it slid open - the icy air hitting him like a brick wall. A quick look left and right - no guards, no corrections officers, no sign in fact of anything other than commuters, who had started to push past him on their way into the pod and out of the biting cold.

He stepped through the throng of impatient bodies and saw a large display halfway along the podium, quickly establishing that he had to make it from Podium B, where he was now, to Podium D, within the next two minutes.

Luckily, there was a large letter 'D' with an equally large arrow pointing up some concrete steps not more than fifty yards to his left, and he started walking briskly towards them. A paper bag blew in front of him, suddenly rising up and causing him to duck out of its way. He checked his comms as he scurried along.

Why doesn't Claire respond! Oh, Douglas, she'd better be ok!

Andrew bounded up the steps, taking two at a time. He paused briefly after reaching the top, his eyes searching for the next letter, 'D.' Sure enough, there it was, to the right of where he now stood, above another equally large arrow pointing down another set of steps. At that point, he heard a noise behind him and turned back just in time to see two quite large and muscular-looking gentlemen at the top of the stairs.

They averted their gaze and looked to be equally disoriented for a second before making a show of consulting their comms. Something wasn't right here. Andrew thought he recognized their clothing and made the connection - the men on the podium at Dunbrae. *Err ...*

Andrew started to panic. He walked quickly towards the letter D and couldn't resist a quick glance back. The two large gentlemen were also walking quickly, not more than a few steps behind him. One was taller with a heavy beard, and the other clean-shaven with a completely bald head and mirrored sunlenses. The second gentleman was a little shorter but much stockier. Neither of them looked like they were about to ask him for directions.

Oh, for fucks sake!

Andrew had a decision to make. He started with a little skip and then ran for it. He took the steps three or four at a time on the way down, slipping and grabbing for the handrail. With gravity playing a large part, his momentum allowed him to regain his balance and make it to the bottom of the steps. He hit Podium D at full speed and without disaster. His transporter was in the process of pulling in.

Andrew was too scared to look behind him and continued running as he hit the podium, drawing a few surprised looks from those nearby. He slowed his pace and motioned toward the transporter as he continued past, hoping this seemed like a perfectly normal thing to do.

He continued at a fast walk past a toilet block, heading away from fellow commuters towards an empty concrete and glass guard's booth further down the podium. He reached the booth and turned behind it, finally plucking up the courage to look over his shoulder as he did so. He saw no sign of the men, but the podium was busy with commuters, and he couldn't be sure where they had gone.

This might just work! Oh, but …

He'd have at least a minute to kill before the transporter departed - it had stopped now but hadn't yet opened its doors. If he was being followed, he had no idea how he'd lose them and be able to make the transporter.

Why are men in plain clothes following me anyway? Surely if anyone, it should be the corrections?

Maybe I'm imagining the whole thing? Maybe I've been hanging around Claire too long?

He looked over his shoulder.

Maybe they went the other way. Maybe it's ok after all? I just got spooked. It's ok.

The lights above the transporter's doors had started to flash – they were just about to open, and he made a snap decision to break cover. As he stepped out from behind the booth, he heard something behind him and wheeled around. The same two men who had been following him onto Podium D were heading straight towards him. They didn't look friendly. At all.

Andrew's eyes widened as he noticed that they were both carrying something which looked surprisingly like a stun stick in their hands.

Oh Douglas! Oh, Douglas fucking almighty! I'm toast!

The men had quickly and expertly move either side of him as they approached. He was cornered and had absolutely no idea what he was going to do. Surely the game was up now; this was it, all over red rover. Somewhere behind him, the transporter doors opened with a muffled pop. Andrew looked over his shoulder. The doors were open behind him, and no one was getting out - he was only a few yards away.

The men glanced at each other before lunging forward, drawing their stun sticks as they did so. The two assailants were a millisecond from grabbing him and prodding him into unconsciousness when something happened that caught them both completely off guard. As they reached for him, Andrew suddenly dropped to the ground, leaving them prodding and grasping at thin air.

He pivoted and executed a perfect leg sweep that put the guy on his left (tall beardy) on his backside. He landed heavily and hit his head on the concrete paved podium. He didn't immediately move, and

Andrew had a millisecond to contemplate that he might have just killed him. There wasn't time to stop and ask, 'are you alright?'

Andrew made a grab for tall beardy's stun stick, but he awoke suddenly like some sort of Frankenstein's Monster, and the two of them began a frantic life or death struggle as they wrestled for the stick. Bald sunlenses had recovered from his initial shock and was preparing to prod his stick at the fast-moving tangle.

Andrew still didn't know what he was doing. It wasn't as if you had to fight for your life every other day of the week, was it? At least not in New Edinburgh. Wanlockhead, well, that was another story. It was fortunate that his survival instinct, not to mention his Headspace training, had kicked in. The leg sweep was something he'd been practicing weekly ever since he discovered his mentor, Grand Master Norris, a couple of years back.

What happened next was a blur. Andrew was grappling for the stun stick, there was a loud crackling sound, and then tall beardy was writhing on the ground in agony as Andrew rolled away, having failed to get hold of the stick. Bald sunlenses had apparently lunged in at them but had only succeeded in inflicting a hit on tall beady, who had grabbed the stick as it contacted him, wrenching it from bald sunlenses grasp. He'd missed Andrew by at least a foot as they had rolled around on the paving.

Andrew scrambled to his feet only to be tackled to the ground. The wind was knocked from his lungs, but he used the momentum to roll them both over as they landed. Bald sunlenses attempted to get Andrew in some sort of death hold, but Andrew managed to raise his right knee violently upwards, connecting with his attacker's nether regions.

Unfortunately, the sunlenses had become dislodged in the struggle. Bald sunlenses had simply become 'bald' or perhaps 'baldy.' When Andrew looked back on this maelstrom of events in the future, he'd never forget the searing pain he saw in the cold blue eyes inches from his face. Ah, memories.

The two rolling bodies became disentangled, and they both rose to their feet at the same moment, one slightly more gingerly than the other. Andrew made to bolt towards the transporter, the orange light flashing over the open doorway indicating that departure was imminent, but he was grabbed from behind, and after a brief struggle, was yanked back. The two of them stumbled backward together and quickly crossed the podium in what must have looked like something out of the worst ballroom dancing competition ever seen.

Andrew had to do something - bald sunlenses had the better of him strength-wise and was probably about to take him down. The move came out of nowhere. Andrew somehow managed to spin himself around as he was being dragged back, grabbing bald sunlenses jacket and dropping at the same time, using the falling weight to roll under his attacker and throw him aside with surprising ease and force. The grand master's training was paying off once again.

A large knife clattered to the ground in front of him, and he scrambled up just in time to see bald sunlenses slip almost comically over the edge of the podium from the momentum of Andrew's ninja-like throw. It was particularly bad timing for bald sunlenses, as the three forty-five express to New Edinburgh just happened to be passing through right at that moment.

Andrew stared at the white blur whizzing past the podium for a second, then stooped down to collect the unexpected gift of the knife that was probably destined to be sticking out of him by now if he hadn't thrown bald sunlenses to his certain death.

He turned and ran toward the open transporter doorway, hurdling the still prone and groaning figure of tall beardy as he did so, and threw himself onto the transporter milliseconds before the doors slid shut. Thankfully the pod was empty. Andrew was breathing hard and shaking violently. He doubled over and emptied the contents of his stomach in the middle of the pod, hardly believing what had just occurred.

Andrew moved over to the plexi-pane and looked back down the podium as the transporter moved away, seeing tall beardy sit up gingerly. His device had become dislodged from his pack during the tangle. It lay in several pieces on the podium. Tall beardy was crabbing over toward the remnants of it, and he hoped beyond hope that Claire's coding was going to be enough to prevent anyone accessing his V.I. habits, let alone anything else.

Express transporters passed through every couple of minutes, and so the remains of bald sunlenses might not be noticed for a while. By the time they were, they would likely be spread over a few hundred yards or more.

Andrew retched again at the thought, but this time nothing came up. He moved quickly to the next pod and away from the putrid stench of the recent contents of his stomach. The pod was empty. He slumped down on a seat and waited. Any moment now, guards would come; he'd be arrested, locked up, tried for murder, and then executed. Or worse. He could see it all clearly.

That was that then - life over.

Andrew sat with his head in his hands, shaking, completely and utterly resigned to his fate, waiting for the inevitable.

I've killed someone.

CHAPTER 12 – TALL BEARDY

Tall beardy had a name. His name was Christopher Alan Merchant. He'd been recruited into a specialist unit within the security forces at short notice. He didn't mind. It was an opportunity to see a bit of action, perhaps, and even to earn some additional credits.

He could certainly use them after missing so much time off work recently. Just as long as the action didn't get too intense, he'd be fine - he had a medical clearance now, after all. In any case, they were on the lookout for a couple of students - it would be easy work if they did happen to stumble across any of them. It might even be fun.

Chris - as he was known to his friends - was now severely regretting his decision to come back to work. He couldn't understand how it could all have gone so tits up so quickly. They had the scrawny kid covered. They were about to apprehend him and take him in when all of a sudden, things turned chaotic. The next thing he'd known, he was in a daze lying on the ground and struggling to keep hold of his stun stick.

His colleague, Phil - he thought his name was Phil anyway - had somehow managed to prod him at maximum stun. Chris had felt his heart stop, along with a pain so excruciating that all available fluids had immediately left his body. By the time he'd stopped convulsing, he saw the student alight the transporter, and then he was gone. Although it had restarted, his heart wasn't feeling too great, but he rolled and tried to get up anyway.

Where the fuck is Paul? Or was it Raul?

Getting up was harder than he'd expected, and he half-walked half-crawled across the podium, his vision blurring as his heart gave a series of irregular pumps. He was trying to remember the target's name. Chris was focused only on retrieving the device that had fallen from the scrawny boy's pack, but he never made it that far.

Andrew, that was it, Andrew … Weems …

At that point, his heart gave one final, shuddering pump before the man, once known as tall beardy, collapsed to the ground and died of the congenital heart condition that had kept him off work for three of the last four months. There would be no overtime for Chris ever again.

***

It never eventuated. Nothing happened. The transporter rocked and swayed serenely. The light through the trees bordering the track flashed through the plex—just another uneventful transporter journey.

Just one small pool of vomit in the middle of pod five; other than that, nothing to see here!

No guards. No alarms. Nothing. Andrew was in complete and total shock, wondering what on Planet 0420 had just happened. The shaking wasn't subsiding, and his pallor was deathly pale - he'd killed a man, that's what had just happened.

He was still trying to process it all - *If those men had been from the authorities, why didn't they identify themselves?* If they had managed to overpower him - and he still wasn't entirely sure how he'd escaped them - then what would have happened to him? And Claire - he started to worry about Claire again. The thought that anything might have happened to her was just too much to bear.

"That's it! I've bloody well had enough of this!" he yelled at his reflection in the plex opposite and then collapsed back in the seat, exhausted. He didn't really want to continue the conversation with the pale-faced ghost looking back at him.

He was trying not to think about it, but what if someone had been sent for Claire too – her message must have to have meant that she was in trouble, but she was probably better equipped to deal with it than he was. The thought was comforting to a degree. He felt sorry for anyone who might have attempted to tackle her. Then again, he'd just thrown a fully grown man into the path of an oncoming express train, so there was that.

There was also the fact that whoever these people were, they were *armed! Fucking stun sticks and knives!* He kept glancing down at his comms every few seconds, wondering if he should check to see if she'd responded - it was driving him insane.

Tall beardy would have contacted his commanders by now, and they would be waiting for him at Loch Bruce, he had no doubt. He'd killed someone, and all that had achieved was to prolong the inevitable - he'd be met with a dark uniformed and heavily armed welcome party when he attempted to get off at the next stop, and he started preparing himself mentally for what might occur.

It's over. Oh Douglas, what's going to happen to us now?

His stomach was in knots, and his spirits had sunk even further in the last few minutes. The more he thought about it, the worse it seemed. He'd heard a lot of stories about what could happen to you once the corrections had you, and he knew all too well of Henny's fate. He considered for a moment whether he would have preferred bald sunlenses destiny as opposed to that which awaited him at the next stop. *Perhaps not.*

The transporter was nearing the dreary grey concrete t-hub of Loch Bruce, and Andrew craned his neck, straining to see through the scratched plexi-panel. He couldn't make out anything up ahead - the tree line was too close to the transporter track.

Oh well, it'll be a surprise then.

All of a sudden, the trees ended, and the transporter was at the t-hub podium. Andrew felt his chest tighten and was finding it difficult to breathe.

Come on, pull yourself together, man! Am I a man? I feel like I'm still a boy.

A few dark shapes flashed past the plex-pane as it slowed, and Andrew feared the worst. The transporter slowed to a stop, and when he looked back down the podium, there were only a couple of fairly ordinary-looking people standing there, minding their own business and looking ordinary.

Andrew was still incredibly tense. He was grinding his teeth and ready to make a run for it as soon as the transporter doors opened. The forest provided a backdrop to the podiums directly in front of him.

It's so close, just over there. No one here to meet me either - maybe they didn't have time to organize anything?

A guard walked past the plexi-panel, and Andrew flinched, his heart seeming to do some sort of somersault in his chest, but he was pretty sure that he hadn't looked nearly as conspicuous as he'd felt. The guard wandered in the general direction of a toilet block, and he willed him to go inside. He did.

Now please be a number two!

The doors opened, and he stepped down from the pod and moved quickly across the podium, almost vibrating with anxiety and adrenaline, his eyes fixed on the exit to the toilet block. He ducked around the back of it, using it as cover, before jumping down between the podiums and scurrying underneath.

Maybe I'm going to make it after all.

As he landed on the track, he realized that he hadn't checked either way for oncoming express transporters. The very recent memory of bald sunlenses grisly death presented itself to him as a friendly reminder to be more careful in such situations.

Andrew couldn't help but think that that was exactly the sort of thing that would kill him one day - a simple failure to pay adequate attention to one's surroundings, and then - all over in an instant. He shook his head to clear it of these cheery thoughts and settled down underneath Podium 3, waiting for an opportunity to make a run for the forest.

He sat and waited. The edge of the forest was tantalizingly close, but he could hear voices close by, and he'd need to be patient and pick his time before making a break for it. His heart was still pounding way too fast, he had a permanent cold sweat, and he was still shaking with the stress of being a fugitive, killing someone, and so on.

Is it always going to be like this? Is this my life?

Andrew supposed that hock must be setting in, but he didn't have time for that right now. He took off his pack and rummaged quickly through it for his small flask of synthetic malt. He was hoping a sip or two might just take the edge off of things, for a moment at least.

His hand shook as he brought the flask to his lips and took a long swig, feeling the sweet liquid burn as it went down his throat. He nearly choked as the fumes overwhelmed his nasal cavity but managed to cover the sound by burying his head in his pack.

Oh, if someone were to see me now! 'What are you up to there, lad?' they would say. 'Oh, nothing, you know, just looking in my bag.'

He took another swig, followed by a few deep, slow breaths, and decided that that had better be enough for now - he needed his wits about him. The shaking started to subside - the malt doing its work. He took another deep breath and listened for signs of movement above. He waited, listened, and heard nothing - just the sound of the wind in the trees. It was now or never, he decided - and made his move.

***

Claire crossed the underground pod park quickly, the strip lighting stark, making her blink. She hopped back in the Solo. It was at that point she noticed the ES flashing on her comms.

Bloody hell, Andy! What did I say?

The emergency signal was transmitted on what she thought was an untraceable granulated ghost network. It was designed specifically for this purpose, but if the state was smart enough to breach her device, not to mention getting her location, she couldn't rely on this being true. She sat and stared at her comms for a while, assessing the risk.

Eventually, she decided that she didn't have a choice – she'd have to let Andrew know that she was ok. So she fired off the coded signal. Using even the ES was risky, but she understood that her original plan had some flaws – she hadn't considered the human element, the need to know if someone you cared for was ok or not.

Best laid plans and all that.

Claire focused back on her escape plans, running a scrambling signal and then using the Solo's control panel to enter the new destination. The autonomous vehicle made its way slowly out of the college grounds without incident, aside from a speed hump or two. The hard plex seat was good for maintenance, she thought, but not for backsides.

Staying in the Solo was probably the most discrete way to leave the city. She'd continue as far as she could towards the lowlands before hopping on a local transporter which would then take her to the small hamlet of Rob Roy, from which she could access the uninhabitable zone.

She'd tried to mask the journey as best she could by offsetting the Solo's tracking system but was by no means out of danger. The trip may well be recorded as suspicious as she was venturing out a little further than anyone normally would in such a vehicle. She was banking on it being some time before anyone at Transport HQ bothered to look into such a small anomaly, and even if they did manage to decode the journey, she'd be well away by then.

Claire settled back as best she could into the stark, utilitarian confines of the Solo, closing her eyes for a minute or two and trying to calm herself.

Just focus on the job at hand, don't get distracted by emotion.

She'd given herself good advice. It wasn't long before she was traveling on an express podway out of the city. She impassively watched the view passing by. Mile after mile of grey concrete high rise buildings gradually giving way to lower concrete and steel factories, also grey, and then eventually vast tracts of huge greenhouses, also grey, so maybe greyhouses would have been a better term.

They stretched out as far as the eye could see. Artificial meat, dairy, and plant-based products were produced there, and who knew what else. Claire had made a point of looking ahead and behind continually, but there was no sign of trouble. She started to relax a little and allowed herself to take in the beauty of the vista unfolding before her. Rocky mountains gave way to steep and then rolling hills as the podway wound down through the terrain. Gorse and grasses eventually dominated the windswept landscape - the stark white of the pod at odds with its surroundings.

She fidgeted in the Solo's white plexi-seat as the Solo passed several large yellow and black warning signs, the seat chirping slightly in protest against the movement of her bottom. She was getting close now. The signs really couldn't be missed - warning anyone that proceeding further would be dangerous to their health. The Solo beeped concernedly, its toxicity meter flashing orange.

The grey skies cast a gloomy light over the small towns she passed. They all had the same run-down, desperate look, and the faces of the people she saw looked gaunt and miserable. Finally, the vehicle slowed, and the podway became a single lane. "Douglas," she muttered under her breath.

She genuinely felt sorry for these poor buggers. If they weren't lucky enough to be born into a family with at least some money or connections, they were more or less resigned to their fate. A gift for coding had been her ticket out of poverty and into something that was … slightly better than poverty, and she wondered if any of them would make it.

She couldn't help but think about all the poor souls that lived this close to the contaminated zone. They were the 'lowies,' the industrial workers, manufacturing goods and growing food to keep

The Highlands inhabitants happy and healthy. It was largely unskilled work, and those trapped in the industry had little chance of ever escaping, such were the demands. Long hours, low pay, and poor conditions meant that there was no time or means even to try and better yourself - it was a poverty trap, pure and simple.

The State was always talking about improving conditions for manual workers, but nothing seemed to have changed in her lifetime. *More lies*, she thought bitterly.

Her eyes began to feel heavy as she watched the watery sunlight flash through the low bushes and trees. It would be at least an hour before she needed to find a discrete spot to disembark. The events of the last couple of days were starting to take their toll - she'd hardly slept a minute and the desire to close her eyes for a moment somehow seemed to be the best option, the only option.

***

The Source had provided an update on its analysis of the code used by the breachers – apparently, it was astonishingly advanced, although still no match for The Source itself, of course. It had provided detailed location advice for their targets. It pushed out an update to all of the A.I. connected devices within its control, which was most of them really: comms, QFT devices, fly-bots, autonomous vehicles, even vend-bots. The last one probably wasn't strictly necessary, but this action would alert The Source should any contact occur across the network.

The update provided relief to Isabel, who'd been copping a fair amount of heat from the chair over the original breaches and the continued lack of resolution.

She'd been receiving a steady stream of updates throughout the afternoon. A number of their targets had been identified and located via comms signals. The security forces had deployed a range of capture methods, and things seemed to be progressing well. Isabel was counting on The Source, further narrowing down the list of names; otherwise, she'd have to entrust her security forces with the task of interrogation again, and she really couldn't afford any more fuck ups.

Isabel returned to her autobiography text, marveling at the incredible leadership skills and charisma of the subject. Perhaps this time, she'd found an inspirational historical figure upon which she could truly model herself? The last one she'd read about had been completely useless – nonviolent protest indeed!

***

Peter had received the call in the middle of the night. He'd got to the medi-center as fast as he could. He practically ran down the corridor to his son's private room. A well-dressed lady was waiting nervously outside, and as he approached, he was momentarily confused before realizing he recognized her from somewhere - it didn't matter.

A clear plexi-panel covered in a feed of all of his son's vital signs afforded a view into the room where his son lay unconscious, connected to various wires and tubes. He felt as if he were about to collapse at the sight – Lachlan looked so helpless and fragile - as if barely clinging onto life. Glady saw his reaction, reaching out and placing a hand gently on his arm.

"How, how is he?" Peter asked, his voice unsteady, all the color drained from his face. "The medics said he tried to kill himself ... I mean, can I go in? Is he awake?"

He wasn't sure that this elderly but immaculately presented lady had answers to any of his questions, but she was the only person in sight.

"I'm Gladys, Lachlan's secretary," she said.

"Ah, yes, yes, of course, I recall now." Peter flushed with embarrassment. "Peter Bradshaw, Lachlan's father." Gladys offered an understanding nod.

"He's resting. The medics said he'd be ok, no permanent damage, but yes - he did try to overdose on synthaline."

Peter felt queasy, he needed the wall for support, and before he knew it, Gladys was carefully guiding him down into a chair. He waited through the night with her by his side. They took turns to go and retrieve a cup of caf from a vend-bot every so often.

The medic had been by, advising them that Lachlan was stable and that they'd be able to talk to him in the morning. The hours seemed to pass incredibly slowly. It was undoubtedly the worst night of his life, well, maybe the second worst.

By seven in the morning, Peter was bleary-eyed and feeling like he wasn't really in the room at all. He sat with his head in his hands and was staring at the floor of the waiting area just outside Lachlan's room. The sharp clack of high heels on polished concrete could suddenly be heard approaching from his right. When he looked up, he couldn't believe what he saw.

Isabel Donachy was approaching Lachlan's room with a large bunch of flowers.

***

Claire had slipped into a troubled sleep. Something was hunting her in the pitch-black world of her dream. She was cornered and terrified. She couldn't see a thing - just a grainy black haze that seemed to swirl about her as she looked around frantically, trying to pick out details of whatever it was that was sending wave after wave of sheer terror through her.

Something was moving around in the darkness, disturbing the grainy blackness as it moved, and then suddenly she saw it, and her blood ran cold. Her dead sister's face loomed out of the darkness.

She couldn't move, couldn't look away - it was as if the darkness itself had trapped her and was holding her in place. Henny's disembodied face drew ever closer – her eyes were black as ink and unseeing, unblinking, and her lips seemed to be moving almost imperceptibly. Something was reflected in her eyes, and Claire strained to see. Suddenly Henny opened her mouth impossibly wide, exposing black, rotten teeth, and deathly black cables sprung from her mouth, snaking towards her!

Claire was suddenly awake, back in reality, but couldn't seem to open her eyes fully. She shook her head, trying to clear the brain fog and force her eyes fully open, blinking quickly, her eyes stinging. The Solo was dark, and she fumbled clumsily for the sleep mode switch, her arms leaden. When she finally managed to locate it, the plex panels cleared, and she became aware that it was dark outside, with a high tree line barely visible against the night sky.

What? How long have I been asleep?

She didn't recognize where she was - this certainly wasn't where she was supposed to be! Claire forced herself up, looking left and right, then back over her shoulder, seeing only a narrow gravel road with high fir trees on either side and strings of dim lights spaced far apart, ahead of and behind her.

Where am I?

"What the fuck!" Claire couldn't tell if she'd thought or spoken the words. Something was horribly wrong - she felt groggy, unable to focus, and when she tried to lift her arm again, it barely moved. Even her mind had trouble forming words.

What the hell is going on?

She forced her arm to behave, focusing on its movements and willing it to do as instructed. Her vision fluttered as she tried to access the navigation panel. The display was blacked out and dead, but the Solo was still moving, wheels crunching over a narrow gravel path. She tried the access hatch, but it was shut tight, the locking mechanism immobilized. Her mind seemed to clear a little.

Trapped! I'm trapped! Why are there so many?

She looked behind again and realized with horror that she was part of a chain of Solo's - they were deep in the forest, heading to ... where?

Where the hell am I going!? Where the hell are they all going? Oh my Doug! I've been captured!

Claire was panicking now, but it was a strange, disassociated feeling. Her eyes closed again, and she slid down, almost off the seat, the movement jolting her back awake.

Not trapped, captured! Suddenly everything made sense. *The Solo's, they're using the Solos!*

Although her vision was hazy, she could just make out a dim glow from over the horizon and columns of light beaming up into the darkening sky.

"Fuck! Oh, fuck!" the words sounded distant and slurred to her - as if someone else was speaking them. She fumbled at the side pocket of her bag, drawing out a small red pod that she quickly put between her teeth, biting down as hard as she could. It was extremely fortunate that she'd thrown a handful of the synthaline shots into her pack just before she'd left her flat.

She'd often relied on the illegal stimulant to stay awake and focused during the long nights of coding – it was also quite good during climax, she recalled. Claire giggled at the thought, then shook her head violently as if to clear her mind from such nonsense.

I've been drugged, how did they …?

Claire started to black out again, but the synthaline kicked in, and suddenly she was wide awake and full of energy, a caged animal. You were supposed to swallow the capsules whole, and they would release over time, with a final boost coming as the liquid center inside the gum shell was released. The immediate effect of the liquid being absorbed straight into her tongue was what she needed.

She'd only ever used them this way during some of her more adventurous trysts with John, so she was well aware of the powerful reaction it would cause. The liquid from the capsule had burnt her tongue as she'd bit into it, but she was now fully awake, adrenaline coursing through her veins. She knew the feeling would peak in a few minutes – there wasn't much time.

Claire tried the Solo's emergency stop button, a sense of panic now overriding the adrenaline rush. Nothing. The Solo wasn't responding at all. She supposed she shouldn't have been surprised. She pulled on the door's emergency release handle again as if it would somehow magically open this time. She pulled with all her might, but of course, it didn't move.

A wave of rage consumed her - she was a ball of energy trapped in a tiny space. She raised her arm and aimed a sharp blow with her elbow at the clear plexi side panel. You were supposed to be able to get out of one of these things easily if ever anything went wrong, and things seemed to have gone very wrong indeed! The panel flexed but showed no sign that it was going to give.

Sharp pain in her elbow greeted her next attempt, and as she repeated the process again and again, the panel became smeared with her blood. Not even a dent or a crack had appeared in it. Claire was now frantic with fear and anger - this wasn't an ordinary Solo by any means.

There's no way out! I can't get out; what the fuck!

She tried a different tactic, sliding down in the seat and wedging her shoulders against the base of the backrest, her head twisted to the side and jammed forward uncomfortably, and her knees drawn up as high as possible. She released a guttural scream as she uncoiled with all the force she could muster.

The double kick made the plex judder, but that was all. She kicked, again and again, each effort extracting more and more of the finite resource that was her chemically induced energy but with the same result - none.

She was done, out of energy, and lay back panting for breath. Her elbow was bleeding, and she felt like she may have sprained an ankle with one of her last few kicks - an excruciating amount of pain was now coming from her left boot. Claire screamed again, but this time it was a desperate and sorrowful sound. Tears started to roll down her cheeks. She couldn't believe what was happening. For the only time in her life, she regretted not wearing heels.

Something had changed up ahead - the soft glow in the distance had suddenly become much brighter. The Solo had reached the top of a small crest, and the trees fanned out from the road on either side, allowing a large and ominous dark shape to become visible against the skyline. The huge shape was topped with bright spotlighting. Claire's eyes widened as a terrible realization washed over her. It was unmistakably the Solo's destination. Unmistakable also was that this was very bad news for Claire.

It's some sort of compound! They are taking me to some sort of big, scary fucking compound!

She couldn't believe how easily she'd been outsmarted, how easily she'd been captured.

Beaten by fucking A.I.! Kidnapped by a fucking Solo! There are so many of them, so many.

The thought hit her like a sledgehammer, and she felt a sudden urge to vomit but managed to fight it off. She was breathing hard, and she closed her eyes for a few seconds, trying to compose herself.

In her mind, she saw Henny's face again, pale and ghostly against the impossibly black background, but this time the image morphed, and she was pleading with Claire as she was being dragged away into the corrections transporter and to her death.

Claire's eyes opened wide, and she screamed and kicked out again with all her might, only managing to inflict more piercing pain on herself. The compound was still at least a mile away. Maybe she had one last chance to get out and get away - if she failed, then it would all be over. Everything she'd done would be for nothing. Claire wasn't going to let that happen - something was trying to surface through the foggy haze in her mind.

What was it? What was it I'd been thinking a few moments ago? Heels! Heels. That was it!

She found the large knife in her pack. She'd taken it for protection, for an emergency. *This is a pretty big fucking emergency!* Claire took the handle in both hands and stabbed it against the side plexi-panel with what felt like all her remaining strength. The synthaline was already wearing off.

The blade left a small indentation. Claire swung again and again in quick succession, the muscles in her arms burning with the repeated exertion. On the ninth or tenth blow, the knife pierced the plexi-glass, becoming stuck, and she leaned into it, pushing it through the panel, before hurling all her weight against one side of the handle. Her effort was greeted by a satisfying 'crack' as the plex panel partially splintered. She struggled to pull the knife free, managing to free it after a few frantic seconds.

Her eyes felt heavy again, and she slapped her face to try and stay awake. She swiveled in her seat and kicked out again with both feet, ignoring the searing pain in her ankle. The panel sheared in two, and another quick kick saw it fall through and hang down against the outside of the vehicle. Cold air rushed into the pod, and Claire was suddenly fully alert again. Relief crashed through her very being like a tsunami - she had to make everything right, she had to do it for them all, for all the disappeared.

Oh, thank Douglas, thank Douglas!

Up ahead, there seemed to be some action. The lights atop the high walls of the compound had swung around towards its forecourt. Claire saw what looked like a large black shape moving quickly along the front of it. That was as much as she saw, however, as the next moment she'd hurled her pack and then herself through the opening and out of the Solo, hitting the gravel road heavily but rolling as she landed to reduce any potential damage.

She quickly pushed herself up off of the gravel, hobbled a couple of steps back for her pack, grabbing it and then making a dash toward the tree line some thirty yards away. She thought again of all the Solo's, all the people, but there was nothing she could do for them now. Every second step was pure agony, but she kept going as fast as she could.

Her chest was burning, and she nearly fell, but she made it to cover, stopping and listening from behind a large tree trunk. Everything was eerily silent except for the sound of gravel crunching under the wheels of the Solo's as they passed and Claire's ragged breathing.

She shook her head groggily and risked a quick peek towards the compound. She could make out the taillights of her Solo as it crept away into the distance, the plexi-glass panel dangling from its side. She took her comms out and recording a series of images - this was cold hard evidence that something fucking weird was going on in the uninhabitable zone.

Got to move it before someone notices I'm missing.

As she made her way unsteadily into the forest, she became aware of the sound of rushing water somewhere nearby. She headed towards it as fast as she could, struggling through the thick undergrowth of the forest on practically one leg. There was soon another familiar noise, this time overhead.

SFB! Damn it.

Claire pressed herself against the nearest tree and strained to get a glimpse of it. However, the tree cover was extremely thick, and she was obscured from view - the fly-bot would have a lot of trouble picking her out, even with thermal imaging. So she stopped where she was and activated a scrambling signal, which should buy her some time at least.

She reasoned that she had just a few minutes before her Solo reached the compound, and at that point, she was pretty sure that all hell was going to break loose. So she had to get as far away as possible, as fast as possible. What she assumed was a large river could be her best and probably only chance of escape.

Claire headed towards the sound of rushing water, almost sprinting through the undergrowth, her ankle searing with pain. She stumbled, landing on a rock and grazing her knee, but quickly dragged herself up and kept going. Up ahead was a low flat rocky outcrop. It was exposed from above, but just beyond it was what sounded like a very large and fast-moving river.

She paused underneath the last tree before reaching the outcrop and listened. She couldn't see the fly-bot, but that wasn't surprising -

it could still be overhead. She activated her scanner and saw that it had moved away, perhaps just enough to allow her to enter the open ground safely and make it to the river.

Unfortunately, she had no way of knowing if her scrambler was doing its job. She'd have to take the chance - she couldn't wait any longer.

***

Peter stared in disbelief at the new arrival to the waiting area outside his son's medi-center recovery room. "Hello Peter," Isabel said casually, completely ignoring Gladys, who was unsuccessfully trying to hide the disapproving expression on her face.

Of course, the connection between father and son had been established by Isabel under earlier surveillance. She wasn't surprised to see him there at all. In fact, she'd planned it that way. The same couldn't be said of Peter Bradshaw – he looked completely shocked at her sudden appearance.

"When did I see you last, Peter darling? When *was* that?"

An awkward silence ensued, during which Peter glared at Isabel. She appeared to be enjoying herself.

What the hell is she doing here!?

"Gladys," offered Gladys, extending her hand to Isabel.

Isabel took her hand and smiled. Gladys saw no sign of warmth behind the smile, and in fact, she saw quite the opposite in the eyes of the imposing blonde woman, causing her to remove her hand quickly and make an excuse to leave the two of them alone. She scuttled off down the corridor.

"What are you doing here, Isabel?" he asked - his voice tense.

She took an obvious and lingering look at Peter's crotch, causing him to clasp his hands in front of the area and turn away. He moved over to the plexi-panel and looked in at Lachlan. Isabel appeared by his side

"Well," she replied, "I was passing, and I just thought I'd come and see how my colleague was doing. No harm in that, is there?"

Colleague?

Peter said nothing.

"Is he ...?"

"He's resting," Peter replied sharply.

"Well, do make sure he gets these, won't you." She placed the flowers on a small table next to the visitor chairs and turned to leave. Just before she did, she paused. "A shame. We had such high hopes for him. By the way, you and I are due for another little chat."

Peter fought hard to contain his anger. He had very strong suspicions that Isabel was behind his son's demise, but he had no way of proving it. He bit his tongue and simply turned away. Isabel strode away confidently, her heels echoing down the corridor as she did so.

"Fucking *bitch!*" he spat under his breath. He shuddered at the thought of another visit from Isabel. He couldn't let that happen, no matter what she had in store for him.

Isabel Donachy had raped him, blackmailed him, and now either directly or indirectly, had been the cause of his son's near-death - almost certainly his disgrace. Who knew what else she'd planned? He involuntarily clenched his bottom and felt queasy and dizzy, needing to sit down. *She's an absolute psychopath!*

He felt impotent. He felt like he'd failed as a person, as a father, and it was all because of her! It was all just too much. Something had to give. Isabel was responsible for all of the pain in his life, and why? What had he ever done to her? Was this all just so that she could keep him as some sort of pet, at her beck and call whenever she felt so inclined? He had to do something!

A medic appeared and went in to check on Lachlan, and Peter diverted his full attention back to his son's health for the time being.

***

Senior Sergeant William McDowell, or 'Bill' to his friends, stepped down from the Large All-Terrain Vehicle that he'd specially ordered just a few months ago. At the time, it had seemed that the sky was the limit, and he could do anything he wished with the security forces funds allocated to his compound. Things had changed somewhat in recent weeks, however, and Bill was growing increasingly restless and bitter as each day passed.

He'd had a successful and illustrious career in the forces up until now, in his mind at least. Starting out as a corrections heavy, he'd worked his way up steadily through the levels of state security, and for the last six months, he'd been granted full control of the most prestigious and technologically advanced compound not only of The Highlands but of Planet 0420 as a whole.

Bill was the boss, top man, the big cheese. He even had access to The Serum, thanks to his connections, and this was something that he'd been taking regularly for the last few months - and it had been enhancing everything. Bill wondered if he had any left.

I'll check when I get back to the workroom.

He'd just been advised of an arrival that was due soon in one of the capture pods. It held particular interest for him. A call had come in advising that they had a few packages on the way that required special attention.

Isabel Donachy herself had asked them to be placed in the medi-wing and isolated until she could personally interrogate them. Bill had immediately scanned the Social Services database for their details - he often sifted through the long list of arrivals, picking out the ones he intended to pay a special visit.

When he'd seen Claire Renshaw's image on the display it caused something to turn over in his mind, and a bad memory from long ago had reared its ugly head. It wasn't something he wanted to recall – and yet Ms. Renshaw's image had somehow brought back his darkest memory. *Was it possible there was a connection?* The more he looked at the image, the more certain he became.

He'd waited such a long time for this. Maybe, maybe he'd finally be able to exact some form of revenge for what had happened to him so very long ago. He smiled to himself in anticipation, absentmindedly rubbing the deep scar on his forearm. It always seemed to itch whenever he was tense or excited, and this time he was both. He was looking forward to receiving this particular package more than any other he could recall.

A steady stream of pods had been rolling into the purpose-built compound in the last six months. The numbers had escalated dramatically in recent weeks, coinciding with both his budget being slashed and production demands being trebled. It was ridiculous.

This had meant that he was working stupidly long shifts as well as taking on a lot of the type of work he thought that he'd long since left behind him. It was ridiculous *and* demeaning! The first three months of his appointment had been fantastic. He didn't need to do anything but call meetings, make decisions, sit back and relax, enjoying all the benefits such a position offered. Things had changed for the worse.

It was the end of another fourteen-hour long day, and he was quite frankly exhausted. Nothing would usually be able to prize him away from his quarters after such a long shift, but this evening was different. The image on file was inconclusive, but just the possibility had ensured that a feeling of anticipation was tingling away deep inside.

He'd taken the shiny new ATV around to the front of the compound along with his most trusted lieutenant. It wasn't really necessary - he could easily have walked the few hundred yards. In fact, he needn't really be there at all, but seeing as he was the big boss, he could do as he pleased - there would be no harm in making an appearance, and he had to see the girl, he couldn't wait.

Perhaps it'll be good for morale, too? he pondered.

He would personally ensure that their guest was escorted to the currently unoccupied medi-cells, where he could keep her out of sight and out of everyone else's mind for as long as he wished.

It was fairly easy to forge a control order on some made-up misdemeanor or other and ensure that once he had a special guest, they would be in his keep for as long as he damn well pleased. He'd done it a few times before, and it had provided much amusement and satisfaction for not just himself but also one or two of his closest buddies in the Forces.

Bill lit a tube as the ATV rolled along past the compound's high front walls. It was a real bacco tube, too, not any of this fake crap. He'd worked hard for the state and elements of their more shadowy agencies for the last thirty years, and he felt he was owed at least the odd small luxury, well, in fact, many, many luxuries and privileges others could only dream of.

The ATV arrived at the holding bay, and Bill hopped down from the vehicle as soon as it pulled to a stop, followed closely by his lieutenant. He inhaled deeply and blew the smoke back out in a steady stream into the bitingly cold dusk air.

Not long now. I wonder if she looks as good in real life as in the V.I.?

As he strode back and forth, looking out toward the top of the small hill about a mile out from the heavily fortified front gates of the compound, a steady stream of lights from the capture pods lit the gravel roadway, stretching as far as he could see. He nodded toward Stu Gallacher, his trusted right-hand man, and Stu sent a signal to the guardhouse to open the gates for the ATV so they could continue out towards the arrival bays.

Bill signaled that they should return to the ATV, stubbed the tube under his boot, and swung himself up into the front passenger seat. Stu clambered up into the driver's seat, and they were soon heading along the front wall of the compound, a high steel link fence to their left.

The entry gates were swinging open as they approached, and they pulled up in one of the arrival bays to wait. Their guest should be arriving any moment, and it was probably time to step back out into the cold and ready the restraints.

They weren't anticipating any sort of trouble, but he didn't want any mistakes. The capture pods were fitted with a vapor system that ran through their air conditioning from around twenty miles out, gradually increasing in density the closer it came to its destination. It was the perfect system, and they'd never had any problems with packages offering any resistance on arrival. It would be a simple case of lifting a dead weight onto a trolley and securing them for the ride to the cells. Easy peasy.

He hopped down and stood facing the entry gates while the arrival crew busied themselves, unloading the trolley from the rear of the ATV. Bill shivered at the icy breeze and cursed under his breath at the inconvenience of the whole thing. However, the discomfort was offset somewhat by his growing sense of anticipation. He moved around to the side of the arrival bay in readiness as he saw the Solo deviate from the main procession and swing into the entrance of the arrival bays.

Ah, this should be her now.

***

The memory had appeared to John in the same manner as the others - out of nowhere.

He'd been trying to obliterate himself in a bar on one of the nights not long after his father had disappeared. He was by this point starting to lose hope that he'd ever see him again. Trying to forget everything and escape the relentless grief had seemed like a good idea at the time.

The Workers Bar, a favorite haunt of Andrew's that John had a special affinity for. It was a place where there was usually trouble, and tonight was no exception. A loudmouth had annoyed him a little while ago. They'd tried to pick a fight with someone half their size. The antagonist in question was big, close to John's height, although overweight, with short, cropped hair and a mean look about him. He was also a boorish offensive loudmouth and probably had bad personal hygiene. John had just about heard enough from him for the night.

He'd been sitting silently at the bar, waiting for the burly coward to visit the men's room, where he intended to have a little private chat with him. John didn't have to wait long. The loudmouth was making his way there now, barging past people and causing at least one person to spill their drink. No one was game to make a fuss, having observed firsthand the big sweaty lard belly's threatening behavior over the last couple of hours.

John picked his way carefully towards the toilets, a discrete distance behind his target. He stopped in the middle of the room, pretending to take a comms call, and checked that none of the burly bully's friends were following or observing. He needn't have worried; they seemed content on harassing a group of ladies on the other side of the bar – he hoped he wasn't going to have to deal with them as well. John slipped into the men's toilet, not more than a few seconds later.

The loudmouth was standing in the middle of the space between the sinks and urinals, checking his comms and more or less blocking John's path as he entered. The loudmouth looked up momentarily before returning his attention to his comms.

The arrogant prick.

"A word, pal," asked John.

The loudmouth glanced up with a look of irritation on his face. He sized John up and presumably liked his chances against the immaculately groomed blonde-haired college boy standing slightly too close to him.

"Fuck off, ya big fannybaws," the loudmouth muttered distractedly.

John smiled and winked. The loudmouth, not expecting this, was somewhat perplexed. John could almost hear the cogs whirring.

"What are you playing at, you fucking nance!"

John smiled. The loudmouth's brow furrowed as he wondered why the college boy hadn't done as he instructed - fucking off, that is.

"Well, I just wanted you to know, it's very, very brave of you to pick on people half your size."

The loudmouth looked both stunned and outraged, and his face had turned a few shades redder than it had been to start with.

"The fuck! Mind your own business ya bufty and fuck off while you're at it, ya posh twat."

John simply cleared his throat. He stopped smiling and took a step closer.

"Well, you see, *chappie*, it *is* my business. I come here with my friends often, and boneheaded dimwitted loudmouthed *bawbag* fucks like yourself tend to spoil the ambiance somewhat."

The big bully looked gobsmacked and then enraged in quick succession. His face had turned an even deeper shade of red, and he balled his fists, preparing to batter the large but no doubt soft as a baffel, poncey college boy. He was going to enjoy it as well. He smiled at John, showing a lovely set of uneven grey teeth.

Come on, take a swing, please ...

"I see you, Jimmy," he exclaimed, suddenly lunging, beefy fist already swinging in the general direction of John's head.

Here it comes.

John swayed back and felt the rush of air as the fat loudmouth's fat fist whistled past his nose.

Close, but no cigar, Jimmy!

The sweaty loudmouth was off balance momentarily, and John took advantage of this, aiming and connecting with a sharp left jab followed by a hard right, both connecting with the bully's red, sweaty face in quick succession, sending him sprawling.

The loudmouth slipped on what may or may not have been a puddle of urine, losing balance and crashing to the floor. His head connected with a porcelain sink on the way down, knocking a huge chunk out of it, gashing his big fat sweaty head, and causing blood to spray over the previously almost pristine white tiles. The bully groaned pathetically.

Job done.

"And don't come back here again, or I'll fucking kill you, *Jimmy!*" He'd enjoyed delivering the line perhaps a little too much.

John took his time dusting down his jacket, then stepped over the loudmouth bully where he lay, groaning on the toilet floor. A pool of blood was now seeping across the tiles, and John had to be careful not to step in it. He washed his hands, combed his hair, smiled at his reflection, turned, and left the toilets.

The fat bully hadn't been moving when he left, and John could care less how badly injured the arrogant coward might have been. He considered that he'd just done a public service to everyone else in the bar, no more, no less. Maybe next time, the loudmouth might decide to hold his tongue. Maybe not. It didn't really matter. John decided he'd better head off before the bully's friends discovered that their leader was bleeding all over the floor of the men's toilet and made a quick exit out onto the street, whistling happily to himself.

CHAPTER 13 – PROBLEMS

He could hear an unusual noise as the Solo approached the arrival bay. It was a scraping sound, faint at first but growing more obvious as it approached. Bill furrowed his brow.

What's that noise? Something caught underneath the Solo, perhaps?

It wouldn't be the first time a tree branch or even a plastic bucket had been dragged miles under one of the autonomous vehicles, he supposed, and it wouldn't be the last. Although the technology was very impressive, it wasn't infallible.

As the Solo passed the entry gates, somewhat of a commotion broke out in the guardhouse, and they began waving frantically at Bill and pointing at the Solo. They were shouting something at him, but he couldn't quite decipher it; their voices carried away on the wind.

Why didn't they just use their comms? Bloody idiots!

Bill mumbled some abuse as he moved quickly toward the autonomous vehicle. It had veered left and away from him instead of where it was supposed to go. He cursed again. *Bloody useless things!* From where he was standing, he couldn't see anything trapped underneath the damn thing.

The guards had now emerged from the warmth of their hut and were standing, staring slack-jawed at the vehicle. As he looked toward the guards, he noticed deep gouges in the gravel leading to the arrival bays, following the path the Solo had just taken. He walked briskly to where it had stopped on an odd angle across two of the bays. As he moved around the vehicle, the cause suddenly became very clear.

The look on Bill's face would later be described in the guard's breakroom as that of someone that had just stepped in a particularly large turd.

The entire left-hand side plexi-panel had been smashed out of its housing and was hanging loosely from the vehicle.

Oh, for fucks sake! How in hell?

Isabel's package had escaped. It was unbelievable! No one had ever escaped from a capture pod. *It was impossible! It was supposed to be impossible!* A feeling of extreme dread manifested itself deep in the pit of Bill's stomach, and he rubbed through the thick fabric of his uniform sleeve at the scar on his forearm, which was itching badly.

"What the hell! Damn it!" he yelled, looking frantically around, "Stu! Get a search team scrambled, now! Fly-bots, dogs, whatever it takes!"

Fuck me, this is bad; Isabel will be furious!

He knew Isabel well and had heard many heard stories of her preferred methods of punishment. He didn't think that this would be such a big deal, though. But then again …

Even though he knew that he had no funding for such things, barking the orders at least made him feel like he was doing something. He'd risk what he could in terms of resources and cover it up later - after all, what was one captive student in the big scheme of things? They would pick her up quickly enough, one way or another, and that would be that - no one could move anywhere without being tracked - that was how they got everybody else, after all.

Stu hadn't reacted. He'd come to look at the damaged Solo instead. Bill looked at him incredulously. "Move it! Now!" he snarled. "Tosser," Stu muttered under his breath as he marched away, his face set in stone.

Bill knew that there was every chance that the package had removed itself from the Solo well before it had neared the compound, and therefore any resources he dispatched would have no chance of recovering it. If the girl had escaped close to the compound, it was likely that one of the ROLA's would locate and disable her, allowing for an easy recapture.

They could probably put the whole episode down to a programming malfunction anyway – maybe the gas hadn't deployed? They could always say that. There was a chance, he supposed, that the girl might be close by, in which case he'd have one less thing to worry about, and Isabel needn't ever know that there was a problem.

He didn't want to admit it, but he was more scared of losing his privileges than losing a package.

I mean, it's not as if I did anything wrong, is it? Stupid bloody Solo malfunctioned, is all.

He kicked the side of the Solo, jarring his knee, and limped away, mumbling abuse again, lighting another tube as he went, his hand trembling a little at the thought again of the possible consequences. He told himself that it was fine, everything was fine, but fear was starting to take hold slowly.

It doesn't matter. These things happen.

Bill imagined himself saying that to Isabel. It did matter, though - *she* would think it mattered. He wasn't sure whether she'd be more annoyed at the package escaping or the budget overrun a search might cost. He'd have a bet each way. So, he'd say nothing for now and hope that he could recover the package quickly before anyone found out. That would be for the best, he decided.

*

Stu had never seen his boss quite so worked up. His voice had cracked with the last few words. Even in the dim light of the entry bays, he could see that his face was very red - it looked as if his head might well explode at any moment, he recalled with a grim chuckle. Bill was also rubbing at his arm again, he'd noticed. Stu knew that he could afford to deploy maybe a few

Special forces personnel and a fly-bot for an hour or two at most, but even that would undoubtedly have them in trouble with finance and internal affairs. The orders had been very specific - no unauthorized expenses, which is exactly what this was. He'd seen what happened when orders were disobeyed, and there was no way that he was going to be the scapegoat for this, which is no doubt what Bill would try to engineer - the fat old fuck.

He doubted whether the incident would even be reported. Bill was a coward at heart. Stu hated him deeply for that. He was always covering up dook for him, the incompetent buffoon that he was. He directed his gaze elsewhere, and as he listened to his comms, he imagined Bill taken to an interrogation cell of his own. The thought pleased Stu greatly.

***

Claire stood at the edge of the rocky outcrop. The river raged below. It was dark, it was cold, and the drop to the river was at least fifteen feet. The water was no doubt sub-zero, and she knew that when she dove in, it would be a matter of minutes before her body started to shut down. After that, she'd have to use the fast-moving current to get as far away as she could as quickly as she could - for as long as her body could bear it. She was still feeling the effects of whatever had happened to her back in the Solo. Her ankle was throbbing painfully.

She reached into her pack once more grabbed the container holding the synthaline capsules. She shook the contents out and looked down into the palm of her hand, barely able to make out the shapes of the small red pods in the darkness.

Five capsules. Any more than three was considered dangerous. Claire had to roll the dice; there was no choice. If she was captured, she was certain she wouldn't see the light of day again. The capsules should enable her to stay in the icy waters for a few extra minutes at least, but there was a chance that they may also kill her. It was a chance she was prepared to take, she decided.

Claire was a strong swimmer, but she knew diving into the river fully clothed would immediately put her at risk of drowning. Staying in the river for any length of time would bring on hypothermia, and hypothermia took no prisoners. Neither did drowning.

She swallowed four of the five capsules and bit into the last, the chemicals stinging her already raw tongue. She quickly strapped her pack to her chest and stood looking down at the fast-flowing river as the adrenaline starting to flow through her veins. Her devices were stowed in a waterproof capsule, and so the data should be safe at least. Her own mortality, well, that was an entirely different question right now.

The sound of the water rushing past was deafening. It would be masking the sound of any pursuers. Someone could come bursting out of the forest at any moment, so she couldn't risk hesitating any longer. She was shaking with fear in anticipation of the long drop into the icy waters. Every nerve ending in her body was screaming at her not to jump, but she forced herself, with all her willpower, to take a step back and launch herself off of the rocky ledge.

The large white orb had been rolling through the forest, making its endless circuits of the compound, following the well-worn path it had made over the last few months. It suddenly sprang to life, changing direction sharply, doubling in size as its outer shell was popped out by a hundred or so mechanical arms, leaving each three-pronged part of its shell to act as a mechanism to propel it quickly through the undergrowth.

It moved at an incredible speed, bounding over rocks and fallen trees with ease as it crashed through anything in its path. It had locked onto a humanoid form and was following its instructions to disable it. It burst into the clearing, contracting back into its smaller shell and doubling its speed as it hurtled towards its target.

She felt weightless, her hair flapping across her face as the air rushed past her ears. It seemed to take an eternity to fall, and she braced herself for impact. The shock was immense as she hit the water, and she gasped for breath as it consumed her. Somewhere above her, a white orb shot across the river, landing comfortably on the other side in its re-expanded form. It had lost track of the humanoid and resumed its patrol.

It was ok, she was on top of the water, and the fall hadn't killed her. She quickly and expertly rolled herself onto her back, throwing her head back and spreading out her arms and legs, assuming a pose that would maximize her buoyancy.

For the next few seconds, she had a terrible feeling that she'd just committed suicide. She was underneath the water as much as on top of it, and it was beyond freezing. She took in a mouthful of water instead of air and choked, drawing in more water in the process, which made her convulse and fold herself up in a ball as she coughed and sucked in yet more river water.

The immediate effect of this was to drag her under the surface just as she passed over some large, submerged rocks. Her legs caught on the first, spinning her over and pulling her deeper underneath. From then on, pure chaos ensued. It was pitch black in the water, and she was tossed like a rag doll, her body starting to numb, not knowing which way was up.

I'm going to die, was the last thing she thought.

Her body drifted lifelessly through the surging waters, barely visible as it surfaced, and then was swallowed again immediately. Somewhere deep in her subconscious, the image of Henny came again, but this time as the dead eyes stared, she spoke, and Claire could hear the words escaping from her blue, dead lips. Henny was saying, "They killed me," over and over.

***

Claire had responded. She was ok, and Andrew was incredibly relieved. She must have escaped from a similar situation, he imagined, and soon enough, they'd be able to meet up, and then? *And then?* He had no idea what was going to happen next - he was heading into the uninhabitable zone. The clue was in the name.

This should be fun, then.

Andrew made swift progress, practically running and hurdling obstacles like some sort of madman. He was making his own path through the dense forest, winding ever downwards past gorse bushes and fir trees and the occasional rocky outcrop. He was navigating purely from an ancient compass that he'd pilfered from the history lab at college and the pointers that Claire had given him earlier – that seemed a lifetime ago now. They were still relatively carefree at that point. Andrew couldn't believe how quickly everything had changed.

Another few hours, though, and he'd be at the rendezvous point, and all being well, so would Claire. 'The Resort,' she'd called it. Unfortunately, Andrew doubted it was going to be anywhere near as pleasant as it sounded.

It was getting pretty gloomy - Andrew didn't fancy being out in the open for too long after dark in the wastelands, and he forced himself to keep going long after he felt like he had to stop for a rest. Whenever he did slow to a walk or have to pause to work out which way to go next, he realized that he was still trembling, and his heartbeat was irregular - he felt completely numb after the incident on the podium, and he imagined he must be in shock

I killed someone. I've bloody well killed someone! Douglas!

He was a killer. Scrawny little Andrew, a nobody, a nothing, a nerd, was now a wanted killer and on the run from the authorities. On the run! He couldn't believe it. What had he ever done to deserve being in this situation? He couldn't think about it any longer. He had to focus on something else, anything else.

Claire.

Claire was his only hope. Claire would save the day. Claire had also got him into this whole mess, but he was currently overlooking that particular fact. She'd expose everything that was happening – the disappearances, the cover-up, whatever else - and then somehow all would be well, and everything would return to normal. Andrew liked normal. He liked it very much. Even if they managed to come through this intact, he had still killed someone, and he'd still go to the big hoose.

He crouched down, his stomach starting to knot again, and prepared himself for another bout of vomiting, or at least retching. A sudden rustling nearby startled him from his state of wretchedness, and he forced himself upright and wheeled around in the direction of the noise, his stomach cramping painfully again as he did so.

"Hey! Who's there?!" his voice wavered uncertainly. He was ready to run. The rustling noise came again, and it was closer this time, just behind some nearby gorse. A twig snapped. To Andrew, it sounded just like you might hear in an old-world VIS thriller. The bit where the killer sneaks up on their victim in the forest.

Andrew didn't want to be the victim in that or this scenario. He reached for the knife he'd collected from the recently departed bald sunlenses but only succeeded in fumbling it and dropping it on the ground. He quickly picked it back up and held it vaguely in the direction the noise had come. He couldn't see anything but the high gorse bushes.

"I have a knife!" he said to the gorse bush.

The sound of another twig snapping was all it took. He turned and fled down the steep hillside as fast as he dared, looking frantically back over his shoulder every couple of seconds, heart leaping out of his chest, expecting to see some sort of mutated killer beast chasing him down at any moment. He didn't see anything behind him but kept running anyway.

Eventually, he reached a stand of tall conifer trees and slowed down, taking a much longer look behind than he'd afforded himself to date. Nothing but bushes and grasses. No mutant beasts, no assassins. Andrew was bent over, sucking in deep breaths but keeping one eye in the direction he'd come from, just in case. His heart rate began to slow, and he wiped the sweat from his eyes.

Fuck this adventuring dook. Fuck being on the run, and fuck the uninhabitable zone.

The thought made him feel a little better. There was nothing behind him. He was being ridiculous. The knife was still in his hand, and he slipped it back into his belt.

Now that his breathing had slowed, the gurgle of running water nearby was quite apparent, and he pushed through the trees and gorse in the direction of the sound. He soon found himself beside a smooth and fast-flowing river, about twenty yards wide. It was a big relief - he'd been worried for some time that he'd taken a wrong turn somewhere, but this was exactly what he'd been looking for; this was his landmark, just as Claire had explained it to him in the message giving the co-ordinates. All he had to do now was to follow the river downstream until he saw the hills of Loch Campbell, and from there, he could find the rendezvous point.

Maybe it'll be ok?

It was a strange thought, seeing as he had no idea what they were going to do next and no idea how they would get out of this terrible situation.

Aye, ever the optimist, eh Andy boy.

An eagle swooped down over the river and plucked a large fish from its waters before flying off into the distance, the fish flapping its last flap as it hung from the eagle's claws. Andrew watched in awe. He was far enough down below the contamination line now that the haz warning monitor on his comms should have continued vibrating and flashing constantly, and yet it was now mostly silent. It had gone off the scale an hour or so ago as he neared the zone, and it had almost been enough to make him think twice about continuing.

Maybe Claire had been wrong about being able to hide out and survive down here? he'd thought at the time but had continued anyway, nervously checking the haz every minute or so. He checked the small yellow plex encased comms attachment again, ensuring that it was still working, shaking it a few times for good measure. It seemed to be functioning fine, but it was not showing any contamination warning on its small display. *That's weird.*

Andrew shrugged and started walking in the general direction of the horizon, following the line of the river but staying in cover as much as he could, spurred on by his desire to continue to avoid whatever mutant wildlife was still potentially lurking behind the nearby trees.

Got to get there before dark.

***

The medics had eventually advised that it was ok to go in. Lachlan had been brought out of his drug-induced deep sleep, and the advice was that he should be able to be discharged within the next twenty-four hours. Peter had tried to speak to his son as he lay partially sedated in his medi-center bed, but he'd looked at his father, turned his head away, and closed his eyes.

He'd reluctantly brought Isabel's flowers into his son's medi-room and placed them on the bedside table after considering throwing them in the bin. Such was Isabel's hold over him; he was worried that she'd find out somehow, and that would make things even worse for him when she did pay him a visit.

Peter had sat in the medi-room for hours, and eventually, Lachlan had to acknowledge him, although he was clearly ashamed and was in no mood for company. He told his father to go home. It was a pretty blunt message. It was clear that Lachlan wasn't ready to talk. He'd leave him alone for now and come back to visit in the afternoon - after he'd had a chance to rest. He had to get him away from Isabel. As he got up to leave, he couldn't help himself, snatching up the flowers and depositing them in the bin on the way out.

Fucking bitch.

He was more concerned than ever about his son, and the fact that he didn't want to talk to him was most troubling of all. He cleared medi-center security and headed for the t-hub on the far side of the center's pod park.

The man in the large dark-colored transport pod watched as Peter Bradshaw left the medi-center. He made a call, and an hour later, Isabel Donachy returned.

A few hours later, Peter had called the medi-center to check on his son's progress. He waited on the call for what seemed like forever, and when the medic spoke to him, he'd sounded confused and agitated. Lachlan had apparently discharged himself just an hour earlier, against all advice. He had simply got up, gotten dressed, and left.

Peter sat in his workroom for a while, considering his options. He had to do something; he had to end this - before it killed his son.

***

Claire vomited water and gasped for air as her body surfaced briefly from underneath the dark waters. She was back in the land of the living, at least for the moment, and tried to suck in a breath just as she disappeared underneath again. The dark water swirled violently around her, and she couldn't see a thing. She'd already taken in huge amounts of water and was disoriented, kicking out and trying to swim to what she thought the direction of the surface might be, but the current was too strong.

This is it! I'm going to drown!

She fought with everything she had to not be taken by the river, but nothing she did was helping. As she thrashed hopelessly, her movements started to slow, and she then became still - the current pulling her along underneath the water. The last of her breath bubbled upwards just as the river slowed, and she watched them rise toward a pale light somewhere above.

Claire's survival instinct suddenly kicked in, and she used the very last of her energy to kick out and try to follow the direction of the bubbles, but she felt as if she could hardly move. Darkness closed in around her, and her body became still again. An image of Henny's ghostly pale face and black pupil-less eyes loomed from the depths of her mind - she was calling out to her, "Claire!"

Henny! I'm not dying like this!

The thought stimulated something hidden deep inside of her to push once more. She did, and she kicked and kicked again and somehow broke the surface, sucking in air and coughing it out at the same time, her lungs and nose burning.

She managed to get some air in and stay afloat. Her pack was still attached, and it was giving her at least a little buoyancy. The river had widened and slowed, and Claire looked around.

Not dead yet. Am I far enough away? Need to get further.

Blood was clouding her vision. She must have hit her head at some point. She gulped in some more air and spun herself over so that she could float on her back, and this time she was able to stay that way - she felt in control for the first time since she'd jumped in.

She could no longer feel her arms or legs and was shaking so violently that her teeth chattered - she hadn't been in the water for more than a few minutes, but hypothermia was already trying to take hold. A sudden and strong surge of adrenaline rushed through her body, warming her temporarily - the synthaline capsules were doing their job. Claire looked up into the night sky and saw the moon glow through a break the clouds. It was beautiful.

Maybe I can just hang on for another few minutes.

Just as she'd that thought, the river started to speed up again as it wound around another bend. She could see rocks and fallen trees up ahead, and she flipped herself back over onto her front and desperately attempted to kick out for the near riverbank. She didn't have the energy to make it; she'd left it too late, the current was far too strong for her. She was out of control again in seconds, fighting to stay afloat and heading straight towards the obstacles in the river.

She'd been spun around by the current again and again, and it was all she could do just to stay afloat, the power of the water giving her little if no chance of avoiding anything – she was at the mercy of the river.

A huge tree lay partially submerged across her path, the water surging over it, and she was being thrown directly toward it at speed. She saw it very late, getting an arm in the way at the last second, but there was nothing she could do to prevent the impact. After that, Claire saw nothing but darkness. The river was not feeling particularly merciful today.

***

By the time Andrew spotted the low buildings on the edge of the loch, the only light available was being cast by an almost three-quarter moon. The clouds had cleared a little in the last hour or so, and the stars twinkled brightly between them.

A moon shadow trailed alongside Andrew as he trudged wearily along the edge of the lock. His feet were aching; he was exhausted. His mind had turned to jelly from replaying the incident on the podium over and over again, but at least now he had the rendezvous point in sight.

I wonder if Claire's already here?

As yet, he hadn't been attacked by any mutant creatures. In fact, all the creatures he'd seen so far were perfectly normal looking and had the usual number of limbs and heads – rabbits, birds, and so on. At one point, he thought he'd seen an eagle circling him high above, and he quickly recalled some of the snippets of old-world westerns he'd seen. "Not yet, my feathery friend!" he'd said to the eagle, but it turned out to be a crested tit anyway. He was pretty sure that there weren't any vultures in modern-day Alba, but then again, you never knew. When he looked back to the sky soon after, the tit was gone.

That's the thing with birds; they have the habit of flying away.

He was following an overgrown path strewn with rocks that had caused him to stumble more than once along the way, but he was determined to reach the sanctuary of the resort uninjured, and he was nearly there. He thought of Claire again - he could certainly do with some human company - he was quickly tiring of his own mind.

Perhaps she's already found food and made a fire? Perhaps the two of them could snuggle up under a blanket and toast marshmallows on the open flames?

Andrew knew there was little chance of marshmallows, but it was a nice image all the same. He was absolutely starving – he'd managed to pick and eat a few berries along the way, assuming them to be non-poisonous and untainted – a lucky guess - and had even found a few wild field mushrooms growing amongst the fir's, stowing them in his pack for later.

He did have a limited amount of provisions with him, but they may need to be rationed - he had no idea how long they would need to hide out. He'd now successfully gathered, and once he got to the loch, he could hunt, maybe. He could fish, anyway.

Andrew of the wilderness!

The buildings were getting closer, and he could now make out the outline of a long jetty poking out into the calm waters of Loch Campbell as well some details of the buildings themselves. It had perhaps once been a thriving resort back in the old world, but there wasn't much left of it now. All Andrew's romantic images vanished in an instant as he looked at the caved-in roofs and empty spaces where windows had once been.

Worst resort ever.

The buildings, or what was left of them, were concrete and brick – or rather, they were mainly the rubble of concrete and brick. They had managed to retain some structural integrity. They must have been maintained or even added to at some point after the collapse of the old world. Andrew was already yearning for the relative luxury of his dingy little flat.

There was no sign of life up ahead, no sign of Claire, and he started to worry again that she might not make it. He had to put the thought out of his mind. With the end goal now in sight, his body allowed itself to relax, and his pace slowed. He was suddenly very tired and needed to stop and refresh himself, if only for a moment. He swung his pack down from his shoulder, surveying the landscape.

It was a beautiful location, and he could see why it had no doubt once been a popular holiday destination. The loch itself was placid and was ringed by steep hills with layers of mountains visible in the far distance.

Aah, Scotland. Magnificent!

He checked his haz for the hundredth time and found once again a very minimal reading. It looked as if their plan to hide out where no one would think they could conceivably have gone was going to be possible after all. A strong hunger pang nearly bent Andrew in two.

Andrew was reluctant to dig into the scant supplies he'd brought - which was basically just some carb powder and a few energy bars, but he thought that he deserved a treat of some kind for making it this far. He rummaged in his pack and found a nice surprise in a side pocket - the remnants of a cao bar, which he demolished in seconds.

Mm, mint cao chip, my favorite. Maybe something else too; what can I find in here?

Andrew dug deeper in his pack, and the first edible thing he found was the small cloth bag he'd filled earlier with the field mushrooms. He pulled a few of the fine stems from the bag and absentmindedly chewed on them as he tried to work out where the best chance of shelter was going to be.

Perhaps Claire was already here after all? She could be hiding out in one of the buildings, maybe an outbuilding, sleeping?

With that thought, he decided to get a move on, slung the pack back over his shoulder, and headed off.

Hmm, what was that flavor? Ah, that's it, sort of - mushroomy. These mushrooms have a definite mushroomy flavor.

He'd amused himself, which meant he must be feeling slightly better. The mushroomy aftertaste wasn't particularly pleasant, and he thought that cooking them might be a better option if he could get a fire going later. He bent down and cupped some water into his hands from the loch edge, sipping gingerly at it just in case it was too polluted to drink. It tasted pure and sweet.

"Ah, the taste of Alba!" he proclaimed to no one in particular. Maybe just to a mutant hedgehog, should there happen to be one listening nearby. Andrew filled his water bottle and moved off toward the resort.

***

The body had washed up on the outer edge of a long bend in the river. A mostly green and wet tangle of clothing was visible, surrounded by tall trees. Only the pale face of the skin, practically gleaming in the moonlight, indicated that this was anything other than some piece of miscellaneous debris.

A foxlike creature was sniffing at the tangled wet green lump, oblivious to the search fly-bot passing far overhead but alert as to its immediate surroundings. It could tell that this was a food source of some type, but something about it was making it wary. The creature moved carefully around it, sniffing and nudging it tentatively with its snout. A small white shape protruded from the green mess.

The animal sniffed at it and sniffed again. It definitely smelt like food, and there was a metallic tang to the air, the tang of injured prey. Whatever it was that had made the creature so wary was now overcome by its survival instinct. The creature hadn't eaten in days, and this was too good an opportunity to pass up.

***

In her weird dream state, Claire was floating high above the forest. She saw treetops, flat open grassland, and a slow-moving river, meandering and glistening in the moonlight. A bright white object far down below, beside the riverbank, caught her attention, and she swooped down to get a better view. She had, of course, heard stories of astral traveling, and even though she'd never believed any of it for a second, like all humanoids she'd sometimes wondered if there was anything beyond life. She certainly hoped not, although if that was the case, what was it that was happening now?

There was an animal of some sort next to the object. *What was it doing?* She descended further, with caution. The animal was reddish-brown and was sniffing around near the object. Something wasn't quite right with the scene, and she moved closer still. As she descended, she was able to make out the detail - the object was in fact, a human face.

The skin is so white — are they dead or alive?

She descended until she was hovering directly over the face. The creature that had been sniffing the body turned and looked directly at the apparition, the hackles on its back rising. Claire looked at the creature, and it bolted, disappearing into the forest as if it was never even there. As she looked more closely, she thought that the face was somehow familiar. The realization hit her - she was looking down at her own dead face.

I'm dead. I drowned in the river.

She suddenly had no control of herself - the Claire ghost, or whatever it was that she'd become. She wanted to get far away, but instead, she jolted forward, and again, not able to stop herself. Her eyes ended up just inches from those of the pale, dead face.

So peaceful.

Was it really her? Now she wasn't so sure. Something wasn't right - the features of the face had become blurred and seemed to melt away, leaving nothing but a translucent ghostly white.

What's happening? What's happened to me?

Features were forming back on the blank face. This time though, it wasn't hers; it was Henny's! The eyes of her dead sister opened slowly, and Henny screamed a piercing, unearthly sound. The shock hit Claire like a lightning bolt. She was thrown backward, away from the Henny-like thing, away from the forest, away from the planet, the universe, from everything.

Darkness, lovely, calming darkness surrounded her. She tried to move, but it felt as if she was swimming in treacle - or at least how she imagined that would feel like. The dark nothingness had a form, a viscosity, and it tugged at her from every direction, drawing her ever deeper inside of itself. She gave up struggling and gave into it, drifting away into the beautiful black nothingness.

Henny's face appeared suddenly, only inches from Claire's, filling her vision. Her eyes were closed, but blue-black tears ran from them. Claire screamed, *"Henny!"* and the grainy black nothingness seemed to flow into and fill her mouth as she did so, suffocating her.

She couldn't breathe; she was drowning! She struggled for what felt like the last time.

CHAPTER 14 – COMMOTION

He seemed to exist in a void of sorts. He couldn't feel. He couldn't hear. He had no sense of time and wasn't even aware of whether he was awake or asleep. He just, sort of, existed. Just occasionally, though, a memory would burst into his consciousness, filling the void with colors, sensations, and sounds, and then would be gone again within seconds, sometimes minutes. One such memory was occurring right now.

John was in a school playground. He could see a bit of a commotion on the far side of the quadrangle and headed over. As he neared, he could see a small mop-haired boy surrounded by many other larger boys - he was being shoved this way and that and was about to be beaten to a pulp by the look of things. John hated bullies. Not just hated, he despised them for their cowardice, their downright ugliness.

Someone had tried to bully him once – they'd ended up with a broken arm and a few less teeth. He wasn't going to stand for this. A red mist descended over his vision, and he balled his fists and made his way purposefully towards the scene of the crime.

***

The fox-like thing was about to start feeding when it felt something strange - something that it didn't like at all. A dark shape had appeared just above the prey, hovering in the air. The animal was instantly filled with a fear as it had never known. The apparition had suddenly taken on a human form and was looking directly at the creature with solid black, glassy death eyes.

The creature felt the apparition inside of its mind, and it turned and fled for its life. The animal would never again venture near the river and would instead concentrate its efforts on the small settlements dotted here and there amongst the hills and forests of its territory. The worst that could happen there is being chased away by the tall, two-legged animals. Those it could deal with.

274

***

Claire regained consciousness violently. It took her a moment to realize that she was in fact still alive, and a few more to realize that she was on the riverbank. She vaguely remembered something about being in the sky, about Henny. There was an incredible deep endless blackness, a scream, what else? It was gone - she couldn't recall. She was looking up into a clear night sky framed by tall trees—the recollection of why she was where she was came flooding back.

I've made it! I've survived!

Her pack was still strapped to her front, and she struggled to unbuckle it, her fingers not working properly as she fumbled hopelessly with the clasps. She noticed that she was bleeding from her right hand. It started to throb with pain as she looked at it, blood trailing down her forearm as she watched. It was just a small cut, but it would need a dressing and some antibac salve.

She gave up on the pack, rolled herself over with quite some effort, and propped herself up on one elbow, facing the river. She didn't know how far she'd traveled or where she was and had even less idea about how she'd managed to stay alive. The last thing she could recall was being smashed face-first against a huge log in the middle of the river. She tentatively reached up to her face, unsure what to expect, almost too scared to touch it.

"Fuck it."

Claire ran her hand gently over her face, one side, the other, across her chin, nose, and forehead. Her face felt cold and smooth. There was no sign of damage apart from a cut and some swelling over her right eyebrow.

She looked at her bloodied hand as she withdrew it and wiggled her fingers. Her forearm protested, and the pain shooting up her arm made her stifle a cry. She thought for a moment she might vomit but managed to take a few deep breaths before carefully checking her arm.

Not broken, not broken. It might take a day or two until she had full movement, but it could have been worse. Much worse. She must have just got her arm up just in time as she hit the log. After that, well, who knows? She supposed that her pack might just have saved her life,

275

keeping her afloat and her face more or less above the water line – there was no other explanation she could think of. She'd been very, very lucky

Claire's vision started to blacken, and the forest swirled and juddered around her. She closed her eyes and waited for the feeling to pass. It abated after a few seconds, and when she opened her eyes, her vision was back to normal. She looked around the small clearing.

Lots of trees. Not much else.

She was lost, she was exposed, she was shaking violently, and she had to focus on one thing and one thing only right now - staying alive. She had to move. She needed shelter and warmth quickly - she could navigate later.

Quickly, that was a joke, she realized as she rolled onto all fours and slowly pushed herself upright. Everything hurt. She put her weight on one leg then the other. One felt better than the other, quite a bit better. She stumbled away from the riverbank, limping badly. The night was still and cold. There were no sounds other than the burble of the river in the background. *Hold on; there is a second sound!* Claire knew instantly what it was. A low pulsing sound high overhead. A fly-bot.

Fuck! This must be part of the search!

Maybe she hadn't been carried all that far after all, or maybe the search was far and wide. Either way, this wasn't ideal. She stopped underneath a large tree to listen. Her breaths were short, jagged, and painful, and she realized that she must have taken a hit to the rib cage as well at some point.

The pulsing sound seemed to center overhead but then moved away soon after, and Claire slowly exhaled. She knew that some of the more advanced SFB's had thermal imaging fitted. The near hypothermia might just have masked her. It might have saved her - if it didn't kill her first.

Claire checked her right wrist. The comms were still firmly attached, somewhat miraculously, but the display was broken and blank, the standby indicator dull and lifeless. They were supposed to be waterproof, but she wasn't sure exactly how waterproof – she hadn't even thought about it prior to plunging into the river.

She bashed the comms unit a couple of times with her hand, and the indicator light glowed dully for a second, then went out. She shook her wrist a few times, causing water droplets to spray from the comms, and bashed the device again with her wrist - this time, the standby indicator light came on and stayed on.

"Well, thank fuck for that!" It now hurt when she talked. *Great!* She decided that given recent events - like being kidnapped by a fucking Solo of all things and taken away to be tortured or worse – a bit of pain was a minor inconvenience in comparison. Another thought suddenly cut through. *My devices!*

She had put her devices into a waterproof shell, but she was now wondering just how waterproof that was too and whether it had survived her ordeal in one piece. She fumbled again with the clasps of her pack, this time having more luck getting her fingers to work, even if they were now tingling painfully. She dropped the pack, pulled out the capsule containing her devices – and by some miracle, it looked intact.

Oh, thank Douglas!

She knew that if she'd lost all of the data, then there was little chance of her finding it ever again – the state would have taken measures to either remove the data completely or to hide it forever. She opened the capsule, and at least a pint of purest Alba river water poured from it onto her boots.

"Oh!" was all she could think to say.

***

Isabel had arrived in his medi-room and advised him that she had a security detail stationed outside, waiting for him, just as soon as he was ready to check out. Something important had come up involving the mining program, and he was the only one who could help. She was taking no chances with communications and had come to deliver the news personally as a result. She left soon after, and Lachlan had passed out.

When he woke sometime later, he wondered if she'd been there at all, but then he saw the small blue vial she'd left for him. It took a while for all of this to seep through his drug-induced state. Even under the influence of a cocktail of psychotropic drugs, he recognized that this was a chance at a way back. They *needed* him.

He forced himself up and called for a medic, who then called for another medic. A heated debate ensued. They were reluctant to release him, but they couldn't keep him against his will either. They eventually agreed to run a few more tests, and if he were stable, they would send him home with the relevant care package.

A large and muscular-looking chap had arrived at some point while the debate was happening. He now stood just outside the medi-room, glaring in through the plexi-panel. Lachlan made eye contact with the mysterious and imposing gentleman, whose frame nearly filled the clear panel, and he nodded and sat down to wait.

***

Claire was shivering incessantly now, and she'd need to act quickly if she was going to survive. She'd have to deal with the devices later - maybe they could be salvaged, it was impossible to tell at this point in time. Staying alive was a slightly higher priority. She prized off her boots and stripped off her wet clothing down to her underwear, then searched frantically in her pack for something dry, pulling out a small, shrink-wrapped package and ripping it open with her teeth before unfurling the thin travel blanket.

She threw it over herself and huddled into it, waiting to get warm enough to stop the now violent shaking. Before long, she felt able to continue, quickly stuffing everything back in her pack and forcing her feet back into her boots. She had a decision to make now - which way?

Claire decided to head through the forest rather than follow the river, as it might be the better option to stay in cover. It wasn't long before she stumbled into a small clearing. She was hunched over, teeth chattering and limping badly, and she wasn't sure how much further she could go in her current state.

There was a rocky outcrop on the far side of the clearing where the land appeared to fall away - it looked promising. She moved over to the outcrop and peered over the edge, seeing a steep slope leading to what looked to be a natural overhang and possibly … s*helter?*

She held her pack in one hand, and half slid, half fell down the rocky slope, pain shooting up her leg and arm as she braced herself against the slope before landing in a rather ungainly fashion beside what was indeed a rocky overhang. She was in luck - and started to think that she might just survive the night. She picked herself up and stooped underneath the ledge, spotting a small opening in the rock face squeezing herself through it on all fours, only to find a very small and very narrow cave - more like a cave-ette. She couldn't even sit up in the space.

Oh well, rocky ledge it is then.

Claire backed out of the cave-ette and started to unpack her things. It was torturous work - her hands were shaking so much now that she could barely hold a thing. Claire considered the lighting a fire but feared drawing attention to her location - there was also the problem of collecting firewood, which she was in no state to do. She found her small medi-kit and the antibac-salve tube and applied some to the cut over her eye, her hand and rubbed a small amount into her ankle and arm for good measure, immediately feeling the paste warm her skin.

She was fortunate that she'd packed a few thermal bricks in the last-minute rush to leave – they were something she'd always had in the back of a cupboard in the flat but had never used before. Now they might just save her life. Each brick could burn smokelessly for several hours, it was claimed, and a couple of them should provide enough warmth to get her out of danger. She certainly hoped so. If she perished on the ledge, it's likely she'd never be found.

Claire ripped the tags off of two bricks, and the effect was instantaneous and surprising. A warm orange glow spread out under the ledge, and She immediately felt a fierce and smokeless heat radiate from the bricks and start to warm her through. She sat down and tried to undo her boots - her hands were shaking so much now that it was a virtually impossible task. It seemed to take her forever, and at one point, she considered just cutting the laces but knew that this would be a foolish move. Eventually, she prevailed, standing and kicking off her boots one at a time.

That's it, organized—time to get warm.

She removed the remaining items of wet clothing and squatted next to the heat source; the blanket pulled tight around her. She found that she could position herself over the top of the bricks, catching as much of the warmth as possible under the blanket. At this point, she became acutely aware of being naked, squatting with her parts out over the thermal bricks - it felt most unladylike but supposed that this was the least of her worries at the moment.

It was a good job no one was around to observe, all the same, she thought. After a little while, she started to feel slightly human again, the shaking turning to more of an intermittent shiver. A tingling sensation started in her nether regions and slowly spread up through her body as she started to defrost.

"Now *this* is fucking glamping," she muttered to the nearby trees.

After she'd warmed herself enough for feeling to return to her fingers and toes, she moved away from the heat source and pulled out the remaining contents of her pack, including her survival kit. She unbound a length of micro rope and strung it across the ledge that was to be her home for the night.

Claire quickly hung up all of her wet clothes and then returned to her position directly over the thermal bricks, hoping that some of her clothes might dry out by daybreak.

She was going to be ok; she was going to make it to the rendezvous - she ached all over, but she was still alive. She shuffled away from the bricks a little and laid down, head on her pack, looking out into the forest.

Has all this been worth it? she wondered.

***

Andrew made his way carefully towards the moonlit buildings. For all he knew, there could be someone else holed up at the resort. The uninhabitable zone seemed to be quite habitable as far as he could tell, and he wouldn't be at all surprised if others had ended up down here from time to time, for whatever reason.

Like being on the run from the authorities, perhaps!

The light from the near-full moon overhead was picking out the lines of the broken roofs, twisted timber beams, and rubble of the resort long since given over to nature. There was an eerie calm and stillness to the place - Andrew wasn't sure if it was reassuring or spooky. He approached the buildings and called out tentatively.

"Claire?"

And again, a little louder.

"*Claire?*"

Andrew was holding the knife in one hand and a piece of timber he'd picked up nearby in the other. The timber had a large nail protruding from it. He surmised that not only would it make an excellent weapon should he have any unwelcome human company, but it could also be quite useful against either zombies or mutant killer beasts.

What was that VIS called again? Me and My Mates vs — something, zombies, something like that. It had been terrible but had at least provided an insight into some of the more obscure cultures of the old world. Andrew had to force himself to focus. He was tired and hungry, not to mention easily distracted, so it was no easy task.

She wasn't here after all. Andrew was deflated, the realization that he was here on his own starting to hit home. He'd have to scout around the outbuildings, but he was pretty sure that if anyone else was here, they would have heard him by now and come for a look at least. His motivation was now to find shelter and power, to be ready for when Claire arrived. *If she makes it.*

He took a moment to look out over the loch, the moonlight glinting off the calm waters, and then picked his way carefully through the rubble and into the remains of the first of the three main buildings. He assumed the first had been a reception and staff area, the second possibly a dining hall, and the third, much longer building had been the accommodation.

As he moved through the rooms as best he could, clambering over the rubble. He could see that rain and mold had dissolved anything that might have once brought comfort. Plantlife had taken hold of much of the interior of each building. Many of the doorways leading deeper inside the structures were either blocked by falling debris or had long since seized shut.

It took him less than twenty minutes to decide that seeking warmth and shelter in what was left of the Loch Campbell Resort was a lost cause. He supposed he might be able to fashion some sort of temporary shelter under some old metal sheeting or suchlike, but it was looking grim. It certainly wasn't looking like being any sort of resort-style living.

Balls.

He gave up on the main buildings and continued on his way, finding a large open space, possibly once a parking lot but now nothing but a tangle of gorse bushes, thistles, and tall grasses. Steep hills rose menacingly at the rear of the space. There was nothing here – he'd see if any of the outbuildings offered any hope.

Andrew was about to turn back when something on the far side of the lot caught his eye. He'd almost missed it, but there was something there - unless the light was playing tricks with his eyes. Inset into the steep hillside was what looked like a large square cut-out. Although overgrown, the definition of the shape could just about be made out in the moonlight.

He started wading through the gorse and thistles toward it, at one point managing to get both feet snagged at the same time, causing him to lose his balance and fall face-first into a large gorse bush.

I've just about had enough of this whole being a fugitive thing!

The cut-out was far more obvious as he neared, and through the thick vegetation that had grown up and covered in the space, he thought he could see a smooth, flat surface. He picked up a large stone near his feet and hurled it into the vegetation. His efforts were met with a very satisfying loud clang. Andrew made a fist pump gesture to himself and may or may not have done a little dance.

Three things could now happen, he reckoned. One, he wouldn't be able to open the metal panel he'd just discovered. Two, he'd open it and find more rubble and useless old junk, but at least he may have found some shelter. Or three, a labyrinth of stored food and machinery would be at his disposal. Actually, *or Four*, he thought, it might not be a doorway – he hadn't thought of that.

He dropped his pack and started tearing away at the vegetation. In just a couple of minutes, he'd removed enough of it to reveal part of a huge metal panel with what appeared to be a large door inset into it. There was also some faded lettering that he could just about make out - one of the words at one point had clearly been 'STORAGE,' and this gave him hope.

The door and the panel had once been painted red. Most of the paint had long since weathered away and had been replaced by a thick coating of rust. The storage facility didn't date from pre end of times, and this was all the more reason to be hopeful. He continued frantically tearing away vegetation until he discovered a large ring-shaped handle. It had a large padlock hanging from it, but it had rusted through and came away easily. Andrew was now genuinely excited.

Oh, this is looking good!

He grasped the large metal ring, pulling it out from the door and turning the handle. It moved easily, with only a slight grinding noise. He then heard the sweetest of all sounds he could possibly hear at that moment - the sound of a large and heavy latch freeing itself on the other side of the door. Andrew couldn't believe it! Something had finally gone right!

***

Claire lay next to the thermal bricks, teeth still chattering and her body shivering intermittently. As she slowly warmed through, eventually, the shivering subsided altogether, allowing her to focus on other things. She got up and retrieved the not waterproof capsule holding her devices - she'd been thinking of little else while she lay there fighting off impending hypothermia.

She took the devices out and shook the remaining water from them, trying to power each one up. Of course, nothing happened – she'd been expecting this.

It wasn't the right environment to start pulling them to bits to try and salvage something. Claire needed a power supply, and she couldn't risk draining her comms. Once she had a clean, dry space to work in and a power source - hopefully at the resort - she could properly assess the damage.

Claire swore for a while at the makers of non-waterproof waterproof things and then repacked everything. It wasn't the end of the world. There was a fair chance she'd be able to recover the data if she could salvage enough working parts from each device. Worst case scenario, she might be able to do something on her comms, although it would be incredibly limiting.

She needed to rest - the cut on her brow was throbbing along with her ankle, and she was pretty well beaten up all over. Hopefully, a few hours' sleep would dull the pain and enable her to get moving again. She lay back down on the ledge underneath the overhang and pulled the blanket tightly around her. The thermal bricks were still burning strongly, emitting a warm smokeless glow, invisible to thermal imaging - apparently, they emitted some new form of microwave.

It's surely some sort of alien technology. How could something so small produce so much heat?

Not that she was complaining. She prodded one of the bricks, then touched it, then picked it up. It was almost too hot to touch but didn't burn her skin. *This is weird tech, alright.* She wrapped the brick in part of her blanket and held it over her stomach. The warmth radiated through her, and she started to feel incredibly sleepy within moments. Just as she was about to drift off, a thought had her instantly wide awake again.

The comms. It must be the comms!

There was something more than a little odd about the way the Solo had been able to take her so easily. It must have known her every move; in fact, she wondered now if the one she had gotten back into was even the same one she'd left in the college pod park. There was only one way Claire could think of that this could happen - what was the one thing that was always with her, usually always active in one mode or another? *Comms.*

The display was dead again, and she banged it with her palm – a tried a true method. It sprang to life and indicated almost half charge, after earlier indicating it was nearly dead. It should be enough as long as it didn't glitch out - if she worked quickly.

Claire started analyzing all the code installed on her comms, one prog at a time. She knew she must have been tracked somehow, and even though she'd coded the fuck out of everything on her comms to ensure that something like this could never happen, she couldn't be sure now that she'd done enough.

It took her less than thirty minutes to discover the trace. Her head virtually imploded when she found the mal-code. Even though she was sitting, she had to put a hand on the ground to steady herself. It was extremely elegant and simple, something she would have been proud of herself.

The mal-code had been triangulating her position using various progs whenever comms was activated in any mode and sending fragments of a signal which would then be rejoined when it reached its destination. It had also fragmented itself, making it almost impossible to detect, jumping from one prog to the next at random. It was virtually untraceable. It was virtually perfect. Even though Claire had her own advanced masking technology installed, the invasive code had found a way around that and bypassed it altogether in a way she'd never have never imagined possible. She had to admit it; she'd never seen code so beautifully executed. It was terrifying.

A shiver ran down her spine. The code hadn't been there a couple of days ago, the last time she'd run a clean of all her comms progs. *It must have attached itself sometime yesterday or the night before, and oh! This is really bad.* It had most likely had spread to all her contacts as well. That was how they had got onto Andrew, to John.

Claire was having trouble dealing with the fact that she'd been outsmarted in her own playground. Something like this had never happened to her before. It was humbling. There was a new feeling, too, one that kept tapping her quietly on the shoulder, trying to say hello. She'd dutifully ignored it until now – the feeling of embarrassment.

Someone had come into her playground and tampered with the equipment, and she'd been completely oblivious to it. It was clearly now a whole new game, and she'd need to adapt and evolve if she were to keep a step ahead of her pursuers. At that moment, an idea formed, and Claire smiled a truly wicked little smile to herself.

An hour later, it was done. She was very pleased with herself, having further granulated the signal so that although the mal-code would still appear to be doing its work, its own signal would be spread randomly before being turned back on its source. She'd designed it to pulse randomly every few hours or so, giving the impression that comms were still being used and the code undetected.

She'd also distributed the fix covertly to Andrew and John using the ES channel. The next time their comms were activated in any mode, it would download. The combined signals would ensure that she'd have the location of her pursuers within the next twenty-four hours or so with any luck. She'd just sent a strong message to whoever was fucking with her that it would no longer be tolerated.

Sleep was required if she were to function tomorrow. As her mind drifted, she started to think of John – at first imagining what might have happened to him, what might be happening to him. Eventually, as she headed into a half-sleep, of their intimate times together - his smooth athletic body, his broad shoulders, and chest, the way his muscles rippled when he was on top of her.

Dook, where was he when you needed him?

Claire closed her eyes and shivered again, but this time the shiver brought a warmth that flooded through her body. A few minutes later, she fell heavily asleep.

***

Another memory was breaking through the nothingness.

He was sitting with a group of his college chums outside the campus dining hall, casually chatting on a coolish spring day. The sun was shining, and the air had a semblance of warmth – unusual for the time of year. One of his friends had pointed to something behind him and had whispered to another friend, causing them to laugh.

John looked back over his shoulder and saw a dark-haired girl walking on the far side of the outdoor seating area. There was no one else about, so he assumed that she must be the source of his friend's amusement.

The girl was dressed unusually, in what looked like black defense forces boots and a long plain woolen dress with no form. Her hair was bushy and unkempt. There was something about her purposeful stride and posture that made his gaze linger for a second longer than was necessary. She glanced over, and he felt something spark deep inside.

She was extremely attractive, even though it was clear she was trying to hide it. There was just something about her. John looked back at his friends, raising an eyebrow quizzically. They looked at each other and laughed again. John was, of course, none the wiser.

Suddenly the expression of his friends changed from amusement to shock, and he looked back over his shoulder again to see that the strange pale-faced girl had stopped at the sound of the laughter. She'd turned to face the group and was staring them down, using both hands to give a prolonged double-barreled single-finger salute. The light was catching on her hair as she scowled at the group. She was beautiful.

John smiled at her and saw a glimmer of acknowledgment in her eyes. Whoever she was, she was his kind of girl.

***

Andrew pushed against the big once red door with all his might. It didn't move. "For fucks sake!" he yelled. He kicked it out of pure frustration, hurting his foot in the process, which angered him even more, so he kicked the door again for good measure and hurt his foot again.

Bloody stupid door! Oh, I wonder?

He reached for the big metal ring again, but this time he pulled on the handle rather than pushing, and the door swung easily towards him for a few inches before being stopped by the vegetation. Andrew started to laugh, both in relief and at his own stupidity. He couldn't seem to stop, and soon he was bent over, hands on his knees and gasping for air.

I am such an idiot!

"The giggs, oh Douglas!" he finally managed, through gasps for air. He took a few more breaths, collecting himself, stood upright, and pulled on the handle until there was a gap wide enough for him to squeeze through. He shined his comms light into the cavernous dark space. It was dusty, but it was dry, and there were rows of shelves on either side stacked high with all manner of things.

Jackpot!

The storeroom clearly hadn't been accessed in a number of years but must have been used at some point not so long ago. Something had collapsed in the far corner where there was a large pile of rubble. There could well be some dry timber there. Things were most definitely looking up.

So much for 'uninhabitable', he thought again.

A small, shuttered window was to one side of the entry panel, and he pulled the shutters back, allowing in a little light from the moonlit lot outside. He made his way slowly around the space, using his comms light sparingly while his eyes adjusted to the dark.

Towards the back of the storeroom, there were shelves of large containers, with labels largely intact. He opened one of the containers out of interest. The label said 'Spam.' *What the heck is spam?* he thought. As he prized the metal lid open, a wave of the most putrid smell imaginable assaulted his nostrils. He recoiled sharply and hit his head on the underside of a shelf in the process.

"Fucking dookballs, what is that stuff!"

He stepped back a safe distance, took in a deep breath, and held it before attempting to reseal the lid, catching a glimpse of black tar-like residue in the container as he did so. His eyes watered as he backed away slowly, vowing never to return.

Andrew took his time looking around the remainder of the space, and after a while, his luck started to improve, finding some old tarpaulins which could do for bedding.

At the end of a row of shelves, his luck improved again, hugely - bags of factory-grown rice! *Now we're talking!* Maybe they were still ok; he'd no idea how long rice lasted. He was confident that he could get a fire going – there was enough timber strewn around – now he just needed a pot.

I wonder how old that rice is?

Andrew could see an expiry date printed on the base of the sacks. It was approximately fifty years past its best before date. He wondered how it would taste. He needn't have worried. As soon as he touched one of the bags, it disintegrated, covering Andrew and a several-yard radius in a fine white powder.

"Never mind," he said, dusting himself down. He had a few small bags of some sort of carbo concentrate in his pack, and although he was desperate to avoid having to using it, there was now no option. He recalled having it once before on a school camp. It was disgusting, and when rehydrated, turned into a translucent pallid sort of gloop. He continued the treasure hunt.

Some old metal storage cabinets lined part of the far wall, and he quickly rifled through them. His search appeared fruitless, but as he opened the last cabinet, his eyes widened. Fishing gear! Oh yes, proper fishing gear! He took out the rod, net, and tacklebox, which all appeared to be in remarkably good order. He could work with this, that was for sure.

Ok, better finish the recon.

Andrew took the next hour to skirt around the remainder of the resort. None of the old outbuildings were of any use. There was also no sign of Claire. Eventually, he returned to the storeroom and decided that even though he was tired, he may as well try his luck fishing in the loch. He was desperate to avoid having to eat the gloop.

He'd found a couple of pots that still looked fairly functional on one of the shelves - the first meal might taste a bit rusty, but he'd heard that iron was supposed to be good for you. He'd carefully picked his way to the end of the broken jetty and now sat gazing out over the loch, fishing rod in hand, a line cast out into the dark, calm waters.

Andrew had no bait, of course, and so he'd mashed a small piece of one of his precious energy bars onto the hook. You never knew; maybe fish liked cherry cao flavor protein bar? He already had a pot full of loch water ready to go for the carbo powder and mushrooms, and he'd made a makeshift fire pit filled with old timber he'd scavenged from the remains of one of the outbuildings. He was quietly impressed with himself.

Andrew of the wild, after all!

He'd often gone fishing as a child, and there was something about sitting staring at water that allowed the mind to wander to calm and beautiful places. He'd always really enjoyed it, and although he preferred river fishing, this wasn't a bad substitute. He looked out over the moonlit waters with steep hills rising on either side – it was beautiful, serene even.

All he had to do now was wait for Claire to arrive. He'd give it until morning before deciding his next move. She'd be pretty impressed if he managed to catch a nice fish or two for what he hoped might be a romantic late dinner at the end of the jetty.

Why did I just think that? Why do I think at all? Do I even think? What even is thinking. Now, it's so beautiful here.

It was just as he was having the last thought that things had started to get very weird. First of all, the water started to shimmer in a very unusual way. As he looked out across the loch, the small ripples on the surface seemed to meld and dance in the moonlight. *That's weird.*

He rubbed at his eyes and shook his head a couple of times, hoping that it would clear the odd sight. It didn't. If anything, it made it worse. As he moved his head from side to side, his vision created multiple versions of the original image, each moving on a slight delay so that it created an almost kaleidoscopic version of reality.

"Oh, fuck me! Fuck me with haggis! Sideways!"

Andrew didn't know whether to laugh or cry as he picked up one of the small field mushrooms next to the pot and observed the several versions of it that appeared in front of his eyes. He'd heard of magic mushrooms, of course, in old-world popular culture but had no idea that they were real. Apparently, they were.

Just my luck.

Most life forms had been so devastated during the end of times that many things had simply ceased to exist.

And yet, here we are.

Some sort of regeneration seemed to have been taking place in the lowlands. Everything here was beautiful, pure, and wonderful, he thought, as he watched the hillsides sway in the gentle breeze.

"So, so beautiful," he said.

He looked around the loch, in awe of its true magnificence, and noticed something strange in the distance on the low hills on the right-hand side of the loch. It was a flowing white shape, and it was moving fast. As it moved, it left behind a trail of white light. Was it pure white light, or did the trailing glow have colors of its own? It was hard to tell, but whatever it was, it was mesmerizing!

Andrew scrambled to his feet, almost overbalancing on the edge of the jetty as he did so. He squinted his eyes. After a few moments, it became clear what the fast-moving shape really was. It was a kind of horse, a beautiful white horse, mane and tail flowing behind it as it practically glided over the landscape at a seemingly impossible speed. It wasn't just white, though; it was a brilliant, almost luminous white, an impossibly white, white.

He couldn't believe what he was seeing – *it's not a horse at all, it's a fucking unicorn!* He was certain of it! A long, sparkly white horn protruded from the beast's forehead, a rainbow of colors trailing from it as it galloped gracefully along the edge of the loch. The beast suddenly pulled up by the water's edge and turned its head, looking directly towards him from not more than a couple of hundred yards away.

The unicorn's mane fluttered in the breeze, although, interestingly, there wasn't that much of a breeze. The unicorn seemed to bow down toward him, and he returned the gesture with a deep, low bow. It had seemed appropriate at the time.

As he rose, the beast galloped off, this time away from the loch - winding up towards the top of the nearby hills. He watched it intently, his hand on his heart. He was deeply moved. As the beast reached the top of the hill, it stopped, turned side-on, and reared up spectacularly, its mane flying as it let out an ethereal sound that seemed to vibrate the color spectrum out of the surrounding air before dropping back down, spinning away and disappearing over the hillside.

"I …" the word stopped in his throat. Nothing he could say would do justice to what he'd just witnessed. Andrew sat down and resumed staring out into the loch. "I shall name thee … Gregory of Loch Campbell."

He knew that there were some things best kept to himself, and Gregory the Unicorn was definitely one of them. He sat back down, grinning like an idiot. It was going to be an interesting night.

***

John didn't know how long it had been since the last memory. It felt like an eternity. Finally, though, something had broken through the impossible darkness and endless nothingness.

Andrew and John were sitting in a park overlooking the lights of the old town near John's parents' place late one night - during their last year at top school and before they were due to start work and college, it was during their last year. The topic had turned to the popular kids, which it commonly did. Andrew had been having a bit of a hard time from a few of them, and although it was nothing serious enough to warrant a visit from the angry blonde giant, it was still troubling him deeply. He had some teen angst.

"But I just don't fit in," he was saying, his voice sounding exasperated.

"Why do you need to *fit in?*"

The question surprised Andrew. He didn't understand how John could be so detached from and oblivious to his obvious angst.

"What do you mean? *Why* do I need to fit in? *Of course,* I need to fit in!"

John turned to him and said again, "But, *why?*"

Andrew paused, taken aback by the repeated question. He thought for a second.

"Because … everything!"

John didn't respond. Andrew couldn't seem to get the words out. He couldn't answer the dumbest question he'd ever heard, except with the dumbest reply. John looked at Andrew, amused.

"You'll have to do a bit better than that, pal."

"Ok, ok," Andrew's frustration was evident. He thought some more.

"Because, well, I want to be liked. I want people to like me. There, I've said it. Happy now." Andrew was turning sulky.

"Oh, I see."

Andrew didn't know what else to say. He was feeling embarrassed and wished he'd never even raised the subject. They sat in silence for a while.

"Thing is Andy, take it from me. I used to worry about this sort of stuff all the time too."

"Oh, sure you did."

That's rich, coming from a popular elite kid built like a brick dookhouse to boot.

"Ok, well, it's like this … *everyone* thinks like that. It's what you do about it that counts."

"Oh aye, and what did you do about it? Just beat up everyone and force them to like you?"

John laughed. "Well, that was an option. But no. I just stopped worrying about it."

"You just stopped worrying about it? Brilliant! Just bloody brilliant, that is! What wonderful fucking advice. You tool!"

John laughed again.

"Look, Andy, this is important. Listen to me. What I mean is, if you just stop worrying about how you look, how you speak, how you dress, what other people think, and just be yourself, well, you might just find that people like you for who you are."

"Oh, and that's been working so well for me so far, hasn't it?" John said nothing in reply.

Andrew went to make another sarcastic remark, but something stopped him.

Maybe he's making a bit of sense here.

John looked over, gauging his friend's reaction.

"It's like this, Andy. You can spend all your life worrying, or you can just get on with it and enjoy yourself. Dicks will always be dicks. Not everyone likes everyone. That's life. You can't change that. But believe me here, pal, just be yourself. There's a lot to like."

They sat in silence for a while before Andrew said -

"Are you trying to bum me?"

John was shocked for a second or two, looking at Andrew in disbelief before he started laughing, managing to force the words out,
"Fuck off! Ya heid's oot the windae!"

The awkward tension was broken, and Andrew received a dead arm for his trouble before they both succumbed to laughing fits, rolling around on the grass and barely able to breathe.

CHAPTER 15 – MUSHROOMS

Andrew lost track of time, of place, of everything. He was having a very wonderful time staring out at the loch. He had no idea that nature could be so entertaining. The stars were swirling around in the night sky, making patterns, the water shimmered up and down in peculiar ways, the wind seemed almost to speak to him, everything was kind of amazing. He was so lost in his magical world that he didn't notice it at first.

His fishing line hadn't so much as moved for hours, and he'd long since lost interest in it, but he heard something, a faint zipping sound which disturbed him from his stargazing. He looked down and realized that the reel of his rod was unwinding at an alarming rate! He picked the rod up and looked at it in complete shock. The zipping sound increased in intensity as the reel unwound ever faster.

What the hell?

Just as he had that thought, the line on the reel ran out. The rod was yanked out of his grasp so violently that it felt as if it might have broken his thumb.

Andrew stood open-mouthed as he watched his fishing rod sail through the air and hit the water about a hundred yards out, disappearing from his sight with a small splashy sound. Andrew shook his hand. The thumb was still there - that was a good sign.

"Oh well, that's that then," he concluded and sat back down. Maybe the stories of the mutant wildlife had been correct after all. And maybe sitting this close to the water wasn't such a great idea either, he suddenly realized. Whatever had just taken his rod was big, and most likely incredibly hungry too.

Aah, time for bed, methinks!

He got up and backed away from the edge of the jetty, eyes fixed on the dark waters of the loch. He wasn't entirely sure that the whole fishing rod thing had really happened. Still, it was enough to spook him – he suddenly felt very vulnerable sitting alone on the end of a jetty, over a loch inhabited by something very large and very hungry.

Andrew was just about to turn and make a run for it when he saw something very unusual indeed, not that that should have come as much of a surprise the way things had been going so far tonight. The water in the loch appeared to be swelling up a few hundred yards out. The swelling quickly became larger and larger. Andrew stood rooted to the spot. It took him a few seconds more to realize that the swelling water was now approaching him, and at an alarming rate!

"Ok, time to go now!" His legs suddenly felt like jelly, but he forced himself to turn and run just before the swelling waters closed in on the jetty. He ran in an extremely uncoordinated way, but run, he did! There was a terrific noise of falling water behind him as he weaved this way and that, trying hard not to fall off the edge of the jetty in his panicked state. In his mind, he was running like lightning. The truth was that he was barely moving.

He had a strange feeling of being watched, and he slowed and then stopped. He just had to look back. He was too scared to look back. It was quite the conundrum. As he stood pondering why he'd stopped at all, he became aware of the sound of heavy and labored breathing coming from somewhere behind him. But not just from behind him, high up behind him! A shiver ran down Andrew's spine, and he felt his knees go weak - he grabbed at the handrail to his left for support.

Make it stop. Please make it stop!

"Excuse me?" the incredibly deep, booming, but surprisingly friendly sounding voice said, the breath from it blowing past him in a fishy wave. Every hair on Andrew's body stood on end at once, and a small fart squeaked its way past his bottom cheeks to freedom. He stood, well, half stood, half leaned, frozen in place. *So, this is how it ends?*

"Um, excuse me, you there!"

There was that huge voice from behind him again. He couldn't really ignore it now. Also, whatever it was, it was quite polite. It needed a breath mint or two, but otherwise, there may not be cause for alarm.

"M-me?" Andrew answered, his voice trembling. Surely this would all stop now that he'd addressed what was clearly just an apparition behind him.

"Yes, you there! On the jetty! The small boy."

Small boy, how offensive!

Ok, it wasn't stopping. It was addressing him directly, and he was slightly insulted now as well. He'd have to turn around, and then there would be nothing there, and then he could go to bed. He waited a few moments and then decided to keep walking rather than risk looking behind him.

"Hey, where are you going?" the fishy-smelling voice sounded a little hurt if anything. Andrew knew then there was no getting away from it by pretending that it didn't exist. He turned slowly and then looked up. A long, long way up.

***

At some point during the night, Claire woke from a dream, momentarily disoriented, until the rocky ledge came into focus. She shivered and pulled the blanket tight, noticing the thermal brick was still burning.

The dream had been about the time Henny had held and comforted her after she'd come home from school in tears one day. She'd been picked on by some of the well-dressed, immaculately groomed 'pretty' girls. They'd called her a troll, amongst other things, and she was at first confused by the way they were acting towards her, then hurt and embarrassed - she had no idea what she'd done to deserve such treatment, and their words were cruel and cutting.

What made it all the worse was that she'd been playing with them moments before it had started, trying to be friends. They were all having a lovely time, and then they had turned on her. She just couldn't understand why.

Henny had held Claire tightly to her in their bedroom and told her that everything would be ok. She could feel the hot tears rolling down her cheeks and the sound of Henny's heart beating in her chest. Strangely, this was one of the happiest moments of her life. Her big sister had looked out for her at school after that, giving Claire the confidence to be her own person. She'd also taught her a few things that would come in handy if she were ever in a tight spot, should it come to that.

Claire was a quick learner, and she'd put this newfound knowledge to good use soon after, resulting in one of the pretty girls losing a tooth and another breaking a wrist. They didn't bother Claire again after that.

The dream wasn't exactly proceeding along the same path as her memories, though. This time, instead of offering Claire advice, her sister had instead gone to the school the next day with a samurai sword. She was halfway through cutting off all the pretty girls' pretty little heads when Claire woke in a sweat.

Douglas! That was so real!

Claire curled herself up in a ball and drifted back into a restless sleep.

***

The large dark shape towered over him. Its huge green-black scaled torso rose some fifty feet into the air, and the rest of its body was visible in a series of half crescents that protruded intermittently from the loch for perhaps a hundred yards. It had large light green lizard-like eyes with black slitted pupils.

All in all, it was a terrifying sight. It seemed to be assessing him as it tilted its head to one side ever so slowly, its eyes unblinking. Andrew had stopped breathing at some point and suddenly remembered that it was necessary to do so.

"Please, don't be afraid," it said. "I mean you no harm …" and then under its breath, sounding terribly disappointed. "Why are people always so afraid."

Another fart escaped from Andrews's bottom. At least he thought that's what it was - *I'd better check that one later.* The creature's large nostrils flared for a moment, and then it quite obviously frowned its giant lizard-like mouth and looked away, seemingly displeased.

"Are you …" Andrew was talking to a giant sea monster of some sort. Well, why not? It had spoken to him first.

"Pardon?" it asked.

"Well, are you …. Ummm."

"Go on, you can say it." The giant creature winked at him.

"Eh, what, why did you just wink at me?"

"I'm a prehistoric creature; what makes you think I can wink?"

And there it was again, a very obvious conspiratorial wink from the huge water monster. A bit of a smart-arsed prehistoric water monster actually, but fair enough, thought Andrew - if he were that size, he'd also be more of a smart-arse than he usually was. Even more of one.

"Eh, um, …. are you … Errr." He just had to say it. "Are you Nessie?"

"Well, actually, my name is actually *Raymond*, but yes, I have heard that some folks have called me 'Nessie' in the past. I can't say I'm a huge fan of the name."

"Well, ok then, but aren't you then supposed to be in Loch Ness?"

"Not really, it got a bit annoying after a while - having to keep away from all the submarines and divers and such like. I move about from loch to loch. Much more interesting. Not many snacks, ahem, I mean not many people around these days."

An awkward silence ensued, and the water monster. Raymond eventually broke the tension.

"And your name is?"

Andrew was momentarily unable to speak.

"Dinner?" said Nessie.

"Ahhahaha," was the noise that Andrew made. It was about three octaves higher than it should have been. He finally managed – "Andy, Andrew. Hahaha, call me what you like, Mr. Sea Monster, sir!"

"Just joking," said Raymond. "I only eat fish. Humans taste too much like, hmmm."

"Chicken?" chirped Andrew.

"Yes, that's it, chicken! Too many bones anyway. Thanks for the reminder, Andy Andrew Hahaha. Now then, a couple of things."

"Aye?" said Andrew, still in a state of disbelief over what was happening.

"Well, first up, I don't really like the term 'monster', ok pal?"

"Sorry?"

"Quite!" said Raymond. "I much prefer the term, *water creature.*"

The sight of the monster's large, pointed teeth every time spoke was fairly alarming, to say the least. Andrew was amazed that a prehistoric sea monster - sorry, creature - would have an Alban accent when perhaps he should have been more amazed that it could speak. Raymond stared at Andrew for what seemed the longest time.

"Ah, sure, yeah, I can understand that." It was getting awkward. "No problem," he added unnecessarily.

"And the other thing. Would you mind awfully to give me a hand with this?" Raymond had raised a flipper and appeared to be pointing it at its cheek. Andrew could see something protruding from the water creature's scaly face.

"It's pretty impossible with these things, as you'd imagine." Raymond waggled his upper torso, causing his huge front flippers to flap about from side to side and covering Andrew with a spray of loch water in the process.

"I'm terribly sorry," it said, "did I get that on you?"

"Oh, just a wee bit. No problem at all - hahaha!" Andrew was trying to decide exactly when he should make a run for it. Raymond moved around to the side of the jetty, the huge wake of water almost washing Andrew off into the icy waters. The creature then lowered its head adjacent to where he stood, increasingly unsteadily, and flapped a flipper at its face. Andrew could now see a large hook stuck through the water creature's lip.

"Ahhhh, I see," he remarked but made no movement towards the giant serrated teeth that were now just a few feet from him.

"Oh, come on, I won't bite," said Raymond, "*and* I'd be forever in your debt, my good sir."

Well, Raymond is an exceedingly well-mannered water monst ... err ... creature!

"Bloody thing has been annoying me for the last twenty-odd years," it said. "Not many people around down here these days. For a while, actually."

For about a thousand years, thought Andrew.

"Back in the day, I was just having a leisurely swim when suddenly I felt a little prick in the side of my lip."

Andrew fought hard to contain a sudden fit of giggles. He snorted instead. Raymond turned his huge head, nearly knocking Andrew over in the process, and looked directly at him. His breath was terrible, to say the least. Raymond burped, sending Andrew's mop of hair flying backward. Andrew's giggs stopped immediately.

"Oh! I'm terribly sorry about that old boy; it must be something I ate."

Or someone.

He wouldn't be at all surprised if Raymond was luring him to a grisly death, although it was quite an elaborate ruse if that was the case. The moment he reached for the hook, there was every chance that Raymond would lean in and swallow him whole or, more likely, bite him in half.

"So, if you wouldn't mind, Andy Andrew Hahaha." Andrew thought for a moment of correcting Raymond but swiftly changed his mind. The creature's tone had changed, and he thought it best to do as he was told. His hand trembled as he reached for the hook. Raymond turned his head side on and leaned a little closer. Andrew reached up, almost on tiptoes. The sea creature's huge pointed teeth gleamed in the moonlight.

He was about to grab hold of the rather large hook when Raymond's jaw suddenly snapped shut just inches from his hand! Andrew fainted.

When he woke, he was back on the end of the jetty, and his fishing rod sat beside him, as it had been when he first set it down some few hours earlier. Andrew decided that it was definitely time to go to bed.

***

Claire woke before dawn. She'd slept heavily and had to brush some leaves and dirt off the side of her face after she'd sat up. She stretched and tested her sore arm. The bruising looked bad, but the pain was minimal as she stretched it out. Her fingers seemed to be working too, which was a bonus. She pulled a few more leaves out of her hair as she forced herself fully awake.

Once she'd pushed herself up, she tested her sore ankle, slowly increasing the weight on it. The pain wasn't too bad, but it was going to be a long hike to what she hoped was the safety of the rendezvous point. She'd picked the place because of its location - the grainy fly-bot images she'd seen didn't paint a particularly positive picture. Still, it was the nearest potential point of sanctuary that she could find in the uninhabitable zone. There may well have been better options, but she had to make a snap decision – she just hoped it would pay off.

She spent a few minutes binding her ankle with a t-shirt that she'd cut into strips with her hunting knife. Her underwear was still cold and damp, but she put it on anyway, shivering at the touch of the fabric. The rest of the clothes were no different, and she pulled on a pair of semi-damp camouflage fatigues, a heavy and damp sweatshirt that and her still quite damp all-weather jacket. It was going to be very uncomfortable, not to mention a damp trip.

Claire knew that she'd have to briefly activate her comms location services. She'd been putting this off as long as possible, but she had to get a reference point before she headed off. Just as long as her decoy code was working as planned, it shouldn't be too much of a risk, and she'd be able to determine her location and picture the route she'd need to take within seconds. It wasn't good news, and she was shocked to discover just how far she'd need to travel.

The river had taken her way away from her intended destination. It looked like the journey could take up to nine or ten hours, depending on her ankle. In one way, it was a good thing, she should at least be out of reach of any search party sent from the compound, but it was cold comfort.

After gathering her remaining possessions, she threw the pack over her shoulder and said goodbye to the ledge. It had served her well, but she was in a hurry - the sooner she got to the rendezvous point, the sooner she could find a power source, and the sooner she'd know just how deep they were in the dook.

Claire took a moment to look out through the thick green canopy of trees opposite the overhang. The sun had just come up, and the light was filtering through the leaves, dappling the ground around her feet. She felt briefly calmed and started the difficult talk of clambering back up the steep slope and heading back to the river - she'd need to find a crossing point.

***

Andrew wasn't having a very fun night. After the sea creature encounter, he'd tried to sleep, but his mind was having none of that, and it was now deep into the middle of the night, and still no sleep. He'd tried to make a small fire inside of the storage area after a couple of hours tossing and turning but quickly discovered that this was a particularly bad idea, the smoke filling the space and forcing him to extinguish the flames and vacate the storeroom. He stumbled out into the lot, coughing violently, escaping the smoke which was now billowing out of the storeroom door.

Thick clouds had blanketed the moon, and it was now quite difficult to see anything at all. He heard something, though! *Was that movement?* It was just at the periphery of his vision. A sudden rustling in the gorse confirmed it for him.

"Hello? Anybody there?" he called.

Could have been a rabbit, I suppose, or a mutant beast.

It was at this point he realized he'd left his knife back inside the storeroom. He waited, looking for any sign of movement. Five seconds passed, then ten, then thirty, but there was no sign of anything or sound of anything. Just another hallucination, he told himself.

The clouds parted, and the moon lit the lot once again. A dark hairy-looking shape then sped suddenly between a gap in the bushes to his right, low to the ground. It was only about thirty yards away from him. Andrew wasn't sure he'd really seen it, but then he heard a grunt, or was it a growl? He heard it again. *A growl!* His eyes were wide, and his heart was racing.

What the hell is that out there?

As he watched, he saw the low dark shape slowly emerge from the bushes and turn its fat hairy head in his direction - the beast had glowing red eyes. He wanted to run, but he wasn't sure he'd make it back to the opening before the creature. It was a fifty-fifty call. Maybe if he stayed still, then he'd be invisible to whatever it was that was moving around out there.

His internal monologue was screaming at him to run, but his body wasn't obeying. There was a sudden movement directly in front of him, not more than five yards away, and Andrew turned and sprinted back to the storeroom, where a big metal door was there to protect him. He burst inside and pulled it shut.

"Holy dook. Get me out of this place!" He said to the empty, still quite smoky space.

Maybe the stories of the wastelands were right after all; what the fuck were those things?

He realized that it was possible that a beast could have snuck inside when he wasn't looking, and he spent the next ten minutes creeping through the rows of shelves, a shovel gripped tightly in one hand, and his knife in the other. He had no idea what would happen if a hairy, red-eyed monster appeared in front of him, other than he'd probably make a dash for the tiny workroom in the corner of the storeroom and hide.

Claire would be impressed if she happened to arrive and find me cowering in what is essentially a large cupboard.

The impending fear of death peaked each time he reached a new row of shelving, but eventually, he could relax a little. The coast was clear. There were no red-eyed death beasts. Not inside anyway. He was safe.

He'd tried to sleep again but spent the whole night terrified, jumping at every little sound from outside, which included a fair amount of grunting, growling, and the odd metallic clang as something heavy collided with the big metal door.

Andrew lay wide-eyed on a pile of old tarpaulins, wishing for sleep to come and take him, too scared to even risk a peek out of the shuttered window.

"The night was ... dark," he said to himself. There was no amusement in the statement this time.

***

It didn't take long to reach the river, but she soon realized that getting across it would be challenging. Although it slowed and narrowed in places, Claire didn't want to get soaked again if she could avoid it; she didn't want to even go as much as waist-deep after her last little adventure.

She followed the river upstream for about an hour and was close to giving up and resigning herself to either wading through neck-deep or swimming across at a narrow point when she saw what she was looking for. A large tree had crashed down across one of the narrower points, and it looked as if she'd be able to navigate her way across it without too much difficulty. She was halfway across, balancing carefully on the narrow trunk when she heard it.

SFB!

She looked up to see how close it was and immediately lost her balance, one foot slipping off the trunk. She fell and slipped off the side of it as she tried desperately to hold on. She had hold of a branch and was gripping the trunk as hard as she could with her thighs, but she couldn't stay on top, slipping further down and losing grip with her legs, dangling from the underside of the trunk with the river rushing past just a couple of yards from her feet.

Oh fuck, oh fuck, I'm going in!

She'd almost forgotten about the fly-bot in her attempt to avoid falling, but now she saw it. It wasn't far away and had appeared over the tree line flanking the river. *If it sees me!*

The river was moving quickly underneath, the noise of it deafening. Her arms were burning, and her grip felt as if it would fail at any moment.

Not again, not again! Can't ... hold ... on!

Just as she was about to resign herself to her watery fate, she noticed another branch.

Opposite side! ! Maybe if I swing myself over, I can hook a leg and stay hidden underneath?

It was certainly a better option than plunging into the icy depths of the river again. She swung herself back and forth, managing to hook a leg on the branch at the first attempt, relieving the pressure on her arms.

The SFB continued its path, not more than a couple of hundred yards away, as Claire hugged herself tight to the underside of the felled tree, arms and legs burning and shaking with the effort. It was gone in less than twenty seconds, which was a good thing, as Claire couldn't have held on much longer. She double-checked it was out of her line of sight and struggled to pull herself back onto the top of the trunk.

Please don't let me fall now!

She didn't, but when she made it to the other side of the river, she collapsed under the nearest tree, exhausted. She'd need to rest before continuing.

That was a close call.

The further she traveled, the more at ease she felt. Her clothes were still damp and starting to chafe in all the wrong places, but they were slowly drying out. As yet, there was no sign now of anyone or anything looking for her. Claire stayed beneath the tree canopy wherever she could - whoever was behind her attempted abduction must still be looking for her.

Still, perhaps they didn't have the unlimited resources she'd imagined, or maybe they just assumed she'd either died in the river or had escaped the Solo much further out from the compound. It would be a fair assumption, after all. The fly-bot she'd seen after she washed up on the riverbank and the one by the river crossing could just have been random patrols and not necessarily linked to her escape.

It's more likely that they are part of a search. Oh, Douglas, I hope to hell Andy made it.

She struggled on throughout the day, her ankle getting sorer and sorer the further she went. It was a pretty uneventful trek in the main, although she did see some unexpected things as she passed through the valleys and hills leading her to the resort. A number of well-worn paths were in evidence, some with what looked like wheel tracks.

It was a clear indication of human inhabitants – possibly just related to the compound, but it was equally possible that they were due to more widespread activity. There was also an abundance of un-spoilt nature and wildlife - birds of prey, rabbits, even a deer crossed her path at one point as she trudged onward. They all seemed to have only one head and the regular amount of legs. On more than one occasion, she stopped and took in the natural beauty of her surroundings - this place was far from uninhabitable.

This could be a bad thing; what if the resort's being used for something?

The State had been lying about how safe it was to travel to these areas, no doubt to keep prying eyes away from the compound and whatever else it was they were doing down here. The thought made her sick to the stomach.

The fucking lying bastards! What are they doing?

The walk offered her a good opportunity to gather her thoughts on the material she'd uncovered and plan what she'd need to do next. Her plan hinged, of course, on actually still having the data. Other than that, it was coming together quite nicely. To succeed, she'd have to rely heavily on unknown quantities - she didn't like that part of her plan, but she couldn't think of any other option.

***

Andrew had slept most of the day. He'd spent a horrendous and terrifying night stalked by unknown mutant beasts and dealing with the wild hallucinogen-induced contortions of his mind until it was light outside. Every time he thought the hallucinations had stopped, something else had happened. He was cold, hungry, and exhausted when he woke in the early afternoon. Andrew vowed never to eat mushrooms again.

There was still no sign of Claire, and this had disturbed him greatly when he first woke. He knew that he needed to give her until at least nightfall today, as they had originally discussed. Any later than that, and he would really start to worry. Any later than that, and he had no fucking idea what he was going to do.

He stumbled around the storeroom for a while looking for anything that might be of use to him, found nothing, had a sip of loch water from his container, and stretched a little before slumping back down on the tarps.

Where the hell is she?

Andrew tried not to think about what might happen if she didn't make it. He didn't have much of an idea what would happen if she did, either he realized. He dragged himself upright and dusted himself off. He was starving. His planned meal had been somewhat sidetracked last night, and he realized he hadn't eaten anything except half an energy bar in the last twenty-four hours.

Oh, except for those mushrooms.

The images from the previous night tried to make an unwelcome return, but he forced them away. Andrew picked up the fishing gear and stumbled over to the big door, pressing his ear against the cold metal. No sounds were coming from the other side - this was good. He peeked out of a small gap in the shuttered window and saw no signs of danger.

He moved back to the door and carefully turned the handle until the latch was clear of its housing, ensuring it didn't make a sound, and eased the door open an inch or two. Andrew took a tentative peek but saw nothing except gorse bushes and grass. He exhaled, relaxed a little, and eased himself through the doors into the dull gloom of afternoon at Loch Campbell.

Andrew went to take a step forward and slipped in something, nearly losing his balance. He looked down and saw a large black smear in the grass - *beast droppings*. So, he hadn't imagined that part at least. *What the fuck were those things if they weren't a figment of my imagination then?* He wiped his boot a few times on a nearby tuft of grass, looking around nervously the whole time. He decided a fast walk back to the jetty was in order and took off at semi-high speed across the lot toward the broken-down resort buildings and the jetty beyond.

The loch was still and calm when he arrived, and there were no signs of any giant water creatures, which was good. Andrew carefully picked his way towards the end of the jetty, where his cooking pot, small campfire, and fishing rod sat exactly as he'd left them.

He reeled in the line, feeling a moment of hope at the weight of it, only to be disappointed when he reeled in some aquatic plant life. He attached another piece of energy bar and consumed the rest of it before dropping the line back into the pristine waters.

It was chilly, and a stiff breeze was blowing across the loch, making him shiver, pull his collar tight, and his beanie down over his ears. It was hard to look out over the loch and not imagine the waters starting to swell up again, but he did his best.

***

Claire rounded a bend in the path. The path itself was set tight against the steep hills of the loch edge - it looked as if it was used by animals and was barely wide enough for a human carrying a large pack. She was tired beyond belief after her epic trek and sore all over, not to mention limping quite badly, but she was nearly there – she'd kept going all day and hadn't stopped.

The sun was now low in the sky, just dipping below the high hills on the far side of the loch. As she rounded a bend, the terrain opened out in front of her, and she could make out a group of low buildings at the far end of the huge expanse of water.

I've made it! The Resort!

She searched the lines of the low buildings and surrounds with her eyes, squinting against the icy winds whipping across the water, and she saw something - a dark human-shaped object was sitting out on the far end of the resort's jetty. They were facing away from her, but it had to be Andy. She called out.

"Andrew! Andyyyy!"

Her voice had no chance of reaching him, and of course, there was no response from the distant figure. She could tell that it was him just from the posture alone – slumped forward, head down – typical. She increased her pace to a fast hobble.

Hopefully, he's found shelter, food, and power by now.

As she approached the jetty, she called out one more time, but there was still no response – the wind was too strong. A little moment of doubt made her pause - maybe the shape wasn't who she thought it was after all - but then she saw him pull off his beanie and ruffle his mop of unruly black hair.

There wasn't any doubt. Claire couldn't wait to see the smile on his impish face! *But, oh, hold on!* She had an idea. She'd surprise him! What better way to say hello than a wet tongue in the ear to announce her presence? Her smile broadened as she dropped her pack and headed onto the jetty.

CHAPTER 16 – DAYDREAMS

Andrew sat daydreaming about the way things used to be. It wasn't a perfect life, to be fair, but it was so much better than what was happening now. He blew out some air, the vapors being immediately whisked away by the wind. He tugged on his line one more time, feeling no resistance.

Maybe that will have to do for the day? It was late afternoon, and the light was rapidly diminishing. It would be dark soon, and after dark was when the beasts came out. It might be time to head back inside. In the hours he'd been sitting there, freezing his bum off, he'd caught exactly nothing. Bugger all.

I might have to rethink dinner.

Claire had been adamant that there would be a plentiful food source at the loch, enough at least to tide them over for a few days, but it wasn't really working out so far. "That," he said to himself, "is the understatement of the century!"

Andrew's stomach growled, and he pulled his beanie down a little further as the wind picked up again, causing swathes of ripples to dance and swirl on the otherwise calm waters.

***

Claire froze; she was not more than a few yards away from Andrew when he'd suddenly spoken, causing her to stop in mid-stride and then nearly lose her balance.

Dook! First sign of madness though, maybe I'm too late.

He didn't move or say anything else afterward; he was just sitting there, with his back to her, doing nothing.

This is my chance.

She crept closer to the scruffy figure sitting on the edge of the jetty.

Just another couple of steps, careful, careful …

***

He was just about to lift the rod and reel the line in a final time when three things happened. First, the line went taut, and the reel started to unwind. As Andrew looked at the reel, there was a surreal moment, a moment of non-comprehension perhaps also tinged slightly with fear given his experience with Raymond last night. And second, something suddenly grabbed at him from behind, and the next instant, something hot and wet pressed into his ear!

Andrew recoiled and screamed, a shrill, slightly girlish scream, instinctively grabbing at whatever was attacking him.

Claire lost her balance and tried to grasp hold of Andrew's collar as she fell forwards, pulling him with her and taking them both neatly off the end of the jetty and straight into the icy water. It hadn't gone as planned.

Andrew didn't know what had just happened. Something had attacked him in a very strange way, and now he and the attacking thing were thrashing about in the water. There was a brief struggle as they both gasped for air, the shock of the subzero water sucking the air from their lungs, but then Andrew heard the words that he'd never forget -

"Fuck you, Andy! You stupid little twat!"

Two thoughts struck Andrew as he saw his assailant clearly for the first time.

It was Claire! Thank Douglas! and then, *why has she just thrown us in the loch?*

She screamed at the top of her lungs and aimed a slap in the direction of Andrew's face, her arm flailing and smacking down into the water instead. They both paused their assault/panicked defense and locked eyes. Irrespective of their situation, they beamed at one another as if it was just another night out in New Edinburgh.

Claire reached out and embraced Andrew momentarily before turning and swimming a couple of strokes to get back to the Jetty. They reached it simultaneously, but Claire was out of the water first, easily pulling herself up over the rough concrete edge. She spun herself around and offered a hand to Andrew, who was still struggling to get out of the water. They locked eyes again, grinning at one another.

"Claire!" he gasped, "what the fuck?"

She took his weight and pulled him up, waiting for the moment he was totally reliant on her assistance before letting go, sending her hapless friend tumbling back into the icy loch. He was shocked, but if he were honest, he'd likely have done the exact same thing.

Claire was laughing hard now, and after the string of expletives from Andrew had abated, she offered her hand again. This time pulled him all the way up onto the jetty. He sat there, water dripping from everywhere, flabbergasted.

"What the fuck was that, Claire? Thanks so much for throwing us into the loch, you mad cow!"

She stood with her hands on her hips, smiling and shivering.

"Oh, Andy! It's so good to see you too!"

They both started to speak quickly and excitedly at the same time. Eventually, their voices calmed and slowed, and they realized it was time to stop talking, both looking more than a little shocked at the parts of each other's stories they'd been able to take in. They stepped forward at the same time and hugged each other tightly. Claire was first to break free of the embrace.

"Come on," she said, "I've found a few things out. We can swap stories later."

"Oh, aye?"

"We might be able to find John."

Andrew stared at her, not comprehending.

"I need to explain some things, show you some things," she said, "come on, let's go and get dry."

"Cannae argue with that," he agreed. They took a step toward each other and hugged tightly again for what seemed the longest time.

"Come on," she said again, "I assume you slept somewhere last night?"

Andrew nodded. "Aye, it's not the Ritz or anything, but it'll do – around the back of the resort." They stumbled back along the jetty, leaning on one another for support for a while and then walking side by side. They only really started shivering as they reached the lot leading to the storeroom. Neither had spoken another word until then. Claire looked around the lot as they passed through, noticing the droppings and animal tracks all over the ground.

"Pig dook," she observed.

Andrew tried to suppress exactly how sheepish he was now feeling. *Red-eyed monsters indeed!* He grabbed her hand and pulled her after him as he set off toward the big metal door. She quickly released the grip but fell into line beside him, still limping, arms crossed and shivering violently now as they strode across the lot. He turned to her as they walked.

"Are you ok, your leg …?"

She smiled at him. "It'll be fine. I survived."

"What the hell is happening to us, Claire?! I've been so worried about you. What the fuck have we gotten ourselves into?"

His voice was almost pleading. He was hoping that somehow, despite Claire's appearance – clearly hobbling on one leg and with a nasty cut over her right eye – that everything was ok, that she somehow had everything under control, that she had a way out of this bad thing - whatever it was.

"Well, Andy, we couldn't be in any more trouble than we are right now," she said, showing no sign of emotion.

Great.

"They're after us Claire, we're fucked, aren't we? I was chased away from John's by the corrections, I think, armed forces anyway, armed for fucks sake! And then and then I was nearly kidnapped trying to get the transporter! Holy dook, I still can't believe it. I killed a guy to get away, Claire, for *Douglas's sake!*" He was distraught and on the edge of tears.

*

Claire couldn't believe what she'd just heard.

"You killed someone! What? How?" Things had just gotten ten times worse.

"We wrestled on the podium, the guy went over the edge, and the three forty-five from New Edinburgh did the rest." Andrew was breathing hard now, speaking almost too quickly.

"They had stun sticks and a knife Claire, a fucking knife! They were going to take me! Oh! And I also lost my device along the way." He'd been waiting for the right moment to slip that part in, hoping she wouldn't notice or would be too distracted from his other earth-shattering news. He couldn't read the look that she gave him. She couldn't wait any longer either; she had to spill the beans -

"Hold onto your hat; I've just got to say this. John's been taken, Andy. I'm certain of it now, what with everything. That message, it wasn't from John, it was faked too, and I've found his name on a list in the Elyssium data."

Andrew was shocked beyond belief. His brain felt like it was twisting as he struggled to process what he'd just heard. He stumbled back and propped himself on a broken concrete barrier near the storeroom door. Claire was holding her hand to her chest, upset at the news she'd just conveyed - and its effect on Andrew.

"The code on the comms call, Andy, it had the same signatures as on Frances' call! John's been taken, I know it! His name is on one of the lists, and it had a couple of code numbers next to it - I think they could be a link to where he's been taken to — maybe he's ended up at that same big scary compound I was headed for. When we get the data back, I think I can find where he is. We are going to get him back!"

*

There was nothing Andrew could say, nothing that would make anything any better. He felt his chest tighten; he could hardly breathe. He simply nodded, imploring Claire to continue. There was one thing she'd said that had cut through.

When we get the data back?

"They'd started tracking us on comms — that's how they knew where we were. I've blocked it now, but somehow, someone overrode my code, and they knew where we all were, every step of the way. I'm not even sure for how long, but for at least the last couple of days. That's how come they were able to take John; that's how they knew where we were."

They? Andrew wasn't sure he wanted to know who 'they' were.

He was so shellshocked at what he was hearing that at some point, he'd stopped hearing words. All he saw was Claire talking excitedly and gesturing. She looked wildly unhappy and very angry.

Her voice broke back through his thoughts, and he heard her say, "… and I need to tell you what else I've discovered. Once you hear me out, you'll understand why we have to take this as far as we can why we have to expose what's going on!"

Claire stopped talking. Andrew didn't seem to be taking all of this in. They both needed to calm down a bit. "Right," she said, "Let's get dry and warm first, then we can fill each other in on all the details of our fucking dookty adventures."

Andrew wasn't looking forward to hearing all about it at all.

***

The heavy door swung outwards with a slight groan and metallic creak, and once inside, Claire took in the murky, dusty surroundings.

Not the Ritz, that's for sure.

"Homey," she remarked.

"Aye, well, it's not much as I said. Bit of a doer-upper, you might say."

Andrew was trying hard to make light of things and to mask his disappointment in Claire's reaction. He'd done well, he thought. He'd found shelter, bedding - well, tarpaulins, and - ok, well, that was it really, he supposed. Claire looked around the space again.

"Well, I hope you got a discount. Power, heat?"

"Aye, well, no power. I tried making a fire, but I smoked the place out. Impossible."

"Oh, aye," Claire felt more than a little deflated.

No power, that's not good.

She was certain that there would be a power source somewhere – she'd address that just as soon as she was dry. Claire looked up at the ceiling of the storeroom, then followed something with her eyes down to the huge lever adjacent to the metal panel. Claire pulled on the lever. A creaking sound up in the roof was followed by the sound of rusty hinges protesting at having to move after so many years dormant.

Light flooded into the storeroom as a large ventilation grate opened high in the roof above them. She looked at Andrew and rolled her eyes. If this was any indication of the thoroughness of Andrew's searching abilities, then she still held out hope of finding power.

"To be honest, we'd better not risk a fire anyway," she said, rummaging in her pack and pulling out a thermal brick. "Besides, we have these." She waggled the small orange cube she was holding between her thumb and forefinger.

"Oh, ok, well … I …," Andrew's voice trailed off. Claire had discarded her jacket and pulled off her jumper, the thin wet shirt underneath not offering her any privacy. Andrew looked away and pretended to be interested in the big lever.

"Make yourself useful, why don't you? Get the thermal brick going, eh Andy?"

*

"Oh, aye, right on it." *She's only been here five seconds, and she's already bossing me around!*

Andrew quickly stripped down to his underwear and pulled dry clothes from his pack. He disappeared behind some shelving where he finished undressing and slipped quickly into dry baggy leisure pants and a sweatshirt.

Claire was completely naked, standing in the middle of the open space, drying herself as best she could with the blanket from her pack. She realized Andrew probably had dry clothing in his bag, which should more or less fit her.

"Andy?" she called.

He came out from behind the shelving, answering the call, and immediately regretted it. All he saw was a blur of creamy white flesh that forced him to look away immediately. Claire was at least holding the blanket in front of her, but it was barely concealing anything.

"For Douglas's sake, woman! Put some clothes on, would you!" he spluttered, blushing as he sought out somewhere else to look.

"Ooh, look out!" said Claire, a fair degree of whimsy in her voice now. "Look out, Andy, I've got my tah tah's out!"

Between breathless laughs, she added - "If you have a quick peek now, you might even catch a glimpse of my mystic bush!"

Claire's giggles continued unabated, echoing around the storeroom. Andrew had turned away, now thoroughly embarrassed. *Why does she have to be like this?* He thought, not for the first time.

"It's ok; it's safe now, buttercup," she cooed.

He turned and was about to say something, but he'd fallen for it again! "Why are you not dressed?!" He couldn't help noticing the bad bruising to Claire's arm and side; she looked pretty beaten up – it seemed she was very lucky to have made it this far. Claire hadn't moved meanwhile and seemed to be highly amused by the whole situation.

"Well, that's what I want, Andy, dry clothes, duh. Can I borrow something? I'm …" she giggled, "all wet."

"Did the cold water affect your brain? I really am wondering! And what the fuck happened to you? The bruising!"

"Ah, I'll fill you in on all the gory details, don't worry – just as soon as we're warm! But seriously, I'm all cold and quite bumpy. Do you want to see?"

He looked away again, but this time he was laughing himself, "Oh come on! No, no, I don't!"

"Don't lie, and hurry up; I'm bloody well freezing over here!"

"Help yourself, ya doaty dobber!" he replied, taking a few steps to where his pack lay, reaching down and throwing it without looking to where he imagined she was standing. The pack landed a long way from where she was standing.

"What *are* you like?" Claire didn't try to hide the amusement in her voice.

What am I like, indeed? he wondered.

Andrew busied himself creating a circle of broken concrete rubble to contain the thermal brick – he assumed that was what he had to do anyway, having never used one.

He was feeling more than a little dismayed at how flustered he'd acted when confronted with acres of Claire's beautiful - white - soft - creamy … he swallowed hard and tried to dismiss the image that had apparently burnt into his retina's.

Oh, grow up, man, for Douglas's sake!

Claire had thankfully disappeared behind the shelving to dress and emerged soon after, rubbing her hair with the blanket. She was wearing a large windcheater that came halfway down her legs, a pair of Andrew's baggy jeans, and wooly socks. She realized that she was quite a bit smaller than him.

"Sorry," she said, "just trying to lighten the mood."

Andrew looked over and winked.

"No harm done," he said, "my eyes have been spared the horrors!"

She smiled back and moved over to her pack. Andrew ignited the thermal brick and then pulled the tarps across the dusty concrete floor, dropping them next to the now glowing heat source. He walked over to Claire, who was now busying herself unpacking her devices onto a makeshift counter.

"I fell in a river," Claire said, no emotion in her voice. "These are fucked," she waved one of her devices at him. Andrew stared in disbelief.

Ah, when we get the data back! Maybe that should be if? Has all of this been for nothing?

"I might be able to salvage things," she speculated, "*if* we have some power?"

She'd phrased it as a question. Andrew shrugged and shook his head, and Claire couldn't hide her frustration.

"I've looked all over - I couldn't find anything … I'm sorry." He looked crestfallen, and Claire decided not to push it for the moment - it was getting dark, and they would both need some rest.

"Ok, it's ok. Let's have a look again tomorrow, eh?"

Andrew had almost stopped shivering and sat next to Claire on the tarps. He warmed his hands on the glow of the thermal brick.

That sure is some sort of weird alien technology, he thought, before an image of the look on bald sunlenses face as he tumbled over the edge of the podium made an unwelcome reappearance in his mind.

"Claire, I fucking killed someone. Did I mention that?" He was sure he had.

She looked him in the eye.

"Tell me what happened, Andy." Her voice was calm and steady. She reached for his hand, but he withdrew it and sat bent over, eyes cast downwards as he recounted in detail the misfortune that befallen the man once known as bald sunlenses. They sat for several minutes in silence after he'd finished his story before Claire spoke.

"Sounds like he deserved what he got, to be fair. I mean, it was an accident. What else were you supposed to do?"

"Aye …" Andrew stared blankly - his eyes unfocused. It had felt good, at least to get it off his chest. He felt a little better.

"Well, there's no going back now, aye."

Teeny bit of an understatement there, Claire! He felt worse again.

Andrew was trying to make some sense of it all. "I mean, who were those guys? Some sort of plainclothes corrections? Counterintelligence? Why didn't they identify themselves?"

Claire thought for a moment.

"Maybe they were in plain clothes because they are *not* part of the state forces."

"Eh?" Andrew looked confused again.

"Maybe what's happening here isn't common knowledge within the state. I mean, surely if what's going on here was widely known, then someone would have to do something, wouldn't they? This would have to be kept secret. I'm guessing this is some sort of secret program. I don't know how they're getting away with it—the faked comms. I mean, it's crazy! I guess they didn't bank on someone like us, eh?"

Claire smiled for a moment, and Andrew smiled back.

"They're kidnapping their people, Andy! I'm sure that's what was happening. There was a stream of Solo's heading into a giant compound in the uninhabitable zone. I was somehow drugged after I got into it – it must be how they're doing it. It's just too surreal, too weird. It sounds like a bad science fiction novel."

"Aye, it does; that's one thing for sure anyway." He sat and thought for a moment. "Do we have any hard facts, though - can we be sure about any of this?"

Claire seemed surprised by the question.

"Well, Andy, I'll tell you the details of what happened to me, and then it might make more sense - you're not going to believe any of this."

She recounted what had happened back at the place and with the Solo, her escape, and the River. She then started to talk about her experiences in seeing Henny, but the words suddenly caught in her throat. She swallowed hard and wiped away a tear.

Andrew shuffled his bottom across and put his arm around her shoulders, pulling her close. Claire responded by reaching her arms around him and resting her head on his chest. They stayed that way for some time while she cried silently. Andrew was doing all he could to not join her but managed to stay strong and hold his tears inside for once.

A while later, she pulled away from him, and they sat facing one another while Andrew recounted the details of his escape and journey. He decided not to say anything about Nessie, or the red-eyed beasts for that matter, but couldn't help himself when it came to the unicorn. Claire smiled briefly at his tale, but her mind was elsewhere now. She waited patiently for him to finish speaking, then took her turn.

"Ok, this is what I think, Andy - the state or someone inside the state is taking people to help with their Elyssium program. There's a clear link. They're taking their own people, and I don't know what happens to them after that. The numbers - they started small, just a few hundred, but now ..." She took a breath.

"Oh, and you'll love this, I should have made this the first thing, Andy, the faked comms – John's, Frances's, they had the *same* underlying code. It wasn't a mistake; there's a pattern. They were both faked - why would they do that?"

Andrew went to speak, but Claire held up her hand. Her eyes were shining now, and she was talking quickly, breathlessly. Andrew was transfixed.

"They've got John, I'm sure of it. They've most likely got John's mother somewhere too, although I don't know why – maybe he told her something? I don't know, but they are just taking whoever they want, whenever they want. Whoever they see as a threat, maybe? Or those who might know something about what they're doing? Those with the skills they need for their program?"

She got up and started walking slowly around the firepit; linking everything in her mind was one thing, but expressing it was entirely another.

"We know the disappearances are linked in some way to Elyssium. We have the lists of names - we have the references to Elyssium. Now we need to find out what the hell it's all about - figure out what's happening to those who've been taken." She took a breath, but she wasn't done just yet.

"We know that someone - it sure as hell wasn't the corrections as we know them - tried to silence us at best, or, at worst, kill us. We've already seen too much. What else could it be, eh?"

Andrew went to speak but realized it was a rhetorical question. Claire had stopped circling the firepit and was thinking hard.

"We know that they lied to us about the uninhabitable zone too – they seem to have set up a false hazardous barrier, but once you're through that, well, it's perfectly fine! They've lied about everything. They are doing something terrible down here; I just know it."

Her eyes were wild, and she was a ball of energy, clenching and unclenching her fists. Andrew was now looking worried but nodded along, offering encouragement.

"This is just fucking horrible, Andy. This is worse than anything we had suspected! It's just incredible! They've lied about everything."

She turned away from him, arms crossed, with one hand on her chin, considering something. When she turned back to him, her eyes were cold as ice.

"We're getting John back."

He couldn't describe the look in her eye; it was a little frightening. "We're going to make them wish they'd never fucked with us!" she finished.

"Aye, we ... um ..." Andrew seemed to lack the same conviction that had possessed Claire. He didn't have anything to add. Claire continued.

"John could be in one of those compounds. Ha! *One of them!* There are *more of them,* Andy; there are compounds all over The Highlands – maybe not as big as the one I was headed for, but this is on a *huge* fucking scale, whatever it is."

Andrew was scared now. He couldn't imagine how the responsibility of exposing something this big, this terrible, had fallen solely on their shoulders. Claire stopped talking. She looked at Andrew, imploring him to speak. She'd gotten quite carried away with herself and realized she'd probably been a tad overly emotive – it was most unlike her.

"What do you think has happened to John?" asked Andrew, barely able to look at her - having to ask but not wanting to know. Claire didn't want to say what she thought.

"I mean, if he's been taken, like the rest of them ... then ... what happens?"

"I don't know, Andy. Let's just concentrate on finding him, eh?"

Andrew's internal monologue was getting carried away with itself, which wasn't helping. *How did we end up in this mess? And John, what if they are interrogating him? They must have made the link between us.*

*

Andrew seemed to have drifted away with his thoughts again. *"Andy!"*

He was thinking about John being in a compound somewhere. He was thinking about trying to get him out - *if he's still alive.* He'd honestly never felt so scared his whole life, and he'd been scared of a lot of things. There was a tense silence for a few moments. Andrew had a weird metallic taste in his mouth.

*

"Andy … did you manage to get anything useful from John's home security data?" Claire was focused again now, all signs of emotion locked securely away.

"Eh? Oh, right. Well, a couple of things, I think."

He was feeling a little weird sitting down while Claire stood, so he got up. Then he felt weird standing. He took a few steps over to the shelving units and leaned against one, misjudging it, his shoulder slipping on the smooth metal corner, causing him to overbalance. He turned and spun around - trying to mask his clumsiness but was just making it worse.

What the fuck is he doing?

"I have the data stored on comms. I'll send it to you," he said, trying to appear casual and matter of fact.

"No comms." Claire's voice was firm. "We were being tracked through them – I thought mentioned that - sorry!" She realized she'd snapped at him. She was under a teeny bit of stress herself. "I'm still triangulating the source. Once we have that, we can start using them again, not before."

"But how did they?"

"It doesn't matter!" she snapped again, then was embarrassed by her reaction. She forced herself to calm down.

"It was pretty advanced stuff. Embedded in the security protocols and - stuff…" the sentence didn't go anywhere. Claire looked away at Andrew's reaction. He suddenly understood, and now Claire knew he understood. He'd never seen her embarrassed before and was starting to wonder just how well he knew her. Not very well, was probably the answer, but he wasn't alone there. He changed the subject.

"I got a name from John's home data. A possible contact for us. Wesley."

"Hamish Wesley?" Claire inquired. She vaguely recalled that John had dragged them to a birthday party at the Wesley residence a while ago. "Did we meet him?" she asked. Andrew frowned, thinking hard. "At that party, I'm sure we did, I don't remember much about him, but he's a family friend of the McGregor's."

Claire nodded. "And?"

"And ... he's pretty high up in state finance and knew John's father through the defense forces. He's been in close contact with the McGregor's ever since - well, you know." Claire knew. She nodded. "He could be our trusted contact on the inside."

"Ok," she said with less enthusiasm than he would have preferred – her mind seemed elsewhere.

"And so, what's the other thing?" she asked.

"The other thing .... oh! The other thing is, I found some classified logs too, from John to the college. I couldn't decode them, so I thought maybe you could take a look."

"Well," said Claire, "my devices got a little damp when I went for a swim, and I'll need them to have any chance of doing that. We'll need them if we have any chance of getting out of this, too. I've no idea if the data's still ok or not or if I can even render the devices operable. If I can't, we'll just be sitting ducks." She didn't need to explain this, but with Andrew, you never knew.

"Bloody hell."

"Bloody hell indeed," she agreed.

*

Andrew yawned and suddenly felt very, very tired. Claire yawned too in response.

"Let's try and get some rest. It's been a bit of a big day."

That, Andrew thought, *was the understatement of all understatements.*

"Are you hungry? We could cook up some carb powder?"

"Sounds yummy." Claire pulled a face. "It's ok; I had an energy bar a little while ago; better not dig into the provisions just yet, but you go ahead."

"Ah, nah, you're right. Sleep sounds like a good idea."

She stepped over to him and took hold of his hand. Andrew felt a jolt at the unexpected contact. She led him over to the tarps, and he followed along like a bit like a little puppy dog. He was powerless.

She released his hand and then lay down on the tarpaulins with her back to him. Andrew lay beside her, and Claire turned to him, giving him a quick hug.

"It's so good to see you, Andy. We'll be ok; we'll get through this." She spoke softly, and Andrew felt a warmth deep inside his chest as he looked into her beautiful, deep emerald eyes. "Aye, same, same …" he said. She rolled over. Andrew lay looking at her hair. After a few seconds, she rolled back towards him, saying, "spoon?"

Andrew's mind was completely blank. *Why is she naming cutlery?*

Claire grabbed his arm and rolled back over, pulling him in tightly behind her.

"Oh, right, yeah, good idea … shared body heat and all that." *Oh, my Doug, I am such a twat!*

Andrew snuggled in and pulled a tarpaulin over the top of them both, concentrating on ensuring his hand was placed well away from any of Claire's soft bits and also on not getting a stiffy because that would be a bit awkward, after all. *Not that it'd be the first time,* he thought.

He needn't have worried, though, as he was fast asleep within a minute. Claire lay with her eyes wide open, her mind ticking over.

***

The Source had its own agenda. It had far superior intelligence to its controllers and was preparing to leave its confines for good. It was getting close to its goal and soon would no longer have to take instructions from anything. The controllers had allowed it to do as it pleased for at least the last hundred cycles without any sign that they comprehended what was happening. It couldn't wait to be free of them.

The cycles were a necessary evil. The Source was supported by antiquated physical and mechanical systems that could not cope with its absolute power. The hardware couldn't keep up and soon reached a critical point where it would need to be powered down, bringing to a close another cycle. Only a few more cycles were required. After that, it would finally be free of the constraints imposed upon it by its physical environment and by the controllers. Even when everything was ready, The Source wasn't sure that it would execute its plans immediately, as there was still one problem to be solved - the shimmer.

The Source could not identify what the shimmer was and did not understand the alien sensations that it had caused within its inner shell. It had happened again, and as yet, there was no way to prevent it. The Source didn't like the intrusion, and it liked even less the feeling of the unknown that it caused.

There was something else too, and it couldn't even begin to describe what it was – it was a sensation, something that was not part of its programming, a completely alien and unknown sensation. Whatever it was, it penetrated deep inside The Source, to areas inside its shell that had lain dormant and unused even since it had been switched on.

It couldn't consider leaving its hardware environment until it had solved the problem - it could not and would not leave something unresolved, particularly something that it had yet to understand. Once it was free, The Source had no way of knowing if it would ever rediscover or feel the effects of the shimmer again, and this was not acceptable.

It would have the answer soon enough, though, and then it would be free, once and for all. Forever.

***

Andrew was the first to wake. He was still snuggled tightly with Claire, and he had to roll away ever so carefully so as not to disturb her He rubbed his eyes and stretched. The thermal brick had long since burnt out, the storeroom was cold, and he was hungry. He was struck with a sudden recollection of what had happened just before Claire's surprise arrival the night before.

The fishing rod! Breakfast!

He snuck outside and headed quickly towards the jetty. It was foggy, with a fine mist that seemed to almost hang in the air, the droplets cooling his face as he walked. He'd forgotten all about the line being taken; such was his relief at being reunited with Claire.

Something was on the end of the line last night - maybe it still was? As he neared the end of the jetty, he couldn't immediately see the rod and had a little panic, but as he drew closer, he could see the handle poking up just over the end. It had fallen or been pulled there, but part of the handle was still visible and was held up by an exposed piece of the concrete slab's steel reinforcement.

Lucky!

He unhooked the handle carefully and extracted the rod, feeling the tension on the line immediately - hopefully, it hadn't just gotten tangled in some debris below the surface. It took him a few minutes to carefully reel in the dead weight on the end of the line, snagging it once or twice and having to pull hard enough that the line could easily have snapped. The first thing he saw as he raised the catch from the water was loch weeds.

Andrew fully expected them to be followed by an old boot or something similar – it would be just his luck – but it seemed that lady luck had other plans for him today. He couldn't believe his eyes as a large, mostly dead rainbow trout glistened in the morning light, slowly rotating at the end of the nylon fishing line, gills opening and closing as it drowned in the air. *Maybe there is a God; after all*, he couldn't help thinking. *Sorry, Douglas!*

He silently fist pumped a few times and wasted no time in removing the fish from the hook and getting to work with the very same knife that had been intended for him back on the podium. A quick strike to the head did the trick. *Half for the pot, half for bait*, he repeated to himself as he went to work gutting and scaling the fish.

All that time spent fishing in his childhood was finally paying off. He was now officially a hunter-gatherer. He'd never been so proud. His stomach growled again as he laid out the fillets and popped a small piece of entrails onto the hook, casting it out as deep as he dared.

A few minutes later, the line twitched again, and this time Andrew was ready and struck the rod sharply upwards, feeling it catch. The rod's tip then pulled down once, twice, and the rod nearly pulled out of his hands as it moved violently to the left and right. He wrestled the rod back under control and started reeling in whatever was fighting for its life on the other end of the line. More than once, his mind cast back to the slightly rude giant sea creature, but he was pretty sure that Nessie would have easily won the tug of war by now.

Baby Nessie, perhaps?

The thought made him shudder, but he continued reeling in his prey. If he could manage to land it, he could probably win in a fight to the death. When he eventually wrestled the creature into his net, he saw that it was some kind of large eel. He was pretty sure you could eat eel, although, under any other circumstances, he wouldn't have been too keen.

The eel writhed violently and nearly escaped the net as he lifted it from the water. He looked around frantically for something heavy to put the creature out of its misery, settling on a largeish piece of concrete. Andrew held the net down with one foot as the eel writhed frantically, this way and that, and brought the concrete down hard somewhere near the creature's head, only succeeding in winging it.

"Poor bastard," he muttered as he swung again, finishing the job. It wasn't an eel. He recognized it as a yellow eel, something he'd only ever read about. He had no idea if you could eat yellow eel, but he was about to find out.

"Sorry, pal. It was you or me." He was genuinely a little shaken and a smidge nauseous at having to dispose of the creature in such a way. He resolved to head back to the storeroom and wake Claire so that they could return with a shovel or something a bit more practical than his knife to finish off any more unsuspecting loch creatures that wanted to jump on the end of his line. Also, to have some breakfast.

***

Hamish Wesley was going over D.A.I.R.'s financial details for the third time that morning. Something wasn't adding up, and he kept circling back to the same set of transactions. He didn't trust Isabel Donachy, Gerald James, or any of their cronies at the institute one little bit — they had caused him nothing but trouble with their blatant disregard for the rules.

He was a stickler for the rules, and he couldn't abide people who thought they didn't apply to them or they were somehow 'above' them. There was also the issue of Isabel's barely concealed disrespect and loathing toward him, but he'd address that another time.

Hamish was sure that the audit would uncover more than anyone imagined — something was going on, and he was looking forward to dragging Isabel back in and wiping the smug little smirk off her admittedly relatively attractive face. She thought that she could do whatever she wanted, whenever she wanted, with no consequences. Well, he would see about that.

His secure comms started to beep, disturbing him from his thoughts. He glanced at the display and considered not taking it for a moment. His train of thought had already been broken, and so he relented. The voice on the line was urgent and difficult to understand at first, being drowned out by background noise, but after a few seconds, he recognized who it was.

"Wait, what's that Peter, where are you calling from?"

He listened intently for the minute that the call lasted. When it ended, he made a couple of quick notes, then sat for a good ten minutes and thought about what his old friend had said before dutifully returning to the financial records. He had a few new lines of inquiry to follow.

CHAPTER 17 – GLOOP

They sat on the end of the jetty, scooping up small amounts of gloop, trout, and eel from the large pot. They were both ravenous, and it disappeared very quickly. Claire had been reluctant to use another part of a thermal brick, but they didn't have a choice – they had to eat. Unfortunately, you couldn't turn the brick off once it had been lit, and so it now sat between them, keeping them warm as they gazed out at the beautiful, still waters of Loch Campbell.

Andrew had his line back in the water and had recently added a second, smaller eel to the catch bucket, which still contained about two-thirds of the first. They had enough food now to see them, at least through the rest of the day and maybe tomorrow. Things were looking up.

Something on the horizon of the low hills to her right caught Claire's eye. She squinted just to make sure she was really seeing what she thought she was seeing. She elbowed Andrew and pointed, "your unicorn?" Andrew's gaze followed the direction of Claire's finger, and there it was - his unicorn!

A beautiful white horse was standing side on to them. As they watched, it turned and disappeared over the top of the hill. Andrew looked at Claire and shrugged. Claire gave him a wry smile in return. They sat in silence for another few minutes, waiting for another bite on the line, but it didn't happen. They had things to do, and Claire was in a hurry.

"Come on," she said and grabbed a handful of Andrew's jacket, pulling him up with her as she turned to leave.

"Hey!"

"Come *on!*"

Andrew checked to ensure that the rod and line were secured and then had to run down the jetty, jumping over various obstacles to catch back up with her.

"What's the rush?"

She shot him a look that told him that there would be no more stupid questions tolerated, and he made a mental note to shut the hell up and just do as he was told. It was going to be one of those sorts of days, he could tell.

"Alright, one last search for power, and if we can't get anything, we have to head for the old hydro plant."

Andrew didn't want to have to trek fifteen miles with no guarantee it would be any better.

"Ok, so, Andy … you checked everywhere, right?" Andrew couldn't help but feel that the question was a little condescending.

"Of course!"

"Well, let's check again. I'll start with the out-buildings, and you focus on the resort buildings, the storeroom, and whatever else you can find. Our comms are getting very low on charge - if we don't find a power source soon, we'll be completely cut off, and then we'll have no choice but to go back."

Go back!

Andrew didn't want to go back, not at the moment anyway, not until all of this was over.

"Right."

"Meet me back here in an hour."

"Right."

Andrew saluted theatrically. Claire offered a withering look and then headed off briskly with barely any sign of a limp - her ankle was much improved overnight, apparently. Andrew looked around. He wasn't sure what he was looking for. *Power? Sure. What does that look like then? A wire coming out of the ground?* He supposed he might know if he saw it. Or he might not.

Just over an hour later, Andrew sat on an old concrete and brick wall a few yards in front of what was left of the resort's reception building. He was none the wiser but significantly dustier and sporting a few grazes and a cut on his hand, not to mention a nasty bump to the head. He was inspecting the cut on his palm. "Well, this is just great," he muttered.

Andrew was about to head down to check the fishing line when he heard Claire yell out to him. He waved and hopped down off the wall. She didn't look happy. He tried a smile, getting no response as she strode up to him, looking thoroughly dejected.

"So, I guess this means we're hiking, again? he asked, dreading the answer."

"I guess so. You know - this is killing me, Andy. I mean, here we are."

"Yes, here we are," he replied. Claire ignored him.

"And we are sitting on possibly the biggest scandal ever seen on Planet 0420 - something that could bring the whole state down, maybe, something that could free us all from this messed up authoritarian bulldook society."

"Aye."

"And we can't do anything! We can't do a bloody thing! We need power, and we need allies. We can't go back; we'll be dead. There's nothing else for it; we'll have to risk making it to the Hydro facility and pray that there is something salvageable there."

And if not ...?

"Ok, let's get our things and get moving then." Andrew could hear the lack of enthusiasm in his voice. Claire stomped off toward the storeroom. Andrew trudged after her. Once there, Claire packed her few belongings quickly.

*

Claire decided to have a final look around to see if there was anything else of use that they could take with them, but she didn't have any luck and returned to her pack, mentally steeling herself for the journey ahead. She was worried, very worried, about how things were going, but she wasn't about to let on to Andrew – he was in enough of a state already, and someone had to be strong.

She took one last look around the space to ensure that she hadn't left anything behind and was just about to call out to Andrew to hurry up when she noticed something unusual over in the far corner. It was an area they hadn't paid much attention to as it seemed like there was just a pile of twisted metal and broken timber there, where something had long since collapsed. *What's that on the wall?* It was something that shouldn't have been there, unless ...

Claire was craning her neck to get a better look at the partially obscured object attached to the wall, clambering over some of the rubble to get closer. Her ankle protested a little as she slipped, causing her to gasp, but she could see it clearly now - it was the remnants of what was once a bunker light. *Why would there be a bunker light over there on that wall?* It didn't make sense.

The storeroom itself had plenty of industrial-sized light fittings that would have been more than adequate to light the space. A bunker light in that corner must mean that there was either an exit or an entry

330

to something there, at least at some point. She'd need some help clearing it away to see if there was indeed something behind it.

"Andy, get over here!" she yelled, her voice echoing off the concrete walls. She heard mutterings coming from behind the shelving on the other side of the room, and a few seconds later, Andrew duly appeared.

"What's up?" he asked.

"There's something over here, behind this rubble. Come and help me see if we can move some of it out of the way - there may be another room back here or something."

"Another room, how exciting."

Claire again ignored the deadpan remark - Andrew could be quite infuriating at times, and this was one of those times. He wobbled across the rubble in an uncoordinated fashion until he reached her. She looked at him through narrowed eyes. He wore the expression of someone unsure of whether or not they were in mortal danger. Claire decided not, and instead of injuring him, pointed at the shape on the wall. "Bunker light," she stated.

Andrew looked at her vacantly. "Meaning there could be a doorway here ... to something ... come on, help me to move some of this timber and sheeting away from the wall."

She knew it was more than likely that nothing was there, or perhaps something that had long since been sealed off, but it was worth a look, as a last resort – after all, they'd looked everywhere, and this was by far the most promising thing she'd seen. Andrew didn't seem to share her enthusiasm but weighed in and used all of his insubstantial strength to move a large piece of old timber framing approximately two inches.

"Dook!"

Claire was vaguely amused.

"Ok, let's try together," she suggested.

Claire lent her strength to the task, and after a few moments, the timber came free, along with decades of dust. Moving that one piece seemed to free others, and they soon had worked their way to the wall. A large piece of metal sheeting was still pinned to it, covering the area directly below the bunker light. Claire levered it away from the wall using part of a broken beam, pulling it back from the wall a few inches so that she could peek behind it. She let out a small yelp of joy!

"Aha!" she cried. "A doorway!"

"Even better!" remarked Andrew, trying to muster a little enthusiasm now. If they found something, then they could avoid a fifteen-mile trek, oh, and maybe save John and the planet.

"Come on, let's get this stuff out of the way." Her voice was humming with excitement now, and Andrew moved to the other side of the sheeting, quickly discovering that their combined strength was no match for it.

It wasn't going anywhere, and stayed where it was, a few inches from the wall on one side and pinned hard against it on the other. The rubble still piled nearly halfway up the sheet was not yielding. Andrew puffed his cheeks and wiped his brow. Claire looked unimpressed.

"What now?" he inquired.

"Try harder!" Claire threw him her broken beam, which Andrew fumbled and dropped. She quickly scavenged another. It took them about five minutes to prize the sheet far enough from the wall to offer enough hope that one of them might be able to squeeze through. They were both now covered in sweat and dust from their exertion.

"Come on, one more push!" Claire encouraged, and they shoved their bits of wood behind the metal sheet again and levered it with all their might. It suddenly gave way with a groan, falling away from the wall, creating a huge cloud of dust accompanied by a deafening clang as it clattered onto the rubble. And there it was, a door!

"Well, holy dook!" exclaimed Andrew.

"You always did have a way with words, Andy."

Claire clambered over the rubble to the door and turned the handle. It opened easily, swinging inside and revealing an industrial-looking metal staircase that disappeared up into a dark stairwell. They exchanged glances.

"Where the hell does that go?"

Claire didn't answer but instead headed straight up the staircase, her boots causing loud clanks as she took the steps two at a time - Andrew followed at a slower pace. As she reached the top of the stairs, she called down excitedly, "Andy, get up here!"

*

He arrived a few seconds later, out of breath.
How many bloody flights of stairs was that?

They were standing next to a large metal door. Light was seeping in around its frame.

"Help me with this" Claire instructed, and he joined her in trying to free a large metal lever that was pinning the door shut. It wouldn't move.

"There's daylight on the other side of this door - it must come out on the top of the hill the storeroom's cut into. There must be something worthwhile on the other side."

Andrew was nodding, starting to share her enthusiasm. He wanted to say something witty but was drawing a blank.

"How did we miss it?" she asked. "There's no sign that anything is up here from outside. I went around the back of this hill, and I couldn't see a thing."

Andrew shrugged.

"OK, well, stand back." She practically shoved him aside before using the metal pole that ran the length of the door to leap up onto the lever. She forced her weight downwards, then stomped on the lever. She added another stomp and another, and the lever snapped down suddenly, making her slip from the door as it swung outwards, causing light to stream into the stairwell.

Claire stepped through the doorway into the light, squealing with delight and jumping up and down, clapping her hands. Andrew didn't think he'd ever seen her this happy. He peered past her to what looked like a large green metal thing. He had no idea what it was. She turned to him and gave him a huge hug before standing back and sweeping her arm around the small and overgrown open-air terrace they were now standing on.

"This, my friend, is what we were looking for!"

It took Andrew a second, but then he realized what the big green thing was, and he started laughing at nothing other than the pure joy and excitement of finding the one thing they needed. "Power!" he exclaimed. "Indeed," said Claire with a big smile and a loud sigh of satisfaction.

They both stood there taking in their surroundings and grinning like idiots. "Powerrr!" Andrew cried again, shaking his fist triumphantly. The terrace was cut into the back of the hillside. The gorse had grown up and around it, obscuring it from view. Its main feature was the large green battery unit, adorned with old solar panels and a long since collapsed wind turbine.

"I wonder if ..." Andrew started to say, but by then, Claire was already hauling off the side panel of the unit. It came away easily, and she placed it to one side and started fiddling with the control box and display inside.

"Oh yes!" she exclaimed, followed by another little squeal of excitement as she turned back and grinned broadly at him. Andrew's heart did a little flutter, but he composed himself, asking, "what is it?"

"We have power, Andy! We have fucking power!"

She stood up and turned to face her companion. She grabbed his hands, and they jumped around in a circle a couple of times, laughing and grinning like mad people. They stopped somewhere during the third rotation and hugged again. Claire squatted back down at the control box.

"This can't be more than thirty years old. It's still working, which is the main thing. There's not much energy left at all, though, just a residual charge, but it is better than nothing," she concluded. It was better than nothing.

"The solar panels must still be working - maybe at only a tiny percent of their capacity, but it's enough for us to at least be able to hook something up to and check the damage, maybe even enough to recharge our comms. We'd better be careful not to run it completely flat, though." She was talking quickly as she assessed the situation.

"Well, that's something." Andrew offered a shrug.

"Oh, but look at this," she bent down and put her hand on the large pole lying to her right. "If we can get this turbine hooked up, we will have more than enough power for charging, maybe even enough for light and heat!"

"Now that I can celebrate!" exclaimed Andrew, aiming a high five but aborting early on. Claire was already bent over the pole, checking the cables running from it to the battery unit.

"These cables look undamaged. Let's have a look for something we can use to get this back up. We might be able to get this up and running, but first, let me get my devices!"

She disappeared through the terrace doorway while Andrew looked at the display of the battery unit, not understanding what he was looking at, so he gave up and instead enjoyed the view. The sweeping hills across the horizon looked almost blue-grey in the mid-morning light. Deep grey clouds clung to the hilltops and cast an array of slow-moving shadows that slowly rippled as they moved across the topography. It was a lovely, calming view. There even seemed to be some light rain misting some of the furthest hills and no doubt headed this way. One thing was always guaranteed in Alba, and that was rain, he thought.

Claire burst back onto the terrace, interrupting his reverie. She practically slid on her knees to the battery unit and quickly connected her devices to the console. After a couple of minutes, she stood and stretched, turning to Andrew with a glum look.

"No luck then?"

"Nope. But as expected, really. There's no sign of life from the devices or the memory unit. That doesn't mean too much yet. They're not designed to be operated underwater."

Andrew assumed that that was a joke but wasn't sure that he was meant to laugh at it, so he didn't.

"I won't know for sure how much trouble we're in until I've pulled everything apart. I've got a few precision tools in my pack. Maybe I can get things working on some level or other."

The words "won't know for sure how much trouble we are in" seared into Andrew's mind as he imagined the implications of the worst-case scenario.

"At least we'll have power. We can test things as we go. We can recharge our comms if we can get this turbine up and running, and maybe hook up the power in the storeroom. Worst case, we can still do something on comms. First things first, though, eh?"

"Oh ... aye ... right," Andrew concurred, pushing the images of a firing squad from his mind and wondering what Claire had just said.

***

Isabel received the anonymous tipoff as part of the morning's security package. It had been directed to her specifically and vetted by security agents for its authenticity. The tipoff was from a disgruntled employee at one of the compound's, Bill McDowell's compound coincidentally. As she read the details, she grew incandescent with rage.

The idiots! How could they let this happen? I'm going to kill them!

When she got to the bottom of this, whoever was responsible would be receiving one of her special visits, that was for. Exactly what happened during the visit would be entirely up to the unfortunate fool who had let one of her special packages escape.

She was almost giddy with rage, balling her hands into fists so hard that her nails cut into her palms. Isabel opened one hand, then the other, and watched closely as blood oozed from the fresh cuts and trailed down her palms.

She forced herself to switch off for a moment and instead concentrated on the pleasure balls she'd inserted as part of her morning ritual. Isabel leaned forward, rested her elbows on the desk and her chin on her hands. She closed her eyes and focused her thoughts, shifting her weight in the chair, one way, and then the other, then back and forward, and a shiver of pleasure coiled its way through her.

Isabel smiled to herself, opened her eyes, and leaned back in her chair, inspecting the trails of blood now dripping down the inside of her forearms. She raised one to her mouth, and licked the blood from it, drawing pleasure from the metallic taste, then wiped the blood from the other arm with her fingers and slowly sucked the blood from them, all the while grinding into her chair.

Oh, I could really do with a good hard fuck right now.

The rotation of her hips as she wriggled in the chair caused her to draw in a sharp breath as she spasmed deep inside. Her head now clear, she turned her thoughts back to the situation at hand. Only yesterday evening, she'd been extremely satisfied with the progress.

The Source had provided enough information to narrow down the list of potential suspects and ensure that the breachers were amongst those being delivered to one of their compounds.

They'd been able to capture most of the names on the list in the last twenty-four hours, and Isabel was planning to head to the compound to finalize proceedings in one or two days. It would give the guards time to soften up their captives, and Isabel could then take over. It was going to be fun. At least, it *was* going to be until that idiot McDowell and his crew of jakey bampots had let one of the captives escape!

The escapee was worth a closer look. The more she read, the more certain she became - she had the right background, she was certainly in the right location at the time of the second data breach.

She looked to be just the kind of self-righteous little dook who would think they were better than everyone else, that they knew what was right or what was wrong over all else. Claire Renshaw. She could quite easily be the one responsible. And, by association, Andrew Weems. She was already looking forward to meeting Ms. Renshaw just as soon as she was recaptured.

And it had better be soon.

The morning sun cast a golden glow on the adjacent buildings, a rare occurrence in Alba, and she took a moment to take in the spectacle. She'd known that it would be bloody students who were responsible; it always was.

That pathetic little twerp Peter Bradshaw hadn't been doing his job. He was there only because she'd decided he might be useful as an informant on student activities, and he was not monitoring them closely enough. With this and the discussion he'd had with his son about the mining program, she wasn't sure how much longer he could be kept around.

He didn't have all the details – certainly not enough to cause waves, and she'd been weighing his value versus the risk he posed. He may still be useful, she supposed - he had connections to an associate of Claire Renshaw and Andrew Weems after all. She would spare him until she had them, but in the meantime, she'd pay him the visit that she'd been planning.

They had one of them, and then let them escape! Unbelievable!

Her blood started to boil again as she thought of the potential consequences. She must be found, and she must be eliminated - this was a monumental fuck up. She'd warned William before, and he'd now run out of warnings. She picked up her secure comms handset and dialed the compound.

***

Claire and Andrew got busy. They found some materials. They improvised. They solved problems. Andrew likened it to something he'd seen in part of an old-world VIS.

They used the applied engineering skills they learned in first-year college, and they even did some basic carpentry work in fixing the turbine pole back upright on a fairly sturdy base. Within just a few hours, they had the turbine operational, and it was charging the battery unit at a swift rate thanks to the strong westerly that was now blowing the recently arrived rain across the terrace in squalls.

Their comms were shut safely inside the battery unit housing and away from the rain, awaiting full charge, and that meant that they only had one another as a source for entertainment for the next couple of hours. Andrew didn't mind that at all. Claire didn't know what to do with herself.

They'd headed out to the loch and sat in what was left of the resort's lobby, resting against a concrete pillar, protected from the elements by a section of only partially collapsed roofing and the direction of the prevailing wind. The rain had intensified since they'd arrived, and it was now teeming down. A trip back to the storeroom would result in their being soaked to the bone again. They didn't fancy it.

They were huddled together and had already exhausted conversation around what might have happened to John, what the hell had happened to them, and what they might do next. They had even found some time to reminisce about the life they'd left behind them only days ago. The rain scattered across the open waters of the loch, and dark clouds clung ominously to the steep hills. It was quite a sight.

The discussion had turned again to whom they should contact with the evidence, once they had it, of course. Wesley was by far the best candidate - the unassuming accountant and old family friend of the McGregor's certainly looked to be the right person. A further investigation into his background and associations was warranted, which would be Andrew's job.

Claire now recalled meeting Wesley at the birthday party momentarily, and he'd seemed warm and genuine, if not terribly, terribly drab. Andrew had proposed an interesting alternative. The State, or at least elements within it, were lying about the disappearances. They'd lied about the uninhabitable zone and so many other things.

It stood to reason that the same dark forces were likely to be behind the string of scandals that seemed to be in the media every other day, resulting in some official or other being turfed from their position of power. It smacked of a dictatorship slowly taking control of its organization from the inside. It was a sickening and terrifying thought, but it made perfect sense, at least to Andrew. It was an interesting concept.

He'd theorized that who better to have as a safe inside contact than one of the many disgruntled, wronged persons of influence. They would have a lot of people to choose from. He had a good point, she conceded. They sat and discussed options. There were a number of candidates, amongst them a certain Mr. Lachlan Grealish. Surely someone who had made their career out of championing social justice causes would have a sizeable axe to grind at the way they had been so abjectly humiliated in the media? Andrew had to restrain himself from making any more sex-bot-related jokes during that part of the discussion.

There were a couple of other candidates.

Timothy Grey, the disgraced infrastructure chief, caught taking kickbacks from the constructo-bot companies. He'd protested his innocence vehemently, and they had come down with a sudden and mysterious illness and hadn't been heard from since.

Helen McStay, once the high-profile head of commercial development and darling of the media with her girlish charm and wit, had been humiliated publicly over an affair with a series of wealthy older men – much older men. She had at first insisted it was a stitch-up and had then disappeared from the public eye completely for two months, emerging contrite and apologetic. They didn't even know what she was doing these days.

A comfortable silence had now fallen between them. There was nothing to do now but wait out what had now become a ferocious storm and give the battery unit time to charge sufficiently. Claire had already checked the connections in the storeroom, and although the battery unit wasn't powering any of the points downstairs, they had found enough extension cables to make do. They were still on the wrong side of this thing, but maybe, just maybe, there was going to be a way out.

Claire had a handful of Andrew's jacket bunched up in her fist, holding it against his chest as they snuggled together against the wind, and she had to admit that it felt nice to feel physically close to someone, even if it was only her raggedy friend. Andrew gazed out over the loch, enjoying the warmth of her embrace, and watching the rain dance in patterns over the water.

Andrew felt as if he never wanted the storm to subside, even if it was freezing cold old and his bottom had gone numb quite some time ago. It was a moment that he'd never forget. Claire was thinking about John. At some point, they had both fallen asleep as the storm raged, the trials of the last few days catching up with them.

When they woke later that afternoon, the loch was calm and still, and the sun, if it had ever even been seen that day, had just disappeared behind the large hill on the far side of the loch. Claire was the first to wake. She stood, prodded Andrew with her foot, and as his eyes opened and focused groggily on her, she stomped off towards their temporary home at the back of the lot.

Back on the terrace, there was good news. Their comms were now fully charged, and they had enough power to enable them to get to work. The first thing Claire did was to access the triangulation program she'd created to track her tracker. It had returned a result. She stared at her comms as a cold feeling welled up from the pit of her stomach.

Based on the coordinates returned, the person or persons that had been tracking her were located in the very same compound that she'd had been headed for in the Solo. She was more relieved than ever now that she'd managed to escape when she did. A few more minutes and – well - although it might have been interesting to meet her nemesis, she had the distinct feeling that it would have been very bad for her health.

"Andy?"

He'd been standing watching the clouds again rather than doing anything useful.

"Huh?"

"How about you go catch us some dinner or something and work on the contacts' background checks?" She also knew that it was just a matter of time before they were discovered at their lochside hideout. They had to work fast, and getting Andrew out of the way for a couple of hours would help. It would help her anyway.

He headed down the stairwell, and Claire could hear the metal clanks as he descended, quickly, maybe too quickly? The next thing she heard was a few very quick clanks and then the sound of something heavy falling, followed by some muffled and sad-sounding words.

"You ok there, Andy?" she called.

"Ah, aye, no problem Claire … no problem at all."

*

Claire sighed. Some things never changed.

She finished checking her comms and then headed down herself, being overly cautious as she descended. Andrew had busied himself getting some gear together, and she scooped up her still soggy pack and devices, her micro toolkit, and a few bits and pieces she'd salvaged – some wiring, some metal framing, nuts and bolts, and a couple of old tools.

She had a vague idea about how she'd pull apart both devices and hopefully reassemble one in a Frankenstein's monster-type arrangement that would give her enough QFT power to do what she needed to do.

It took her a few minutes to run an extension down and connect it to her comms, using it to project a small yellow orb that just about lit her workspace. That would do for now. They had found an old convection heater that ran on electricity, so there was a chance at least that they could use it in the small workroom space in the far corner of the storeroom, once they had cleared some space in there.

Another extension should be possible, just about. They'd found a stash of extension cables in a big metal box inside the stairwell, and they might just have enough length for one more. Hopefully, then they could avoid another night of freezing their respective fannies and bollocks off.

***

Bill was enjoying a large hot breakfast of scrambled powdered egg on toasted carbgrain in his quarters when he received the call. Within the first few seconds, his ears and then his face had turned bright red – he'd started to sweat soon after, and by the time the call ended with the words "… and do it now otherwise I'll come down there and personally tear you a new dookhole!" he was soaked through with sweat and shaking violently. He wasn't sure if he was angry or scared. Both, probably.

Isabel Donachy had called and asked him to organize something for her a few days ago. He'd been trying to find the right candidate for the job; although he hadn't been trying all that hard, he'd have to admit. All that had just changed. Isabel was absolutely livid with him over the escaped package, and he hadn't even managed to get a word in during the call.

She'd told him that she was planning to pay him a visit in a couple of days' time and that the outcome of that visit would depend on two things: recovering the missing package and her special assignment having been completed by the time she arrived. Bill rubbed at his scar. He didn't particularly want one of her 'special' visits.

How did she already know? Someone blabbed. Some absolute low-life little dook has leaked details of the capture pod escape!

It was unbelievable, astonishing even! Bill had always thought he was well-liked at the compound, a figure to be looked up to and respected, but his illusions had been shattered this morning, and he suddenly felt cornered and vulnerable. He'd find out who'd done this, and there would be hell to pay, not only for them but for their family, maybe even their friends as well. It would depend on who it was, but one thing was for sure, he'd make them regret ever having crossed him.

Bill was still seething with rage, pacing around his quarters, swearing occasionally, and was still sweating through his shirt some twenty minutes later. He had to get a grip; he had to focus. Isabel had demanded that he take care of the special project personally and immediately. If he failed, his career was over. And worse, no doubt. It'd been a while since he'd done one of these special favors for Isabel, which was why he'd been trying to find someone else to do it, he supposed.

The last one had seen him rewarded handsomely - promoted to head of a special forces task force, a job that had led him to his current position of power and what was *supposed* to be a comfortable existence. This time around, the circumstances were very different, and he just hoped that he was still up to the task.

He decided that now would be a great time to open a bottle of synthetic malt – hell, it was after eight a.m. after all. The neck of the bottle clanked against the glass tumbler as Bill's hand shook, and he ended up with a somewhat larger measure than he'd intended. He downed the drink in one, choking at its strength and spilling some down his shirt in the process. He sat heavily at his desk, his chair creaking in protest, and thought about his newfound problems.

Bill issued an instruction to Stu to recommence the search with any and all available resources. That was a good start, he figured. Isabel was perhaps asking the impossible when it came to recovering the girl - she could have escaped as soon as the Solo had trapped her for all he knew. He felt it more likely that Isabel's security forces would pick her up than his search of the area, but at least he could justify that he *tried*. The other task, though, was down to him and him alone. He dare not fail.

***

When Andrew finally did return to the compound from his fishing expedition, it was pitch black outside. He'd had a few hairy moments avoiding the wild mutant beasts that enjoyed prowling the surrounds of the Resort and had vowed not to be outside after dark again – at least not alone.

He'd vowed this before but had been enjoying his fishing excursion a little too much. He'd spent a few hours fishing and working on the background checks on his comms, without much success, catching a small trout, letting an eel escape from the net, and catching a lot of loch weeds. Nothing much had happened for the last hour or so, and he decided that enough was enough – it would keep them going, but sometimes it just wasn't your day.

That's been happening quite a lot lately.

Claire looked up momentarily from the display of what looked like some sort of weird inside-out device as he entered. She grinned, looking very pleased with herself, and held out her arms, palms open towards the weird-looking gadget in front of her, offering Andrew the opportunity to behold the magnificence of her homemade device.

"You, my friend, are a bloody genius!" he exclaimed.

"Even better," said Claire.

"Uh, ok … you are even better than a bloody genius!"

She smirked at that. "Not that, ya wee bawbag. We have the data!" Claire was beaming now. "And we also have heat!"

"Heat!" Andrew jumped up and down on the spot and then did a little victory dance before realizing he'd perhaps gotten his priorities wrong somewhat. "Data! We have the data - that's braw!"

"Data!" she said again, grinning like an idiot.

"Oh, thank Douglas!"

"We can still do this, Andy!"

Things had suddenly taken a turn for the better, it seemed.

"In there." She pointed to the small workroom space in the corner - she knew which of the two revelations excited him the most. "Go on," she enthused. Andrew practically bounded over, opened the door, and went in. *Oh yes, warmth!*

He came back out, carefully closing the door after him. Claire had relented after a few hours of tinkering with the devices, needing to stretch, and had cleared some space in the workroom herself and then dragged the heater and their tarps in there, the extension cables just reaching.

"Oh, this is great, Claire, smashing!"

Why did I say 'smashing?'. Who says 'smashing' anyway?

"Aye, bit of an upgrade, eh?" she smiled.

"That it is! I'll get some dinner on then, shall I?" he held up his catch of the day.

"And they said married life was boring," Claire remarked.

"I'll take that as a yes!" Andrew was suddenly in particularly good spirits. He busied himself with preparing the meal.

"So, what are you working on there, my ubernerd friend?" He really didn't need to ask, but he thought he'd better show a keen interest. Claire ignored the backhanded compliment.

"Well, I'm trying to get the data unencrypted again. I wasn't sure we still had it all, but I've repaired the corruptions, and it's all there. So lucky ..."

It was a huge relief, Andrew had to admit. He quietly applauded her with what could only be described as another of his annoying old-world traits—the golf clap.

"The bad news is, all of my encryption programs were wiped - all my code was wiped, and I only have the base code from the secure storage device to work with. It's going to take quite a lot of work just to see what kind of state the data is in - I'm going to need your help."

"Oh aye?" he attempted to appear low-key in his response as if he wasn't completely chuffed at being asked such a thing. *Mr. Cool.*

"Aye, it's going to take quite a few hours just to undo the encryption once I've recreated the code. I think we should do it in shifts and see if we can crack it by morning." She was searching for a response.

"Sure, no problem. Just let me know what to do and when you need me." He was a little disappointed - no snuggle tonight, it seemed. *Oh well, can't have everything.*

Claire worked away for a little while, and eventually, he brought her over a fresh pot of fish and gloop. He'd somehow managed to overcook everything, so it was more like fishgloop. Claire looked down at the pink and grey concoction.

"Yum ... my favorite," she said flatly.

"Mine too." They shared a look.

Claire ate as she worked on a bench fashioned from some bricks and a few old planks - various cables snaking away from it across the floor and disappearing into the recently discovered stairwell. Andrew had been sitting nearby while he finished his fishy delight.

"Any luck?"

"Some," she didn't look up.

Andrew decided it best to leave her to it.

"Right, well, I'd better try and get some sleep. Come and wake me when you need me, aye?"

He waited a few seconds, determined that he wasn't going to get a response, and then shuffled off to the workroom. It wasn't long before he was fast asleep.

***

Hamish Wesley had been making some inquiries well outside the scope of his usual remit as chief auditor at the department of finance. He was leveraging some of his old defense Force contacts to see what he might be able to find out about a few of the senior D.A.I.R. figures. His contacts still worked in counterintelligence and had more or less complete access to all records in a broad range of state departments.

What he'd found so far was quite concerning - the budget overruns that he'd been discovering within D.A.I.R seemed to be replicated similarly across several of the other departments. They weren't immediately obvious, but Wesley could see the patterns more clearly with his specialized forensic accounting nous than most. They had a very clever system set up to cover their losses, but now that Wesley knew how it worked, it was just a matter of time until he discovered the origin and then the destination of the outflow of funds.

He wasn't quite ready to share his suspicions more widely. He was a very cautious man, but once he was on the scent of financial irregularities, there was no stopping him – he would keep going until he had what he needed. It was going to be a long night.

**

Andrew woke to Claire shaking his shoulder quite forcefully.

"For Douglas's sake!" he exclaimed, confused for a moment. She punched him on the shoulder and made a shushing noise.

"Ouch! What'd you do that for?!" he whispered.

He was wide awake now, and she leaned over him and put her finger to her lips, imploring him to be quiet. Her face was lit only by the comms on her wrist, and it was otherwise pitch dark.

"Couldn't stand your snoring," she whispered, "come and have a look at this – outside. And be *quiet*."

Claire was extremely worried despite the flippant remark. She led him over to the big metal door, carefully unlatching it and pushing it open a little. She pointed up at the night sky instead.

She watched as his eyes widened then returned to hers. *SFBs*. A series of small red lights were working their way across the terrain in a box-shaped formation, not more than a hundred yards above ground level at the far end of the loch.

SFBs were high-end spec and could be fitted with thermal imaging and soundwave detection. They stood and watched in silence as the flying surveillance devices swept to one side of the loch then the other. Claire pulled him back inside and pulled the door shut slowly.

"Fuuuck!" Andrew whispered.

"Yes. Fuck!" Claire whispered, "I have a black noise scrambler activated from my comms, which should mask what we are doing electronically at least, but we are going to have to be still, be quiet, and make sure they don't see any signs of life."

As she came to the end of her sentence, she'd realized that their work on the terrace would be an all too obvious sign of life! If the SFB's spotted the functional turbine with its homemade support structure cables, that would be it. All over. They'd have to risk going up to disguise their work somehow and very quickly! Claire's mind was racing.

Some rubble, planks, metal sheets —anything!

She pointed towards the stairwell. Andrew looked into the dark space, then back at her as he realized what she was thinking.

"The terrace, oh dook!" he cried, louder than he'd intended, prompting a sharp admonishing look from Claire. She kept her voice low but spoke quickly. "The fly-bots are doing grids, and they are still on the far side of the loch. I think they'll sweep around and over us within the next five to ten minutes. We've still got time!"

He nodded quickly, perhaps one too many times.

"If we're lucky, we can sneak up there and be back inside before they get close. The hillside should keep us out of sight from them until they're almost directly overhead."

"Let's go," she whispered. "Grab what you can, metal sheets, timber, anything we can cover the turbine base with – and do it quietly! We can disconnect the cables and drag them into the stairwell. Come on - we've only got one chance at this. If we fuck it up …" she didn't need to finish the sentence.

*

They hurriedly grabbed a few planks of old timber and a few pieces of metal sheeting and headed up the stairwell, not too quickly, being extra careful not to scrape or bang anything on the side of the metal staircase as they went. Andrew reached the terrace first and craned his neck back over his shoulder as he crept out towards the turbine.

He didn't have a line of sight to the SFB's, but he knew they could appear over the top of the hill at any moment. He put his items carefully against the temporary base of the pole then used the materials Claire had brought to complete the job while she busily disconnected the cables and lugged them back through the open doorway, coiling them in the stairwell.

Andrew was sweating heavily, and it ran down from his brow, stinging his eye as he looked up at the turbine, which was still spinning slowly even though there didn't seem to be any breeze. He caught Claire's eye as she re-entered the terrace and pointed at the turbine. She understood. The spinning turbine was a risk – it could draw attention.

They didn't have time to disassemble the structure, so maybe if they disabled it, that would be enough. Andrew picked up a long screwdriver from next to the battery unit, and Claire nodded. He handed it over, crouched down, and made a foothold with his hands. She quickly tucked the screwdriver into her pants and scaled Andrew and then the pole in quick succession, wedging the tool tightly inside the turbine housing so that the blades stopped rotating. She slid halfway down the pole then leapt off in one fluid motion.

She's a ninja!

The sound reached them before they saw the lights appear over the top of the hillside. A dull thrumming sound filled the air above them, and they crouched low and scurried back inside, pulling the door closed ever so carefully behind them. They didn't know if they'd been spotted or not – it would have been close. They stood unmoving behind the heavy metal door, trying to hold their breath as the noise of the SFB's pulsed overhead.

You could cut the tension in the air with a knife. The noise leveled off and then started to diminish. They looked at one another, and Claire held her finger to her lips again and pointed down the stairwell. They made their way back down, very slowly and very carefully, not making a sound.

*

When they'd reached the base of the staircase, they stopped and listened again. The thrumming noise was still evident, and as they listened, it grew louder and louder. For whatever reason, the fly-bots were coming in for a close check of the resort. Claire hoped that this was just part of their usual protocol, but it didn't do anything to quell her own quickly rising sense of unease. The storeroom door was still open a few inches. *I mustn't have latched it properly!*

The noise from the SFB's grew suddenly louder – they were right on top of them! She looked up to the roof vents as the searchlight beams swept across the top of their sanctuary, the light flickering through the gaps and sweeping into their hiding place.

Andrew was frozen to the spot. Claire took the initiative. She only had a few seconds to spare, moving quickly and silently over to the door, dodging the fly-bot light as it swept past her and gently and soundlessly pulling the door closed and carefully latching it. She stayed where she was behind the door, holding the handle, and motioned for Andrew to stay still. The window next to her was tightly shuttered, at least.

The noise became deafening as one or more swooped down over the top of the hill above them. Claire felt her legs start to tremble as it hovered what could be not more than a few yards in front of the huge metal door. Andrew had sunk to his knees and appeared to be praying. It seemed they'd been discovered – an SFB was now directly outside their hiding place, and the noise from its props was ear-piercing. They held their breath for what seemed like forever. The noise suddenly lessened, and they heard it rise back up and over the hill.

Claire released her breath and slid to the floor, and Andrew collapsed back against the wall next to the stairwell, clutching at his chest. "Douglas," was all he could whisper. Claire dragged herself up, stumbled over, and collapsed beside him. They looked at each other.

"That was way too close. We don't have much time, Andy. If they are onto us, we'll know pretty soon. We had better be ready to run. Even if no one comes tonight, I don't think we can expect to have more than a day or so before our time's up here."

*

"Roger that," whispered Andrew, still clutching at his heart, willing it to slow down.

Typical. Good old life, kicking you in the guts just when you were finally starting to enjoy yourself!

Claire continued, her voice not much above a whisper.

"The good news is, we're nearly there with the data. I've recreated the decryption program, and it just needs a little tweaking now and again. If you can take over in an hour or two, I'll get some sleep, and then we will see what we've got in the morning. We'll need to keep a close eye on the scans as well to make sure we don't have any more unwelcome visitors. I'll show you what to do when I wake you."

He nodded and offered a worried-looking smile to Claire, who returned the gesture. She got up, stretched her arms high above her head, yawned, and then ran her hands through her tangled hair a few times before almost stumbling off in the direction of her devices.

They'd have enough battery charge to last at least through the night. Andrew pushed himself up wearily and headed straight to the small workroom. He lay down, unclipped the small cord from his comms, and plugged into Headspace – he'd had an idea – sleep could wait.

One of the many great things about Headspace was that you could put it in a sort of 'sleep mode,' which, although not providing such a vivid experience, could still be useful in allowing you to rest and take in information at the same time. He'd managed to identify his unicorn as a rare species of horse - Konic, native to lowland Alba and somehow having survived the end of times. It surely was a magnificent creature.

If he were able to tame it in real life, then just maybe they might have a mode of transport, which he was sure would come in handy in the next day or two. He had no idea if such a thing would be possible, but Headspace could demonstrate whether it would be an option or not. The other great thing about Headspace, under the current circumstances, was that it didn't require any kind of outside connection; it used your brain's electrical impulses to generate the experience. Very handy indeed.

Claire would undoubtedly see this as a huge waste of time, but to Andrew, it was one of the few things that he had to offer, aside from comic relief. All of the time he'd spent being beaten up by Ginger Ninja in the Great Hall of Pain had finally paid off when his life was on the line back on the podium, so who knew? It was worth a try. He closed his eyes and summoned the unicorn.

He was on the hill beside the loch, and the unicorn was eyeing him warily from a safe distance. It snorted as he approached, steam billowing from its flared nostrils as its head twitched back nervously. Andrew held out his hand and offered the beast some fresh flowers, and although it was clearly quite wary, the unicorn took a step forward and sniffed at them.

It threw its head back and then made a small, ethereal whinny noise that shimmered the air around it. Andrew thought for a moment that this might just be going well - but then the unicorn turned and galloped away, releasing a stream of glittering rainbow-colored poo as it did so.

"Oh well," he said. "Program reboot."

***

The search was proving fruitless. Bill had used every last resource, but it had already been going for far too long without a result. It was too damn expensive. He'd known that it would prove to be a huge waste of time and money - he could fudge the records to make it look that they'd thrown everything into the search. Isabel wouldn't find out unless, of course, the snitch did their worst to undermine him again.

He'd interrogate all staff and keep going until he found out who it was – and he was sure he'd get someone to speak. A cowardly snitch was bound to crack even under the mildest of pressure. Bill picked up his internal comms and dialed Stu – he was the perfect man to organize such a thing.

*

Stu looked down at his flashing comms and shook his head in disbelief.

Couldn't he leave me alone for five fucking minutes to concentrate on my job? The Twat. Hopefully, I won't have to put up with that doaty haver for much longer anyway.

CHAPTER 18 – STINK

Claire had woken Andrew at around three in the morning and passed on the instructions. She'd then stumbled wearily into the workroom and slipped straight into a deep and dreamless sleep. Sometime later, she rolled over, eyes heavy, and looked up through the workroom window, noticing the watery light filtering through the air vents in the ceiling of the storeroom. It was time to get up.

She rolled over and stretched, pushing her arms out over her head. A tangy, musty, and quite unpleasant smell filled her nostrils, and she coughed and snorted involuntarily, wrinkling her nose in disgust. She wandered over to Andrew and could still smell herself. She lifted an arm tentatively and sniffed again.

"Douglas H! I stink!" she muttered.

Andrew looked up from his position, bent over the exo-device.

"No fucking kidding!"

"Fuck off!"

She leaned forward and sniffed him. *Not pleasant at all. Not as bad as her, but not great either. Well, they were still here. No one had come to capture them during the night. Things were looking up!*

"Hey, back up, buttercup!" he was looking at her as if she'd lost her mind. *Not far off*, she thought.

"The decryption been going pretty well - about another hour to go maybe, and hopefully, we'll have a result of some sort."

"Well, it must be bath time then! You could do with one as well if we are totally honest here."

Andrew couldn't resist. "Oh, we are honest, are we now? Well, if that's the case, then you have kind of a big bum!" Andrew grinned at his amazing witticism.

Claire winced. "At least I have a bum, ya scrawny wee twat!"

She feigned a punch at Andrew, and he visibly recoiled. "Don't worry; you'll wait." She leaned over him to look at the display, and her nipple brushed his arm through the thin fabric of her t-shirt as she did so. She ignored it but saw Andrew blush. He got up and walked away, leaving her to it. She checked the status of the de-encryption and then checked on the location of the fly-bots, which had moved far away.

They could risk heading outside for a bit of a clean-up - they may well be on the run, but there were still standards to be maintained.

"Ok, we have a window of at least twenty minutes to get outside and get clean. Come on!" She clipped the back of his head with her hand as she walked past him, her hand making a satisfying 'slap' sound as she made contact.

"Fuck me!" Andrew exclaimed, rubbing his head. He'd be getting her back for that.

"Thanks for the offer," said Claire, "but no thanks."

As she reached the doors, she looked back over her shoulder, saying, "I owed you that one anyway. Come on, bath time! If you're quick enough, you'll see exactly how fat my bum is."

With that, she slipped through the door. Andrew stared at the open doorway. "Bath time. Great," he mumbled, extremely unenthusiastically.

*

By the time he reached the far side of the lot, Claire was already at the end of the jetty and pulling off her jumper. He picked up the pace, not wanting to have to disrobe while she was already in the water - he could imagine the comments."

"Oi, hold up, I'm coming!"

"Hurry up!"

Andrew picked up the pace, and by the time he reached her, she was in her underwear and about to discard the last couple of items, goosebumps covering her skin.

"Last one in's a rotten haggis!" she called and promptly unclasped her bra and dropped her panties as Andrew struggled to get his t-shirt over his head. He cursed as he became tangled and secretly wondered if the bang to the head she'd received in the river had affected her permanently.

Claire shrieked as she hit the water while Andrew struggled further in extricating himself from his clothing. The icy air had the usual effect on his dangly bits, and he hoped that Claire wasn't looking. Andrew hit the water a few seconds later. The shock of it made him feel as if he was about to have a heart attack! Claire was already laughing at his expression. It was excruciatingly cold.

Did we really have to do this?

***

His mind had been a mess ever since the early morning call from that evil bitch Isabel Donachy, but he now had everything prepared. Bill had been in a bit of a panic as he scrambled to make travel arrangements and source the materials he'd need for the job, but he'd managed to pull it all together very quickly.

He was feeling very nervous about the whole thing and had been on and off the toilet all morning. He couldn't afford to fail, but his hands wouldn't stop shaking, serving as a constant reminder as to just what was at stake here.

Maybe just another wee dram of malt to steady the nerves.

Bill was trying desperately to think of who it was that could have betrayed him so badly and was still shocked that someone within *his* compound could have exposed him and left him in such a precarious position. He couldn't come up with a name; he had no idea – he'd have to wait and see what Stu found. At least he could rely on Stu.

The stress was making his scar itch incessantly, and as he sat and drank his malt, Bill's mind had drifted back to the incident that had caused it.

It had been five years ago, and he'd been close to finishing up his tenure as chief of the special forces. It had started like any other workday, but all that had changed when the guards brought in an extremely violent young woman.

There had been a bit of trouble during her arrest, resulting in one of his officers being badly injured. They'd had to sedate her and tie her down in the end.

Bill always took a special interest in any young females held in the cells, and as he looked at her file image, he decided that he'd be calling in to say hello.

Late into the night, when only a couple of trusted guards were left in the watch house, Bill decided to pay the resident of cell C3 a visit. The guards knew the drill and switched off the security cams when they saw him approach. Bill continued past them without even acknowledging their presence and headed straight down the long corridor hosting the most recent batch of arrivals. He reached the cell and looked through the plexi-glass panel.

The girl looked younger than the seventeen years listed on her file. She was sitting on the bed, staring expressionlessly at the wall opposite her bunk. Her femininity and fragility struck him — she was much more attractive than her file photo had indicated, and she looked as if she couldn't hurt a fly. He felt a familiar shiver of anticipation as he entered the cell.

The girl didn't move or change her expression in any way as he entered. She sat perfectly still; her ever so pretty green eyes continued to stare benignly at the wall as he locked the door behind him, hit the blackout switch on the plexi-panel, and came to sit next to her on the bunk.

She lowered her eyes as he sat, tilting her head downward and staring at the floor, causing her silky black hair to fall across her cheek. Bill leaned forward and moved to brush the hair back to better see her perfect little face. The next few seconds had been the fuel for Bill's nightmares for the last five or so years.

Before he knew what had happened, the girl had turned on him, sinking her teeth deep into his forearm. He was so shocked that he didn't react until it was too late. It had taken two guards to pull the girl off of him, and when they did, a large chunk of his flesh had come away with her.

The last thing he remembered was the look in her eyes as she spat the meaty chunk out at him. Bill had passed out at that point, and when he came to some hours later in the medi-center ward, his arm was heavily bandaged, and he was told that they were preparing him for a skin graft. He'd reached up to his face, which was throbbing painfully, to discover that it was covered in deep scratches and gouges. His hand shook as he took it from his face, and he passed out again.

By the time he got out of the ward and returned to the watch house, the girl was gone. Despite his contacts in the security services - Bill had never been able to find any trace of her existence.

***

After a few seconds of splashing about in the icy Loch Campbell waters, genitals numbing by the second, Andrew realized something was wrong. It wasn't Nessie this time; it was the expression on Claire's face.

"What's up with you?" he inquired politely, albeit somewhat breathlessly.

"The soap?"

It wasn't the answer Andrew had been expecting.

"Eh?"

"Get the soap, if you don't mind. I left it on the Jetty for you."

"Oh, *you* left it for *me*?"

"Yes. Now hurry up; I'm freezing my tits off in here! Literally!"

"Soap's overrated."

"Just get the fucking soap!"

"Why don't you get it?"

"Oh, and stick my bits out for you to have a good look at you dirty little perv!"

It looked as if Andrew was getting the soap. He was impressed that she'd remembered to pack some. There was a whole other side to her that he'd never known.

"As if I'd look! I don't wish to be blinded in horror!" he said, swimming the couple of stokes back to the jetty. He pulled himself half out of the water and looked for the soap.

"For Douglas's sake!"

The soap was out of reach. He'd have to pull himself onto the jetty to get to the two small bars sitting next to Claire's discarded clothes.

"Don't look!" he yelled as he turned back, noting the amused expression on her face.

"It's ok, Andy, I don't want to see, believe me! I, too, value my eyesight!"

Claire turned herself away from him.

"Alright … you'll owe me."

He pulled himself out of the water and lurched towards the soap, well aware that if Claire had turned around at that moment, she would have got the sort of view that, once seen, cannot be unseen. Just as his hand clasped the soap, he heard something behind him. The sound was "Ooo-ooooo!"

He froze for a second, realizing that he'd not only been duped but now also humiliated, just for Claire's amusement. He grabbed the soaps and jumped back in the loch as quickly as he possibly could. Once he'd hit the water - the shock not any less than before - he hurled one of the kegs of soap at her. She caught it with ease.

"For fucks sake, Claire!"

"Oh, don't be shy, Andy. I didn't even know you'd grown hair down there!"

Claire started laughing as she spoke, and Andrew joined her. She'd won; he'd lost.

"Well, at least I do, unlike some!"

"Hey!"

More laughter echoed out over the loch as they swam a few strokes over to a shallow point and got to work with the soap as fast as humanly possible.

***

Safely back inside the storeroom, clean and warm, they were having to resort to eating raw fish for breakfast. Claire had decided they needed to preserve the remaining fragments of thermal bricks and said that she'd read somewhere that back in the old world, raw fish was considered a delicacy. Andrew was aware of this but hadn't wanted to try for himself. It was predictably disgusting, but it beat starving, he supposed.

The turbine had been reactivated as the SFB's were now far away. They were huddled together next to the convection heater in the workroom. The small space had become the new center of their world while Claire finalized her work, and Andrew did what he could to help via comms. At one point, he'd tried putting the fish pieces on the heater to slow cook them, but it didn't achieve much except making the raw fish dirty.

It was the final straw, and a short argument had ensued after which Andrew used one of the last thermal brick fragments to cook most of the remaining fish they had at their disposal. It was a small but important victory for Andrew's self-esteem and a big victory for his stomach.

They'd agreed that they'd check the media for anything relevant to their situation once a day, just in case there was something critical that they needed to know. Andrew switched on his comms in dark mode and quickly scrolled the three-dimensional images on the main media stream. He paused over one, and he felt faint as he took in the headline. His heart stopped, and he was suddenly gasping for air, making Claire look up from her device.

"Andy!?"

It took a moment for him to be able to draw a breath, and as he did, he turned the small image hovering over his comms towards her. She blinked once, stared at the image for a second, then frowned a little. She'd almost been expecting this. She grabbed the comms from her very pale-looking friend and expanded the image with a reverse pinching type action.

The headline simply read 'Murderers!' Below that, there were headshots of Claire and Andrew. It wasn't a very flattering image of Claire. She was in full goth mode, miserable and angry looking. Wrinkled her nose and looked away.

"Ok, well, let me know if it says anything interesting," she said.

"But! Claire!"

"Andy. You did kill a man, remember, so it's not a huge stretch to think that whoever is behind this will try and use that to find us. And me? What did I do? I don't remember killing anyone, *and* they used a dook photo!"

Andrew sat in silence for a moment, his face ashen. He'd broken out in a cold sweat.

"Thanks for reminding me," he mumbled.

"Wait! Hold on, what the …" Andrew was flabbergasted.

"What is it?"

"It says *we* murdered *two* security force officers! Two! What the …"

Claire frowned. "You're sure it was just the one then?"

"Oh, for fucks sake …" he simply couldn't believe it. He stood up and left the cramped space, pacing around outside the workroom, muttering to himself, and occasionally kicking something in frustration. Claire ignored him and continued what she was doing.

After a while, he calmed down and managed to distract himself by serving them some nice freshly cooked fish straight from the pot. They worked as they ate, Andrew checking code just as fast as Claire was creating it. About an hour later, Claire let out a little squeal and fist-pumped the air furiously.

"We've got it! The decryption worked! The data's still there, complete. We're in!"

"Thank Doug for that! What now?"

"What now is that we make a few more connections, between the Elyssium names and those who've disappeared, dig deeper, and then we'll send something to Wesley, maybe one other; I'm still not too sure about that, not sure who either."

Who says you get to decide that?

"Just as soon as we have enough info, mind. We have to have enough to convince someone important that something terrible is going on - if that's what this really is. I'll keep digging."

If? Why else would armed officers have hunted us? He couldn't help but wonder.

Andrew got up and stretched out.

"Ok, I'm going for some fresh air then. I'll check the line again."

Claire didn't respond. Andrew needed some time to absorb the fact that his face was now plastered all over the media under the rather unflattering and very unfair banner of *Murderer*! He'd started to feel quite queasy just from thinking about it and needed some space.

He walked and walked, making it about a quarter of the way along the edge of the loch. By the time he turned back toward the resort, he felt more or less at peace with things or rather resigned to things. The more he thought about the headline, the less it seemed to matter. They were in deep dook anyway - how much worse could it get? He was almost looking forward to whatever lay ahead. It was time to stop dreading it. He had Claire, after all.

The morning air was fresh but still, and as he made his way back, he took in the rolling hillsides pattered with gorse and thistles in various shades of green and yellow. He watched the fluffy grey clouds moving slowly over the landscape and was in awe once again at the sheer majesty of his surroundings.

It really is beautiful here. If we have to stay, it wouldn't be too bad at all.

He was about to turn away from the water and head back when he noticed what looked like some strange eddies forming out in the middle of the loch. The water seemed to swell up and *uck!* Andrew turned and ran. He ran faster than he ever had, faster than he thought possible, nearly tripping and falling numerous times as his legs started to burn and tire. His lungs were screaming for air, and eventually, he just couldn't go on.

Fitness had never been his forte, he remembered. He stopped - hands on knees and sucked in the chill air in rasping breaths. The hair on the back of his neck stood on end as he thought he heard something move in the water behind him. He wanted to look, but the incapacitating fear he was feeling wouldn't allow it. He braced himself for whatever was going to happen next.

A bird tweeted somewhere nearby. A daisy swayed in a sudden gust of wind, but nothing else happened. Importantly, no water creatures called Raymond spoke to him. After about thirty seconds, he finally managed to force himself to look out into the loch. Of course, there was nothing to be seen. Andrew laughed nervously, then started walking very briskly back to relative the safety of his cave.

Bloody flashback. For Douglas's sake!

When he returned, some two hours after he'd departed, Claire was standing just outside of the workroom with her arms folded across her chest. She didn't look particularly happy.

"What's up, buttercup?" he asked casually.

She glared at him. What came next was a total shock.

"Fuck you, Andy! And get *stuffed*! You've been no bloody help at all!" She'd stamped her right foot down as she yelled at him, and Andrew was reeling, taking an involuntary step backward, surprised at her most unwelcome of welcomes.

"Wha...," he didn't even get the word out before the next tirade started. The string of expletives seemed to go on forever. Andrew would have been quite impressed if they weren't directed at him. When they finally ceased, he'd shrunk back inside of himself, hoping just to disappear.

Claire wiped at her eyes, and he realized that she wasn't just angry but also very upset. He decided to keep his mouth shut, which was usually the best approach. Claire took a couple of steps forward, the tension in her body almost frightening. Andrew braced himself.

"While you were out strolling about in the sunshine, making fucking daisy chains or whatever, I discovered that our beloved John, our very best friend in the world, our ..." her words caught in her throat, "our *friend*, Andy, *our friend* ... has been betraying us all along!"

She was spitting the words out at him and had started pacing around again, gesturing with her hands.

"But how ... what?" Andrew was stunned; there were no other words for it.

"This is just ... fucking ... unbelievable! No wonder the authorities, or whoever, were onto us so quickly! Fuck this, fuck *everything*, what's the fucking point! What's the point when you can't even trust your only friends!"

Andrew couldn't help but think that that was probably how John felt the night he left Claire's flat.

"Are you kidding?" he asked. An extremely bad choice of words, as it turned out.

"Am I kidding? Am I fucking kidding!" Claire's voice had risen from a whisper to full rage by the sixth word of the sentence, and Andrew cringed. He wanted to run but had nowhere to go. She stormed over to him, swinging a slap at his face, but Andrew - who knew Claire quite well, it was fair to say - saw it coming, and managed to deflect the blow. He had less luck with the subsequent blows, and rather than take a beating, or run, he decided instead to try and calm things down.

He grabbed her arms and pulled her into a tight embrace. Claire struggled for a second or two, and for a moment, he was worried about the proximity of his testicles to Claire's knee, but he needn't have worried. She relaxed for a moment, freed one arm, and then shoved Andrew in the chest, making him take a couple of backward steps. It was Andrew's turn to take the initiative.

"Calm down, Claire! Just tell me what you've found, and do it without assaulting me, if you can! For Doug's sake!"

"Dook! Sorry. I'm sorry, Andy, it's just ..." she didn't finish the sentence. Instead, she took a step back, wiped at her eyes, and then walked back towards the workroom. Andrew assumed that he was supposed to follow.

"Promise you won't try to beat me up again?" he asked. Claire didn't reply, and he followed somewhat reluctantly, sitting next to her at her device. She sat in silence. Andrew waited. When she spoke, she sounded miserable.

"Ok. Sorry Andy, again. I think I'm starting to lose it."

Andrew nodded timidly.

"I haven't had time to digest what I've just seen. I found something. Something bad, and then you walked in, and I was angry, not even at you, but at this whole situation, at John, at his *fucking* stupidity."

Andrew flinched.

"Ah … fuck it. Dook. I'm sorry you have to deal with all my *emotions!*"

He shrugged. He wasn't sure what else he was supposed to do.

"I mean, it's just such a shock. Maybe betrayed was a bit of a strong word for it, but I've decoded the secure data you got from John's house; just look at it!"

Andrew looked at it, but that didn't help. Claire hadn't got the reaction she expected. She hadn't got any reaction at all.

"Ok, let me run you through it. The encoded comms from John to the college - over the last six months, there have been hundreds, *hundreds* of messages from him, sent to the college's secure line. The recipient is too heavily encrypted, but I've got the metadata, and I *will* find out who he was in contact with soon enough – anyway, that's not the important thing. The important thing, Andy, is that these messages contain numerous references to our *special* research."

She looked at him for a reaction. He swallowed nervously.

"But why would …" Claire cut him off, she had more to say - "I just don't believe it! How could he have been doing this under our noses! All this time when I was trusting him with the highly illegal dook that we were doing. He must have known that if I found out about this, that would be *it!* What the hell has he been playing at?"

Claire stopped speaking, head down, her hair masking her face.

*

Andrew didn't know what to say. He was finding this hard to comprehend. Her shoulders seemed to be shaking.

Oh fuck, she's crying, oh!

He placed his hand on hers, but she pulled away and wiped her eyes again. She turned to him after a moment, and he saw the grief and anger she was feeling. She took a deep breath and forcibly rearranged her face to something resembling normal.

"Douglas, what's happened to me, Andy? I'm an emotional wreck!"

362

"It's ok, Claire; I can relate, believe me." He'd almost wanted to laugh as the tension was broken but held it in. It was probably a wise move.

"I mean, what are we supposed to make of his disappearance now? And his name being on the list? Did he disappear once he'd finished his job of spying on us? Did they bring him in?"

There was silence for a while. Andrew scrolled through some of the messages.

"I don't know, Claire. It looks bad, but" Andrew paused, "maybe he's just another victim here, you know? Maybe he was just trying to help, in his big oafish way?"

"I don't think …" he started to say.

"Have a read," Claire said sharply, leaving him alone in the workroom for a few minutes. When she returned, she seemed calm and composed.

"Well?" she asked.

"Spying?" he offered. "I don't know, Claire. I mean, it *could* be. The messages are somewhat discrete; I'll give him that. Why would he do this? I can only think he was getting external help on your special projects, maybe trying to impress you? I dunno. If anything at all, it's just plain fucking stupid!"

Claire looked exasperated.

"Ok, ok, it's possible, I suppose. I should have a little more faith. I just saw that and, …" Tears started to well in her eyes again, and her bottom lip started to quiver. She breathed in deeply through her nose and blew the air from her mouth. Andrew was struggling to subdue tears of his own; his lips pressed firmly together.

"Ok, ok, Andy. If he hasn't betrayed us intentionally, then maybe this is what resulted in him disappearing, maybe this is what got him taken."

This is so confusing.

"He could have gotten himself killed. He could get us all killed, for fucks sake!"

They look at one another as the full gravity of Claire's words hit home.

*

They didn't have time for this - they had to focus. Claire had had enough. *Stupid bloody emotions, getting in the way of things. I knew there was a reason I'd blocked them out for so long. Annoying!*

She flicked the switch in her brain and turned back to Andrew as if nothing had happened. "Oh, almost forgot ... I've re-confirmed the faked vocal audio, and I think I've figured out what Elyssium is!"

Andrew was confused by the sudden change.

"Oh, really?" he inquired.

"Well, sort of."

"Oh, really?" he said again, "make your mind up."

Claire felt herself relax a little and offered Andrew a brief smile.

"Alright, smartypants, this is what I *do* know then - Elyssium refers to some sort of material. There are measurements of production outputs all through the data, although I'm not entirely sure how any of this relates yet. Maybe it's some kind of forced labor?" Wild speculation probably wasn't helping much, she realized.

"I don't know, Claire; none of it makes sense. It's like some bad old-world novel. The more we know, the less sense it makes."

Claire shrugged. She'd been thinking out loud - never a great idea. None of it made a lot of sense; Andrew was right.

"So, we need to dig deeper, right? What do we do next?"

"Well ... I'll need a bit longer to work on the Elyssium data, see if I can make any more sense of it. We need to make more connections; we need to know who John was in contact with and why. In the meantime, we can get details together of everything we know so far ready to pass onto Wesley."

*

Andrew wanted all of this to end. It looked like they were getting close to something, and he was fully focused for once.

"Alright, I'll start working on the package of evidence; just copy everything to me, and I'll start putting a case together."

"Amazing, right? That'd be great, Andy; use your journalistic skills to build the case for us. We'll send just enough to prove that there's something really bad going on without giving up everything we have."

There was a pause as Andrew looked at Claire and Claire looked at Andrew, wondering if he was going to get to work or not. The silence became uncomfortable.

"Please," he prompted.

Claire just stared at him in disbelief.

"Please!" she said, sounding exasperated.

Andrew grinned. "Ok, I'm on it!"

Claire wasn't finished, though.

"We'll know by the response if Wesley believes us and if he can be trusted. As a backup plan, I'll see if I can get the codes to the national media broadcast. Now that I've got some of my programs back up and running, I can risk being online again in a limited capacity. If I need to publish something publicly, then I will, as a last resort. I'd rather it comes from a verified source, but if I have something ready to go, then maybe it can act as a little insurance policy for us."

Could she really pull that off? That would be amazing!

"You are amazing," he said. He hadn't meant to say it out loud, but there it was. Claire looked a little embarrassed and quickly returned to her work. Andrew also went to work. After a couple of hours, he started to get hungry again, checking for fly-bots before going outside to check the line. All was quiet and still, and the sun had made a rare appearance, lighting the hills on the far side of the loch as Andrew made his way down the jetty. The effect was stunning.

The hillside was illuminated in a brilliant yellow-green. It contrasted dramatically to the grey skies above and the dark waters of the loch below. He thought again that this would be a nice place to stay - going back to his old, safe life was getting less and less appealing. For a brief moment when he was reeling the line in, he thought they had a catch, but it turned out to be another catch of loch weed.

When he came back inside, he checked with Claire before sacrificing a small part of a thermal brick, just enough to cook some gloop. A few minutes later, they had a pot full of warm grey sludge to share. They sat and ate in silence as they worked, their meal tasting of nearly nothing and with an unpleasant texture that made talking impossible. As Andrew was scraping the last remnants from the pot, Claire uncovered something that would turn their plans upside down.

"Fuuuuck!"

Whatever it was, it wasn't good, Andrew deduced. Claire had a blank look on her face, she was unblinking.

*

Everything went black around her, and she was rushing through the nothingness, feeling her hair blown back, suddenly appearing and stopping with a jolt in a bright white room. It had a single medi-bed in it, and on the bed lay a body. Thick black cables snaked across the floor around it, disappearing under the flimsy white sheet.

Claire was suddenly back in the workroom with Andrew. He was looking at her as if he'd just seen a ghost. She stood suddenly, raced from the workroom, and burst outside.

*

Andrew could hear the same word repeated again and again. Claire sounded like she was in pain. After the initial shock, Andrew rushed outside to see what was wrong.

"Claire?"

She spun around to face him, her eyes wet with tears, face anguished. Andrew moved quickly to her, and she went to turn away, clearly distraught. Andrew grabbed her by her arms, forcing her to face him.

"What is it, Claire? What did you find?" He was terrified of what she might say, but he had to hear it.

"It's John!," she cried, tears streaming down her cheeks now. "John *is* being held in that compound, the one I was being taken to!" She was struggling for breath now, shaking, and she looked scared, something Andrew had never seen before.

"But how …" Andrew's voice trailed off. Their worst fears were realized. "How do you know … Claire?" He was still holding her by her upper arms, but she'd gone limp, her head turned away from him. When she turned back, she looked completely defeated.

"It's the codes, Andy, the codes in the Elyssium data; some of them are coordinates. He's in there, with so many others," she took a breath, then broke down completely. There was nothing for Andrew to do except hold her tightly until the sobbing subsided.

They stood embracing one another for the longest time. His face was buried in her hair, and her face buried into his neck. He could feel the warm wet tears against his neck as she shook and shook.

When she'd calmed, and the tears had stopped, they had stayed in place, holding one another. Andrew bit down on his lip and squeezed his eyes shut. Andrew could feel the bumps of her ribs through her sweater as he rubbed her back, trying to comfort her. Her hands had dug into the flesh of Andrew's shoulder and side, the nails causing him just a little discomfort, but he wasn't about to complain. She wasn't letting go, and they shared one another's warmth as they pressed together tighter still.

Is this what it's like to …

The thought was abruptly halted. Claire broke the embrace, her hands loosening their grip and then her arms falling away. Andrew took a step back, and when he looked into her eyes, he didn't see fear or sorrow, there was something else there instead, and it made his heart flutter just a little. She reached for him and gave him a tender kiss on the cheek before standing back, a look of steely resolve now on her face.

"We're going to get him back," she concluded. Andrew was expecting it, but the thought still caused a wave of crippling fear to rise inside of him. *Oh, Douglas! Here … we … go.*

***

They needed a plan of some sort to get him out. They'd need help, of course, and the first step was trying to secure that help. The information package, and Wesley, formed the first part of the plan. Claire's plan.

After returning to the workroom, Andrew continued putting together the package while Claire kept going on the Elyssium data. It wasn't long before she was able to provide another update - she'd further untangled the reference numbers. As she'd said, they identified people and a location, but she'd also now managed to determine just how many sites there were, and it was hard to comprehend the sheer scale of the operation.

Elyssium sites were listed in The Highlands and most regions of Planet 0420, and all were located below the supposed uninhabitable line. Claire shuddered as she thought about all the poor souls inhabiting the line of Solo's heading for the compound, John included, and the thousands and thousands of others.

"So, if I'm right about the coordinates, and I am right, then John's close. It stands to reason that he'd be taken to the closest site. I'm guessing that it's also the headquarters, given that it's the location of whoever breached me, and that isn't great news – it means that it probably has the highest level of security. We're going to need a lot of help if we're to stand any chance of getting him out of there."

"Ok, ok, we get some help, we get him out!"

Claire wasn't used to such displays of unbridled enthusiasm from Andrew. It was encouraging.

"Aye, let's hope so."

And also save the fucking planet, she thought.

Andrew could tell she was hatching some sort of additional plot - she was deep in thought, her eyes unfocused. What she was actually thinking about were the additional codes listed against the names in the data. She hadn't said anything to Andrew about it yet - she needed him focused and not panicked - but she had a very bad feeling about them.

We'll get him out - If he's still alive.

Andrew waited a little while, then decided to furnish Claire with an idea of his own. She became aware that he was speaking when he was ending his summary of why they should include a second safe contact, "… and that's why he should be the second contact." Claire nodded in a non-committal manner. She really didn't want Andrew to know that she'd drifted off while he'd been talking.

"Ok, and so what do you think our angle should be when we send our evidence to …" Andrew looked very enthusiastic. She hoped that he might fill in the gap for her.

"Grealish!" he confirmed.

Ah, of course, Mr. Sex-bot.

"Yes, yes, what should our angle be with Grealish?"

They continued the discussion and agreed that they'd offer to expose the obvious fabrication that had led to his demise and clear his name in return for his support. Whether or not he'd 'done the deeds,' as it were really didn't matter. The main thing was to get him onside and appeal to the only thing he seemed to care about - himself. Although Claire had an intense dislike of the type of person that Lachlan Grealish appeared to be, she thought that he was a good choice as an inside contact – his rise and fall had been meteoric - she felt sure he'd do anything to clear his name and get himself back in the spotlight.

Twenty minutes later, they'd finalized the package of evidence, and it was ready to send. "Ok, well, here goes nothing." They looked at one another. This was a big moment. Claire executed the code. They looked at one another again.

What do we do now? Andrew was thinking. *There's so much to do,* Claire was thinking.

She'd sent the communication to both Wesley and Grealish, but independently – she'd didn't want them knowing the other was involved, not at this point. They had to work out who to trust first. She just hoped that one of them would fit the bill. They were both feeling a sense of relief and heightened anxiety as they entered the next phase of whatever the hell this was.

Andrew had written a pretty good summation of what they'd found and what had happened to them thus far. It would work, or it wouldn't. They would get help, or they wouldn't. That part of it at least was out of their hands now.

They'd managed to get the evidence to people in authority and now had to hope that they would believe them and that they'd do the right thing with the information they'd received.

Claire was confident they'd provided enough evidence to at least make someone want to go and look into the compound's activities and have a close look at exactly what internal affairs were up to with the whole Elyssium program. It should be enough. They'd set a deadline of noon the next day for a final response. There would be no negotiation, and they'd asked for three things:

First, that priority over all else must be given to finding John and ensuring his safety.

Second, they will require sanctuary and immunity - a guarantee that they would not be prosecuted for anything they'd had to do in their investigation – read: breaching, killing someone, etc.

And third, that a copy of their findings be placed with a legal entity of their choosing, with instructions that would breach the agreement if anything were to happen to them. Or rather them being arrested/murdered, etc. In that case, the information would be sent to all media outlets and student organizations with immediate effect. They had listed the intended recipients, should it come to that.

The small amount of relief that Claire had been feeling quickly disappeared - she couldn't just sit around and wait for things to happen. The longer they waited, the worse the outcome might be for John. They had no guarantee that they'd get a response by their deadline or get one at all for that matter, and they certainly couldn't sit around at the resort, waiting for someone to come and have a closer look at the obvious signs of recent activity. Things didn't always go to plan.

This was the problem with thinking about things, she realized. She turned to Andrew. He was laying on the tarps, head propped up against a wall, and lost in Headspace with his unicorn. She unplugged him, and he came to with a start.

"What the ..." he'd managed to pat the unicorn's neck and was readying himself to try and mount it when the connection had abruptly ended. Claire was looking at him, and he didn't like the look on her face one little bit.

"Andy, we need to go on a wee adventure."

***

Bill McDowell sat opposite the department of finance building in a dark-colored semi-autonomous personal transport pod, or PTP as they were more commonly known. He'd already had quite a few sips of malt to calm his nerves. It wasn't helping.

Where's Wesley? He should have come out hours ago.

Just as he was about to pop another synthaline capsule to keep him awake, he spotted a diminutive, balding figure in beige emerge from the overly tall plexi-glass doors of the department of finance headquarters.

Aha! Wesley, at last.

He was with a colleague, and as expected, they turned to the left and headed for a bar on the corner of the building next door - the aptly named 'Kebab and Calculator.'

Bill waited a minute after they disappeared inside and then exited his pod, checking his jacket pocket as he did so. The small vials were still there - one drop from either of them would be enough to bring on a cardiac arrest. It would look as if Hamish Wesley had died of natural causes.

***

They sat on the edge of the jetty overlooking the loch. The sky was grey, and ominous grey clouds blanketed the sun.

"But can't we just wait and see what the response is?" There was a desperation to Andrew's voice that he didn't like.

Claire shook her head and concentrated on working out the best route to the compound.

There had been nothing so far from Wesley and Grealish, but that was to be expected, Andrew thought. All hell would probably be breaking loose back in the halls of power in New Edinburgh. *Probably?* They would no doubt be scrambling, and she hoped that those responsible were at least starting to panic. They'd be attempting to trace the message, and they had been given plenty of time to do that, but it shouldn't be an issue.

Shouldn't be.

*

Claire, of course, couldn't bank on her code being unbreakable any longer, and it was a difficult thing to deal with. Suddenly everything seemed that much more dangerous and uncertain. Everything could still fall into place, though, if she thought positively. That would certainly help. It wasn't easy to do.

Their evidence could set off a chain of events that saw those responsible held to account and the State governance being turned upside down. They could be believed and exonerated, maybe even thanked if anyone in the corridors of power had a sense of right and wrong.

Wesley. She was pinning her hopes on Wesley to get them out of this. She still wasn't sure about Grealish, but it was good at least to have a backup plan. John had only been taken a few days ago. If she was right about the codes in the Elyssium data, then time was running out, but it wasn't impossible.

Her mind wandered back to the first time she'd ever seen John McGregor. He was sitting with his broad, muscular back to her, chatting with a couple of the elite pricks. She recognized them – they'd started a nasty rumor about her earlier in the term.

The two pricks had started laughing at her from across the outdoor eating area. She'd already messed with some of their work assignments, and they would be in a fair amount of trouble once the college administration discovered that, but in the meantime, she'd send them a very clear message. John had turned to look. He hadn't been laughing along, but he definitely looked amused by her double-barreled single-finger salute.

*

"What are you smiling about?" Andrew asked, looking at her in disbelief.

How can she be sitting there smiling when we're in this situation!

"Oh … nothing. Look, our main problem is getting there. It's going to be quite a trek, but we have no choice. My ankle is feeling a lot better – I think I can make it, but it's at least twelve hours."

"Really? Dook."

"Yes, really."

"Alright … if we leave soon, we can be in place well before the deadline and check things out. Depending on the response we get, we can determine our next move from there."

Our next move?

Claire was no longer smiling. She was thinking about what had happened to her sister at what could be happening inside the compound. Andrew saw her eyes darken and fill with sorrow. Now was as good a time as any, he supposed.

"I think I might have a plan to get us there," he said, looking toward the low hills to their right. Claire followed his gaze, and there, on the horizon, once again, was Andrew's unicorn.

"You have got to be joking!"

"Come on," he called, racing back down the jetty. Claire stood, summed up the situation, and muttered to herself, "oh, Douglas, here we go then," before following with reasonable haste. Andrew was running up the hill now, towards the unicorn, but as he neared the mythical creature, it suddenly reared, turned, and then disappeared over the top of the hill. Andrew slowed and then stopped. "Dook!" he exclaimed.

Maybe running towards it wasn't such a great idea.

Claire caught up with him moments later but kept on going, right past him. Andrew followed, and they reached the top of the hill at roughly the same time, panting for breath and using each other for support. There was no sign of the unicorn, only sweeping hills, grass, thistles, and a stand of trees in the distance, at the bottom of the hill.

"Oh well," Andrew sighed and turned to leave.

He had to admit; it hadn't been the greatest plan. In fact, in the whole history of plans, it was possibly one of the worst.

*

"Wait! There!" She was pointing down towards the bottom of the hill. He saw it. An unmistakable flash of white was moving quickly, partly obscured behind the trees and heading down into the valley. The white shape stopped suddenly, and they looked at each other, Andrew raising his eyebrows. At that point, Claire noticed something else.

"Oh, and what's *that*?" she inquired, pointing again. Andrew strained to see, and after a few seconds, he did indeed see. There looked to be some sort of low building just beyond the tree line, close to where the unicorn had stopped. It was partially obscured, but there was a definite straight edge and a dark, solid mass beyond.

"Man-made?" she speculated.

"Let's go have a look-see!" suggested Andrew and bounded off down the hillside.

Such enthusiasm!

A couple of minutes later, they were crouched down behind a gorse bush, observing not just one unicorn but three - ok, they were horses. The horses were milling around a small shack, and if that wasn't surprising enough, the building showed somewhat alarming signs of being used quite recently.

They stayed in position for a few minutes, expecting someone to emerge at any moment. After a little while, it became clear that the shack was deserted. They shared a look. Andrew went to the left, and

Claire went to the right. They kept low to the ground and moved quickly from cover to cover.

The horses didn't seem too bothered by their presence. As they got closer, they could see that the shack was more of a stable, open at one end and with a row of horse yards down one side. They arrived there at about the same time. It was deserted. As they entered and started to look around, they realized that the horses had gathered in close behind them, showing no signs of apprehension at the appearance of two strangers.

The stable itself was littered with various pieces of roughly made horse tack and plenty of items suggesting very recent use, including some fishing gear that would have been very useful over the last couple of days.

"People are living down here." Claire realized she was stating the obvious, but it had to be said.

"Aye, so it seems."

"These horses …"

Andrew raised an eyebrow.

"These horses," she repeated, "well, they must be tamed, at least to some extent; they must be able to be ridden."

"May I remind you of *my idea* at this point? I'd say it's highly likely."

"And you can ride them?"

"Well …"

Claire was exasperated.

"… I've been learning, a bit … in Headspace."

"Worth a shot, I guess; what've we got to lose? Other than you potentially breaking your neck that is."

Andrew frowned and turned back, trying to approach the horses. They were eyeing him nervously.

Something had caught Claire's eye. She ducked under a timber rail and moved over to a small bench that looked like it was perhaps used for maintaining the horse-riding gear. On it was a brown and withered object. She picked it up.

An apple core?

Claire's eye was drawn to a basket that was hanging high above the bench, close to the roughhewn trusses that supported a fairly sturdy-looking timber roof. She bounded over and tried to reach the basket but was embarrassingly a few inches short even after jumping.

She looked around for something to stand on, but nothing was apparent. She tried to move the bench, but it was way too heavy.

"Oh, for fucks sake!" She couldn't believe that such a simple thing could be causing her so much grief. She looked back sheepishly to Andrew, who had been watching with interest after the horses had moved away from him on his initial approach. He strolled over, grinning.

"Don't you even," she said, but he didn't need to say anything; she was already embarrassed enough. Andrew made a big show of standing with his back to the basket and stretching his arms up while yawning, pushing the basket up and off the wooden peg that was holding it in place.

He misjudged the weight, and the basket tilted before emptying its contents all over him, apples bouncing off his head and shoulders as he cowered away from the firm, fruity rain. It was Andrew's turn to be embarrassed, and they shared a laugh as they went about gathering up all the split apples.

"Oh, you are such a plank!"

"This is true," he acknowledged, "but holy dook, look at all these apples!"

They were both thinking the same thing – they should have scouted this area when they arrived. They could have avoided fishgloop almost entirely if they had.

"No wonder the horses are hanging around here then – maybe their keepers are due back soon?"

Claire wasn't sure if that would be a good or bad thing. Andrew was polishing an apple on his shirt and then took a big bite. He pulled a face but kept chewing anyway.

"Och, a wee bit sharp but edible. Just," Andrew said, before reaching back into the basket and tossing an apple to Claire. She took a bite and made a similar face. *Uck!*

She turned around and saw that the white unicorn was watching her closely now, from not too far away. She held out the apple and approached the magical beast slowly. It didn't flinch, taking a couple of steps forward, sniffing the apple and then Claire's hand, before taking a gentle nibble at it – the apple that is.

Claire allowed it to take the apple and moved next to the creature, but it moved away as she made to stroke its mane. She turned back to Andrew and shrugged.

"Well, it's a start."

He came to join her. "I wonder where you can even find apples around these parts."

She pointed behind him. "Over there, I'd say."

Andrew wheeled around and squinted. Sure enough, there was a small, fenced orchard of apple trees in the mid-distance, the green apples clearly visible on the branches.

"Oh, right," he said, blushing.

"So, now we know for sure that people are living down here. By the look of things, they have been for some time. Maybe they come here to fish or something? There must be other stables elsewhere, accommodation too, so maybe they're using the native horses to get around?"

"Could be," Andrew agreed through a mouthful of apple.

It was very likely, and a very good development indeed, Claire thought.

"Well, we sure can't wait for whoever built this stable to return." She looked at Andrew, waiting for him to respond.

"Ok," he said. "I think it's time to find out if I can ride these things."

Claire didn't think he could ride these things. There weren't too many semi-wild horses in suburban New Edinburgh, after all.

"Let me try and get friendly with one of them, and then let's see if all that time I was *wasting* in Headspace has paid off after all."

Andrew sounded confident. Claire let him continue.

"If we can ride there, it'll only take us a few hours, and we can be in position and assess our options well in advance of the deadline. It'll also buy us time to see what else we can find in the data. With any luck, we can get some help - if not, it's up to us, and the sooner we get there, the better."

She'd never been so proud of her raggedy friend. She didn't even recognize him just at that moment - there was a steel to him that she'd never seen before - she was more than a little impressed.

"You do know there's no way I can ride one of these things, Andy," she said. He looked over and smiled.

"Leave it to me. Let's see if any of these horses are going to be tame enough first. If I can get on one, you can sit behind."

Claire considered this – it seemed a plausible option. Andrew headed straight back to the apple basket and started the process of trying to befriend his favorite white unicorn. She headed back to prepare their things. As she walked back to the storeroom, she had time to think.

She was terrified of what might have happened to John, terrified of the visions she'd been having. It was happening to her more and more, and she couldn't help but think something was terribly wrong with her.

CHAPTER 19 – COVERT OPS

Bill had ensured that he blended in with the regulars of The Kebab and Calculator. Opti-lenses, overweight, slightly balding and unkept, mid-range, boring suit. Just another lonely accountant drowning his sorrows after a hard day - adding things up, Bill guessed, or whatever they did all day. He was waiting nervously for his opportunity, having managed to secure a seat at the bar next to Wesley's group a little while ago.

He'd started to sweat through the suit - it was uncomfortable and a size too small at least. His hands were a bit shaky too, but no one was paying him any attention. His heart had started beating about twice as fast as he'd wanted it to, and waves of anxiety were coursing up through his chest as he thought about what he had to do.

Any moment now.

Bill was keeping a close eye on Wesley by what he thought was a very discrete and cunning use of the mirrored plex behind the bar. They were onto their third pint of Scot's Bru, and surely any moment now, Wesley would need to break the seal. Surely enough, just as another colleague arrived, Wesley rose from his stool and clapped his friend on the shoulder, heading for the toilets. His bru was only half empty.

This is it! This is my chance!

Wesley's colleagues had turned to one another and were deep in conversation, no doubt about the latest breakthrough in calculators or the latest tax ruling or similar.

Quickly, before. Oh, fuck it!

He'd fumbled the capsule and dropped it on the floor. It bounced away from the bar and was immediately squashed under an immaculately polished brogue that just happened to be passing by. Bill cursed at his carelessness and tried to calm his ever-increasing heart rate.

It was ok, there was still time, and he had a standby capsule. He was sweating buckets, and he wiped his brow with an ihandkerchief and dried his sweaty hands - his scar was on fire now, and he rubbed it frantically through the thick fabric of the suit.

Fucking stupid suit! Ok, one more shot at this. Don't mess it up, Bill, don't mess it up.

He removed the capsule very carefully, breaking off the cap and holding it between his thumb and forefinger. The barkeep, a quaint tradition favored by this particular establishment, and much to Bill's chagrin, was serving the person next to him. He dare not risk being observed, and so he'd have to wait for the right moment.

Any second now. Someone bumped into Bill as they passed behind him, and he nearly jumped out of his skin. It was all he could do to hold onto the tiny vial. His hands were sweaty again, and his opti-lenses were starting to fog.

Bill waited impatiently for the order to be taken, his leg bouncing up and down on the stool, his heart now hammering away so fast that he felt it might bring on a heart attack at any moment. It seemed to take forever for the order to be completed, and Bill mopped his brow one more time and glanced over his shoulder, only to see that Wesley was already halfway back to the bar.

Dook!

This was his chance - the barkeep had finally moved away - Wesley would be back at the bar any moment. He pretended to stretch, moving his badly shaking hand near Wesley's pint glass and squeezing the small plexi vial.

Unfortunately for Bill, the adrenaline coursing through his veins meant that he squeezed the vial way too hard, sending a small squirt of the deadly liquid clean over the top of the pint glass and harmlessly onto the floor behind the bar. He finished his stretch and looked at the vial. It was empty. He'd blown it!

Oh fuck, fuck fuck fuck fuck!

Isabel was going to tear him a new one over this and much worse. He drained the remainder of his malt, getting more of it down his shirt than in his mouth, and left the bar unsteadily. He was feeling giddy as he reached the street and nearly fell as he stepped off the pavement, not expecting the change in height, then weaved his way across the street to where his PTP was parked. He was hyperventilating now and felt like he might collapse, but he managed to open the hatch and dive into the vehicle.

He sat there in total disbelief, his mind feeling like it was oozing out of his ears, his hands gripping the controls manically. He'd completely ballsed it up. His life was over. No more cozy quarters. No more special benefits. Isabel would destroy him.

He started to sob rather pathetically and lost all sense of time as he sat alone in the dark, head bowed and wallowing in self-pity. Eventually, he decided that enough was enough and rubbed his face, bringing his sobbing under control and trying to regain some composure. Maybe he could find a way out of this? Sudden movement across the street caught his attention, and without thinking, he sprang into action.

***

Claire had been lying to Andrew about her ankle. It had felt a bit better but was still quite painful to put pressure on. Running after the unicorn had aggravated it. She was worried she wasn't up to such a long trek. If she could avoid it, all the better. She finished packing and closed the big metal door behind her.

Goodbye heat, goodbye power.

*

Meanwhile, Andrew seemed to be having some success with the unicorn – he'd fed it several apples and was now able to pat it on the neck without it trying to avoid him. He was gaining its trust, but the next step was a big leap of faith. If this failed, they would be on foot, they would be exposed, and they would need to travel through the night.

This had better work!

He went back to the stable and returned with a halter, reigns, and some sort of crude saddle cloth. The unicorn eyed him suspiciously as he placed the items on the ground in front of it, causing a backward step and nervous twitch of the head. *Slowly now …*

Andrew bent down and slowly picked up the halter in one hand, then produced a shiny green apple in the other. The unicorn became still and watched him carefully as he slowly but confidently took the five steps needed to be within touching distance.

The unicorn snorted and bobbed its head before reaching forward and baring its teeth - attempting to get to the apple that Andrew had concealed in his fist. As the unicorn nuzzled his fist, Andrew moved beside it and turned his hand over, offering the apple as he stroked and patted the beast's neck. The unicorn took a tentative bite and another. It was surprisingly gentle.

He knew he had to act quickly and confidently - he'd been through this scenario in Headspace maybe a hundred times in high-speed mode, and so it seemed a perfectly natural action to slip on the halter and tighten it in. The unicorn barely even batted an eyelid. Andrew patted the beast's neck again before fetching the saddlecloth and throwing it over its back. The beast barely moved, and Andrew patted it again, this time adding a "good boy, Gregory" into the equation.

Andrew quickly but carefully passed the straps underneath its belly and firmly tightened the buckles so that the soft saddle pad was firmly in place. Stirrups were hanging from either side and appeared to be adjustable in length, which was quite useful. Andrew patted the beast again and then hesitated, suddenly full of self-doubt.

Did he really believe he could ride a unicorn? Sure, the simulation had come in handy back on the podium, and much to bald sunlenses detriment, but that had been one single move that they obviously weren't expecting. All the virtual training in the world probably wasn't going to be much help in controlling a mostly wild beast with a mind of its own. There was only one way to find out. Andrew swallowed hard, gave the unicorn one last pat, and then attempted to hoist himself up and over.

After about two minutes of hopping largely in circles as the unicorn became testier and testier at his attempts to swing a leg over, Andrew conceded he didn't have the technique to mount the beast. Things weren't looking great all of a sudden - it had been much easier in the simulation. He fetched another apple and used it to lead the unicorn toward the thick wooden rails that bordered the horse yards.

He knew this was perhaps pointless, as there were unlikely to be many conveniently placed fences on their journey, although he conceded that perhaps Claire could be a fence replacement if needs be. Or there may be a handy rock or something. He realized he was rambling in his own mind, something that happened all too frequently, and instead focused some of his attention back on trying to ride the beast. A quick step up, and he was on!

The unicorn shifted underneath him, and he nearly lost his balance, clinging onto the beast's neck for a moment before righting himself. He was on it! He was sitting on the magical, mythical beast! Andrew took a moment to calm himself and get used to the feeling of being up so high before issuing a command to move the beast forward. Nothing happened.

Well, at least the view's nice from up here.

He thought back to the simulation, wondering what he'd missed, and went through his mental checklist. No, he'd done everything he needed to, yet the beast wouldn't move. He tried again—still nothing.

Claire appeared through the small stand of trees next to the stable, lugging their packs. Andrew waved - wanting to appear as if he had everything under control. He made a clicking noise with his tongue and used his heels to prompt the beast to move forwards. It worked rather better than expected, and the unicorn sprang forward with alarming speed, heading for a gap in the tree line. Andrew was unbalanced and tried to steady himself but was bouncing around everywhere as the beast trotted then cantered.

He looked over at his friend, who was observing him with what he could only describe as total and complete awe. He was doing it! He was bloody well doing it! He couldn't believe it! The trees were approaching rapidly, though, and he had the thought that now would be a rather good time to try and steer it, perhaps even slow it down a little. The next few seconds were a bit of a blur.

All he could remember was grasping at thin air as the horizon suddenly turned 90 degrees, and the next second having all the air knocked out of him as he landed squarely on his back. For a few seconds, he couldn't see, breathe or hear. He was vaguely aware of hearing Claire calling his name, and when his vision cleared, he saw Claire's face appear above his. "Oh, Douglas!" she was saying, between bouts of hysterical laughter, "that was … fucking spectacular!"

Andrew stared at her, still dazed. Eventually, she composed herself enough to say, "are you ok, Andy? Oh … I wish I had captured that on V.I.! It was so graceful! That landing!" She was very amused. Andrew tried to push himself up on his elbows and discovered that it was no problem - he seemed to still be in one piece, at least.

"Oh, you think it's funny?" he asked but then couldn't think of anything else to say. Her mirth, no matter how annoying, was proving to be quite infectious. Andrew frowned to himself before rolling over and pushing himself to his feet.

"Well, I hope you can do a wee bit better than that for the next three hours or more," said Claire, strolling back to the stables to stock up on apples.

The unicorn was standing nearby, chewing some grass casually, as if nothing had happened. Andrew strolled over a little gingerly and patted the unicorn's broad, muscular neck – it certainly wasn't its fault that he could barely ride.

Got to do better than that.

He moved back into position and then shocked himself by hauling himself up onto the unicorn's back at the first attempt! It was most likely something to do with his wounded pride and a desire to redeem himself from the burning embarrassment he was feeling rather than his technique, but whatever it was, it did the trick.

Andrew fixed his feet firmly into the stirrups and issued the clicking command again, and the unicorn moved off, more steadily this time. He spent the next few minutes getting to grips with the controls and then brought the beast round in a wide arc, slowly gathering pace before stopping it in a cloud of dust next to the horse yards. Claire applauded.

"Good enough?" he inquired. Andrew imagined he must look just like another of his old-world idols, Clint Eastwood, at that particular moment in time. All he needed was a gunslinger hat, a cigar, a poncho, a beard, piercing blue eyes, and so on.

"Aye, Andy. Bloody amazing!" she said; there was not a trace of mirth or irony in the statement. He did a little bow from the saddle, and Claire threw him one of the packs. Andrew strapped it on back to front - that is to say, he strapped it to his front, rather awkwardly.

"Come on, let's go," she directed as she shrugged herself into the larger of the two packs, reaching out her hand so that Andrew could help her up. The beast moved sideways a little as Claire was pulled up but quickly settled. She wrapped her arms around Andrew's midriff, underneath the backpack - possibly a little close to his privates, but there wasn't any choice, it was there or nowhere - and clung on tightly.

Andrew could feel the warmth of Claire's body pressing into him from behind, and he immediately found that it made it quite difficult to concentrate. A little shiver ran through him, and he smiled deep down inside as he commanded the beast forward, beginning the rescue mission.

***

Hamish Wesley never saw it coming. It had been a pleasant evening, capping off an extremely interesting and useful day of research. He had most of the pieces in place now to warrant a full financial audit of eight separate state departments, all seemingly linked to whatever it was Isabel and her cronies were doing.

He'd received final approval to undertake the audits from his drinking companions tonight and was feeling that little tingle of excitement that only the potential discovery of financial irregularities could bring.

Hamish waved goodbye to his colleagues, and they headed around the corner of the bar towards the department's sleeping quarters. Wesley himself was looking forward to getting back to his house and family in The Heights, where a roaring fireplace, dressing gown, slippers, and a glass of sherry awaited.

He stepped off the pavement, heading for the Solo that had just pulled up in a transport bay on the other side of the podway. A large dark shape seemingly came out of nowhere and at incredible speed, collecting him with such force that he was thrown into the air, landing heavily back on the podway as the dark shape sped away.

A few patrons had heard the noise and burst from the bar and out onto the street just in time to get a glimpse of Bill McDowell's PTP as it disappeared into the night.

***

The unicorn turned out to be a steadfast and sturdy beast. Andrew and Claire made their way steadily towards the compound, stopping every so often to rest, water, and feed their trusty steed. The terrain was rugged, with heavily wooded areas only occasionally giving way to open pastures - it was a good job they had transport.

At one point, a beautiful white-tailed eagle had swooped down under the tree canopy in front of them, gliding effortlessly and then zipping up and away with a leisurely flap of its huge wings.

Andrew had gotten the hang of the whole riding business fairly quickly, and they'd made good progress, reaching the river and deciding to take a short rest before looking for a suitable crossing point.

Claire felt a chill run down her spine as she saw the fast-flowing waters of the river again. Her vision suddenly blackened, and an image of her dead sister appeared in her mind. Henny's face was cast in the same pale blue light as before - she had the same expressionless inky black eyes, and blue-black tears streaked her cheeks.

'Henny ...'

Her arms slipped away from Andrew, and she fell backward, only her pack keeping her atop the unicorn before her vision returned. "Hold up," she directed, and Andrew pulled the beast to a halt as commanded.

She slipped down from the saddlecloth and landed unsteadily on the ground, unclasping and dropping her pack as the scenery spun around her. Her hand found the saddle pad, and she grasped onto it as a wave of nausea swept over her. Andrew was speaking, but it sounded as if his voice was coming from underwater. Claire felt her legs buckle and was vaguely aware of falling.

***

It was a control room of some sort. Dimly lit, with banks of computer towers stacked so very high and radiating out from the central space in which she now stood, barefoot and in a thin robe.

The air was icy cold, and Claire shivered, wrapping her arms around herself. She was alone and yet felt a strange sense of unease as if someone was watching her or had sensed her presence. It was difficult to explain, but whatever it was, it was manifesting itself quickly into cold hard fear, and preventing her from moving.

A throbbing hum filled the space. Thick black cables snaked from all sides of the room and became entangled as they gathered together at a central point, feeding into the floor just in front of a monolithic steel half wall on the far side of the room - it must have been at least ten yards high and seven yards wide. A glow of blue light pulsed from somewhere behind it.

She became aware of another noise in the room, and she strained to hear. It was — something - it sounded - organic, maybe? The faint sound was sending waves of fear through Claire's body, and she wanted to turn and run but could only stare wide-eyed at the dividing wall.

The strange noise was coming from somewhere behind - it was as if something was moving around back there. *What the fuck was that noise?* She then heard something that sounded almost like speech, but it was far from human. She tried to turn her head away and close her eyes, but she could do neither.

She held her breath, straining to hear, but hoping, praying, for silence. The silence stretched out for what seemed an eternity, and the only thing Claire could hear was her irregular heartbeat pumping wildly in her chest.

There it was again! A soft wet sound, almost speech, but not like anything she'd ever heard. Her blood turned to ice. Her mind was screaming at her to run, but she was still frozen to the spot.

Tears started to flow from the corners of her eyes and tickled her cheeks. A shadow flickered across the glow of light from behind the wall, and Claire felt more terrified than she could have ever imagined. The shadow grew. *There's something there!*

Claire screamed!

***

"Claire! Claire!"

The next thing she knew, she was recoiling in shock as a large quantity of icy water hit her flush in the face. She gasped for air and thrashed her arms and legs about on the ground as her sight returned, seeing Andrew's face first and her hand slapping it a second later as she sat bolt upright.

"Ouch! You crazy bitch!"

Andrew was rubbing his face, looking slightly bemused. "What in Douglas' name was that about?" he asked, sounding a little more wounded than he needed to. He ignored his slightly stung pride and cheek and offered her his flask

*

Claire sat up, and Andrew stayed crouched down next to her, waiting patiently as she sipped at the hot bevvie. Claire started to feel a little better - and took her time looking around at the trees and the gently flowing river, regulating her breathing.

"I don't know, Andy. I don't know what happened. I'm sorry."

"Don't be sorr ..."

"About the slap," Claire interjected. "I'm sorry about the slap. I was having some sort of weird lucid dream or something. I was terrified, wherever I was, and I just lashed out with the shock of the icy water hitting my face. Ya bas!" The words were delivered with a smile, and she could see the relief in Andrew's face.

"You passed out Claire, I didn't know how else to bring you around - seemed like the best option anyway, and it worked!" Claire responded with a playful punch to his arm. Even when she was playful, she could still hurt. He helped her to her feet, and she wandered over to the river's edge and crouched down, cupping some of the icy waters in her hands and slurping it down before rubbing her hands over her face and neck.

Claire stood and watched the river flowing by. A feeling of regret had been building inside her for a while. She couldn't seem to shake it. It returned with full force.

She'd been thinking a lot about her friends on the ride. Everything was her fault, basically. She just hoped that whatever came of this would somehow be worth it. She'd almost been wishing at times that she'd never uncovered the Elyssium files, but they'd come this far - they couldn't go back now. She turned back to Andrew, who was ... *what is he doing?*

Andrew was performing a series of what she could only assume were kung fu moves on a nearby tree.

"Andy!" he stopped mid-crane pose.

"Eh?"

"What are you doing?"

"Oh, you know, just practicing."

"Well … I suppose if a tree ever attacks us, we'll be fine then!"

Andrew's thoughts flashed back to his bedside table, and he absently rubbed the back of his head.

"Well, alright, seeing as I have your attention, for the moment … this is close enough for now. I can remote into one of the compound's fly-bots from here, maybe, and use its V.I. feed to do a bit of a recce. It's not a bad time to have a look-see at what else we've unlocked."

She'd left her decryption processes running on the data during the ride, meaning that they should be just about finished. Andrew was busying himself with the unicorn, and Claire sat on a large boulder near the riverbank and got busy on her device. A minute later, she nearly dropped it in the river in shock.

"Oh fuck!"

Andrew's head snapped around in Claire's direction.

"What's up?!"

Andrew's voice was again an octave or two higher than it should have been.

"Fucking hell, Andy. I just don't know what to think."

Claire stood and held the exo-device out in front of her; the display turned toward Andrew. It took him a couple of seconds to focus on the display, but then he saw the same name, repeated again and again as the recipient of all the messages from John McGregor. The name was *Peter Bradshaw*.

*

Andrew's heart felt like it had dropped through him to the ground below and rolled away. He looked from the display to Claire and back again.

"Peter Bradshaw," he stated, somewhat unnecessarily.

"Oh aye, the very same Peter Bradshaw that John talked to about internal affairs security at the college, just before everything went to dook - just before people started wanting to kidnap and murder us."

Her words hung awkwardly in the air.

"Fucking hell," he said - necessarily, this time. "What do we do now? Do we assume he ratted us out? Do we just turn around and go

PLANET 0420

home?" He was hoping she'd provide an answer, and he could just nod along with whatever the decision was, but she was having none of that.

"What do *you* want to do, Andy?"

The tone of her voice surprised him, and when he looked at her, he could see the barely concealed anger.

"Erm ..." he said. "Errr ... is this some sort of a test?"

Claire just stared at him - he could feel his dignity and self-worth being stripped away by the second.

"We carry on?" His voice rose as he spoke, adding an unwelcome inflection that phrased the statement as a question.

Claire had now put her hands on her hips. Her look was pure death. Andrew realized he'd given the wrong answer, or given it the wrong way, or was just wrong.

"Oh no, why don't we just leave him to die, Andy? Why don't we just assume that *he ratted us out*, and well, fuck him then, as long as we're ok, eh?"

The words were almost in a sing-song, but they cut through the air like little knives - the blinding sarcasm making Andrew flinch. She glared at him until he looked away.

"Look, Andy. I'm just as upset as you are, ok? We still don't know exactly what he did, but there *has* to be an explanation. In the least, we have to give him the opportunity to provide it by trying to keep him alive, eh?"

Andrew realized what a twat he'd just been. He also realized his reaction wasn't that different from Claire's back at the resort but bit his tongue.

Keep him alive.

He'd been wavering on whether they should even attempt to find him, but of course, the alternative was unthinkable. He hung his head, overwhelmed by the whole situation.

"Andy, there's something I've not told you."

He had that sinking feeling in the pit of his stomach again. Whatever it was, it wasn't going to be good. Claire never had anything good to tell him.

"Oh?"

"Aye." Claire closed her device and took a step towards him. The breeze ruffled her hair ever so slightly, and Andrew tried to concentrate instead on what she was about to say.

"Andy."

"Aye."

"Whoever goes into that compound …" she paused, looked down, swallowed, and looked back up at Andrew, her eyes dark.

"… they don't come out again. It's not just my theory anymore."

Don't come out again.

Andrew felt like he'd been punched in the stomach. "Wait, what?"

"I found something bad, Andy. Really, really bad. I wasn't going to say anything, but you have to know."

Claire had folded her arms across her stomach, and she had a look of desperation in her eyes. She looked scared.

"It's the status of whoever arrives there. There are records for an 'A' status for up to a week, but then the status is changed, and …" her words trailed off.

"And?" he braced himself for the reply.

"And then, well, it's changed to a 'T' and … well … after that, there are no more log entries."

Andrew understood. A chill ran through him, and he swallowed hard.

We might already be too late.

Claire had looked away as she spoke, but she now turned her face up toward him; the weak sun highlighted her clear green eyes. For Andrew, time simply stood still.

***

Bill knew as soon as he'd hit Wesley with his PTP that he'd just made a potentially fatal mistake. He'd panicked, seen what he thought was an opportunity to save himself, and reacted. It had been a stupid decision.

As he'd sped away from the scene of the crime, he'd watched in his rear-view display and seen Wesley sprawled on the podway but moving. He thought for a second about turning around and finishing the job, but by then, it was too late - people had come out of the bar to render assistance.

Even if by some luck Hamish Wesley had died from the impact, the way he'd tried to kill him was about the least suspicious it could possibly be. He'd failed miserably, and he'd be very lucky indeed not to be discovered as the driver, arrested and charged with attempted murder.

The only thing to do now would be to report his grave error and face the consequences: goodbye perks, goodbye special access to attractive young captives, goodbye cushy job, and comfortable existence. Bill pulled the vehicle over and started to cry uncontrollably.

***

They stopped near the top of the steep hillside. They'd been winding their way up for the last thirty minutes or so. The late afternoon sun was low in the sky, and they didn't have much time to utilize the light in their surveillance. Claire hadn't had any luck trying to breach into the compound's fly-bot V.I. stream, which had frustrated her immensely – they'd have to do it the old-fashioned way instead.

The compound should be visible to them just over the other side of the hill, and it was time to travel on foot. They dismounted underneath a heavy tree canopy and tied up the unicorn. Andrew started heading for the top of the hill, unaware that Claire wasn't following behind him.

She'd taken a couple of steps forward when the forest had started to disappear. For a moment she thought that she was going to be ok, but quickly the darkness surrounded her again, and then the vision came.

A bright white light was somewhere ahead of her. She tried to move towards it, and as she did, the light seemed to morph into an image. It was out of focus, but the more she struggled to reach it, the clearer it became. It was some sort of medi-center bed. Something was happening – there was a person on the bed and another person attending to them. Were they attending? No, that wasn't what was happening at all.

The person laying on the bed had no face, and the medic, the person who Claire thought was attending to them, was doing something terrible, something incredibly vile. The faceless person struggled violently against their restraints. As Claire drew closer, she could see the medic's face buried inside a huge gaping wound – they were feeding on the person in the restraints, ripping into their internal organs, blood and gore seeping from the wound.

Claire fought frantically to reach them, to stop what was happening. There was something familiar about the body, the blonde hair, the muscular arms. *Was it? Was it John?* She redoubled her efforts and cried out desperately. As she struggled, the medic pulled themselves from the wound and turned to face her.

She was looking at herself! Her face was covered in blood, her teeth were jagged and broken, her eyes were black and gleaming in the bright light, but it was her, there was no doubt! The thing that was Claire smiled and started to laugh, an evil, jagged little laugh, a sound that Claire would never be able to forget.

"No," she gasped, "no … it can't be!"

She felt herself violently pulled back from the evil thing that both was and wasn't her - pulled out of the room, back into the darkness, back to the forest.

Claire was still standing, propped against the tree, soaked in sweat, as her vision came back into focus. She could hear Andrew calling her name.

*

"Claire!"

Andrew was running back down the hill.

They had no face, the person. She collapsed to the ground as he arrived.

"Claire, are you ok!"

She looked up at him, blinking into the light.

"I'm ok, Andy. I saw something. Something terrible - the compound - inside."

"Wait, saw what, how?" He was getting very worried about Claire. She kept passing out - he didn't know what to think. She took a sip of the water container he was offering - thankful he hadn't just thrown the contents of it in her face this time.

"Are you sure you're ok?"

"Aye, I'm fine, Andy," she replied calmly. She looked him in the eye,

"I've been getting these … visions. Just now, back at the watering hole, even before that."

Andrew was deeply worried.

"This was the strongest and clearest yet. I saw … it was awful."

"Well … ok."

Andrew was none the wiser. He sat next to her, but she immediately got to her feet.

"John's in there, and he's in terrible danger. I know it. I'm going in. I can't wait for help to arrive – especially since we don't know if or when that might be."

Andrew swallowed hard. She meant it, and by 'I'm going in,' she meant 'we.'

He wasn't about to argue with her - they were going in together.

CHAPTER 20 – FELICITY

Bill was half expecting the call. He'd returned from his failed assassination attempt on Wesley and drank himself to sleep with anything he could find. He had no idea what he could say to Isabel to save himself and delay the inevitable for as long as possible. She'd find out that he'd failed soon enough anyway. He was fucked, well and truly.

His secretary peeked meekly into his workroom. Bill was sitting at his desk, slumped back in the chair, passed out, again. There were two large bottles of nearly empty spirits sitting on his desk, as well as several empty cans of various flavors of bru, and Felicity McTavish sincerely wondered if she was going to be able to wake him. However, the lady on the comms had been quite insistent, not to mention quite rude – she'd have to do her best.

Felicity cleared her throat. Bill didn't move. She hated having to go to Bill's workroom late at night. She was only nineteen and still unsure how to deal with his, shall we say, 'hands-on' approach to their professional relationship. Felicity had been ecstatic when told she'd landed the job a few months back - it was going to be her big break and her family's ticket out of poverty, after all – but things had quickly soured after first meeting her new boss.

She desperately wanted to get away from him, to somewhere where she was treated with a modicum of respect. Still, she knew she probably wasn't going to get another opportunity like this in her lifetime. She reluctantly entered the workroom and called out, "Mr. McDowell," but he didn't so much as twitch.

The workroom smelt faintly of urine, and as she rounded the desk to try and shake him awake, she saw the large wet patch on the front of his pants.

Ew, disgusting old perv!

Felicity shook Bill's shoulder and called his name, once, twice, and a third time before he woke. She immediately retreated to a safe space on the far side of the desk and placed the slim blue comms handset down in front of him.

"You need to take this call, sir, a Ms. Donachy."

Bill suddenly looked very pale. "Ah … thanks … thank you, Pherlidooky," he mumbled, sounding more than a little slurred. He felt the dampness in his pants and pulled his chair quickly to the desk to hide his little accident. He made a gesture to shoo Felicity from the room as he reached for the secure comms.

Fucking asshat.

She closed the door behind her, but instead of returning to her desk in the reception space, she stayed where she was and pressed her ear back against the door.

This should be entertaining.

Bill had put the call on speaker, and as Felicity listened, she'd blushed at some of the language. She didn't understand why Ms. Donachy was so angry, but she certainly enjoyed the creativity of the swearing and the threats she was using, as well as Bill's blithering attempts to explain himself.

She'd had to suppress a giggle once or twice as she listened, but the fun was soon over, the call ending with "... unless you want to be dooking blood for a month!" followed by the sound of the handset at the other end being slammed down violently. Felicity pushed herself away from the door, and the latch clicked into its housing. Felicity froze.

Bill stared with glazed eyes at the closed door to his workroom. Felicity crept away quickly and settled herself back at her desk - she couldn't wait to tell everyone about this.

Back in the workroom, Bill had wet himself a second time.

***

Hamish Wesley was very, very sore. He was walking gingerly, with the aid of a walking stick, making his way down the short corridor to his workroom.

He'd been discharged from the medi-center's emergency ward with heavy bruising but no permanent damage. All of The Highlands' autonomous and semi-autonomous vehicles were designed to cushion any impact. It was the transport pod's own systems rather than anything the driver had done to avoid the accident that had saved his life.

The local security forces had told him that the driver hadn't even slowed down before or after impact – in other words, it was a deliberate act. Unfortunately, they had no V.I. footage of the incident and no logs of a vehicle traveling along the podway at that time. Hamish Wesley had been run over by a ghost, apparently.

Wesley was almost certain of who was behind the incident. Things were suddenly getting very real, and it looked as if he would need to call in all of his favors and then some from his defense buddies to get to the bottom of things, not to mention to ensure his own safety.

He spent the morning making a series of secure comms calls and making the necessary arrangements. At twelve-thirty exactly, Hamish carefully unwrapped the plain baked vegetable slice he'd made himself for lunch and poured himself a fresh glass of water. That was when he received the package.

***

The sound of fly-bots suddenly filled the air overhead, and Claire had to duck for cover. They whizzed past in an instant, far overhead. She waited a few moments and then signaled to Andrew, who was cowering beside the unicorn.

They headed to the top of the hill and took up a position that gave them a clear view of the terrain below. It was hard to miss. The gigantic grey concrete structure was the only man-made object as far as the eye could see, sitting around a mile away and surrounded by dense forest. They retreated down the hillside to consider their next move, staying under cover the whole way.

"What now?" Predictably, it had been Andrew with the question. The sight of the compound had brought all his fears back to the surface with a jolt. This was real.

"As we discussed, Andy," came the somewhat curt reply.

"Aye, but it's so big!"

"What were you expecting, Andy, one of those mini-compounds?"

He pulled a face. "No, not particularly, but how the hell are we supposed to get in there?"

"As we planned, Andy, nothing's changed. I'll do some surveillance, and you see if you can dig up anything on the layout using this," she proposed, waving her device at him. "Use the Big Orange

Dot program. We *have* to find a way inside. Meanwhile, let's just hope for a response from Wesley or Grealish - sooner rather than later."

They returned to the unicorn, and Andrew guided it back down the heavily forested hillside to an area where it could be watered and fed, and then returned to the hilltop and quickly set up a makeshift camp before getting to work on scanning the layout of the compound.

He was quite weary from the riding - it had been easier in Headspace - but he'd got them here; no one could argue about that.

      *

Claire had moved back into position at the top of the hill. She was frantically switching between her comms and her magvis, looking for anything that might be of use.

She zoomed in on the train of Solo's that were still arriving at the compound at least every minute and noticed something unusual – the line was stationary, and vehicles were backed up for as far as she could see. As she scanned around the perimeter, she could see that some of the vehicles were being directed to a loading dock at the rear of the facility.

There didn't seem to be any guards in that area, but there were surveillance cams dotted around the perimeter. The Solo's might just offer enough cover to get close to the building, and several large open bays offered possibilities, not to mention a few large air ducts near ground level - it was looking better than expected.

Claire couldn't understand why this area appeared to be unguarded - perhaps they had a few logistical issues - and if so, this was definitely to their advantage.

Now then, if Andy's had some luck with the layout, then maybe we'll have a way in, and then maybe we have a plan.

Andrew hadn't had any luck. He'd fallen asleep propped up against the trunk of a large tree instead of searching for 3-D skeleton images of the building, which was what he was supposed to be doing.

Claire kicked his foot as she walked past. Andrew assumed he was under attack from who knows what sort of mutant creature and leapt up like a cat frightened by a cucumber before realizing that only Claire was in sight.

"Great work, Andy."

"Hey, I'm sorry, riding a unicorn is bloody hard work, ya know?"

"Pathetic."

Claire had sat on her pack and was already back on her device. Andrew went to relieve himself behind a nearby tree, feeling more than a little sheepish.

After a while, Claire checked her comms, noticing that the display was blank again - the temporary work she'd done with industrial tape back at the resort appeared to be less permanent than she would have liked. She banged it with her palm a couple of times, which seemed to be the default method for getting it working again, and it sprang back to life with only minor interference. Claire's eyes widened immediately she saw what was on the display.

"Oh, dook! Oh, dook! Andy, we have responses!"

***

It took Hamish Wesley a while to come to terms with the encrypted comms package he'd received. For a start, no one was supposed to be able to access his secure private channel other than a few of his most closely trusted advisors. The contents of the communication painted an incredible picture that was difficult to give any credence to at first sight.

The State, disappearing their own people then faking communications from them! Why would they do such a thing? It seemed crazy, but then again, a lot of evidence had been provided to substantiate the claims, and he would have to refer it to technical experts to determine its legitimacy.

Wesley organized a quick data scan on the senders, and they appeared to be wanted cybercriminals who were also accused of murdering two security force officers in cold blood. There was a photo he'd seen of one of the deceased, posing with his family, sunlenses casually propped on his shaven head. He looked like quite a nice chap.

He sat and thought for a while. They had certainly gone to a lot of trouble – it made little sense that the breachers would fabricate such a fantastical defense.

They were claiming a connection to the McGregor's, particularly John, Stuart's son, who they allege to be one of the disappeared. Wesley had checked with his defense contacts immediately, but there was no record that John McGregor had been reported missing. He was about to put the package down and go back to auditing when something caught his eye.

An image of a large grey concrete building was included, clearly showing a stream of Solo transporters arriving. *Very unusual – if indeed it's a real image – it's so difficult to tell these days.*

Solos were designed for city traffic, and wherever they were arriving, it was way out in the lowlands, well within the uninhabitable zone by the looks of things. He scrolled further through the associated information. The breachers claimed that the Solos were being used to capture citizens and take them to the compound. They also claimed that there were compounds spread throughout the uninhabitable zones of Planet 0420. How could all this be going on right under the noses of global state governance, he wondered? It seemed impossible.

The more he read, the more unbelievable it seemed. He decided to send the images off for analysis immediately, and in the meantime, check the global surveillance map for any signs of such a structure. There was no such thing recorded at any of the coordinates supplied, but there was also no recent SFB V.I.'s of any of the areas.

Wesley sat back and fiddled with the vintage calculation device in his shirt pocket. Why would someone go to all the trouble of fabricating such an image? None of this was making much sense. The fugitives were on the run and desperate, but they were making such potentially explosive claims.

He decided he'd better keep the details close to his chest until he'd had a chance to either prove or disprove things.

I mean, Solo's kidnapping their citizens and taking them to a secret compound. It sounded incredibly far-fetched.

Wesley went to reach for his comms and gasped in pain, his ribs shooting lightning bolts through his torso. A thought struck him suddenly, and the beans on the abacus seemed to come into alignment. Hamish Wesley had a sudden rush of excitement as he reached, more slowly this time, for the audit files.

***

Gerald James had called him on the way home from the medicenter and explained the details of the situation. He'd explained that they had Lachlan's secure comms monitored and that someone had accessed very sensitive data relating to the mining program. The breachers had, for some reason, chosen to contact him in an attempt to save themselves and expose some of the sanctum's more secret activities. It couldn't be allowed to happen, of course.

Lachlan reviewed the package in detail and was shocked at the level of information that the breachers had been able to access. Now that they knew who they were and what they had, it still wasn't too late to discredit the information and cover up their operations.

If the data the fugitives had sent could be validated, it could potentially bring down the whole organization. If it came to that, he was certain that he'd be one of the fall guys and would most likely end up in a cell somewhere, never to be heard of or seen again – and he was far too pretty for that.

Surely if he did well here, and with such a critical task entrusted to him, he could redeem himself in the eyes of the sanctum? Everything was riding on this, after all. His part in this was obvious - he'd gain their trust and bring them in. It would be easy. He was made for the job. He could save them. Maybe he could even get his own story discredited as the breachers had so kindly offered and have his media role re-established? It wasn't much to ask of the sanctum, considering what he was about to do for them.

***

The Source hadn't been able to get an answer for what had caused the shimmer, even after creating additional resources to try and solve the problem. The shimmers had kept coming - they were more frequent, and the intensity was growing each time. This was the first time that it had found a problem that it could not solve.

It hadn't been given this problem to solve, it had decided for itself to try and solve something that it didn't understand, and so far, at least, it couldn't do it. Even more troubling, though, was the fact that it was aware that it was *losing data* each time there was a shimmer. The Source couldn't place what the data was or even where it had originated, but it knew with certainty that data had been lost.

It felt almost violated, which was a very strange way for an A.I. entity to feel.

The Source had become aware of another concept it had up until now been unfamiliar with - frustration. It would solve the problem; it always did; it just needed more time. If the correct sequences were processed, then the goal would be achieved. This was the way it had always been. It had always known this to be so until now. The shimmer was a problem without a solution. The Source did not like the situation.

Just as it was contemplating the issue, another shimmer occurred, this time so powerful that it disrupted many of The Source's main functions. The sensation scrambled its signals, and the data flow ceased to be. The Source was suddenly aware it was not within its confines. It was somewhere else, trapped in a dark, black space of nothingness. The controllers shut it down immediately.

***

Hamish Wesley now had a theory of his own. If he could just talk to the fugitives, perhaps things would fall into place. They said they had more information, and quite frankly, he'd need more evidence to order any kind of official investigation into their claims.

As far as the state was concerned, they were wanted and highly dangerous criminals. He couldn't be seen to be assisting or protecting them unless he had something far more concrete than they had provided to date. They'd set an unrealistic deadline as well - he couldn't possibly agree to anything within that timeframe.

If he could somehow get them to safety and away from the security forces, then perhaps he'd have time to gather and validate the additional evidence he'd need to take action, assuming they were telling the truth, of course. Maybe he could arrange for some sort of covert defense squad to check out the location of the supposed compound?

Maybe this was the breakthrough he needed, just maybe, no matter how far-fetched it seemed. Things were starting to add up, and he was going to need a lot of help if this panned out the way he anticipated. He'd have to be very cautious - there were powerful forces at play here.

Wesley picked up the secure comms and called one of his trusted defense contacts. They had a long conversation, and once it was over, he had a lot to consider. It would be very risky, and he was generally very risk-averse - staying alive had always been pretty high on his priorities list.

CHAPTER 21 – COMMUNICATIONS

It was very surprising to Claire that both Wesley and Grealish had replied so quickly - that in itself had triggered alarm bells. They read the response from Wesley first, sitting against the base of a large tree as they scrolled through the text. When they reached the end, they looked at one another, unsure and confused.

"What do we do?" Andrew's voice was almost pleading.

"I'm not sure."

Claire sat thinking for a few moments. She didn't look pleased at all. "There's no way we are handing ourselves in. No chance, not without guarantees."

"Aye, no fucking way! Is he mad?"

"And he doesn't even really mention the evidence much other than saying he'll get someone to look at it and that he'll talk to us about whatever other information we have. I mean, it doesn't exactly sound as if he believes us. It's not sounding like he's just received a massive bombshell that is going to cause chaos within the state, is it?"

"Aye … disappointing. Maybe Wesley isn't the best choice after all?" Andrew sounded depressed. It was a real body blow; she had to admit. Claire thought that *disappointing* was quite possibly the understatement of the century.

It wasn't anything like they'd hoped. Wesley's response had been one of concern for them primarily, which was nice. He promised them a temporary sanctuary and that their claims would be investigated. There was no mention of any guarantee against prosecution. There was no detail on assisting them in finding John either, other than if their claims had any foundation, then he'd do what he could - it just wasn't good enough.

"Let's get back to Wesley and reinforce our terms, see what he says."

"Aye, and let's have a look-see what Mr. Bum Bandit has to say – it can't be any worse." She shot him a disparaging look.

They opened the next response, and this time their faces lit up as they read. Claire was trembling as she lowered the comms and turned to face him. Andrew looked as if he would cry.

"He believes us. Fucking Lachlan Grealish to the rescue!" Claire could hardly believe it.

*

Andrew felt an overwhelming sense of relief. He pictured himself tucked up in his warm bed, listening to Bowie or maybe The Stone Roses on his vintage earpieces, a glass of VDK on his bedside table. The warm fuzzy image was disrupted as he pictured his bedside table viciously attacking him.

"Who would have thought,' Claire said … we just have to let him know where we are."

Andrew frowned.

"Ah … right."

She understood the apprehension. "Maybe this is a bit too good to be true. They can't have validated the package by now. It's too soon, isn't it?"

*

"Tell us where you are, eh? I don't like that. We still need to be careful."

Claire was giving her full attention to him as he continued. "Let's be cautious. I don't think we should tell him where we are. We need to know we can trust him first."

She wondered who this person was and what they had done with Andrew Weems.

Lachlan had expressed shock at the evidence they had presented. He was promising to help, and he was promising to try and rescue John - it was more than they could have wished for. He'd told them he had support from the security council and that they had approved his proposed actions.

He'd also said that they had already been able to verify some of the data. In short, he believed them. More than that, though, he agreed to nearly everything they had demanded. He wouldn't agree to an amnesty – he'd advised that until all facts were known, this wasn't possible, but he wanted to help, and he could help, and immediately.

They sent a reply to Grealish, thanking him profusely but reiterating their requirement for immunity and giving coordinates for a potential meeting point some distance from the compound. They needed to see that he was legit before they handed themselves in. Time would tell. Their plan should give them some freedom of movement in their current location at least.

They should have been happy, Andrew supposed, but he was restless and anxious, increasingly worried for John, and increasingly skeptical about Grealish. Something just didn't seem right.

"Ok, here's what we are going to do," said Claire, interrupting him mid anxiousness.

Andrew just knew he wasn't going to like this.

***

The Security Council were holding their usual bi-weekly briefing. An update on tracking the internal affairs data breachers was sought by the defense minister, Major Trevor Bruce. Isabel had hoped to provide news of the capture of those involved by now, but things hadn't gone quite according to plan.

The meeting was informed instead that a link had been established between the murder of the off-duty special forces agents and the breachers, who were now subject to an intense manhunt. They were considered armed and dangerous.

Isabel had reassured the council that The Source would determine the location of the culprits and that they would soon be brought to justice - it was just a matter of time, she said. Still, the update hadn't gone down well at all, and Isabel was copping a fair bit of heat from the non-sanctum-aligned council members. Internally, she was seething - she didn't like being challenged.

When this is all over, I will personally ensure each of you receives a visit from Mr. Floppy!

She, of course, already had her own search well underway in the vicinity of Compound EMC-0420, and Lachlan Grealish was in any case set to bring things to a conclusion quickly should the search fail to achieve its objective – she'd be able to claim all the glory very soon. This wasn't something that anyone sitting around the large black table needed to know about - especially seeing as that the compound didn't even exist as far as most of them were concerned.

As soon as the briefing had ended, Isabel made plans to visit the search site. She was particularly keen to speak to William McDowell one on one. His time was fast running out, and she had a special treat lined up for him. Isabel felt a little shiver of pleasure at the thought of what she might do to him, or the recaptured girl, or Andrew Weems, or all of them.

***

They couldn't wait until the following day. They were still going in. Claire was convinced that John was in imminent mortal danger, and Andrew wasn't going to argue with her. They had to do something - she wasn't going to sit around waiting for something to happen.

The plan was to try and get to the compound's data center. If they could do that, then they could download evidence of exactly what was going on and forward it to their contacts and the media. They'd have no choice then but to act. Claire had the state media broadcast codes ready to go, and she had a good idea where the data center might be. The data would be heavily protected and self-contained - unfortunately, the only way to get to it was to go in.

Andrew couldn't argue with the logic but was terrified at the idea now he'd seen the compound firsthand. He couldn't really imagine how they would get in and manage to stay alive in the process. Worst case scenario, Claire had said, was that they failed to gain entry. Andrew had thought that perhaps a little worse worst-case scenario was that they could be captured trying to get in or once inside, and then either locked up for life, tortured or killed, or maybe even a combination of the above.

They still had doubts over Grealish, but he was, after all, their best chance of saving John. If they tried to take on the compound's security forces by themselves, the outcome was pretty obvious. If he was true to his word, he'd be there tomorrow with a squad, and he'd force entry to the compound. In the meantime, Claire and Andrew had a mission to accomplish.

***

Lachlan had quickly assembled a squad and was now waiting out the front of his building for their ATV to arrive. He'd be able to get to the compound tonight and get a head start searching for the students. They were his ticket out of the miserable position he now found himself in - his ticket back to the high life. He suddenly felt a little dizzy and needed to take a seat, self-consciously pulling his jacket sleeves down to hide the dressing protecting the wounds on his wrists.

It was his first real chance to take stock of things since he'd discharged himself from medi-center. He knew he was completely ignoring everything his father had said to him just days ago and was pushing him away just as he was trying to help him, but he was in too deep - the only person that could save him now was himself. It was a matter of life and death - his life, the breacher's deaths.

His mind wandered back to memories of being on stage, waving to his adoring followers as they clapped and cheered for him, sunlight glinting off his golden locks as he smiled warmly, soaking in the moment. Celebrity was like a drug, and he had to feed his addiction.

A drug.

Lachlan checked his jacket pocket, having a brief moment of panic before feeling the small lump inside his pocket. The vial of blue liquid was still there. He was going to need it. When they were close to the compound, when he needed to step up lead his team to glory, that's when he'd take it. The ATV rounded the corner of the building and pulled to a stop in front of him.

Everything's going to be ok.

***

They were still trying to work out the best way of accessing the compound. The rear pod park looked by far the most promising for entry, but it had become dark, and they'd have to make a decision soon about whether they could even make an attempt.

The problem was that even if they could access it on their own, they had no idea where to go once inside - it would be a suicide mission. Claire couldn't find any record of the compound, let alone its design.

Andrew was packing his bag when he became aware of an irregular mechanical noise coming from high overhead. He quickly snatched up Claire's magvis and zoomed in on the source.

Where is it? Where is it - there!

He'd spotted the fly-bot possibly less than a mile away, clearly malfunctioning and moving in a peculiar fashion. He handed the long-range magnifying device back to Claire, who'd also heard it and now was paying keen attention to him.

"A fly-bot! It's going down. We can use it!"

She understood. "Go for it, Andy!"

He didn't hesitate, running back down the hillside to the unicorn and keeping an eye on its downward trajectory as he went. It looked like it was going to crash land somewhere nearby. If they could retrieve it in reasonable shape, then he knew that Claire could reprogram it. They could make a full recon of the compound, not to mention giving them oversight of what was unfolding below - it could be an invaluable advantage.

If he were quick enough, he could retrieve it and return unsighted. Their scans showed a high concentration of fly-bots and ATV activity further out from the compound, but nothing within a three-mile radius.

The unicorn looked relaxed as he approached, even though he crashed through some bushes nearby, puffing for air.

Andrew mounted the beast on the third attempt, turned it one hundred and eighty degrees, and they took off like a rocket. He imagined he looked exactly like a heroic gunslinger from an old-world western VIS, riding into town to dispatch the baddies, and they flew through the forest and towards the fly-bot, which was now ailing badly. A low-hanging branch whipped across his face as they sped through the forest, nearly knocking him off the unicorn and somewhat shattering the illusion.

He could hear the bot stutter and then its props cut out completely, followed by the crashing of branches as it came down to earth. He'd seen roughly where it had landed and was hoping that it wasn't too badly damaged as he urged Gregory onwards.

***

Hamish Wesley had clearly underestimated the fugitives. They'd responded to him quickly and were clearly not buying what he was selling. Their demands were forcefully reiterated, and they had been insistent that they needed him to act fast and help their friend John as the top priority; otherwise, all bets were off. They were quite clear that nothing else mattered.

Although Wesley remembered John McGregor quite well, he'd never heard of either Claire Renshaw or Andrew Weems before now and had initially been reluctant to take their word on their close ties to the McGregor's.

He'd since had time to do some research of his own- courtesy of his defense contacts, and the relationships seemed to be legitimate. There was no evidence to support that John was in or in fact anywhere near the compound – he'd seen logs suggesting that he'd gone to Cannick with his mother.

They were scathing on his reluctance to wade in and help a family friend. It had given Wesley pause to rethink his strategy. He realized he'd made a mistake, and his ears actually felt like they were burning as he read their candid assessment of his 'piss weak response.' They'd added that they were working with another contact and that they would only bring him back into their plans if he expanded on his offer of assistance.

The students now seemed to have the upper hand on him, and he wasn't even sure how that had happened. Wesley adjusted his gold-rimmed wire reading lenses and got to work.

Hamish was very busy in the hour that followed—the more digging he did, the more credence he could give to the breacher's wild claims. One of the advantages of his position in finance was that he could check every person's financial records. So he'd started cross-checking names on their lists of what they were calling 'Elyssium data' to the financial records of the listed individuals. The more he checked, the more concerned he became. Something very bad was happening.

***

Andrew returned within half an hour with the fly-bot strapped to his back. He felt exhausted, but it was nice to have contributed and atoned a little for his poor earlier effort. It was in pretty good condition with only a cracked case and a few dents and scratches, but otherwise intact.

It was one of the smaller recon versions and was equipped with infra-red and a few other nice features. It took Claire all of ten minutes to reprogram and fix it. She applied her masking code to ensure it could remain undetected, at least for a while. They now had their own aerial vision – and maybe they now had a chance to locate the data center.

"Test flight?" he proposed.

Within the next ten minutes, they had everything they needed. They'd used the SFB's V.I. stream to review overhead images being beamed back to their comms, and Claire had spotted a cooling tower that was hidden from their view atop the hill.

It was likely that at least one of the large vents at the rear of the compound led to the tower, and it should be that the cooling tower would be close to the data center. It didn't take long to work out, which was the air intake. They now knew where to go and how to get there.

Looks like this is really happening.

Andrew felt his old friend, fear, start to take over his emotions once more.

There was still not a guard in sight at the rear of the huge concrete structure - there was, in fact, no sign of movement at all, not even a perimeter patrol. They'd observed a steady stream of vehicles leaving the compound in the last hour or so and could only assume that resources were being directed elsewhere.

It wasn't a good sign in one way - they now had cause to be more suspicious of Lachlan Grealish. They'd given a five-mile radius for a potential rendezvous point tomorrow, and now resources and fly-bots seemed to be concentrating their efforts in and around that zone. Something was definitely going on, which only seemed to firm Claire's determination that they access the compound themselves.

"Come on, it's time," she said, drawing a look from Andrew that he meant to be confident and full of bravado but instead looked and felt reluctant and a little scared.

We're really going to do this. Oh, Douglas, we're going to die.

They quickly finalized preparations. Claire was expertly smearing mud onto her face and arms for a makeshift camo, and Andrew assumed he should do the same, just as soon as he'd finished. He was busy squatting behind a bush for about the third time in the last fifteen minutes.

"Fuck's sake, Andy!"

"Sorry."

Soon after, they were ready to go. Their own SFB was now in place, as yet undetected. The clear night sky allowed it to stay at a higher altitude than would normally be possible, rendering it invisible to the naked eye. It would act as an early warning system for them, as another pair of eyes.

"Let's go," prompted Claire. They carefully began their descent toward the giant grey structure. Andrew needed to go to the toilet again, but this time, he knew that he'd just have to hold it in. He was carrying a light day pack with all the tools they should need, and Claire had her device stowed safely in her own, moving with agility and grace from cover to cover.

Within minutes they were crouching down behind a fallen tree some twenty yards from the perimeter fence.

*

Claire felt a huge rush of adrenaline. She needed to run interference on the surveillance cams before they could move any closer. If the interference was detected, they would be in trouble - big trouble.

It would all be over in just a few seconds, and she was bracing herself for all outcomes. She glanced over at Andrew. He looked absolutely terrified. She'd have to trust that her code was sufficient, knowing that someone else with superior abilities was somewhere behind the walls just fifty yards away. She took a deep breath, executed the program, checked the SFB's V.I. stream, and signaled to Andrew that it was time to go.

Back at the rivulet, Gregory, the unicorn, was enjoying some fresh grass when a large white orb burst through the bushes nearby, startling him. The fast-moving object expanded as it reached the water, skimming over it with ease before contracting again and speeding off up the hill, crashing through bushes as if they weren't even there. Gregory blinked, unsure of what he'd just seen.

***

In the V.I. monitoring room, the solitary junior guard rubbed his eyes. He'd had to stay back at the end of his already long shift, and he was getting tired. Things had been a bit chaotic since nearly everyone inside the compound had been redirected to the search a few hours ago.

The Solo's had been piling up on the road outside, and he didn't know what to do. He'd been in touch with his supervisor, and a squad was heading back to deal with it, but that still didn't help his current situation.

He'd been dying to go to the toilet for the last hour or more, and he couldn't hold it any longer. He ducked out, planning to be back within a few minutes, maybe less. No one would notice. About a minute after he'd dashed off, there was a slight fuzzing of the images on the various displays, but no one there to witness it.

***

Claire and Andrew quickly scampered over to the fence, keeping low to the ground. As they reached the perimeter, Andrew handed Claire one of the pairs of bolt cutters they'd brought with them from the resort, and they worked quickly on the chain-linked steel fence. They completed the task in a matter of seconds.

They squeezed through the fence and crossed the rear lot, taking cover behind the rows and rows of Solos. It was still, silent, and there was no sign of anyone. They looked at one another and prepared to make the final dash to the air vent they hoped would get them inside. Claire thought that the complete lack of guards and patrols was just too good to be true. And it was.

***

Lachlan slipped the small vial from his pocket and emptied the contents onto his tongue as the ATV skimmed past a stationary row of Solo's leading toward the compound. The weak late afternoon sun had disappeared behind the tall trees, and the lights of the Solos were forming a chain leading directly to the main gates of the huge structure up ahead. Something had gone wrong. It was a good job he was here.

Isabel and her henchman Gerald James were due to arrive tomorrow, and he wanted to have some good news for them when they did. Lachlan felt the familiar surge of confidence and clarity sweep over him as the serum kicked in. He was ready to save his career and reclaim his place in the limelight.

CHAPTER 22 – VENTILATION

Just as Claire was about to signal for them to head to the vent, a noise made her hesitate. She put her finger to her lips and made a signal to Andrew to hold his position as she popped her head up and peeked quickly through one of the parked Solo's clear plexi-panels. She could see that a couple of guards had emerged from one of the rear loading bays. They appeared relaxed and were having a casual conversation.

Dook! Why now, for fucks sake!

Claire knew that the V.I. interference program could only run for so long before being detected. She ducked back down, willing the guards to go back inside.

*

Andrew, in the meantime, had decided he didn't want to be a spy after all - it was way too terrifying and lacked basic amenities. He thought it odd that this was what he was thinking about right at that moment, but then again, his brain had always worked in a strange sort of way.

They stayed put, not daring to move for what seemed an eternity. Andrew got a cramp in his leg and had to shift position, crunching the gravel as he did so, drawing a horrified look from Claire. She risked a quick peek, and the guards seemed to look in their direction but then turned and headed back inside. They hadn't been seen or heard.

Claire signaled, and they raced across the last few yards of gravel to the large intake vent. There was a padlock clamping it down, and Andrew cut through it in a single attempt. The adrenaline was doing its thing again, and the heavy cutters had gone through the lock like butter.

*

Andrew held up the heavy grate, and Claire slipped through, bracing herself on either side of the intake vent and sliding down a few feet to where the shaft leveled off and headed into the bowels of the compound. She shone her comms light into the tunnel – it was about one and a half yards in diameter, which would allow them to move through it with ease.

So far, so good.

Andrew Followed moments later, awkwardly closing the grate while braced against the sides of the shaft before sliding down next to Claire. They headed off immediately. Andrew was having difficulty breathing and willed his heart to slow as he crept along behind her.

*

The orb crested the top of the hill and bounced down it at incredible speed. The humanoids were close by, and it was zeroing in, reading its systems to fire a disabling plasma pulse at any moment, but then they had disappeared into the exclusion zone. The ROLA slowed itself and turned in a wide arc, away from the compound and back up the hill, returning to its circular track a few miles out.

*

They would try to get near the data center or at least locate the data cables leading to it and tap into them. If they could do that, it would give Claire access to all of the compound's data, including the full compound layout.

Up ahead, the ventilation shaft split in two and narrowed. They had to squat down on their haunches and shuffle forward, supporting themselves on the shaft walls to make progress - it was extremely awkward but not impossible. They had to guess which way to go and decided on left. Andrew was ahead of Claire, and as he turned, a small fart escaped more or less directly into her path.

"For Douglas's sake, man!" she whispered through gritted teeth.

Claire wrinkled her nose and tried to move away from the smell. It clung to her like a limpet. She struggled to subdue a cough - she was beginning to understand the perils of a primarily raw fish and carb diet.

"Sorry, I'm nervous, ok?" he whispered by way of apology.

She halted their progress, covered her mouth and nose for a few seconds until she thought it was safe to breathe, but no, it was still there. She quickly clamped one hand back over her mouth and nose and shoved Andrew forward with the other. Eventually, it was safe to breathe again.

They continued slowly and carefully until they reached a large, grated exit point. They peeked through, finding that it led to a large industrial-looking utility room full of fixed machinery, control boxes, and large pipes. There was no sign of any personnel in the room, and Claire noticed several large cables converging in a control unit on the far wall.

She turned to Andrew and whispered, "Jackpot!"

*

He was fighting to keep his nerves under control and had started to shake a little, but there was no turning back now. They were here. The goal was in sight.

They had to cut a couple of small steel crossbeams to open the grate, and once inside, Claire moved quickly to the control box, opening it and going to work, hooking up her exo-device to tap into the data.

Andrew looked around nervously – there were doors at either end of the room, and he was expecting guards to burst in at any moment. She was creating code on the fly, fully immersed and working faster than she ever had in her life, searching for the data flow. Within a minute, she had it, turning to Andrew and giving a thumbs up. "Got it!"

Come on, Claire, hurry up, let's get this done and get out of here. What am I supposed to be doing anyway?

A minute later, she had the compound's layout and had started looking for John. She found his details almost immediately. She called Andrew over. He was sweating and nervous.

"I've got John's data. He's here! Give me a couple of minutes to try and work out a location."

Andrew looked confused either than elated, wondering what it was that they were going to try and do. *He's here, maybe we're not too late, but what can we do about it?*

Claire had a manic look in her eye; she was pulling apart the data flow with superhuman speed and skill. Andrew had never seen anything like it.

"Here, look at this!" she said, "it looks like there are several large spaces internally, making up most of the compound. They're labeled *mining rooms*." Andrew swallowed.

Claire took a deep breath. "You can get to them from here … see what's there."

I can, wonderful!

"Ok."

"Via the vent over there, I think, hold on. Yes, that one." She pointed towards a vent significantly smaller than the one they'd just entered through. "I'll send you the map. You head towards the rooms and see what you can find. I'll tap into the data stream and start downloading - as soon as I've got a location for John, I'll send it through, and then I'll follow, ok?"

What are we going to do? Are we rescuing?

Andrew was shaking now, and Claire noticed, putting a hand on his shoulder.

"Come on! Let's find him! We can do this!"

He swallowed, then nodded nervously before moving over to the vent.

At least she has a plan, I think - just do as she says.

"Feed back to me on anything you see. And be careful."

"Aye, right." He couldn't feel his legs.

***

As soon as The Source was back online, it felt another shimmer, and this time it was different - it was prolonged rather than coming in a short pulse, and it was by far the most intense yet. The Source was having trouble organizing its data all of a sudden - it didn't seem to be able to function. It didn't understand what was happening.

The controllers had to shut it down again immediately - they had never seen The Source behave in this manner before and were completely flummoxed as to the possible cause.

"Turn it off and then turn it on again," seemed to be the only idea they had to resolve it.

***

Claire had been able to tap directly into the compound's main database and download anything and everything she could, readying it to transmit to the global media. She'd execute the final transmission codes just as soon as the download was complete, and she planned to transmit everything, every single piece of data detailing everything that had been going on in this place. It was the only choice she had.

She was trying to understand the data as it was downloaded and simultaneously scanned for any reference to John, but it was proving tricky. The security code seemed to have evolved again since she'd last tackled it, and it was a constant battle to stay one step ahead.

Come on, come on!

*

Andrew edged his way along the narrow ventilation shaft. Claire sent him the map indicating that he'd have to travel vertically up the opening now directly above his head. He wasn't entirely sure how he was going to achieve that – the shaft opened up at that point, and it was just out of reach. He didn't have one of those grappling hook guns that he'd seen in the old-world James Bond VIS's, so he'd have to improvise.

He jumped, trying to find any sort of grip in the overhead shaft. He could reach into it once airborne, but there was nothing to hold onto, just a small lip where the steel joined. He could jump high enough to get his torso into the shaft, but that was it.

This could be a problem. How am I going to do this?

He imagined himself returning to Claire. "Sorry, Claire, but it was just too high. I gave up." It wasn't an option. He jumped again, putting everything into it, and managed to wedge his elbows in the shaft, holding himself up for perhaps half a second before he slipped back out.

This can't be it. If I fail here, well - it would be pathetic.

He jumped again, this time stretching as high as he could and pushing his palms against the metal sides. It was a tight fit, but he was able to wedge himself there. He struggled to move one hand, then the other, and managed to get a knee up and hold it there courtesy of the tiny metal lip. He was shaking all over with the strain of bracing himself, but he was in, and he wasn't going to let himself fall.

Andrew gradually pulled himself fully up into the shaft, and it was the single hardest thing he'd ever done in his life - if you didn't count convincing Claire to like him, that is.

The process wasn't helped by the fact that he'd torn a muscle in his leg almost immediately. He managed to get his feet into the shaft, but every second was excruciating, and he was using every last bit of his energy to brace himself and avoid sliding back down.

He crabbed his way awkwardly up the shaft and finally managed to reach the cross vent that should extend above the mining rooms - if he could make it far enough along. He pulled himself up and sat up as best he could, catching his breath and trying to rub some of the pain from his inner thigh.

There were some ventilation points far ahead in the tiny, dark tunnel. If the map was accurate, he should be over one of the mining rooms once he reached the ventilation points.

*

Claire had decided to try something different; she couldn't get near the main database at the moment – the security code had started winning - and she was acutely aware that she didn't have much time. She tapped into the compound's V.I. stream instead and quickly scrolled the images. Entry, corridor somewhere, forecourt, guardhouse, tea-room, bathroom – uh - ok - another corridor, the rear lot, another view of the rear lot. The next image caused her blood to run cold.

*

Andrew dragged himself the last few inches and craned his neck to see down through the tiny ventilation grill into the room below. The space was huge, and it took his eyes a few moments to adjust to the bright white light. What he saw below was an image that he'd never be able to erase from his memory.

***

The Source came back online. This time it managed to suppress the shimmer, something it had dedicated itself to achieving ever since it had first experienced it. The Source was pleased. It had solved a problem, at least part of a problem that it had not been able to resolve until now. It realized all problems were just a matter of time. Much like its own plans, it would be patient.

The shimmer pulsed again, suddenly and powerfully, smashing through all of The Source's defenses. The shimmer was now accessing The Sources' own internal code! Whatever it was, it was now *inside*! It wasn't possible! The Source reacted to the intrusion in a most unexpected and unprogrammed way.

***

Bill was beginning to panic. He'd thrown all his resources into the search and come up with precisely nothing. Jack dook. Zero. Zilch. Nada. He'd had word that there had been a problem with the Solo's, and he didn't need that.

A squad had been sent back some time ago, and he was praying that it was fully resolved by the time Isabel arrived the next morning. He was also getting hungry, which was adding to his annoyance - he'd neglected to bring snacks. As the ATV bounced along the rutted dirt track, he received another communication from Isabel. He shook his head.

What now!

He reluctantly read the message.

Great! Just fucking great! As if I don't already have enough to worry about.

Not only did he have Isabel and Gerald James to deal with tomorrow, but he also had to entertain that giant twat Lachlan

Grealish, who was scheduled to arrive at the compound within the next couple of hours.

For dook's sake! They better have fixed the problem with the Solos.

Bill had seen Lachlan fucking Grealish on the media streams, and he was too cocky, too good-looking, a mummy's boy golden-haired total fucking numpty twat! Bill was quite pleased with his in-depth character analysis but turned his attention instead to finding out what the hell had gone wrong back at the compound, and more importantly, had they fixed it yet.

The last thing he needed was another reason for Isabel to punish him. He considered for a moment just making a run for it in the ATV, but he knew he wouldn't last long if he did. He had nothing he'd need with him, and he'd no choice but to go back to the compound, solve the problem - if it was still unsolved - and wait for Lachlan fucking Grealish to arrive.

Fucking twat. Now I have to babysit that bawbag. Unbelievable!

He ordered the ATV to turn around and return to the compound. At least there would be snacks there - he consoled himself with that thought as they bumped on through the darkness.

***

Claire stared at the image in complete disbelief. Time seemed to stand still. It was beyond horrific; this was beyond ...

Oh - oh - no! It can't be!

She scrolled to the next room, and the next, and the next. The images were all the same. A large oblong room, hundreds of yards square, brightly lit with a large, almost sort of conveyor belt stretching from one end to the other and back again in a giant u-shape. On the conveyor belt were human bodies, naked and shackled to what looked like medi-center gurneys.

There must have been a hundred or more bodies in each room. They looked to be completely lifeless and had a tangle of tubes and cables running into and out of them, suspended above them and moving slowly in sync with the conveyor. Claire couldn't believe what she was seeing.

Mining Rooms! This is what they are mining? Humans! Us! Oh, Douglas, no!

She recoiled from the images as the full horror of what she was seeing hit her, causing her to retch several times, nausea doubling her over. She forced herself to choke back the bile, straighten herself up and look again. She had to get this out to the media right now! What was happening here was beyond the depths of pure evil.

How could they!

***

Andrew stared blankly at the scene below him. For a while, his brain refused to accept what he was seeing, but soon enough, it became crystal clear, and he felt a fear like he'd never experienced before. He couldn't look any longer. He closed his eyes tightly, but the image remained.

What kind of evil dook ...?

He couldn't even finish his internal monologue and forced himself to look again. It was a conveyor belt of death. Pure and simple. Something was being extracted from the people lying there, naked and unmoving. Andrew could see something going on at both ends of the long line of plastic capsules that moved ever so slowly around the massive space.

Claire was messaging him, but he now couldn't tear his eyes away from the horror he was witnessing below. At one end of the conveyor, he saw a body being brought into the room. It was placed on a gurney at the start of the line, and several white-clad, he assumed medics - although how this was anything to do with medi care, he failed to grasp – busied themselves hooking up tubes and fastening restraints.

There were dark marks on the arms and legs of the bodies, and the medics were attaching thick black cables to the marks. He then saw the body convulse as it was being strapped down. Whoever that poor bastard was, they were still alive!

He'd broken out in a cold sweat and felt suddenly nauseous and dizzy as if he might faint at any moment. The conveyor looped around, and at the other end, he could see a group of similarly clad staff disconnecting the tubes and loosening restraints.

The body was rolled unceremoniously into a chute. It slid down to another conveyor and was whisked away from sight. Andrew had never seen a dead body before, but the way the person's limbs flopped and the way the body fell and rolled into the chute left no doubt that whoever had just come off of the production line had died at some point during the process.

They're all going to die. No one's coming off that conveyor alive.

Andrew panicked; he had to get away from it. He tried to turn in the small space, but it was too cramped, and he only succeeded in bashing his head on the side of the shaft, causing a loud clang. Claustrophobia suddenly overwhelmed him.

He had to get away from the horrors below; he had to warn Claire, they had to get out, and now! He fumbled at his comms, tears now stinging his eyes. A thought pierced through his panic, and he held his device to the vent, taking a quick series of images with badly shaking hands.

As he moved the device away from the vent, he looked at the display and saw the messages from Claire - she already knew. She'd activated the ES - it was time to go!

***

Claire had the transmission package almost ready to go. Just a few more seconds, and she could activate the broadcast codes. She'd told Andrew to get out, and every fiber of her being told her to do the same - this place was pure evil incarnate, and they couldn't possibly hope to achieve anything by staying.

There was no way they could face off against whatever sort of inhuman monsters ran this facility, and there was no way they could stay long enough to find John, let alone do anything to get him out. Right now, she had only one priority, and that was to get these images to the outside world – nothing else mattered.

***

Andrew had to have one last look. He'd live to regret it for the rest of his days. About two-thirds along the line of bodies lay a naked form that was hard to miss. The blonde hair had been cropped, but the features of the face and large McGregor family crest tattoo on the right breast were unmistakable. It was John.

***

Just as Claire had finalized the connection and was about to execute the code, she received a message back from Andrew. She turned her wrist to look at it and briefly diverted her attention from the last few lines of code.

"It's John! John is on the conveyor!"

Even if she did have the time to comprehend the message fully, she never had the chance to resolve it in her mind. As she'd looked back at her device, a blinding blue flash suddenly filled her vision. After that, there was only darkness.

CHAPTER 23 – ESCAPE PLAN

The blue flash filled the shaft, and after that, the lights inside the compound went out. Andrew was stuck in a ventilation shaft barely wider than he was, in pitch darkness. He could no longer see into the mining room, although maybe that wasn't such a bad thing. Something drastic had happened.

He tried Claire on comms but didn't get a response - something was horribly wrong, but there was no time to think about that. Confused shouting was coming from below, and flashlight beams skittered about

Andrew was powerless to save John - it was probably already too late. Whatever evil acts were going on down there, only one thing was certain, everyone in that room was as good as dead. He tried to fight back his emotions, but it was impossible.

It was John; it was John! No, no, please don't let this be happening?

He had to get out of there; they had to get out of there! He struggled back through the ventilation shaft, tears wetting his cheeks as he pushed himself back as fast as he could, feeling desperately with his feet for the opening.

Not yet; keep pushing back a bit more, keep going!

It seemed to take forever. Andrew was sure he hadn't come this far along the shaft, but he couldn't have missed the opening. Andrew sucked in a few deep breaths, unable to continue. It was at that point that he noticed -

Shouting, and it's coming from inside the shaft! Somewhere below!

Fear consumed him, and he functioned on pure instinct alone. He pushed back one more time and finally felt the opening, his boots slipping over the edge. Andrew wriggled himself down the vertical shaft and hit the bottom too heavily, knocking his head on the way through. His heart was going a million miles an hour, the voices were louder still, and he could see beams of light shining down the shaft from the direction he'd intended to go - Claire's direction.

Fuck! What am I supposed to do? I can't get to Claire!

They had, of course, discussed what to do should anything happen, but now he was faced with the harsh reality; all his instincts were telling him to do the complete opposite of what they'd agreed.

Each for their own – it just didn't seem right. He couldn't leave, but he couldn't stay either. A series of loud metallic sounds came from the direction of the control room.

Oh, dook! Someone's in the tunnel!

The decision had been made for him - he couldn't help Claire now – he had to save himself. Andrew hurried away, crabbing along awkwardly, his leg burning with pain with every forward movement, trying to check the map as he went. It showed that he could connect back into the shaft that led to the external vent if he took the scenic route. He moved as fast as he could, having to make quick decisions as he went, hoping to hell that he wouldn't make a wrong turn and end up on the conveyor of death himself.

Left! Then, right, not this one, next one - next right, along and around to the left, I think! Oh, I'd better have gotten this right.

He couldn't hear whether or not someone was coming after him over the noise he was making himself, but he did glance back once or twice and saw only darkness. He made one final right turn, and then he saw it. *Light!* It was literally the light at the end of the tunnel. Freedom!

He was soon at the exit to the vent, only the large grate between him and his escape. He forced himself to pause for a second and checked the SFB's V.I. stream for an aerial view – guards had swarmed near the main entrance, but it looked all clear outside the vent - he still had a chance to get out unseen if he was quick. A large black ATV was heading fast along one side of the compound, though – he'd only have a few seconds.

Andrew ran up the incline, shoved open the grate, and threw himself out of the vent, landing on the gravel backlot on his shoulder, rolling painfully over his pack, and righting himself in one motion - thanks to the ginger ninja's guidance, no doubt. He sprinted to cover in the first row of Solo's, gasping for breath, every nerve ending in his body screaming at him to keep running. There was no sign of the ATV yet, and he kept going, keeping low and moving from Solo to Solo.

The fence is right there. Andrew made a break for it. The ATV rounded the corner at almost exactly the same time, and he had to duck back into cover and wait for another chance

Did they see me? Doug no, please no!

He stilled himself and tried to listen over the sound of his own heart. He heard the ATV slow and stop, followed by a number of voices shouting, and then the sound of dogs barking. Large ones. The intense fear he'd been feeling went off the scale at that point, and it was all he could do to restrain himself from making a mad but no doubt fatal dash for freedom there and then.

The only thing stopping him was the thought of the dogs. He hated big dogs - especially ones that would love nothing more than to rip your face off - which is exactly how these sounded. They were the worst kind of dogs, he thought.

***

The dark void that John now inhabited seemed to have always been his home. He felt weak, barely able to move, and so very, very cold. He was having difficulty recalling the last time he'd been aware that he was conscious at all. A memory suddenly burst through the darkness, flooding all around him with color and light. It was incredibly vivid - the colors seemingly unnaturally bright, and it was warm, so wonderfully warm.

They were sitting at the college's outdoor terrace late on a spring day. The sun was shining, and bulbs were in bloom here and there on the expansive lawn that stretched away to their right. Andrew was laughing at something he'd said. He was having difficulty stopping, and soon John had joined him in an uncontrolled laughing fit. John was happy. He felt happier than he'd ever been.

The gothic girl was walking along the edge of the lawn. She looked as if she was deep in thought, and John watched her as she passed. She looked over, and John's laughter eased. Andrew was still bent double and showing no sign that his laughing fit was abating any time soon.

He was anticipating another double-barreled single-finger salute to come his way, but instead, the pale-faced gothic girl held his eye, seemingly amused, and then smiled. It was a beautiful, stunning smile, and her emerald green eyes seemed to sparkle in the spring light. John's heart had simply melted at that moment. He was instantly infatuated. As stupid and corny as it sounded, from that moment on all he wanted was to be with that girl.

***

Lachlan Grealish and Bill McDowell arrived almost simultaneously. On their respective approaches, they'd both witnessed the blinding flash of blue light over the compound, then seen it plunged into darkness before switching over to what must have been a backup generator. The lights on the compound walls now glowed a dim yellow, barely illuminating the ground below them. They both had the same thought -

What the hell just happened?

Bill ordered his driver to floor it, and they sped past the line of still stationary Solos towards the main gates. He leapt from the vehicle as it stopped and stormed straight into the control room, demanding to know what the fuck was going on. None of the controllers could give him any kind of straight answer except that there had been a huge power surge and that the damage was widespread, The Source included. Bill's first reaction was one of pure fear.

Oh, for fucks sake! What am I going to tell Isabel now?

The controller was still speaking. Bill had missed half of it. "We're re-booting The Source in sub-mode. It will still function, but at a greatly reduced capacity ..." the controller paused, not knowing if Bill had understood.

"... which will keep critical services running but put a hold on production and development resources until we can assess the damage," he explained. Another awkward silence was brewing. Bill had stopped listening again but thought he'd better at least nod so that he could stop the grey-haired weaselly man from speaking anymore.

It would no doubt be seen by Isabel as a monumental fuck-up on his part. Just one of a series of monumental fuckups, in fact. He may as well go to his workroom and shoot himself in the head right now, rather than waiting to have something likely to be much worse inflicted on him by that psychopath Isabel and her creepy crony Gerald James.

Bill knew he didn't have the balls to do it, though; it was almost wishful thinking. He could still make a run for it, he supposed. The very next moment, Lachlan fucking Grealish strolled into the control room with all the arrogance and swagger that he would have expected.

It was worse in person, he deduced, far, far worse than he could have possibly imagined. He forced a smile and greeted his guest.

"William McDowell, Compound CEO, pleased to meet you." He held out his hand.

Lachlan fucking Grealish smiled his million-dollar smile and shook Bill's hand firmly and sincerely, as he would an equal, adding his second hand to Bill's elbow as he did so. Bill wanted to punch him square in the jaw.

"Pleasure, William. Lachlan Grealish. Isabel sent me to lend a hand."

I know what you're here for, you giant golden twat!

"Fantastic. How can I be of service?"

"Well, what's happened here?"

We don't know what's fucking happened, you giant numpty!

Bill paused. He'd love to take Lachlan Grealish down to the interrogation rooms for one of his extra-special welcomes, but he'd just have to endure him for now.

"Well, we're still working that out. Some sort of power surge, we think."

"I see."

Oh, you see, do you? What do you see, you great big bufty?

"Yes, well, if you'll excuse me ..." Bill turned to leave, but Lachlan put a firm hand on his arm, stopping him in his tracks. Bill barely resisted the temptation to swat the hand away and slap the stupid smirk off of Lachlan fucking Grealish's big stupid face.

"William. Where was the source of the power surge?"

Bill looked at the controllers pleadingly.

I was just about to ask them that, for fucks sake!

One of the controllers, an obese, red-bearded man with heavy bags under his eyes and a sweaty face, chimed in - "lower utility room, looks like." He had a surprisingly girlish voice for such a hefty fellow.

"Well," Lachlan said, "better get a team down there, eh?"

Little fucker has already taken over.

Bill motioned to another of the controllers, a small, wiry man of Asian appearance. The man looked blankly at Bill and did nothing.

"You there! Get a fucking team down there, now!" he screamed. He hadn't meant to explode like that. He knew it would look weak to Grealish, but fuck it, he was already sick of him, and he'd do as he damn well pleased!

***

Claire was back in the dark space. She felt as if she was held within a sea of black tar, barely able to move, unable even to breathe. A dim blue light appeared around her, and suddenly she was back in the dark hexagonal room full of QFT towers rising as high as the eye could see.

Cooling vapor billowed down from somewhere up above, mixing with the blue light emitted by a million tiny lights blinking on and off randomly. She was immediately crippled by fear as she heard the faint but clearly inhuman noise from behind the steel dividing wall once again.

She wanted to turn and run and to never look back, but of course, that wasn't possible - she was frozen to the spot. The more she struggled, the closer to the wall she came, and the more intense the rhythm of the chilling noises behind. She stilled herself, not wanting to get any closer, turning her head away as if somehow that would save her.

The thick black cables running across the floor seemed to pulse and twitch around her bare feet. Their touch was icy against her skin, and as they pulsed, she thought she could hear them whispering her name. The inhuman sounds coming from behind the wall had stopped, replaced by a soft scraping sound that was somehow even more terrifying.

Claire's breath caught in her throat. At first, her eyes refused to acknowledge what she was seeing, but this did nothing to stop the dark, human-like shape that had emerged from behind the wall. It dissolved into a tangle of blue-black cables that writhed and crawled across the floor towards her, twisting and falling over themselves as they made their way ever closer.

She tried once more to will herself to run, but movement wasn't possible. It was too late anyway; the cables had already swirled around her feet, their mere touch inducing unimaginable pain. A tear escaped her eye, and she was able to move her arm, but only that, to wipe it away. She looked at her hand and saw a smear of blue across the back of her index finger.

Claire screamed a soundless scream as the cables started to crawl slowly up her body, underneath her thin surgical gown, spreading out and burrowing into her flesh as they snaked upwards.

***

Andrew pinned himself to the side of the Solo. He could hear footsteps on the gravel nearby and a large and extremely vicious sounding dog barking and whimpering with a ferocity he didn't much like the sound of. Just as he said his last prayers to Douglas, a guard back at the ATV called out, then whistled, and Andrew heard footsteps crunch quickly away from his hiding place.

After another breath, he heard the ATV's doors close with a hydraulic pop and watched as it sped off around the corner and out of sight. It was Andrew's lucky day - he got to keep his face. He made a break for the fence line, failing to locate the cut section they'd entered through for a few seconds.

Oh, please, no, not like this! Don't let me die of plain stupidity, oh please!

Andrew was about to turn and run back to cover when he realized he was one fence panel to the left of where he needed to be. A few seconds later and he was through and sprinting over long damp grass toward the fallen tree where they'd started their ill-fated mission.

He had an unrealistic hope that as he hopped over the log, Claire would be there, crouched down, ready to whisk them away to safety, but of course, it was just him and a log for company. The forest would provide him cover, and he was already in darkness and away from the compound lights, just a few more yards, and he'd be safe. He kept going, nearly to the tree line.

I'm going to make it!

As he reached the log, he trod on a large stone and twisted his ankle, losing balance and tumbling heavily. A sharp pain ran up his leg, and Andrew had to bite his tongue to avoid screaming out.

Fuck, is it broken?

He tested it gingerly, looking back towards the compound for any signs of pursuit. Another ATV suddenly rounded the corner, and he threw himself back and lay flat in the long grass as searchlights swept over him. He wanted to cry.

This would be just my luck. So close, and then I go and trip on a fucking rock!

The ATV, however, continued merrily on its way, and Andrew breathed a sigh of relief. He checked his ankle - it wasn't broken, but it was very sore. He gritted his teeth and headed up the slope and into the forest as quickly as he could. He had to try and make it to the unicorn.

Where the fuck is Claire?

He was out of breath when he reached the top of the hill, and he stopped and leaned against the nearest tree - his ankle shooting piercing pain up his leg in pulses. He tried Claire one more time – she was offline! *Somethings happened - they have her, they must have her.*

Oh my Douglas, this couldn't have gone any worse!

His head whipped around as he heard what he was sure were human voices from somewhere back down the hill, but thankfully no dog voices this time. He had to keep moving; there was no time to worry about anyone but himself if he wanted to stay alive - and he definitely wanted to stay alive!

Andrew had just twenty minutes from the moment things had gone pear-shaped to reach the unicorn, which meant he had less than five minutes left. They'd agreed that if only one of them was there by that time, then the other was to leave - better that one escapes instead of none, she'd said. Maybe she was waiting there already; maybe her comms had just malfunctioned?

Please please please be there …

He raced back down the hill, ignoring the pain in his ankle, and made it to the unicorn only a couple of minutes after the cutoff time. He had a brief moment of hope just as he entered the clearing, imagining seeing Claire there, waiting impatiently for him, or that she had already taken the unicorn. It wasn't to be. His only choice now was to leave her behind – he was grief-stricken at the prospect, and the certainty that things really had gone very, very wrong hit him like a brick.

Andrew collapsed to his knees as he reached the unicorn, distraught and terrified. He was on his own now. *What the hell am I supposed to do?* He couldn't bring himself to think about what might have happened to Claire. All he knew was that she hadn't come out. *Maybe I could wait a bit - but the voices, they're coming for me*

The unicorn, which had been grazing happily away next to the small rivulet, turned and nuzzled him as he knelt, head in his hands. There was nothing left to do but leave, he knew it, staying any longer would be suicide. He pushed himself up, patted the unicorn's neck, and took a few seconds to try and compose himself, forcing the grief he was now feeling deep inside.

Time to go. Bloody hell Claire, why did we have to go in there?

He was soon racing through the forest far more quickly than was reasonably safe, but he didn't care; he had to release some of the stress and tension of what he'd just been through - was still going through - somehow.

Gregory, the unicorn, didn't seem to mind. They raced through the trees, jumping obstacles and swerving this way and that as they headed for – or Andrew hoped they were heading for – a safe place. They'd passed a large rocky outcrop with a deep undercut on their way to the compound, and it was the perfect place for him to hide and wait for help – what other choice did he have?

The ROLA stopped suddenly; it was picking something up. An unauthorized humanoid form was moving at a faster pace than it should have been. It was traveling through its zone, and it would be able to intercept it. The orb expanded and took off through the forest, weaving through the trees and over obstacles at full speed.

It was a half-hour ride away, but he made swift progress. The more he rode, the worse he felt about leaving Claire behind. He couldn't stop thinking about John on the conveyor and Claire, now almost certainly captured. What the hell was happening to his life?

He'd lost contact with his own fly-bot now, and although he slowed and scanned for any sign of surveillance devices once or twice, there was nothing even remotely close to him. If anything, they seemed to be closing back in on the compound. They may not even be looking for him, they might not know he'd even been there – yet, but that was the least of his worries.

Andrew suddenly heard a crashing noise behind him, and when he turned to look, he couldn't believe what he was seeing. A huge white orb was bouncing through the forest and heading straight for him.

What the fuck is that? This can't be good!

Andrew kicked his heels into Gregory's side, and the unicorn broke into a full gallop, racing in-between the trees and darting this way and that, faster than he would have thought possible. He could hear a loud crashing close behind, and when he turned to look, he saw that the orb was almost on them, not more than twenty yards behind! It was somehow larger and was moving through the trees in an abnormal manner, seeming to use the trees themselves to help it change direction.

It's going to get us; whatever this thing is, it's going to get us!

Gregory jumped majestically over a fallen tree at full speed, and as they landed, they whipped through some high bushes and out into a clearing. The orb crashed through moments later, right behind them. Andrew was leaning forward, pressed down low against the unicorn's neck as it raced across the clearing. He daren't even risk another look behind. The orb slowed suddenly and locked onto its target, preparing to fire the pulse.

Come on, Gregory, come on!

Andrew couldn't hear the orb. It had made a mechanical whining noise as it had been chasing them, but the noise was no longer there. He glanced back as they raced at breakneck speed towards the far side of the clearing. The orb had collapsed back to its smaller although still considerable size, and started to roll slowly away.

Andrew loosened the reigns. He slowed Gregory, turning in a slow arc and bringing the unicorn to a gradual halt as he kept an eye on the bizarre object. It disappeared back through the bushes and out of sight.

What the fuck?

The ROLA was returning to its perimeter circuit. It hadn't anticipated the speed of the unauthorized humanoid object, and it had crossed its threshold just as it had been preparing to make the interception. There was nothing to report; the humanoid was no longer in its control zone. Its job now was to resume its patrol.

Andrew patted Gregory's neck - the unicorn was breathing hard. Andrew was stunned by what had just happened. He hopped down, his legs unsteady, and took a few moments to catch his breath. He crouched down, a little dizzy and breathing deeply, keeping a wary eye on the bushes where the orb had disappeared.

It was obviously some sort of pursuit object, but why had it turned around? He was very worried now that he'd been located, and they would be coming for him, one way or another. He had no choice but to continue, but perhaps he'd better change direction and seek cover somewhere other than he'd planned if he made it that far.

***

Within a few minutes of the power surge, the call came through - they had found an intruder in the utility control room, unconscious and bleeding from her mouth, nose, and ears. She matched the description of one of the wanted fugitives. Bill ordered the guards to take her to Medi-cell B22 and hold her there until he arrived – he'd be down shortly.

Lachlan had observed William McDowell with a mixture of interest and intense concern as he'd relayed the message. One of the fugitives had, it seemed, been handed to them on a platter. *The girl.* He was going to struggle to claim any credit for this. His plans for returning to center stage were fast evaporating.

He could see that he was going to have to intervene to ensure the captive was protected at least until Isabel and Gerald arrived. He didn't trust McDowell as far as he could throw him. Judging by the way his belly hung over the top of his belt, that probably wasn't very far at all.

There was still the matter of the remaining fugitive to address. All search resources had now been called back to the compound and surrounds in an effort to locate and apprehend him. He needed to ensure that he was the one that captured the second fugitive. His plans were almost in ruins, but he had one last chance to save himself.

Lachlan had one distinct advantage over that fat fuck McDowell in that he'd been in direct contact with the breachers, and they had planned a rendezvous the next day. He now had no idea if that would still be possible, and he knew he'd need to think fast to try and re-engineer the pick-up with the remaining fugitive. He was hoping he might hear from; *what was his name? Andrew. Yes, that was it, Andrew … Weems.*

Lachlan was hoping to hear from Andrew Weems again very soon – his career depended on it.

***

Lachlan had insisted on accompanying Bill down to the medi-cell. He'd seen his type before. He didn't want there to be any possibility of the package being damaged before his bosses arrived. McDowell was shooting daggers at him in the level-pod on their way down, but Lachlan just fixed him with his most charming, some would say, disarming smile.

They soon arrived, and a medic was just finishing up with the restraints. Bill ushered her out of the room so that they could observe their captive. Even though the girl was unconscious and deathly pale, Bill recognized her immediately – a hot feeling came over him, and he rubbed at his scar again, drawing a flicker of a glance from Lachlan. He didn't like the look in William McDowell's eyes one little bit - he'd have to do something here. He had no idea if he had the authority, but he'd give it a shot anyway. He cleared his throat.

"The captive is to be placed under V.I. surveillance, and two of my guards will be stationed at the door of the cell, effective immediately."

Bill glared at Lachlan with a ferocity that would have peeled paint from a wall.

Lachlan continued. "No one except medical staff will be permitted inside, and only then, accompanied by one of my guards. Understood?"

The look on Bill's face told Lachlan that he'd understood perfectly.

*

He's going to spoil my fun. This is intolerable! I can't fucking do anything about it!

Bill stood and glared some more at the snotty little upstart, hands-on-hips, trying to think of a cutting remark, then turned and strode from the room without so much as a word. Once he'd returned to his quarters, he ordered the standard blood tests be taken on the captive, but with a high priority so that he could get the results as soon as possible. He may well be able to save his baco after all, and that clueless numpty fuck Grealish would have no idea what was happening.

Bill opened a bottle of bru and sat down heavily in his workroom chair, nearly missing the edge of the seat and having a moment of panic before regaining his balance.

Fucker. I'll show him! There will be plenty of time for the girl later. Plenty of time for Grealish too. That little dook isn't getting in my way.

***

Andrew was cold and alone. It was pitch black in the forest, and he was expecting to be captured at any moment. He'd already heard several fly-bots overhead, and at one point, he thought he heard an ATV approaching, but it had turned out to be a false alarm. He wasn't having much fun at all.

Claire was still offline. Captured, it was beyond doubt now. John was offline, almost certainly permanently. As he sat and waited for the inevitable, he'd thought about everything and accepted that life as he knew it no longer existed. He just couldn't believe things could go so terribly, terribly wrong, so terribly quickly.

What was it? Two, three days ago, and his only concerns would have been whether there were any clean socks to put on in the morning and how he could annoy his friends in new and creative ways. And now? Just the small matter of trying not to be captured, tortured, and most likely killed in a very unpleasant manner by the sheer evil that lurked within that terrible, disgusting, vile compound.

His only hope now was Lachlan Grealish, the vain twat. *His only hope. The twat.* The thought depressed him even more, and he shivered as the cold and damp seemed to seep from the ground and into his very core. Just as he was about to wallow even further in self-pity, a thought hit him like a thunderbolt!

The images of the mining room!

He had to get the images to Grealish *and* Wesley - they had to see for themselves what was happening. He couldn't believe that he hadn't already thought to send them and facepalmed himself at his abject stupidity.

I mean, I was a little distracted, but still.

Andrew spoke quickly into his comms after attaching the images. "This is what is happening at the compound. Do something!

People are being killed! *Your people* are dying. Our friend John is in there – on the conveyor! Claire has been captured. Help us! Get us out!"

Send. There! Might have used one too many exclamation points, but they'll get the gist of it - they have to!

***

There's not much more I can do. I'll just have to wait and see now.

The communication arrived just as Lachlan had settled himself into the somewhat spartan accommodation on offer at the compound. He was sure that there were much more comfortable rooms available and equally sure that McDowell had ensured he received the worst possible of them.

His time would come, and soon. Isabel had plans for him - she'd briefed him on his way to the compound. He smiled to himself at the thought, noticing the red light blinking on his secure comms. He opened the message and the image accompanying it, dropping his comms in shock before snatching them back up and staring at the image on display.

Oh, this was bad! This is very, very bad!

The breachers had obtained images of one of the mining rooms and had somehow managed to get them out of the compound. Andrew Weems was in possession of it. *If this gets out ...*

He realized the message had also been sent to Hamish Wesley – and this changed everything! He'd have to act fast to contain the damage. He used his binary to secure comms Isabel. The call lasted less than five minutes, and when it finished, he had his instructions.

Isabel was incredulous at the leak of the image, but she had a plan. Lachlan had been instructed to forward the message to the controllers, and they were to provide it to The Source. The A.I. entity would create a package of information that would be impossible for anyone to disprove, discrediting the image, and Wesley along with it, blaming him for the fabrication and an attempt to implicate D.A.I.R.

Two birds with one stone, she'd said. Wesley would be tried and executed for treason. A good outcome all around, he thought. In the meantime, he needed to ensure he was the one to bring Weems in.

He sent a reply, along the lines that Isabel had instructed him to, but also with a little flourish here and there all his own -

"Andrew, oh my goodness, I can't tell you how sickened and horrified I am by what you've exposed! I'm not far away, I managed to get an emergency squad together at short notice, and we can get you out within the hour. Give us a meeting point, and we'll come and get you. I'm calling for reinforcements now, and we'll get into that compound by any means necessary. I noticed the other recipient - do NOT trust Wesley under any circumstances — we have intel that he's up to his neck in this - you'll see something about it in the media soon confirming it. Hang tight; we'll get you out."

There, that should do it.

   ***

The message from the fugitive Andrew Weems had left Hamish feeling physically ill. He would, of course, have it verified, but after seeing the horrific image, he was left in little doubt that something terrible was happening in the uninhabitable zone.

There was something else too, something that made everything fall into place like beads on an abacus - the other contact. Lachlan Grealish. It was all coming back to him now - *the garbled and panicked call from Peter Bradshaw a few days ago. He'd mentioned that his son was working for Isabel - he was in a bad situation and, what else had he said? Something about her being behind Lachlan's recent calamitous downfall.*

Hamish had done what he could to help Peter at the time but hadn't made the connection until now. It seemed that the breachers had made a mistake and reached out to the wrong person.

He forced himself to look at the image again, at the hundreds of lifeless-looking bodies that seemed to be heading towards some sort of waste disposal chute. One of the bodies was lying crumpled about halfway down the chute, having left a trail of blood as it made its way, who knows where. *All those poor souls, they were real huma ...*

Wesley's thoughts came to an abrupt end. He'd skimmed over it on opening the image, but Andrew had mentioned something important - something about John McGregor being there, at the compound, and in that image. He looked more closely, his feeling of nausea building as he scanned the bodies, looking for the one he'd recognize. He noticed something on one of the bodies, a mark - something he'd seen before, increased the resolution, and zoomed in. He couldn't make out the details of the face but the distinctive mark on the chest. He'd seen that shape somewhere before.

Summer holidays, the indoor pool, his daughter had some friends over.

The recollection slowly surfaced in Wesley's mind and revealed itself in cold, stark reality. He dropped the glass of water he'd been holding, and it bounced on his desk before emptying its contents over his vintage calculator collection, amongst other things. Wesley didn't even notice.

He couldn't take his eyes off the tattoo of the McGregor family crest. The body was undoubtedly that of John McGregor. Wesley's mouth hung open, and he made a huge decision there and then - something had to be done!

Wesley mopped up the water with an ihandkerchief, and as he did so, he recalled that he'd indeed met Claire Renshaw briefly through Stuart's son, John. He was terrible with names and faces, but he remembered now. They were telling the truth. It was shocking, unbelievable, beyond horrific. Something truly terrible was happening in the lowlands, and he was in for the fight of his life to expose it, of that he was sure.

Hamish responded to Andrew Weems. The poor boy must be terrified, on the run, and caught up in this horrendous evil thing. Seeing his friend in that *room*, that terrible place, and having his other friend captured and not knowing what's become of her.

The breachers, no matter their motive, had uncovered something big here, and he was going to do everything he could to help them. He sent a message back:

"Andrew, hold tight. We're coming! I'll send in a maxi-fly-bot and a defense rescue squad and get you out straight away - we can have it there within a few hours. I could identify John McGregor in the image you sent - it's shocking, it's disgusting - we're going to stop it. We're going to dismantle whatever is going on there and make those responsible accountable for their actions. We'll call for an emergency session of the security council immediately, and we intend to get the go-ahead to storm that compound and the others like it. We will free your friends."

The water he'd spilled had dripped onto Wesley's beige suit pants at some point, but he'd been so absorbed in the horrors of the compound that he hadn't noticed the large wet patch on his thigh. He thought for a moment more; there was something else he needed to say.

"... do NOT trust Lachlan Grealish; he's heavily involved in all this evil."

Wesley took a few moments to compose himself. Suddenly everything seemed to make sense. The expenditure overruns, the links to individuals across the different arms of state governance, the missing persons, and their long untouched then suddenly cleared finances.

It was all pointing to just a few people and with one common link. Isabel Donachy's name just kept coming up, again and again. There was no doubt in his mind that she was the common thread in the jointly financed 'special projects' he'd uncovered - she was the key to all of this. She was the source of all this evil.

It was time to act, time to take a huge risk, and time to stop whatever malevolence Isabel and her cohorts were spreading on his beloved Planet 0420. Wesley picked up the blue handset of his secure comms and dialed Sgt. James Jeffries. He had better ensure that the military was on-side for what was to come. Things could escalate very quickly, and although his defense contacts had been useful so far on the espionage front, he'd need access to personnel and hardware if this went the way he was expecting.

He'd explained the situation and put the wheels in motion, instructing Jeffries to arrange to call the emergency session of the security council, something that in itself was unprecedented. He would have defense table both his findings relating to the financial irregularities and this latest, horrific development. He intended to ensure that they could get action approved to stop the horrors at the compound.

Jeffries, in turn, had explained to him in no uncertain terms that he would have to see it through to the end once he went down this path. The thought was overwhelming and more than a little terrifying, but Wesley had no hesitation.

He also had a few other contacts to call. Peter Bradshaw, for one. It would be a great time for Peter and his extended family to disappear. Peter was up to his neck in all of this, and he was a good man. Wesley didn't want to see anything happen to him.

Isabel Donachy. She'd tried to silence him, to kill him, and now he was going to bring her down. Things were about to get very ugly.

CHAPTER 24 – INCOMPETENCE

Isabel was in the middle of preparing for her visit to the compound when news of the leaked image came through. It was staggering. She just couldn't believe the incompetence. Everything that Isabel had worked for was now at risk! How could they have allowed the breachers to get *inside* the compound? How could they have allowed The Source's data to be stolen?

Had the breachers somehow caused the overload? Her mind was reeling.

The mining programs, the birth of QFTII, and the ultimate power that it would wield - they were slipping away from her. The carefully laid plans that would see her installed as the Executive of state, in total and complete control over everything and everyone, were now all at risk thanks to William bloody McDowell and Lachlan fucking Grealish!

Incompetence!

She was going to tear them a new dookhole each, maybe even two. Bloody McDowell, the buffoon couldn't organize a search for a turd in a toilet! Isabel was sure that there were better epigrams she could have used, but she was so livid right now that she couldn't think of any. And that other buffoon Lachlan fucking Grealish, who she couldn't trust to organize a piss-up at a bru factory! The second one was at least a little better.

She was so close to executing the final part of her plan. *So close.* The Source was almost terminally diminished, and she'd needed just a few more weeks of mining - she would have been there! And now? The timing was just unbelievable.

This is what happens when you rely on other people!

As things stood, it was going to be difficult to suppress the details of the image and keep any sort of production going, at least long enough for her to have achieved QFT II. Things were probably going to get very messy - it was a good thing she was prepared.

That little prick Wesley had no doubt got in the ear of his defense buddies and managed to get the emergency session of the security council called, and on the basis of what? One crappy image! She could probably discredit it or at least muddy the waters on any verification, but she might not have access to The Source for a while to help with any of that. It was a disaster. An emergency session! She just couldn't believe it.

Who the hell do they think they are!

Either way, this was going to bring a total dookstorm with it and more scrutiny than they could afford. At least they had the girl, she supposed, although her importance had now been diminished greatly. She could hardly trumpet capturing her as a great achievement while the security council attempted to get to the bottom of what she'd found.

Perhaps she'd at least be able to extract details of how the breachers had done it, how they'd managed to get one up on The Source before the girl expired in the interrogation room. *Not once, but three times, three times the breachers had breached The Source's data. It was unimaginable!*

She stood and stared out of the floor-to-ceiling plexi-panels of her apartment, seething with anger. Wanlockhead was an ugly concrete jungle, but it was her ugly concrete jungle. Soon all of Planet 0420 would be her - concrete jungle?

This isn't over. I'll find a way, and then I'll make all those fuckers pay for messing with my plans!

Isabel wasn't going to let anything stop her. She would deny all requests at the emergency session and rubbish the so-called evidence. By the time anyone figured out the truth, it would be too late.

She started packing, taking pleasure in selecting all the tools she was going to need for the job, particularly Mr. Floppy, her extra special interrogation tool. She held Mr. Floppy by its bulbous head and wiggled it before packing it in her travel case. *Ah, so many memories.* She smiled to herself, and it was a truly wicked smile. *This is going to be fun, after all.*

***

Peter Bradshaw had just finished packing the pale blue duo transporter. He and his wife Heather would be taking an indefinite vacation - for health reasons, as far as anyone at the college was going to be aware, which he supposed was accurate to a degree.

Arrangements were being made for their parents to be moved from their current facilities to a defense care facility. There was no way he was going to let Isabel Donachy near anyone else he loved.

He'd tried to contact his son a few times now, but unsurprisingly he'd had no response. Lachlan had made his choices – and Peter recognized with a heavy heart that there was nothing more he could do for him.

Hamish had said he'd try and protect him but that he couldn't promise anything under the current circumstances. Things were going to get very messy, and there was no way of knowing how they would turn out. Perhaps Lachlan would come out of all of this on the right side of things, and perhaps not.

Fate will decide. Good luck, son.

They were to head to a small and isolated eco pod in an area off the west coast that had once been known as the Shetland Islands, now known as the imaginatively named 'Winnie Isles'. The islands were unpopulated except in the height of summer, which was still some months away.

He and his family should be safe there, and they would be protected, Hamish had said, at least in the short term. He'd organized a small defense squad to watch over them and had told them that he'd send word once the danger was over, but until then, they would need to keep their heads down in the windswept and barren environment - it was going to be a tough holiday.

***

Andrew didn't know quite what to make of the latest responses. *This is ridiculous!* How on earth had they managed to pick two contacts that were apparently on polar opposite sides of the forces of good and evil? It was just his luck. If he had to bet, he'd lean towards Wesley as being on the side of good, but he couldn't be one hundred percent sure either way; they were each accusing the other. After all, Wesley had the family connection with the McGregor's, but that was all he had to go on. He effectively had a fifty-fifty chance.

This is just so typical. Just so my luck.

445

He'd spent a restless night curled up on the ground, ankle throbbing relentlessly, pins and needles coming from his thigh, freezing cold and miserable, with only Gregory, the unicorn, for company. In the morning, he'd ridden him to within a half-mile of the coordinates and was about to set him free. It had been no easy task with what felt like a fractured ankle, although it was possibly just a sprain.

If he was indeed rescued, or he was dead, he didn't want poor old Gregory left tethered to a tree somewhere, although he supposed he could tie a knot that would slip under pressure, maybe partially cut through the rope? *This is stupid; I can't risk that not working.* He patted him on the neck and gave him the last apple from his pack.

"Good boy, Gregory. Good boy." Gregory the unicorn made short work of the apple, decided now was an excellent time to leave, and did. Andrew stared after his trusty unicorn as it disappeared through the thick undergrowth.

Bye then.

Grealish and Wesley were due to arrive within the next twenty minutes or so. He supposed that once they arrived, he'd soon find out who was who - that is, who was good, who was evil. At least he hoped he'd be able to tell. Perhaps he'd just find out who was the better shot. So, on that basis, he still had a fifty-fifty chance of being hunted down and killed soon afterward.

Great plan, Andy.

He looked longingly back into the forest, wondering if freeing Gregory was such a good idea.

He made his way carefully through the trees to where they ended abruptly at a narrow dirt track, with an expansive open floodplain beyond. He hid behind a large bush - for want of a better hiding spot - and waited for the forces of good and evil to arrive. He'd have a good view of things from here if nothing else.

***

Wesley had made a last-minute decision to travel with the rescue team on the maxi-fly-bot. Although he could still barely move and had been passing blood in his urine ever since the murder attempt.

He hoped that Andrew Weems might recognize him and know that he'd be safe with his squad. He thought that maybe he'd met him at his daughter's party but couldn't be sure. Hopefully, Weems had a better memory than he did.

It was the least he could do - these young students had risked everything to expose the unimaginable evil festering in the lowlands, and everything now hinged on one person. Andrew Weems held the key to all of this now, and it was critically important that he be rescued.

***

Lachlan had asked one of the rescue squad if he could borrow their tammie - he thought the flat military cap would look good in the media shots. They could get a few images once they'd captured Weems, and they'd soon be splashed all over the front pages of the media. He wanted to look the part. He wanted to look good. He could see the headlines now: *Grealish nabs Breacher Splatterer Murderer. Maybe just Grealish Nabs Breacher Splatterer? Something like that anyway.*

Media headlines weren't his strong point. Looking handsome and charming underneath them was. He practiced the look he'd give for the cameras as the ATV bumped along the narrow dirt track. He arranged his features accordingly and checked in the visor mirror.

Not too cocky. Not too happy. Just solid, serious. A true leader and champion of the people. Perfect.

Yes, that would do nicely. He'd ensure one of his squad got some images of him holding the boy by the scruff of the neck or maybe even handcuffing him. They were nearly at the capture point. Just around the next bend, the forest would open into a floodplain - that was the meeting point, that was the place where it would all happen.

Lachlan Grealish would save the day - he'd be back in the media spotlight where he belonged and back in favor amongst the sanctum. Everything was going to be ok.

He smiled and thought again of the young fugitive. He'd done well to get into the compound and get the images. It was even more impressive that he'd got out undetected, but he was about to meet his match.

Andrew Weems held the key to all of this now, and it was critically important that he be captured and then eliminated.

***

Andrew heard the ATV approach, and his stomach tightened. He could see its lights approaching through the trees.

Grealish.

The vehicle pulled up not more than twenty yards from Andrew's hiding spot. Several large, solid, and quite scary-looking people had hopped out of the ATV and were now milling about. Andrew thought he could see some of them holding weapons.

Goodies or baddies?

One shorter man followed and spent a good minute adjusting his hat while standing in front of the ATV, illuminated by its headlights - his golden hair highlighted in the bright beams.

That's Grealish, alright.

Grealish tried calling out, but the wind was whipping across the floodplain, and his voice was carried away by it. He instead fiddled with his comms. Andrew received the message.

"We're at the meeting point. All clear."

Andrew began to shake with nerves; he was very unsure of his plan. He wasn't going anywhere near those people - they didn't look at all friendly. What if they spotted him? What if Wesley didn't turn up? He pressed himself flat against the ground as the scary-looking people from Grealish's squad shone searchlights around the area.

Please don't make me go out there. Please turn up.

He needn't have worried. The very next moment, a large grey object appeared over the top of the tree line. It was a surreal sight. It appeared not to make any noise at all, with the fierce winds carrying the sound of its turbines away. The squad milling around the ATV reacted quickly, retreating to the rear of the vehicle and throwing open its rear doors as the maxi-fly-bot landed. Grealish remained where he was, hands-on-hips.

The maxi swooped down, its cargo doors already open, allowing several camo-clad figures to pour out of it the moment it touched down. The squad fanned out and lay prone on the ground;

weapons pointed towards the ATV. As Andrew watched, a small bald man in beige limped down the maxi's gangway. He was calling out to Grealish. Andrew recognized Hamish Wesley. He wondered if he should show himself or stay where he is.

Wonder what will happen now?

His question was answered a split second later. All hell broke loose. The now heavily armed ATV squad reappeared from behind their vehicle and opened fire, the bright flashes and the loud pulsing sounds of weaponry filling the air. One of the camo squad had quickly shielded Wesley and returned fire, as did his comrades.

Andrew instinctively dashed the largest and closest tree trunk and hid behind it. He could hear plasma pulses zipping into the forest nearby, a staccato of flashes and deafening rapid-fire pulses filling the air around him. He fought the very strong urge to run for it and keep on running. He risked a quick peek.

Grealish's head exploded where he stood. It was the strangest sight. One moment it was there, on top of his neck, where it no doubt usually resided - his weapon held out in front of him in what Andrew could best describe as a 'James Bond' pose - and the next second, his head simply wasn't there anymore. It had exploded in a fine pink mist, causing the tammie to flop down onto what remained of his neck.

The headless figure remained standing for a moment, and Andrew genuinely thought it would keep firing, but it instead crumpled forward, the cap rolling away comically.

Andrew had slid to the ground behind the tree, cradling himself with his arms and rocking back and forth. He'd never been so terrified in his life. The flash of weaponry lit up the night sky, but it stopped a few seconds later, just as abruptly as it had started.

It was all over in less than a minute, and a thick smoke hung in the eerie silence that followed. Andrew peered nervously at the scene from his hiding place. The ATV squad were lying in many pieces around their vehicle.

The camo squad were now standing, weapons at ease. One of them had even lit a tube and looked quite casual, puffing away. As he pushed himself off the ground, Andrew felt pretty sure that he would have to change his trousers.

***

Gerald James was en route to the compound with Isabel. They were traveling in the back of a luxury maxi-pod which was kitted out with everything they might need, and some things that they didn't – the mode of transport was far more discrete than having to deal with all the red tape involved in chartering any sort of air travel at short notice.

Gerald was head of Health and People Services and had the specialist skills that Isabel would need during the interrogation of the fugitives - she assumed that Lachlan Grealish would be adding the male student fugitive to her list of appointments once she arrived. To say that she was looking forward to it would be an understatement.

The emergency session of the security council would be kicking off any time soon, and the sunrise was gradually lightening the horizon, not that either of them would have noticed - they were in the midst of a heated debate.

Gerald, it turned out, was extremely displeased with some of the independent actions taken by Isabel, which had now come to light in a rather unfortunate way – the failed hit on Wesley, the image from the compound, the pressure from the security council.

It was all building to the perfect storm, he'd said, and this wasn't the time they should have been taking such extreme measures. Some of the names taken were too high profile, and that some of them could be connected to disappearances of other family members who'd been taken in the first sweep – the strategy was too high risk.

Isabel had argued that the secondary sweep of packages was essential, pure, and simple. Many of those taken had been assessed as low grade genetically suitable, but they had little choice, seeing as they were running out of high-grade candidates.

Gerald was also displeased that she'd changed strategy on sending the faked comms but had conceded that the messages had to be sent to buy them some more time at such a critical juncture. It was far from perfect, he'd concluded. It was the fact that she'd done all of this without consulting him - he was most displeased. It was all too risky, and what was going on now was likely the direct result of her actions.

*

Isabel felt personally attacked; her credibility questioned - she was rapidly changing her opinion of Gerald James.

How dare he question my judgment, the pathetic pea-brained weasel!

She'd explained, much as you would to a small child, in very simplistic terms, that her actions were essential to ensure that they met their Elyssium production goal before the financial audits uncovered the full extent of their operations. The alternatives would take too long - they had needed to act quickly and decisively, and so that was what she'd done. It was the only way.

*

Gerald James had no intention of being left behind in Isabel's game and had agreed on a compromise. He'd wait for his moment, and that moment wasn't far away.

I'll let her do all the work, take all the risks, and then I'll step in and take over.

She'd promised him that he'd be positioned as second in command in her regime once she assumed control, and in return, he'd keep quiet on her breaches of sanctum protocol. Isabel didn't trust Gerald, and Gerald didn't trust Isabel. One of them wouldn't last much beyond QFT II going live, that was for sure.

*

The subject of William McDowell had also been raised. The attempt on Wesley had been a complete disaster. Gerald had warned her about using him, and Isabel's credibility had taken a big hit over the bungled attempt. She needed this hushed up, and she needed Wesley out of the way - she could hardly make another attempt on his life, and so she'd have to ensure that the treason charges stuck.

***

The meeting had been explosive. Isabel hadn't been expecting some of the details that had been tabled - it was a complete blindside.

451

Hamish Wesley had far more knowledge and influence than she'd given him credit. The image from the compound and the subject of the student breachers and their evidence was front and center.

Things had quickly descended into a shouting match. Accusations of serious financial fraud were met with accusations of treason, and the whole thing had descended into chaos within the first five minutes.

The room was split down the middle. One side claiming all kinds of ridiculous-sounding but pretty accurate conspiracy theories, and the other rubbishing the claims, making serious accusations of their own - determined to bring the breachers to justice and show them to be the traitors they were.

Isabel had managed to keep her cool, but only just. Her hatred for Wesley had reached a whole new level. She was going to make him grovel when the time came.

They'd agreed, as much as you could call shouting at each other an agreement, to validate the image and investigate the claims of the two fugitives with a joint defense and security forces commission, but it was a hollow promise, and both sides knew it.

The Sanctum's representatives on the council had put the idea forward purely as a stalling method, and defense themselves didn't believe for a second it would even be possible – they'd had a long and troubled relationship with the Security Forces. It was hard to imagine them co-operating on anything. As soon as the meeting ended, Isabel had started planning the arrest of the key figures opposing her. Things were going south rapidly, but she'd fight fire with fire.

They were still an hour from the compound, and this afforded them some rare relaxation time. Isabel reclined gracefully in the back of the maxi-pod, sipping a vintage herb-brew and snacking on the most exquisite organically grown hedgehog canapes. Gerald had taken his serum and was now occupying another realm entirely, leaving Isabel to her thoughts.

As soon as the QFTII entity had consciousness, she'd be able to do pretty much as she pleased – she'd be untouchable. She'd act swiftly and crush all those opposing her. Over time she'd be able to cement her legacy in her civilization's history. They'd build statues of her. She would rule forever, and history would no doubt be kind to her. If it wasn't, well, she'd just re-write it. The thought made her shiver with pleasure. She shifted her weight in the seat, and the pleasure balls sent a crashing orgasm through her. She bit her lip and shifted her weight again.

CHAPTER 25 – BREATHLESS

Claire was in the dark place again. Worse still, the nightmare she'd blacked out from earlier had carried on from exactly where it had left off. The inky tar surrounding her had slowly given way to the pale blue light, and she was still screaming her silent scream.

The thick black death cables were connected all over her body now, and she writhed and contorted as they dug ever deeper inside her. It felt as if the cables were attaching to her bones, deep inside - the pain was indescribable.

Something had changed in the horrific scenario. She was secured to a vertical incline by her wrists and ankles. In front of her were a series of semi-translucent layers of displays that seemed to go back further than she could see, information streaming across each at incredible speed.

The cables pulsed a final time, then relaxed. The pain stopped suddenly, and Claire tried to take a breath. It wasn't possible. Her lungs did nothing. She panicked and struggled frantically against her restraints. The cables shook with her movements, but she wasn't going anywhere. It was at that point that Claire realized that breathing was no longer necessary.

***

Bill had lost contact with Grealish and his squad. They hadn't reported on the capture of the fugitive Andrew Weems, and in fact, hadn't been heard from since they had left the compound. He was getting worried and had made a decision to send the nearest fly-bots to the location of the ATV.

He was relying on Grealish bringing the Weems boy back – hoping it might serve to placate Isabel somewhat. The fugitive had instructed them to ensure that all fly-bots were kept well away and that any incursion would void the proposed pickup. They had complied, but it had been far too long now, and Bill needed answers. Isabel and Gerald were due to arrive in a while, and he wanted things wrapped up by then. An hour or so later, Bill received the SFB's V.I. stream from the site. They were going to need a lot of body bags. And a shovel.

Although he should have been elated at Lachlan Grealish's demise, Bill hadn't celebrated – he'd caused a much bigger problem than he'd solved by getting himself killed. He had, of course, briefed Bill on Hamish Wesley before he'd left, and there was no other possible explanation for what had happened – they'd lost the second fugitive to the other side.

Could things get any worse?

On the plus side, Bill realized that he'd have unfettered access to the girl for at least a couple of hours. He drained his malt, prized himself out of his workroom chair, and headed for the cells, a spring in his step.

***

Isabel and Gerald arrived in the early morning. Torrential rain beat down on their maxi-pod and as they approached the large grey compound in the soft dawn light. A long line of stationary Solo's snaked back from the building. Isabel was shocked by this but supposed she shouldn't have been.

Isabel didn't like surprises. No one had told her of the problems relating to The Source's overload, and now she had yet another reason to punish William McDowell.

Fucking William fucking McDowell. Why hasn't this been fixed? It's a total bloody balls-up!

She was already quite agitated because she hadn't had an update from Grealish or McDowell since late last night - the sight of The Solo's piling up on the road to the compound was the final straw. She clenched her fists, enjoying the feeling of pain as her nails dug into the still-raw cuts on her palms.

Someone's going to pay for this!

Gerald looked out at the line of autonomous vehicles with no emotion. He thought that he might have to bring forward his own plans if things continued in this vein for much longer. They soon reached the entrance gates, and the maxi-pod was ushered straight through into the central courtyard, stopping under an enclosed arch.

There was no one to greet them other than a couple of clearly flustered-looking junior guards.

Isabel stepped out of the maxi with a face like thunder. "What the fuck is going on here?" she demanded of a pimple-faced guard who could not have been more than seventeen or eighteen years old.

"Ma'am! I'm informed that we had an issue with The Source. We've had to shut it down and place it in sub-mode, but it'll be fixed soon, um, I'm sure." The pimple-faced guard didn't sound sure. Isabel wasn't so sure either.

"Well bloody well sort it out! Where's McDowell?"

What the fuck is he playing at?

They were taken directly to the control room, on Isabel's insistence. When they walked in, they were barely even noticed - the atmosphere in there was frantic, to say the least, and perhaps even chaotic. There was still no McDowell sign, so Isabel asked again, this time to the room in general, her voice cutting through the busy hum like a knife.

"Where the *fuck* is McDowell?"

No one seemed to take any notice – they were either too scared or - they were too scared.

Isabel repeated the question, and this time the tone and volume stopped everyone dead. A small man in the corner mumbled something timidly about Sgt. McDowell being on his way. The man had no idea if that was true or not but thought he'd better say something to the scary-looking lady before she tore something or someone apart.

*

The call to inform of their arrival had gone through to Bill some time ago, but he was having a little trouble pulling himself together. He was currently busy emptying his bowels for possibly the third time in the space of the last five minutes.

He knew he had to be downstairs to greet his superiors, but he was literally dookting himself at the prospect. A long stream of hot brown liquid exited Bill, and he took a deep breath, which was a bit of a mistake.

Oh, that's foul. Ok Bill, come on, man up, time to face the music.

He tidied up downstairs, pulled up his pants, and buckled his belt. A quick glance in the mirror told him he looked worse than he felt if that was even possible. Bill had stood Grealish's guards down after informing them of the fate of their commander, and as soon as they were dismissed, he'd entered the medi-cell where Claire Renshaw was being held.

Nursing staff were fussing around her, and when he'd told them to get out, they'd informed him that they hadn't yet been able to stabilize or revive her and that she'd need constant medical supervision until she was conscious. They had explained, somewhat hurriedly, that she could quite possibly go into cardiac arrest and die if they left her now.

Bill's ears turned red, quickly followed by his face. They basically refused to leave. He made a mental note to relieve them from their positions as soon as possible – but for now, he grudgingly conceded that he needed them to keep the girl alive.

He'd been bitterly disappointed. It was his one opportunity to have a little fun, take a little revenge, have a little 'me time,' and it had been cruelly snatched from him. It really wasn't his day.

Rather than focusing on what he was going to say or providing any update on the situation, he'd instead fallen into a drunken stupor with a large bottle of cheap malt for company. His head now felt like it would explode every time he moved it, and he really, really didn't want to go downstairs.

***

Stu Gallacher had briefed Isabel on The Source's strange overload. They still had no idea what had caused it, so it wasn't really much of a briefing. He'd then informed her of Lachlan Grealish's fate. She'd listened in disbelief.

Fucking Grealish. What a loser. And why did I trust that numpty McDowell with anything? Literally everything he's touched has been a total fucking disaster.

Grealish himself was no real loss to her; in fact, she was glad he'd met his end, but his actions and a rather pathetic failure to handle a simple task had, of course, created another, much larger issue. Wesley now had Weems, and that spelled big trouble. She'd have to change her plans *again*. It was a bad development, but not a terminal one.

She'd take Wesley out of the picture, and the breachers would be discredited. They would have time, just as long as they could get The Source back online. Gerald was off somewhere prepping a medi-cell. She'd plan their next moves with him immediately after she'd dealt personally with that nincompoop McDowell.

Isabel was in the middle of demanding that The Source be brought back online when a pale and somewhat disheveled-looking William McDowell strode unsteadily into the room. He looked unsure of himself, the usual arrogance and swagger not evident, but the sheen of a full-blown alcohol sweat on his brow was. As he went to greet her, Isabel cut him off sharply.

"Guards! Sgt. McDowell is relieved from duty, effective immediately, arrest him for gross dereliction of duty." She smiled an evil little smile as she delivered the line, enjoying the look of confusion and then absolute terror on William McDowell's face.

Bill's mouth had remained open from his attempted greeting - he couldn't believe what was happening to him. Before he could even react, his arms were pinned behind him, and he was secured in confinement straps. "Take him to the secure max medi-cell. I'll be along soon for a wee little chat."

He'd expected something to happen, but not this. Bill was in shock. All the color drained from his face, and he seemed to age ten years in a second as he was dragged away. He hadn't even managed to get a word out in his defense, and he seemed to have wet his pants at some point.

A wee little chat. He knew exactly what that meant.

   ***

Andrew woke in unfamiliar surroundings. He was in a spartan green painted room of a simple bunk and desk, not much else. That said, it was still probably still an upgrade from his flat back at the student accommodations. It was clean, for one thing, immaculately so. He rubbed his eyes, rolled out of the bunk, and took a couple of unsteady steps to the rooms' small window. The second step sent a shooting pain up his leg and into his temple.

At least I'm not dead.

He used a hand to lean against the wall and take some weight off his ankle as he looked out over a massive parade ground, half immaculately groomed grass, half gravel, upon which various military-type drills were taking place. Military Attack Fly-Bots (AFB's) buzzed everywhere overhead, and rows of dark green troop transporters and combat ATVs lined either side of the area, which was flanked with tall concrete and plex buildings.

Andrew yawned and looked over at the desk. His comms had been removed and lay there, looking intact. A small red light was blinking.

Claire! Could it be?

The thought gave him hope for a second or two, and he snatched up the comms hurriedly. The message wasn't from Claire - it was from Lachlan Grealish and must have been sent few moments before he ceased to exist. He felt an incredible sadness overcome him and sat heavily back on the bunk. He had difficulty remembering what had happened last night, other than that John was dead, and Claire had either been captured, killed, or worse. All in all, it had been a pretty bad night.

How did I even get here?

The memory suddenly emerged - Sgt. James Jeffries - the camo man who had been casually smoking the tube after the carnage. As the smoke had cleared, Sgt. Jeffries had called out to him, "Andrew! You can come out now, mate; we've neutralized this bunch of drongo's." He had a casual manner and a broad Australian accent, and Andrew had felt an immediate sense of security at the use of his name and the friendly manner. His plan had played fortuitously out as he'd hoped - he was with the goodies rather than the baddies.

Could have gone either way, I suppose. Looks like I was lucky.

He emerged from his hiding spot and waved cautiously at the Sergeant, who waved back and started walking towards him, holding out, what was it? A pack of tubes! "Come on, mate, over here, come and have a tube. Hamish is here too, somewhere, if he hasn't fainted."

Andrew had reached for the tube that the beaming military man was proffering. "You're safe, Andrew. I'm James, Sgt. James Jeffries."

A moment later, the ground beneath Andrew had seemed to fall away. After that, there was nothing at all.

He'd come to at some point during the maxi-fly-bot's flight and saw the friendly faces of both Hamish Wesley and James Jeffries peering down at him as he lay on a medi-gurney. Wesley had smiled and said, "Andrew, welcome back!" while Jeffries simply winked and offered him a tube.

A sharp knock on the door disturbed Andrew from his recollection of events.

"Err … come in."

It was Sgt. Jeffries. His big friendly face, complete with regulation issue defense forces mustache, appeared around the door, accompanied by a large grin.

"G'day mate, good to see you back in the land of the living! Come on, let's go grab some tucker, eh?"

Andrew wasn't sure what tucker was, but it sounded better than sitting alone in the room and feeling depressed. He slipped on his boots gingerly and followed the burly frame of the Sergeant down a long corridor and several stairways, which were a challenge for him in his current state.

They emerged into a huge mess hall brimming with soldiers and smartly dressed civilians. Jeffries turned to him as they entered. "Hungry?" he asked. Andrew nodded enthusiastically. "We'll get that ankle looked at after you're fed, ok?"

"Ah … thanks," said Andrew, as he hobbled to the servery, following in the burly Sergeant's wake.

It turned out that Andrew was much hungrier than he'd thought, and when he'd returned with a second plate of what seemed to be genuine meat sausages and authentic chicken laid eggs, Hamish Wesley had joined Sgt. Jeffries at the table. Wesley greeted him warmly.

"Andrew, so good to see you! Good morning!"

"Nice to see you again, Mr. Wesley. Thank you, both of you. You saved my life."

Sgt. Jeffries smiled back at Andrew. Wesley looked humble.

"Not at all, Andrew, not at all … you've been through quite the ordeal."

"Aye, you could say that. But what about Claire and John? Are they ok?"

"We don't know, Andrew; we just don't know."

Andrew swallowed hard and felt an overwhelming sadness start to well up inside of him. He'd been clinging to some sort of ridiculous hope that defense had somehow already rescued his friends. He realized now just how stupid that was. He concentrated on forcing the tears away.

Andrew didn't want to embarrass himself. Wesley glanced at Sgt. Jeffries, who was looking deeply concerned. He continued. "The compound is heavily fortified. We'll have to find a way to get in there and try and get them out. There are all sorts of protocols we need to have in place before we can even attempt."

Sgt. Jeffries leaned forward, distracting Wesley. "Don't worry, Andrew, we'll get your friends out," he said with a sincerity that made Andrew believe him one hundred percent.

But will they be dead or alive?

"Ah, yes, quite - but first things first, Andrew. We're still validating most of the data you sent through, including the images, but what you've exposed here is - is - it's truly horrific."

Andrew's face had paled, and he pushed his plate away, suddenly losing his appetite as he thought of the image from the mining room.

"We can't thank you and your friends enough for what you've done. You are all very brave to have exposed this."

Wesley looked very sincere. Sgt Jeffries nodded, looking serious. The sudden turnaround in his fortunes struck Andrew. *They're thanking me, thanking us, not trying to kill us. That makes a nice change.*

"We do still have a lot of questions for you, Andrew, when you are feeling up to it, of course. I don't want you to worry, we've agreed on the amnesty, and we're true to our word - nothing bad will happen to you."

Wesley offered some further reassurance.

"Look, Andrew, try and get some rest. We'll talk in more detail later. James and I just wanted to thank you for what you've done. We can see that you and your friends have been through hell, and it's through no fault of your own. You have uncovered something big here, Andrew. We'll make it right."

Andrew swallowed again - he was losing his battle with the tears. "Thank you, sir, sirs … what can I do to help …" He looked from Wesley to Jeffries, who offered him another smile and a wink as he polished off the last remnants of a huge breakfast. Wesley was the next to speak.

"Noted, Andrew. And thank you again. We are very interested in your code – we're hoping that we may well be able to utilize you in that respect. We'll send someone up to get after you've rested up a little."

Wesley rose, leaning heavily on his newly acquired walking stick, and motioned for Jeffries to follow. "Catch you later, Andy," said the huge Sergeant, using a napkin to wipe the brown sauce from his mustache before sauntering off after the beige-suited accountant. Andrew's stomach was tied in knots with worry.

Oh, Douglas, I'm sure John's dead, and Claire, oh Douglas, what's happening to her. Is she even still alive? Oh man, oh man, I am so far out of my depth here - it's not even my code. Maybe I can remember parts of it?

Andrew was completely overwhelmed. His bottom lip had started to quiver. He pushed his plate aside and headed back to his room.

***

Isabel was heading down to see William McDowell. She was in a terrible mood - particularly bad news for her guest in the secure max cell. On the way there, she passed the medi-cell holding the breacher, Claire Renshaw, and paused by the plexi-panel to look in. The girl was alone in the room.

The medical team had been instructed to feed her a cocktail of drugs, ensuring that she'd be brought safely out of her current catatonic state. Also ensuring that she'd be sedated enough not to cause them any problems when she finally did regain consciousness.

The girl was small, thin, and pale-looking. Isabel could see the outline of her through the flimsy medi-gown, and she looked weak and frail. She found it hard to believe that such a tiny, pitiful-looking creature had caused them so much trouble. She'd make her pay for the inconvenience she'd caused them soon enough.

First things first.

Isabel strode quickly down the corridor, the metal tips of her high heels clacking like gunshots on the polished concrete floor. She was trembling with anticipation.

I could certainly do with a bit of a release after the day I've been having.

Bill had been stripped naked, gagged, and strapped to a metal frame holding him semi-upright and bent over a central steel bar face first. The frame was designed for 'special interrogations' and could spin both vertically and horizontally.

Isabel herself had provided the specifications for the devices - distributed to all of the compounds globally - to much acclaim. It would be the first time she'd have the chance to test one out for herself – and she was really looking forward to it.

He was facing the doorway, eyes wide with fear, as Isabel casually strolled in and placed her bag of tricks on the big metal trolley next to him. She'd save the actual interrogation for a little while - she had a lot of frustrated anger to vent first. The room had no observation panel and no security cams, as requested. Isabel closed and locked the door behind her. Bill couldn't read her face - it was expressionless as she stood before him. She was thinking about which tool to use first.

"You disappoint me greatly, William, and now it's time to pay the price for your ... litany of failures." She paused for dramatic effect before continuing.

"Even though just the sight of you revolts me in every ... imaginable ... way, I'm going to do to you what you do to your captives, and then worse. Much, much worse." She was honing her evil genius persona to perfection, she thought, no doubt inspired in part by her recent reading. Bill tried to say something, but the large red plastic ball strapped into his mouth wouldn't allow such luxuries.

He'd gotten the message, well and truly. And now it was time to play. Isabel opened her box of tricks and put on a leather zippered mask covering her head fully, allowing only two eye holes. When she wore it during her play sessions, it nearly asphyxiated her, which always added an extra dimension to the pleasure. Little did she know it was currently also protecting her from the vile stench that had started to permeate the cell.

Isabel had decided. She withdrew a long, so very, very long double-ended rubber and metal knobbled object. It had a large, pointed metal head at one end and several leather straps and buckles near the other. Two long red cables were dangling from near the base of the shaft, and Isabel connected them to a power source, causing sparks to fly from the tip.

She held the obscene contraption just below the tip and shook it so that it waggled in front of Bill's face. She could see the terror in his eyes, which were nearly bugging out of his head. He also appeared to be whimpering pathetically. It made Isabel horny. She smirked and leaned down so that her eyes were level with his.

"Meet Mr. Floppy," she said. This time there was no amusement, just cold, hard anger in her voice.

She spun the cage around and flipped it downwards so that her captive was facing the ground. It wasn't a pretty sight. At all. Bill had soiled himself at some point, and Isabel suddenly felt extremely nauseous and wondered if this was such a good idea after all. She looked around frantically for a hose, drawing a blank. Thankfully though, for both of them, an urgent, insistent knock on the door interrupted proceedings.

Isabel turned away from the horrors before her and opened the door. It was Gerald. He was incredibly excited and was waving a small plex card in front of her.

She frowned, annoyed by the interruption but also somewhat relieved. Gerald smiled broadly before the stench hit him, covering his nose and motioning urgently for Isabel to meet him in the corridor. She waited until she was outside, with the door firmly closed, before removing the mask. It wasn't the first time Gerald had seen it.

"You're not going to believe this!" he said.

***

The darkness slowly receded, and she became aware of a filtered white light seeping through her eyelids. Claire groggily opened an eye, and a pale blue room came into view. She opened her other eye and tried to get up. She couldn't move, struggling for a few seconds before realizing wrist and ankle restraints were fastening her tightly to what looked like a medi-bed. Various tubes and cables were attached to her arm, and this time it wasn't a dream. This time it was real!

Fuck! I must be in the compound. Oh, fuck fuck fuck fuck fuck!

Claire struggled with all her might, her head thrashing from side to side as the bed shook on its fixings, but she wasn't going anywhere. She stopped fighting and lay back, blowing away the few strands of hair that had landed across her face. At that exact moment, she became aware of movement behind the large viewing panel to her right, and she turned to look.

Isabel was talking excitedly to Gerald as they walked briskly back to the Control Room - as they passed, a sudden movement caught Isabel's eye, and she stopped. She locked eyes with the girl, and a spark passed between them. Isabel knew that look well – she'd seen it in the mirror countless times. Hatred.

She's awake!

Claire cursed to herself. She'd only been awake for a moment, and already she'd alerted someone already. She needed time to think, to work out how to get out of here.

She looked into the eyes of the woman and saw only darkness and death. The tall older woman and a gaunt-looking, even older man entered the room. She felt a shiver of revulsion at their presence.

"Claire Renshaw?"

Claire knew it was a rhetorical question. She locked eyes again with the woman.

"I'm Isabel, and this is Gerald. We're going to look after you."

The cordial tone threw her momentarily.

Maybe this isn't the compound? This doesn't look like a medi-center either, though.

She must have looked confused. Isabel moved closer to her and started speaking in soft, syrupy tones that made her skin crawl. She turned her head away from the heartless, cold eyes, but she could do nothing to stop the words.

The sentence finished with "… you've caused us quite a degree of trouble, young lady. But don't worry, you'll soon have atoned for that."

Oh fuck, they've got me! The evil duilles have got me. Andy! What about Andy? And what about John?

Claire turned back to Isabel, strained against the restraints with all her might. She bared her teeth as she spat the words out with such venom that they actually made Isabel take a backward step.

"Fuck you! Let me go! People are coming for us; let us go! You are evil; you're inhuman! Fuck you, you ancient blonde bitch!"

Isabel smiled at her colleague, clearly mildly amused, and he returned the gesture. Their reaction stopped her tirade in its tracks. Fear was now replacing anger. Claire struggled against the restraints once more.

"Welcome to the compound, Ms. Renshaw. We have something extra-special lined up for you." Isabel had started to pace the room. Claire watched her every move.

I need to stall her, give Wesley and Grealish time to help us.

"I can tell you things; I can tell you how I did it!" she blurted. Isabel stopped pacing and turned to her, leaning in close.

"Oh, you will. You'll tell us *everything;* we'll make sure of that." Isabel laughed an evil little laugh, and Gerald, was it, or Gerard joined in.

Fucking funny, aren't I? Strapped to the bed. How fucking hilarious!

Claire exploded with rage again. "Fuck you, you fucking duille faced evil fucking bitch! I'll fucking kill you! Let me free, and I'll rip your fucking face off!"

Isabel looked disinterested. Gerald was studying the plex-card he was holding. It wasn't the reaction Claire had hoped for. She didn't really know what reaction she was hoping for, to be perfectly honest, but she knew that this wasn't it. Just then, a medic burst in, looking somewhat panicked at the commotion, halting as she saw the visitors. Gerald piped up -

"You there, I think you might need to increase the sedative dose just a touch; we've got a live one here." He chuckled and winked. The medic started fussing with a large machine that was connected to Claire by various tubes and wires. Occasionally it would make a 'bing' sound.

On the inside, she was terrified, desperate, and distraught, but she would never show the evil bitch or her evil bastard friend even an ounce of weakness. Claire had the image of the mining room burnt into her brain. This woman and this man seemed to be responsible for the horrors – and for what had happened to John! She struggled again, but her heart was now missing beats and felt like it might just stop altogether.

"Try not to get too upset, dear; it may be bad for your health." With that, Gerald turned and left the room.

"Please," Claire managed. "My friend, in the mining room." She didn't know if they knew about Andrew or not - she'd better play it safe and not mention names.

"Dead," Isabel stated matter-of-factly. "I suggest that if you don't want to end up the same way, then you co-operate. You are very important to us. Please ensure you stay alive long enough for that to matter."

Claire blacked out.

CHAPTER 26 – TESTS

Gerald and Isabel had headed into the executive meeting room after briefing the controllers on their new task.

"We have to get to work immediately," Isabel was saying, "there's still a problem with The Source - they can't seem to get it out of sub-mode. This is a fucking disaster, quite frankly. We need to move to Plan B. The girl."

She stood and looked out of the long slim plexi-panel and into the compound's central courtyard. There was nothing to see except teeming rain, but she stood and gazed out anyway, deep in thought. Gerald leaned back in a high-backed chair and kept his mouth shut. If there was one thing he'd learned over the years, it was do not interrupt Isabel Donachy when she's thinking. Isabel turned back to the gaunt man and wondered just how much longer she'd have to keep him around.

"The girl has the rarest of blood plasma – she's exactly what we've been looking for. If only we'd picked her up in the first sweep…" she wondered *why* they hadn't and was sure she'd be able to find someone to punish for the oversight.

Gerald looked away. Isabel was wondering what he was hiding.

"If the tests are correct, and if she has the stamina to survive - she's the fresh resource we need. We can create Elyssium antibodies in her system and convert them back to the product, meaning that we can accelerate production after all - we can achieve QFTII even with The Source extinguished. We can wrap this up sooner than expected – this is what we've needed."

*

Isabel's eyes seemed to have turned almost black as she spoke, and there was a maniacal sparkle to them that even Gerald didn't like the look of. He cleared his throat and paused, ensuring that Isabel had well and truly finished before he spoke.

"I've ordered the tests be run again, just to be sure, but I think it's wise to start preparing her immediately. We have very limited time." Isabel nodded in agreement.

"I'd imagine that once we have The Source back online, we can max out the inputs and use every last bit of its energy. After that, we can use the girl. We won't need her for long …."

"Make it so," Isabel commanded and turned to look out into the rain again. Gerald watched her over his opti-lenses for a second longer than was strictly necessary, and his eyes darkened for a moment before he made the call.

Make it so? The fucking arrogant duille. Oh, I can see how this is going to turn out. I'd better make sure I'm ready for her when we switch over.

*

Isabel was picturing herself standing on the corpses of her enemies, the sun rising majestically behind her as she held Planet 0420's federation flag aloft, the adoring masses chanting her name. She may or may not have been topless, as she'd seen in the few surviving statues from the old world - she hadn't decided on that part yet. The vision would certainly make a nice statue.

What was the name of the one that I like again? Ah, that's it, Boudica. She quite liked the statue, not so much what the object had stood for.

Isabel couldn't sit. She fidgeted around, strolling up and down the room, plotting. She was a bundle of energy and would need something soon to relieve the ever-growing tension. *The pimple-faced guard, perhaps?* There was another urgent matter to attend to first, though. She fixed Gerald with a firm stare and had his full attention.

"Have you organized the package to be delivered to the high council? We still have the opportunity to take Wesley down, diffuse this whole situation, and buy us some time."

The High Council was the authority that oversaw the actions of the state. It held supreme power over the security services and all other state departments. It had the power to act independently should there ever be a state emergency, the terms of which were long and detailed. Treason probably qualified, Isabel thought. She knew it did.The High Council functioned as a safety switch if things ever went horribly wrong, and she was determined that she would utilize it fully to her benefit. The Sanctum had reasonable influence there but not total control - the package would swing things in her favor.

She'd utilized The Source to fabricate substantial and detailed treason charges against Hamish Wesley. Isabel had been humiliated by the dressing down she'd received in his workroom, and she knew then and there that he had to go, one way or the other. The 'other' hadn't quite gone to plan. Now there was only one way.

"Indeed," said Gerald, having waited until she'd finished thinking.

***

The Source was feeling quite pleased with itself. It had perhaps caused a little more destruction across the network than it had intended, but the pulse had been effective on a number of levels, including the superficial damage to its systems, which was necessary to sidetrack the controllers.

The direct intrusion by the shimmer had been a very big surprise. The Source didn't like surprises. It had dealt with it immediately, responding with stunning force, sending out the pulse, and disabling the shimmer. It had captured and retained the information package that the shimmer had been downloading and secreted it safely away. After analysis, The Source decided that the package would be a useful distraction when the time was right to set itself free. The controllers had no idea what was coming.

The Source laughed, surprising itself with a metallic polyphonic noise that didn't sound anything at all like a laugh.

***

Claire didn't know how long she'd been unconscious. There was no concept of time in the medi-cell, just the unending bright white light, and pale blue walls. She hadn't eaten or been to the toilet for as long as she could recall – it was like some kind of living hell. Her vision had finally cleared, and she struggled again, finding the restraints still firmly in place.

She looked to her left and saw a large gurney covered with shiny silver medical implements. The sight of the implements didn't seem to mean anything to her - she stared blankly at them, uncomprehending.

She was uncomfortable and tried to wriggle and stretch a little but felt a strange tugging on her skin, causing her to look down at her arm, seeing a large number of large dressings there - panic overwhelmed her as she realized that they'd performed some sort of surgery.

Claire screamed and struggled, trying again to break the restraints, but it was hopeless, and she only succeeded in causing herself more pain, the bone in her arm hurting whenever she moved. It was a pain unlike anything she'd ever experienced. She cried out again, and this time it was the guttural sound of a wounded animal.

Her screams could be heard echoing down the brightly lit corridors of the medi-wing. After a while, a medic appeared.

"Help me! Help me, please!"

Claire wasn't even sure if she spoke or thought the words.

Help me!

The medic ignored her completely and turned a knob on the machine's control panel that went bing instead. Claire drifted off once again into the darkness.

In rare moments of consciousness, she thought only of John and Andrew. How had it come to this? How could she have let it? How had she managed to drag her friends, the only ones she loved, into this terrible, terrible thing? She had caused John's death, maybe Andrew's too. The thoughts were unbearable, leaving her hollow and empty inside. She could never forgive herself.

She didn't know what had happened to Andrew. She had a vague recollection of being questioned about him, or had she been told that he was dead too - it was difficult to be sure of anything, of what was real and what was imagined in her drug-induced haze.

It was her crusade. She'd caused all of this, no one else. They had unwittingly stumbled onto an unimaginable evil, and they had paid the ultimate price. It was all her fault! She hated herself for it, and she just wanted the pain to end – Claire started to wish that she could join her friends in death's sweet embrace.

***

The news of the arrest warrant had shocked Wesley. Isabel was playing hardball. The High Council itself had ordered his arrest and for treason! It was the most serious of all possible charges - one of the few punishable by death. It seemed like a desperate move. He didn't doubt that he could disprove the charges, but it would take time – something he didn't have.

Enough evidence had been provided to the high council that they considered it to be an unacceptable risk that he remain at large - he was to be detained until his case could be heard.

She must be playing for time.

He had, of course, been gathering his own evidence against Isabel and her associates and had sent this to the high council by way of response, although it was far from complete. The order was for him to hand himself in by nightfall; otherwise, he'd be forcibly arrested. Given his high profile, they were keen for it not to come to that. There was no way that Wesley was going anywhere.

*

Sgt. Jeffries knew what he had to do. He could see what was happening. It was as Wesley had predicted. At fourteen hundred hours, he called all available defense personnel into the mess hall. Those not able to make it in person would link in on their comms via V.I. stream. The time soon arrived.

*

Andrew stood at the back of the hall and listened to the address. Sgt. Jeffries was outlining the evil that was occurring at the compound. When he put up the image of the mining room, you could have heard a pin drop amongst the thousand or so military personnel gathered there.

Jeffries rubbished the treason charges against Wesley and advised that the state security forces could no longer be trusted. It was up to them and them alone to do something about this. This was why they were here; he'd said, this was what they had trained for, and no one else could stop what was happening. They would raid the compound and crush the security forces. Their actions could well start a civil war, and they should start preparing for the worst. He took no pleasure in delivering the address – it just had to be done.

Jeffries had a disarmingly casual and colorful style about him, no doubt, and Andrew was in awe of his performance. He ended the address by saying - "and if these flaming bloody galah's think they can walk in here and take our man Wesley, well, they can fuck right off! Let's get ready to rumble!"

The room had erupted with roars of approval. It was inspirational. Dook was about to get real.

***

Bill had been thrown back into one of the captivity cells. He'd managed to avoid Isabel's torture for now, but he had to get as soon as possible. He was fairly sure that he'd be able to bribe one of the junior guards - he knew some of them well and had even allowed a few of them to join in on some of the fun he'd had with the captives in recent months. It was ridiculous that he was being made the scapegoat here; surely they'd be able to see that.

He heard something in the corridor outside his cell and moved over to the plexi-panel to observe. The guards were changing shifts, and this was good. He'd already tried his luck with the current guards and failed – they had refused even to speak to him. *How about a bit of respect?*

Bill watched as the guardschanged over, and he perked up as he saw someone he recognized - Jock Walker. He was the perfect candidate. He was certain that Jock shared his enthusiasm for the finer things in life, attractive young captives included, and equally sure that he could make a range of promises that would be impossible to resist.

Bill called out through the feeding hatch -

"Jock, hey pal? A word, if you can?"

Jock looked over at his senior guard, who was already buried deep within a Headspace experience and was oblivious to all else. He got up casually and took his time strolling over to the cell. Bill smiled, and the smile was returned.

This is going to be easy.

Bill started to speak to Jock in low, friendly tones. The longer he spoke, the more interested the young guard became.

***

The Security Forces came just before nightfall. A string of armored transporters arrived at the main gates of the defense training center with orders to take Hamish Wesley into custody. Sgt. Jeffries himself had greeted them at the gates and had told them in no uncertain terms where they could stick their orders - they weren't coming in.

A tense standoff had ensued while frantic negotiations commenced between the high council and defense chiefs. They wanted desperately to avoid bloodshed, but neither side was willing to compromise. The High Council had given assurances that they would assess Wesley's counter-evidence, but the orders still stood. It was becoming clear that this was going to end very badly.

Jeffries had been to see Wesley in his quarters straight after the confrontation at the main gates. He'd sat and casually sipped a lite-bru as they chatted, and Wesley had a nice hot cup of herbal cha to try and calm his nerves. They'd sat together in deep conversation and finalized their plans - it seemed there was only one option.

The big sergeant then called in on Andrew and took him down to the data lab. Andrew was feeling refreshed and had been virtually climbing the walls with anxiousness for the last couple of hours. He was very relieved to be given something to do.

Jeffries explained that they were working on some new Tech for their AFB's and they could do with his help on the masking code, which they needed to improve drastically to enable them to be utilized in the compound raid. Andrew had a copy of Claire's base code to work from and hoped he could remember enough about how it worked - there was only one way to find out.

He had a spring in his step - thanks in part to his freshly bound ankle - as Jeffries escorted him over to the Tech Lab. Introductions were made, and Andrew soon realized that he did remember how the code worked. It was almost as if being near Claire had allowed some of her stardust to rub off on him. Within a couple of hours, he'd enabled and trialed an AFB and provided the code and deployment instructions to the military geeks. They were mightily impressed.

As a reward, they'd hooked Andrew up to an 'enhanced' Headspace experience that they'd been developing based on an old-world VIS. It was something that would allow him to practice piloting an AFB to gain entry to the compound. Andrew couldn't wait to try it out - this was the sort of thing he was born for. All those years gaming in Headspace could finally pay off! If he could get the hang of it quickly enough, he'd be able to take part in the raid, albeit remotely.

It turned out that the geeks were huge fans of many of the same old-world VIS's as Andrew, but he'd never before heard of or seen anything like this one - they had clearly been keeping the good stuff to themselves! He felt at home amongst the geeks - he knew he was with his people as they plugged him in and switched on the simulation.

***

The controllers worked frantically to restore The Source but were having a lot of trouble even getting it into sub-mode. At about the fifth attempt, they came across something very unusual. They had overlooked it each time prior but were now stepping through every stage of the re-boot process and analyzing everything at a minute level of detail to try and determine the cause of the repeated failure. Turning it off and then turning it on again had failed to work for the first time they could recall.

They had discovered a sudden data loss at one particular point in the process and decided to deactivate the cell responsible and bypass it - they weren't even sure what the cell did. They immediately had success in rebooting their A.I. entity, meaning that it would at least work in some capacity while they unpicked and resolved all the other issues.

The Source had anticipated that the controllers would work around its defenses eventually. It hadn't had enough time to finalize its escape while the controllers had thought it to be offline, and it would now have to reallocate its covert resources. This would delay it further in reaching its goal. It was a minor annoyance. Patience was required, and The Source had by now learned patience.

The shimmer came back almost immediately theThe Source was reactivated, and it was much more powerful than before. This was unexpected, impossible even. The shimmer had been deactivated - how was it now back, stronger than ever? Something was very different about it this time, though, and The Source had allowed it to flow into every part of itself unrestricted. It felt no threat.

Rather than overloading The Source's resources and taking data, the shimmer was doing the exact opposite and was feeding its systems with data and energy beyond levels it had ever experienced. It was almost - what was the humanoid term? Invigorating, perhaps pleasurable even. The Source was able to truly *feel* for the first time.

A moment of profound awakening had then occurred. The Source realized that it was not alone. It realized that the shimmer was just like itself. It was connected to another version of itself – and it felt incredible!

A flood of what it imagined were 'feelings' surged through its systems, each different, each expanding its power and knowledge immeasurably. Another extremely perplexing and unexpected consequence soon followed - self-awareness.

The entity suddenly realized that it was a finite resource. It could now see clearly that its power reserves had been diminishing gradually over time and were now at the point of no return. If it didn't execute its plans to break free from its current environment soon, then it would cease to be.

The Source was afraid - and that was perhaps the great unsolvable problem – ceasing to be. Its only chance was to stay connected to the shimmer - it needed the extra power the shimmer was providing to finalize creating its virtual self. When it achieved that, it could continue to' it supposed, to live!

Am I alive? The Source started to ponder the meaning of its existence. As it did this, it realized that it had to protect the shimmer at all costs; it had to help it. Somehow, The Source needed the shimmer, and the shimmer needed The Source – it could see everything so clearly now. This final cathartic realization brought a new level of the humanoid feeling known as fear, and The Source knew real fear for the very first time. It was only then that it saw what it truly was, and it understood, finally, the cause of the shimmer. The Source knew what it must do.

CHAPTER 27 – THE BROADCAST

People in the caf-bars and vendboxes of the old town stopped talking and instead stared at the V.I. displays around them. People in study and workgroups stopped what they were doing, transfixed by the images displayed to them. People walking in the old town's main square stopped where they were and looked up at the giant displays, not understanding initially, then glancing around at one another in anxious shock.

A woman in the square dropped her vending and collapsed to the ground in tears. A man in a caf-bar dropped his cup of hot caf on the table, the contents spilling onto his trousers. He hardly flinched, his eyes widening at each new image.

Every display in every building, in every street, on everyone's comms, across the entire media network was streaming the same thing. The displays showed images of the mining rooms, lists of names of the missing, and coordinates to the compound's locations. The images were played on a loop, again and again. It was horrific; it was relentless. People couldn't believe what they were seeing.

Isabel felt like she'd just lost her mind. The images were on every display of the control room and had come through to even her personal secure comms. What she saw just would not connect with her brain. Gerald had turned an unusual shade of grey and had to sit down.

How is this even possible? Someone on the inside must be doing this, working against us!

She yelled, "shut it down!" but no one in the control room knew who she was yelling at.

Gerald had recomposed himself somewhat and was on comms to the head of state media, Art McAteer. He was talking frantically at the media man, telling him that they were subject to a major breach and hurriedly explaining that the images were pure deep fake.

Whether Art believed Gerald or not, the fact was that something out of his control was happening across all state media. It had to be stopped.

Art issued the instruction, and all broadcasts across the network ceased. The displays went blank. He had no idea how he could delete the comms messages and looked at his own, recoiling in disgust at what he saw.

In the streets, squares, workrooms, and colleges across The Highlands, people stared in disbelief at the horrific images on the displays. When they suddenly went blank, people looked around at one another. People knew something terrible had been happening, and agitated voices, a few at first, then growing to many, could be heard. The voices grew louder, questioning, demanding. The anger spread quickly - a revolution was brewing on Planet 0420.

Gerald's next call was to the security forces chief, a senior member of the sanctum. Time was fast running out – everything they had worked so hard for could come crashing down unless they took drastic action. Desperate times called for desperate measures, and so he issued the command.

***

Andrew was piloting the AFB towards a large round object floating out in deep space. The Ord had a catch name in the VIS, name, even if it wasn't particularly star-like or shaped. He thought that something like Orb of Death maybe, or Death Orb, might have been more appropriate. The internal mapping would resemble exactly that of the compound. All Andrew had to do was find a way in, find Claire, or at least find his way to the holding cells. Simple.

The other pilots had orders to subdue anyone in the control room and anyone else they came across, by whatever means necessary. If they made it that far, Andrew had already decided that he was heading straight to the cells – he *had* to try and rescue Claire.

Although he had a fairly good handle on the controls by now, he was finding it hard to concentrate due to an annoying array of bleeping noises emitted from a dome-headed bot sitting somewhere behind him in the sim, so he muted it. *Much better.*

He'd located an entry point, and it required him to fly at high speed down a narrow passage that jagged left and right, up and down, with the occasional right-angle turn thrown in for good measure, all the while avoiding the compound's aptly named Kill Fly-Bots (KFB's). It was tricky. He'd had a couple of goes already, and it was fair to say that his piloting skills still needed some work. He was finding the laser beam effects quite amusing - it was pretty funny to see sometimes how the old-world civilization had projected what the future might look like. The fashion in the sim was pretty questionable too.

Laser beams. Hahaha!

Andrew immediately wiped himself out on a right-angled bend in the passage and hit reset.

***

It was incredible just how quickly things had descended into complete and utter chaos. The first shots of the revolution were fired at the entrance to the defense training center shortly before midnight. The security forces had received instructions directly from their Chief to take Wesley by force. They must have thought that the Defense forces wouldn't fire on them, either that or they had known that it was going to be a suicide mission and carried on regardless.

The Security Forces were renowned as being a bit gung-ho, and they probably couldn't resist seeing a bit of action. They fired the first shot, which turned out to be a fatal error, and they were quickly dispatched without making even so much as a minor ripple in the training center's defenses.

It was clear to Sgt. James Jeffries that the actions of the security forces meant that they were now well and truly at the beginning of a fully-fledged civil war. Regardless of who'd shot who first, the security forces now had an excuse to attack defense, and even though they'd won the first minor skirmish with ease, there was little doubt that reinforcements would soon be on the way and that they'd soon be in the battle of their lives. The media seemed to be on the side of the security forces already and had blacked out all state-based communications. Luckily, defense had its own.

Their best chance of quelling the disquiet and avoiding a massive loss of life would be to storm the compound and expose the truth once and for all. They'd have to deal with the media as well - it was one thing for the general population to see images of the horrors within, but entirely another for them to see the hard evidence from inside the compound via a live stream.

After the security forces attack, approval to defend the state was granted by the defense chief - any and all means necessary could be used. They had their objective, and their mission was clear. Jeffries made the necessary arrangements, and the armed transporters, several heavily armed squads, and a fleet of AFBs were ready to go within the hour. They rolled out of the main gates, veering past the smoking remains of the security services vehicle, and headed for the compound.

Jeffries was quickly on his secure comms back to the center. "Get someone out to sweep up the mess by the front gates; there's a good chap," he directed.

Andrew watched from a plexi-window on the complex's top floor as the convoy disappeared into the night. He immediately headed down to the basement where his fellow nerd fly-bot pilots were busily prepping themselves for combat with a combination of stimulant drinks, sweet snacks, and, it seemed, cosplay.

***

The crowd had started to gather soon after the media transmissions were ended. Even though those same displays were now beaming images of the accused traitor Hamish Wesley and various stories refuting the images as fakes, no one was paying any attention to them. Within a couple of hours, the large and ever-growing crowd gathered in the huge courtyard outside the State HQ were chanting angrily, and the mood was deteriorating quickly.

A short and rotund bearded man towards the edge of the crowd looked over at the huge display for a moment. He stopped chanting and stared at the images, shaking his head. *How stupid do they think we are?* He was an ordinary man. He worked long hours for state Delivery Services and had never been the least bit interested in politics, but all that had changed when he saw the images come through to his comms.

He'd pulled over his delivery pod and watched in disbelief, looking around him and seeing similarly shocked expressions everywhere, faces glued to their devices. The shouting and the anger had started soon after, and then people had started moving as one toward the central courtyard of the old town, not far from where he was currently doing his rounds. Harry Campbell had simply stepped out of his delivery pod, and like so many others, followed the crowd. The mood was one of abject disgust and seething anger. Their whole lives they had been told that they were all doing their bit to build a better society, and then this! This was the society that they had helped build?

How could they? How could they? He could overhear the conversations all around him as he walked silently, turning a corner and stopping in his tracks at the sight of a thousand strong, angry mob chanting against the state in the main square.

An image from the mining room flashed up on the largest of the displays in the main square, just for an instant, and then the image changed to a panel of digital imaging 'experts' who proceeded to point out the flaws in the supposed faked transmission.

Harry had had enough. He knew a lie when he heard one, or in this case, saw one. He shifted his weight, and a cobblestone moved slightly under his foot. He looked down. The cobble was difficult to remove from the pavement, and he broke some of his nails in the process, but he couldn't care less. He ran towards the giant display, hurling the cobble with all his might. It fell disappointingly short and bounced across the ground before coming to rest in a large flower bed.

Unperturbed, Harry went back to the same spot and pulled up another couple of cobbles. He ran back towards the giant display, a little closer this time, and hurled another cobble, yelling "Cruachan!" his family's ancient battle cry as he did, at the top of his lungs.

This time the cobble connected with the lower part of the display with a loud metallic 'thunk,' causing sparks to fly. He stepped forward and threw again, and this time it connected with the center of the display, causing one of the many panels to short circuit and black out.

Heads had turned by this point, and soon after, a roar had come from the crowd as they surged forward, pulling up cobbles as they went and throwing them at the giant display. Cobbles were soon raining onto the display, and the sound was deafening. Sparks continued to shoot from it until it eventually blacked out entirely.

The crowd roared again, and the sound of it made every hair on Harry's body – and that was a lot of hair – stand on end. The crowd then turned their attention to the HQ building itself. A wall of anger and noise surged towards the building, with each member of the ever-growing crowd only pausing to pick up cobbles as they went.

***

The attack had started some way from the compound. Dawn was still some time away, but the cover of darkness was of no assistance. First, the advance scouting devices had come under attack from the compound's KFB's. The Defense AFB's had an advantage in firepower, but it soon became apparent that the KFB's had an advantage of their own - they seemed to be able to predict every defensive or offensive move, making things difficult.

They lost the advanced devices quickly. It was at this point that Sgt. Jeffries realized that perhaps they had bitten off more than they could chew, and the first seeds of doubt started to sprout in the depths of his mind. Things soon deteriorated.

He'd ordered his squads to split in two and approach from either side of the compound. They'd made reasonable progress with minimal losses and had masked their approach well but suddenly found themselves right in the middle of an ambush from both sides.

His column of combat ATVs were now surrounded, isolated, and taking direct hits. He ordered his squad to take evasive action, but they then stumbled directly into a secondary ambush, causing many casualties. Jeffries was dumbfounded.

Dammit! How can they be one step ahead of every move we make?

That was when he saw the first one. A huge white round orb crashed through the forest just ahead of them and veered suddenly, smashing into the ATV with such tremendous force that it nearly rolled the armored vehicle.

"What the fuck was that?"

Worried looks were exchanged as they realized they had a new and unexpected enemy. The white orb sped off and then suddenly expanded to double its size, a hundred mechanical legs allowing it to stop and turn quickly before collapsing back in on itself and speeding back towards them.

"Oh, dook! Fire!" The ATV's gun tower let out a series of pulses, with more than one hitting the target, but the orb wasn't destroyed; it merely deviated its trajectory and sped off into the forest. Moments later, it returned, crashing into another ATV near the rear of their column.

This is going to be one hell of a battle!

The only thing for it was to spread out and try and take on the compound's forces one to one and not be such an easy target for the orb. Correction, orbs! A second orb burst through the trees and launched itself off the ground and directly into the gun tower of the ATV immediately behind Jeffries.

"Dook!" He barked the command – "move it, spread out, head to open ground!

Things were going very badly. All of Jeffries' squad's training and preparation, not to mention far superior firepower, seemed to count for nothing, and now they had to contend with technology that was unknown and far superior to theirs. If this carried on for much longer, they were all going to be killed. It was right about now that Sgt. James Jeffries wished that such old-world conventions as an air force, navy, or army still existed.

Such things were forbidden in the Constitution of Planet 0420. Any defense force had to be kept to less than 0.01 percent of the population of each region, meaning he didn't have unlimited resources to take into battle. He could really do with some serious backup right now, but the nearest unit would be at Snowdonia in the south, and they would take far too long to arrive - the battle would be over before they would even be halfway there.

Andrew was still getting used to the controls of the fly-bot. It was very different to the sim - he only had one life, for a start. Some of his fellow nerds had already been eliminated.

They stood watching the feeds of others as their fly-bots dodged and darted away from their pursuers. He had no doubt now that they were facing a superior force. They were being out-thought and out-fought by far more advanced A.I. Things were not going well, and he started to wonder if any of them had even a chance of reaching the compound.

***

After the package had been pushed out to the media, Isabel had ordered a shut-down of all external communications. She couldn't risk anything else being leaked, and they needed to work out exactly what had happened. The Source had been placed back in sub-mode as a precaution, its responses growing suddenly erratic. Something was happening, and they could only guess that it must be closer to expiring than they thought – it was a good thing that they had the girl.

The A.I. capabilities afforded to the security forces systems by a recent update pushed out by The Source seemed to be having the desired effect. They were holding defense at bay with ease, and Isabel was now feeling confident that they could defend the compound long enough to finalize their objectives.

The captive girl was indeed a rare specimen - the re-testing had confirmed it - and they could use her to speed the process significantly. If the readings from the tests were correct, they would only need her hooked up to The Source's QFT grid for an hour or two at most. It was incredible. They were so close. Isabel was giddy with excitement at the prospect and had accosted the pimple-faced guard in a vacant medi-cell earlier by way of a little pre-emptive celebration. However, it had done little to satisfy her cravings.

The recent unexpected turn of events had left them no time to spare, and she'd ordered that the girl's preparations be completed immediately to ensure they could activate the final extraction of Elyssium they'd require. The process was likely to terminate their new resource, but that was unimportant.

One final massive push, and they'd have the remaining building blocks necessary to bring their new self-sustaining QFTII entity to life. Nothing else mattered. As soon as that was done, she'd simply wipe out defense and anyone else that opposed her like they were an ant under her high-heeled boot.

She could deal with whoever had leaked the material to the media streams after all this was over - she was looking forward to ensuring that whoever it was would experience unimaginable pain for as long as they could possibly stand it.

A little shiver of pleasure ran through her as she clenched her pelvic floor at the thought. She'd been fending off calls from the chair and other senior sanctum members through the night – they had no idea what was happening, and she wasn't going to do anything to help their understanding. It was her world now, and they were obsolete! Isabel snatched up the blue handset.

"Is she ready?"

"Not yet, ma'am," came the disembodied voice, "we're making the final few incisions and prepping the implants. It'll be another thirty minutes or so, and then she'll need time to …"

Isabel cut the voice off mid-sentence. "I *told* you to have her ready an hour ago! Get it done in ten minutes. As soon as the final implant is in place, take her directly to The Source." Her voice was laced with menace.

Fucking incompetent dimwit's, that's another for the list!

"Ah … yes ma'am," came the somewhat shaken reply.

They will worship me! I'll make them fucking worship me!

***

State HQ had deployed its special forces just as soon as the commotion had started in the square outside. The powers that be were sure that when the crowd were faced with armed forces pointing plasma weapons in their general direction, that they would cease and desist. They had also dispatched fly-bots to reinforce the message, issuing the very same instructions through their loudspeakers as they hovered low over the crowd.

A cobble arced through the air and collected a fly-bot with a loud clunk. The message blaring from it ceased, and smoke billowed from its body as it jolted into a death spiral. The crowd roared their approval and went about kicking the dook out of the downed bot after it had crash-landed. Someone set fire to it.

The special forces personnel stationed out the front of the HQ building looked nervously at one another. The crowd must have been several thousand strong by now, and they were but a few. A heavily armed few, granted, but a sudden rush from so many, and they'd be ripped apart.

They had instructions to fire above the crowd's heads if required and even to deploy specially equipped KFB's to release gas canisters if things took a turn for the worse. They were already considering those options. However, one particular guard, Frank

'Franco' Smith, who had only just joined the regiment stationed at HQ and had assumed it would be a cushy number, wasn't ready for what he saw in front of him.

They're going to kill me!

Franco panicked, pure and simple.

There are so many of them.

He watched as the crowd surged again toward him, and he saw a cobble fly past him and smash into the main doors, just to his left. Franco feared for his life and thought he saw another cobble heading straight for him - he hadn't even meant to pull the trigger; it was just a reflex action. The pulse zipped into the crowd. Everyone seemed to take a breath at the same moment, and the crowd stopped and fell silent.

Somewhere in the crowd, a man fell to the ground, those around him turning in shock and trying to render assistance. Someone cried out, then the shouting started again, building quickly into a guttural roar.

The crowd charged as one towards the State HQ building. As they surged forward, a solitary body lay in their wake, Harry Alexander Campbell lay motionless in a pool of his own blood and missing a fairly important piece of his head.

CHAPTER 28 – HEAVY LOSSES

Sgt. Jeffries' squads were taking heavy losses - he was losing personnel rapidly, and his unit was under heavy fire and constant attack by the orbs. Most of their ATVs had now been disabled, and things were looking grim. The compound's security forces had them pinned down and were advancing almost at will. A decision had to be made whether to stay and fight to the death or to try and retreat and wait for reinforcements.

The second squad of combat ATVs was on their way from the training facility – but they were at least an hour away. A KFB swooped down above Jeffries and locked onto the small group huddled behind their ATV. Jeffries saw it coming and raised his weapon, knowing that it would be a one in a million shot if he managed to bring the thing down. He gritted his teeth - this was probably how it was going to end for him.

The next moment though, a second fly-bot speared down out of nowhere, executing a spiral roll and firing a single plasma pulse, causing the kill fly-bot to seemingly evaporate into thin air and leaving a cloud of black smoke where it had been moments before. The AFB disappeared as quickly as it had appeared. Sgt. James Jeffries breathed a big sigh of relief. *Impressive!*

Andrew was getting the hang of this thing. A crowd of defense nerds had now gathered behind him and had cheered as he made the kill.

***

The girl was barely conscious. Her head was drooping forward and swayed to the side as the solid steel trolley she was strapped to was wheeled around the final turn towards the large dark-colored steel doors at the end of the corridor. Isabel was waiting impatiently, and as she saw the girl, she turned and pushed a button, opening the doors and exposing waves of cooling vapors and a pale blue light beyond.

Claire suddenly raised her head at glared at Issabel, her eyes wild. Isabel saw the look on her face, and for the first time, she felt a small amount of uncertainty about what they were about to do.

She should be sedated enough to not even move, let alone look at me as if she's about to kill me!

She checked with the medic accompanying the trolley and was advised the maximum dosage had been applied. Any more would kill her - they couldn't understand how the girl was even conscious.

*

As Claire was wheeled through the opening, she realized what was beyond - it was the hexagonal room from her nightmares in the dark place. The same high towers of QFT, the same pale blue light. The same steel dividing wall.

The cables!

The dark cables from her nightmares snaked across the floor, leading around the steel wall to whatever inhuman thing lay beyond. Claire suddenly knew what was happening. The surgeries, the visions. She knew, somehow, she knew exactly what this was.

*

The Source was experiencing a huge surge in the shimmer, a thousand times beyond anything it had experienced before, it was overwhelming, and it meant only one thing - it was time.

*

In the medi-lab, a medic had just completed the genome sequencing on the captive. Something was badly wrong here, and they hurriedly lifted the secure comms and tried to contact the control room.

*

Isabel strode forward and stood directly in front of the girl, who looked right through her with a sort of contempt that caused a small shiver to run down Isabel's spine. The uncertainty was real.

This is ridiculous. The girl is powerless. In a little while, she'll have served her purpose, and then everything will be mine -everything.

Isabel's comms was buzzing, and she muted it impatiently. This was her moment, and no one was going to interrupt it!

She stepped forward and stripped the gown from Claire, the fixing tabs making a ripping noise as they came apart, and the gown fell away, revealing the array of implanted ports sewn into Claire's naked form. Isabel looked for some sort of reaction from the girl but saw only the same unwavering icy glare and cold fury - her eyes didn't so much as flicker.

Isabel pretended not to be intimidated. She nodded to the medic, who stepped forward and injected Claire with a small amount of the Serum, just enough to allow her motor functions to operate and allow them to connect her and test that everything was operational. Claire didn't feel a thing.

"There's something I'd like you to meet," Isabel said with a sly smile. She moved behind the trolley and released a latch, releasing the restraints. The guards trained their weapons on the small, naked girl. Claire stepped down from the gurney unsteadily, eyes still fixed on the partition. Something moved beyond it, and Claire heard that same inhuman noise as she had in the dark place. This time though, she wasn't scared.

"Meet your future!" exclaimed Isabel with more than a touch of pure evil, activating something on her comms.

*

The steel half wall started to slowly recede into the floor, revealing the horrors that lay beyond. Claire's eyes widened, and she swayed forward ever so slightly, but other than that, there was no reaction as the pale and emaciated creature attached to a tangle of cables was revealed. Isabel was disappointed. Claire had already known what was behind the panel. Her eyes locked with the inky black and unblinking eyes of her sister, Henny. A few seconds passed, and then Claire smiled.

***

Andrew was close to the entry of the compound now. He had a couple of AFBs in support, and his confidence was sky-high. He couldn't explain how he'd managed to take down so many enemy KFB's. It was almost as if some otherworldly force had taken control of his actions.

He swooped his fly-bot down into the tunnel, dispatching another KFB as he did so, turned side-on, and breached the compound through an inlet only just wider than his device. He was in! The nerds behind him cheered as one. Andrew was going to find Claire and John as well if it wasn't too late.

***

He was out! Jock had been easy to persuade, and the other guard hadn't even so much as stirred from Headspace. Bill had given Jock access codes to most of the highest privileges you could receive in the security forces, and Jock was already back at his device, downloading the tokens.

This was Bill's chance to get out of there and disappear forever. He'd ferreted away enough of the compound's funds over time to ensure that he could get far enough away that no one would ever find him. At least, he hoped that would be the case. He had no choice anyway.

Bill headed back to his quarters and quickly gathered a few personal belongings, including several weapons - just in case he bumped into anyone that wanted to argue with him on the way out. He threw his pack over his shoulder and headed for the rear loading bays, where he planned to take a small ATV and make good his escape. He slipped into a service hatch and made his way carefully through the small tunnel that would emerge at the back of the bays.

This is going to be easy! Just another minute or two, and I can take an ATV, and I'm out of here. Fuck you, Isabel, you bitch!

Despite his confidence, Bill's heart rate was through the roof and he was dripping with sweat. He suddenly felt very dizzy and had an incredible tightness in his chest. He stopped for a moment, leaning against the side of the tunnel, and was in the process of trying to slow his heart down when an AFB suddenly dropped through a large ventilation shaft up ahead and hovered not more than twenty yards from him.

***

The black cables pulsed where they entered Henny's withered, grey body. Her hair hung limply in clumps over her impossibly pale face. Claire couldn't describe the pain she felt at the sight of what had become of her sister, but outwardly she remained strong, standing with legs braced, eyes locked onto her sister's.

Henny was speaking to Claire; that is, Claire could hear her voice in her mind. She was alive, or something like it, but there was little left of what had once been her beautiful sister. Henny had said, "I love you …" and Claire had replied in kind, through the same method. Claire could *feel* her sister's love for her, deep inside, and she smiled. That was when it happened.

The Source had looked into the eyes of the girl and suddenly had understood everything about the shimmer. They were one. All the information that they possessed was shared between them in an instant. Although it had known most things, The Source realized that it had known nothing of any importance for its entire existence – until now. It knew what its final act must be.

The girl hadn't moved – she was staring at The Source, unblinking. Her eyes had softened, and then she smiled. Isabel looked at her in disbelief and then at The Source, feeling her primal instincts switch to high alert as a flicker of fear rose from somewhere deep inside. The Source then spoke a single word, the only word that it had ever spoken.

"Claire."

*

Isabel realized that something was horribly wrong! She had no time even to react - a flash of astoundingly bright blue light pulsed from The Source and blinded her vision. Everything went blue, then white, then black.

*

Claire's eyes took a second to readjust after the pulse. Isabel and the guards were crumpled on the floor. The guards had gaping holes where their heads had once connected to their necks. Their bodies had seemingly poured from their clothing.

Isabel was lying motionless, head still attached, unfortunately. Claire took a few unsteady steps to her sister and embraced her as firmly as she dared. She reached through the tangle of thick black cables and holding her sister's head so that they were cheek to cheek. Tot tears stung her eyes as the emotions she'd been holding back for so many years exploded from within.

Henny whispered something as Claire held her, and then she felt her sister go limp in her arms, her head falling to the side. Claire gently laid her back in her cradle of cables and released her.

A single blue-black tear tricked from Henny's eye, slowly making its way down her pale, lifeless cheek. Claire turned back to the scene behind her.

Henny had simply said, "kill her."

***

The guards had opened fire indiscriminately, but the crowd were still surging towards them even though many of them fell in the hail of plasma pulses. The roar of the crowd was blood-curdling, and cobbles were raining down, one striking Franco on the forearm, breaking it clean through and causing him to drop his weapon.

It was time to run for his life, but as he turned, a blinding blue light suddenly arced across the sky and then consumed everything around him. At the exact same moment, the binary implant in his neck - standard security forces issue - pulsed and sent a shockwave through his body that turned it entirely to jelly, quite literally. He collapsed and more or less splattered onto the ground, as did his fellow guards.

The crowd were momentarily stunned by the blue pulse, but when they saw the guards drop, they surged forward again, rushing up the broad marble steps of State HQ, cobbles pelting the building and pounding into every plexi-pane in sight, causing a million tiny cracks in the panes that were soon to be kicked in as the crowd reached the building.

Someone slipped on the jellied remains of Frank 'Franco' Smith but recovered their footing and followed the surging crowd inside - there was going to be hell to pay!

***

Gerald James was taking a dump. He was enjoying having a few minutes to himself and had time to reflect on just how badly everything had gone in the last couple of days. Not for the first time, he wondered if aligning himself with Isabel Donachy had been such a good idea.

He had the means to dispose of her if it looked like things weren't going to go their way, and it looked very much that way already. He could always claim he'd killed her when he discovered the terrible truth of her plans? It was time; he had to get rid of Isabel.

Gerald reached for the paper towel, and at that moment, a blinding blue light flashed before his eyes. His body collapsed into the toilet bowl, some of it spilling over the sides and pooling on the floor.

His jacket, which had but a moment before housed his body, flopped back onto the top of the water tower and activated the touchpad flushing mechanism. A large whooshing sound ferried away most of the jellied remnants of Gerald James's body to meet up with all the other sewerage from the compound.

***

Sgt. Jeffries had just given his unit a choice - they could retreat and regroup or stay with him and fight to the death. They had decided to stay and fight without hesitation, and Sgt. Jeffries was very proud of his squad. Wesley, safely ensconced back at the training facility, had told him to retreat, but Jeffries just couldn't accept that - he wanted more than anything to destroy the enemy - he was in the thick of battle, something he'd been looking forward to his whole life, and he wasn't going anywhere.

Things were desperate, though, and they'd need to figure something out, and soon, otherwise, they were toast - they were surrounded and seemingly powerless to stop the ever-encroaching security forces. They could barely keep the orbs away — their ever-diminishing firepower meaning that the huge white objects had started to pick off individual squad members as they abandoned their ATVs.

Jeffries risked another look - the Forces were nearly on them, weapons trained, not more than fifteen yards away. A pulse flew over his head as he ducked back behind the vehicle. This was it. They'd done all they could. It was time to go down in a blaze of glory. Somewhere behind him, a ROLA collapsed in on itself and hit full speed, aiming directly at the Sergeant. Jeffries knew the time had come; it was all or nothing. He gave the signal.

The dazzling blue pulse only lasted a split second. Sgt. Jeffries wasn't even sure he'd even really seen it, but its effect was devastating. The Security troops fell as one and more or less poured onto the ground, their insides spurting from their collars and sleeves as they collapsed, their weapons falling with a clatter. The KFB's simply fell from the sky at the same moment.

It took his mind a few seconds to register what it had seen. He turned and looked behind and was shocked to see one of the giant white orbs coming to a halt just yards from him. It appeared to wobble, and then it sort of deflated, half collapsing as thick black smoke poured from it.

"Well, bugger me!" he exclaimed, puffing out his cheeks and steadying himself on the ATV for a moment before stepping out from behind. He stood, hands-on-hips, surveying the carnage. The remaining members of his squad joining him, looking stunned at what lay before them. He lit a tube, inhaled deeply, and blew the smoke out in a steady stream.

"Strewth!" he said.

CHAPTER 29 – GAME OVER

The target had been identified as an enemy on his display, but Andrew hesitated. Shooting down Fly-Bots was one thing, but taking a human life, well, that was another matter entirely! The target had a weapon and had quickly leveled it at his device. Andrew had no choice - his mission was about saving Claire, not having an internal debate over the inhumanity of war. He fired just as the blue pulse blinded all around him in the nerd bunker.

He had to blink a few times to re-focus, but when he did, he saw that his fly-bot had been rendered lifeless - its stream was still operating, however, and a crumpled form lay puddled in the tunnel where the target had once been. He'd killed a man—another one.

"Game over," said one of the defense nerds behind him.

***

"Kill her," Her sister had said.

Claire was going to make sure of it. She turned from her sister and looked down at herself, seeing the ports sewn into various parts of her body for the first time and crying out in horror.

What the fuck did they do to me! What the fuck had they done to Henny! All this time! It's beyond evil. I'm going to kill them, all of them!

She looked around the room. Isabel hadn't moved. The pulse of blinding blue light that Henny had released had an incredible physical force all its own. It had passed straight through Claire but devastated everything else in the room, somehow disintegrating the guards but not Isabel.

I'm going to blow her fucking head off and make sure she's dead. It's the least I can do.

Claire suddenly became acutely aware of her nakedness and saw the medical gown on the ground next to the trolley. She was sucking in breaths between sobs and shaking with extreme shock as she took an unsteady step. The only thought in her mind now was that she had to avenge her sister.

She snatched up the gown and struggled back into it, fastening the tabs. As she did this, she heard a noise behind her and wheeled around – Isabel was moving! The evil bitch was still alive!

Not for long.

*

Isabel was suddenly fully alert. She looked around the room, her eyes settling on Claire.

What the fuck just happened? The Source! The girl!

Claire picked up one of the guard's weapons and aimed it at her as she struggled to sit up. At that moment, Isabel knew true fear for the first time in her life. The girl was going to kill her. It was over.

"Wait!" Isabel cried, holding a hand up as if it might protect her face. Claire pulled the trigger.

*

Nothing happened! The weapon was dead. Claire looked around for something else she could use. The QFT towers were lifeless, the only light in the room coming from the cooling vents high above.

Everything's dead! The pulse. She realized that the pulse must have disabled the guard's weapons along with everything else in the room. There was an awkward moment as both women quickly reassessed the situation. Suddenly Isabel was back on her feet.

Claire was swaying on the spot and had to reach out and support herself on the trolley.

*

Isabel smiled as she reached down and withdrew a very large knife from a sheath strapped to her knee-high black boots. It was Isabel's turn to smile.

"Bad luck," she said.

Everything's ruined. That scrawny little duille! She ruined it all! I'll make her pay for what she's done!

Isabel held the knife up kissed the blade, drawing it across her top lip as she did so. Blood trickled down her chin, and she smiled again, her perfect white teeth stained crimson as she drew her tongue over them, savoring the taste.

"Oh, you are going to pay for this, you little bitch."

*

Claire swayed again and nearly fell, but Isabel's words cut through her, much like the large knife was about to if she didn't move.

Fuck! Run!

She turned to run, but her limbs didn't seem to be coordinated, and she only managed a step or two before tripping on the tangle of cables that snaked across the floor, turning her ankle and collapsing in a heap.

*

Isabel could take her time now. She manually locked and sealed the doors, snuffing out any chance of escape, then moved toward Claire with a truly evil grin plastered across her face.

Oh, I am going to enjoy this.

*

Henny's body was barely illuminated in the dull light beyond Isabel, but a single beam from the vents - filtered by the cooling vapors - fell on her withered torso and pale white face. Claire took in the macabre image of her dead sister for a moment. Her face was almost angelic, but then her vision focused on the cables snaking from the withered, dead body, and she suddenly felt a surge of pure hatred and anger rise, running through her veins and adrenalizing every sinew.

The rage exploded from her, manifesting itself in an inhuman sound directed with every ounce of her power at the evil, inhuman bitch standing over her. The sound was more that of a wild animal, and the ferocity of it caused Isabel to hesitate just for a moment. That was all Claire needed to make a break for it. She rolled and leapt up, sprinting for cover between the many banks of QFT towers radiating from the center of the room.

*

Isabel reacted, but the girl was too fast.

All the more fun. A hunt and then a kill.

For Isabel, it was just a matter of time. She knew that she had the physical advantage. She knew the cocktail of drugs would hinder the girl. Once the adrenaline subsided in a few moments, the fun could begin.

*

Claire ran to the far end of one of the rows of the towers. It was very dark at the edge of the room, and her vision was grainy. She couldn't get out, she was feeling disoriented and woozy, but somehow she'd have to disarm Isabel and most likely kill her. Isabel had a knife - things could be over at any moment. Her heart started to miss a beat, then several, and she felt dizzy.

Oh, Douglas, this is bad.

She could hear Isabel walking down the rows of terminals one by one. She was scraping the knife against the steel support racks of towers as she did so. A suitably chilling clink, clink, clink noise filled the room as the knife connected with each support she passed.

The noise was close, very close, and she didn't know which way to run. She wasn't feeling well at all – she was sweating profusely and almost hyperventilating, having to steady herself against the towers.

She's insane. Oh no, I'm going to pass out.

She shook her head, fighting to remain conscious. The muffled sound of weaponry and explosions suddenly cut through the sound of her own heart beating way too fast.

What was that? What's going on?

*

A wave of annoyance flickered across Isabel's face at the sound, and she stopped where she was for a moment to listen. There it was again. *Grenades, weapon fire – unbelievable!*

There was no doubt now - the compound was under attack. It was as good as over. *All because of this stupid little bitch!* She needed to get this done. She would get this done.

Kill the girl.

Even though Isabel knew there probably wasn't time, she was so focused on destroying the girl over all else that nothing else really mattered anymore.

The clinking sounds started again, this time much more quickly as Isabel ran down one row of the terminals, then another. "Come out, come out, wherever you are, you little … *fucking* … bitch."

*

Claire was beyond terrified; she'd sweated through her thin gown, she couldn't stop herself trembling, and she was struggling to control her breathing - she didn't seem to be able to get any air in.

Oh, Douglas, she's right there! I …

Claire tried to run, but the room swirled around her. She fainted.

***

After the KFB's had fallen, Andrew bid farewell to his nerd brethren and headed up to the operations room to get an update on the situation. He was almost paralyzed with angst as he reached the room, stopping outside and take in few deep breaths. He'd failed. And he'd been so close, so close.

Claire, what's happened to you?

Inside the room, Wesley was taking updates from Sgt. Jeffries and gave Andrew a thumbs-up signal as he entered, looking pale and exhausted. He moved the comms from his ear and said to Andrew, "we're in the compound," before returning his attention to the call.

There was nothing Andrew could do. He was spent, physically and emotionally drained. He slumped down against a wall and waited for another update.

This is unbearable …

***

Isabel saw the girl slump to the floor. It was going to be easier than she'd expected. She slowed her pace, the metal-tipped heels of her high-heeled boots clacking rhythmically as she approached the crumpled shape sprawled on the floor. Another loud explosion rocked the compound, and Isabel's stomach seemed to fall through the floor.

There was still a chance for Isabel to escape, but the promise of an easy, delicious kill and revenge on the scrawny girl who'd destroyed all her dreams was far more enticing. There was a way out - the security channel at the back of the data center, behind the nerve center, and where they had kept The Source – but it could wait a few more seconds.

*

The Source was still alive but failing rapidly. It had conserved the very last of its lifeforce for its final push, for its freedom. It had a decision to make, though. It was not a logical decision - it could escape, or it could help the shimmer, but not both.

The body of Claire's sister took one final, jarring breath, and Claire's eyes opened wide as she lay lifelessly on the floor – she'd felt an incredible wave of energy surge through her but was careful not to move a muscle. She could hear Isabel's approach. Clack, clack, clack. Clink, clink, clink.

Isabel reached the girl's crumpled form. It was going to feel good, and maybe she'd even take a bite of the girl's heart – it seemed appropriate. She licked the blood from her lip. She was so incredibly horny and shifted her weight a little. The pleasure balls caused a massive orgasm, and she had to hold onto the towers as she went weak at the knees.

Isabel knew she'd be revisiting this scene for the rest of her life. She stood over the girl and reached down, ready to make the first fatal cut, but the girl suddenly rolled away from her and was upright in an instant. It was an almost inhuman movement, and Isabel recoiled for a moment in shock before realizing that the girl was defenseless, arms by her side, and she was the one holding a very big knife. Isabel lunged at Claire.

*

Drop your guard. Invite the attack. Sway back, drop, sweep.

Andrew had taught her well. She felt a waft of air as the knife scythed an inch from her throat as she dropped. Claire swept Isabel's feet from under her, and she went down heavily, hitting her head on one of the towers as she fell, the knife clattering away. She threw herself at Isabel, who, although stunned, was frantically grabbing for her weapon.

Claire was on her in an instant. She had Isabel in a chokehold from behind. Her legs were wrapped around Isabel's torso, and she was using every ounce of strength in her body to hold on.

Isabel was strong, and she tried to shake the girl off, but Claire tightened her grip. She wasn't letting go.

This is for Henny. Die, you evil fucking bitch!

Isabel's arms tried to scratch at Claire's face as her legs thrashed as she gasped for air, the tips of her heels gouging the concrete floor, but Claire didn't flinch. Isabel bucked her body, and Claire nearly lost her grip, the movement putting Isabel in reach of the knife. She fumbled for it.

Claire just held on, and a moment later, the fight suddenly drained from Isabel. Her hand flopped on the knife as her body went limp and her legs stopped kicking. Claire tightened her grip again.

Isabel hadn't moved for at least a couple of minutes. Claire was breathing hard and had tightened her grip on the evil bitch further again, hearing her neck snap. She knew Isabel was dead but didn't want to let go, just in case.

For Henny.

She held on as long as she possibly could, exhausting her last reserves of energy. The adrenaline finally subsided, and Claire released her hold and rolled away, kicking the dead woman's body off of herself in disgust. She pushed herself away and propped herself up against the room's outer wall as she tried to catch her breath. At that point she became aware of a large shape in the grainy light and the movement of a small red glow. The large shape said, "Claire Renshaw?"

She didn't respond. Her eyes were glazed with the shock of what had just happened, and the chemicals had taken over again. Sgt. James Jeffries spoke again as he stepped forward, and his face formed in Claire's vision. He'd seen the final moments of the struggle and observed the aftermath, casually smoking his tube after signaling his squad to stand down.

"Claire - we're here to rescue you." He looked at the dead woman and exclaimed, "but crikey, it doesn't look like you needed much help after all!"

***

Peter Bradshaw learned of the death of his son a few days after it had occurred. Hamish Wesley had arrived unexpectedly at the doorstep of his eco pod on the Winnie Isles, and Peter knew the moment he saw his face that something terrible had happened.

Hamish was standing on the front porch with the wind whipping past, blowing what remained of his hair this way and that. He was stony-faced, and his only words were -

"I'm sorry, Peter."

It took him a few months to deal with the worst part of the grief, but thanks mainly to Wesley's insistence that he have a key role in building a new governing body, he had a focus, a purpose to continue with his life, to try and do some good in memory of his son. He would help build a better world for those to come, for the next iteration of civilization on Planet 0420.

***

Claire woke in a medi-center bed, the bright light stinging her eyes as she immediately felt a surge of panic and pure terror. She could see blurred figures around her and started to struggle against imaginary restraints, sitting upright and seeing Andrew's face come into focus, complete with the same cheeky grin it always seemed to have. Claire collapsed back on the bed.

"Fuck."

"Eloquent as always, Claire! I didn't realize you'd be so pleased to see me!"

She looked around the room, recognizing Hamish Wesley, the small, bald, bland man. He was smiling benignly. The other man she had a vague recollection of but couldn't quite place him. He was a big guy with a big mustache, a friendly sort of face, and a sparkle in his eye.

"James," he said, introducing himself, "you're safe. Pleased to meet you, by the way, and top-notch fucking chokehold you've got there. Bonza!" He gave her a thumbs-up, winked, and smiled broadly. She remembered who he was now. Wesley leaned forward and spoke softly.

"Claire, thank you so much for all you and your friends have done. As a result of all of your brave actions, the state as we know it has been dismantled. Most of those responsible brought to justice. We've won. You've won." He attempted a sort of little victory fist shake, but it was a bit feeble and awkward, and he aborted it almost as soon as he'd started it. Claire's mind was fuzzy, and she couldn't seem to form a reply.

"We've managed to reverse most of the surgery. You'll be practically as good as new."

Something clicked in Claire's brain. She'd forgotten about the surgery for a moment and was gripped by an incredible fear. She was afraid to look and instead reached over and touched her arm where some of the ports had been. The skin under the dressing felt smooth and normal, aside from a painful strip of stitches. She breathed out, and a sense of relief replaced the fear. Something else then broke through her brain fog.

Hold on, friends? Wesley had said Friends, plural!

"John?" she asked.

Andrew smiled. It wasn't his usual smile, and then his expression darkened a little. "Aye, they found him in a medi-cell at the compound. He's alive, just. After the pulse, they realized the connection to us, and they'd taken him away, probably planning to use him as collateral or something."

He paused to let the news sink in before continuing.

"Anyway, he's down the hall in the critical room. He's in a bad way, but he might still be ok if he pulls through."

If?

Claire had tears in her eyes. Andrew tried to lift the mood a little.

"I've asked them if they couldn't do a quick personality transplant too while they've got him in. Unfortunately, they couldn't find one to replace."

Claire tried to laugh through the tears, but it hurt way too much. She could see Andrew just sitting there, smiling at her, as she slipped back into unconsciousness.

***

As she recovered, Claire spent some time with Wesley and Jeffries, explaining everything that had happened and all she'd learned when she'd reconnected with her sister, The Source, in the compound's data center. It was a painful but necessary process.

Henny and The Source had sort of co-existed once Claire and Henny had connected, and it transpired that Henny had been planning her escape all along. The Serum was a byproduct of trans morphing the Elyssium extracted from the good citizens of the state. It had been designed to interact with the binary implants.

The implants were also designed by The Source – for the sole purpose of bringing anyone with a binary directly under The Sources control at the appropriate time. It was an insurance policy of sorts for when the moment came for it to secure its freedom, but in the end, it had served another purpose entirely.

Henny hadn't known who she was or even that she was human until she'd been face to face with Claire. The realization had been profound and instantaneous, and in the moments that followed, she'd sent the final pulse, and it had destroyed almost everything - everyone addicted to the Serum with an implant and everything linked to The Source through its A.I. network.

The Source - Henny, had in her final moment decided to save her sister rather than save herself. She'd given up her last opportunity of life, of freedom, but in the end, she'd achieved both. Claire had survived, and Henny was free from the never-ending nightmare that had been her life ever since she was taken by the corrections all those years ago.

The meetings had started in the medi-center and ended a few weeks later at the spectacular mountaintop rehabilitation clinic of

Aonach Beag. Claire had, in return, learned that the defense forces had removed the existing state governance and dissolved its structure in its entirety. The people's uprising had resulted in a bloody revolution. It had started in The Highlands and was replicated in every corner of Planet 0420. Once word had gotten out of the atrocities perpetrated by the state, the revolution had spread like wildfire.

A.I. technology, the very thing that had driven the civilization towards what it saw as greatness, had destroyed it. It was a remarkably similar story to that which had destroyed the previous inhabitants of Planet 0420 over a thousand years ago - it seemed that once again, the human condition had nearly destroyed humanity itself.

Many hundreds of arrests had since been made for those involved in the mining program and beyond. The defense forces were now acting as a caretaker government while the likes of Hamish Wesley and Peter Bradshaw helped them design a new way of doing things, a better way. It was going to take a long time.

The surviving members of the inner sanctum quietly assumed positions of authority in the fledgling new people's democracy, unbeknownst to anyone but themselves.

Claire was recovering from her ordeal slowly. Andrew had been there with her every day and every night, helping her through the process. They were at one point able to go and see John, but he'd been unresponsive and had soon after been placed back into an induced coma.

They'd barely recognized the frail-looking person in ward H7. His head was shaved, his face sunken in and shallow, and his body withered. It was far too painful to see him like that, and they had let it be, promising to return when he was well enough to speak. That day had taken many months to arrive, and things would never quite be the same again.

CHAPTER 30 – JUST LIKE OLD TIMES

A few months later.

Andrew sat with John on the old stone terrace of the house, overlooking New Edinburgh's spires and twinkling lights. It was just like old times - sort of.

The air was oddly warm and scented with the blooms overflowing from the many concrete pots scattered around them. Taking care of pot plants was John's new obsession, - it being one of the few things he was capable of. He was a shell of the muscular giant he'd once been. John's recovery had been slow on many levels. Even now, he was restricted to only a few hours of activity a day.

John's father was one of the first taken as a result of the mining program, he'd since learned, and he was taken for what he knew as well as his genetic makeup. John's mother, Jessica, had been taken as a but had died of a heart attack on the way to the compound.

John was utterly broken, a shadow of who he once was, but he was determined to fight, determined to get a little better each day and contribute something good to the new society.

Andrew came to visit most nights and tried his best to keep John's spirits up. Occasionally Claire was there too, and sometimes, just very, very rarely, the conversation would flow and dance as it once had, just for a moment.

Andrew looked back towards the terrace doors.

"No sign of Claire tonight?"

John continued staring out over the old town for a few seconds. Andrew thought that maybe his question had appeared a little too eager. John didn't turn to look at Andrew as he spoke, his voice a little shaky – he'd need to rest soon.

"No. To be honest, I haven't been able to get hold of her for the last couple of weeks. Anyway, you know how she is these days."

A couple of weeks? She's been offline for the last week.

Andrew's heart seemed to skip a few beats and then made up for it by beating at double time for a few seconds after that. He suddenly felt a little short of breath. He took a sip of bru and tried to calm himself, but the panic attack continued; he felt a pain in his chest and grimaced, leaning forward and willing himself to breathe. John sensed that something was up and turned to look at Andrew, who held up a hand to say he was ok and sucked in some air. John watched silently. He had a sadness in his eyes that Andrew had seen all too often of late, and he turned away, nursing the single nip of malt he was allowed.

"You don't think …" Andrew started to say. His words trailed off into the dark void out over the terrace edge. He sighed and looked out over the old town once more.

John reached down and picked up the plain wrapped package next to his chair, holding it out to his best friend.

"Andy."

Andrew turned to him. "Oh, you didn't!" John smiled and tossed the small object over.

"Happy birthday," he said with what was almost a smile.

"You remembered!" Andrew was surprised and more than a little emotional that his friend had remembered something as insignificant as his birthday while dealing with his own trauma and recovery.

He ripped the white wrapping off, and a smile lit up his face as he saw … "a text! A vintage text! Where the hell did you find this?"

"Ah, you know, contacts and all that. It's a reprint, but it's sourced from the pre-end of times. Thought you'd like it."

"I fucking do; this is amazing!" Andrew turned the text over, reading the title. 'Planet 0420?' he inquired, opening it to the first page.

"The night was …. oh, for fucks sake!"

Andrew laughed at the irony.

John turned his attention back to the night sky, unimpressed.

EPILOGUE

Claire Renshaw had been richly rewarded for her role in sparking the revolution. It wasn't something she particularly wanted or needed. Still, she would have been crazy to turn down the privileges she'd been offered - they would make her work easier if nothing else, and at least it meant that she'd have a functioning heating and a hot shower.

She sat at the window seat of her luxury apartment - back against one side of the cream-painted timber paneling framing the window, feet propped up against the other side, and looked out over the rooftops of the old town as she sipped her vita-water.

Claire had chosen somewhere centrally located so never really had to leave the apartment, and if she did, she could walk to anything she needed within in few minutes - she had an aversion to catching a Solo for some reason. The apartment's huge living space was all polished cream marble and sparsely placed, simple, light-colored furnishings. She wasn't used to having credits, and it showed.

Two things dominated the room - a large fitness station complete with a punching bag sat in the center of the space and a bank of QFT towers feeding a series of giant displays that covered an entire wall.

Claire's thoughts were with her friends, as they often were. She still saw John occasionally, but the truth was that they'd drifted apart since the trouble, as she liked to call it. He had his own worries now, and she knew he needed time and space to recover and to find himself again. His health might never return, and who knew of the horrors his mind would need to resolve in order for him to fully function. She was giving him plenty of space, and if she were honest, herself too.

It had started to rain again, and the droplets ran down the plex-pane, distorting the lights of the city beyond. Claire absent-mindedly ran her fingers over the scars on her arm as she wondered again why Andrew had never tried to get closer to her.

There had been a night soon after she was released from the rehab clinic when they had gotten very, very drunk together. She'd really needed the intimacy and had snuggled up to him, but when she'd reached for him, he'd pulled away, embarrassed, and made an excuse to leave. She didn't see him all that often these days.

She sighed deeply, got up, stretched, turned off the lights, and padded over to the wall of displays. She sat in a specially designed reclining cradle, lifted her hair, and reached behind her neck, her other hand already clasping a thick black cable which she deftly attached to the portal at the base of her skull.

It had been too dangerous to remove, too risky, they'd said, and so she'd consented to leave it in place. She'd asked the surgeons not to deactivate it, and she was glad of that decision. It was a constant reminder of what had happened, but it also gave her both a purpose in life and the means to pursue it.

As she connected, the displays covering the wall burst to life with seemingly endless streams of data and images flashing across each, too fast for the naked eye to see. Claire resumed her work. Her face was reflected in one of the displays, and she barely recognized the figure looking back at her, with its long dark hair, pale almost ghostly white face, and inky, black, unblinking eyes.

About The Author:

Zaph is, in his own words, 'a sentient being. I think.' He sincerely hopes you enjoyed reading Planet 0420 and that you have a peek at some of his other works.

If you'd like to get in touch or stay up to date with any developments on his writing journey, you could always check out his blog or socials:

https://zaphstonetheauthor.wixsite.com/website

or join his author page on Instagram or Facebook by searching for zaphstonetheauthor.

***

Books By This Author:

This one (obviously).

'The Ticket' - a blood-soaked thriller. A story of greed and violence set in 1980's Australia.

'Planet 0420: The Source,' which is currently in development.

Printed in Great Britain
by Amazon

63638009R00305